POPPY & THE BEAST

SYLVIE STEWART

ROLLING HEARTS PRESS

Then Again

Happy New You

About That

Full-On Clinger

Nuts About You

Booby Trapped

Love on Tap Series

To the boys of Old Dominion.
Thanks for all the inspiration and for giving Mac his song.

PREFACE

Poppy & the Beast was originally published as *Game Changer* in 2019. Updates and extras have been added, but if you start reading and it feels familiar, you may have read it in its original form.

You are not crazy.

I repeat, you are not crazy.

ONE

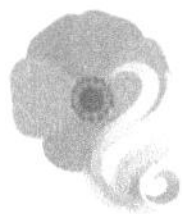

"COOKIE, I'll take this damn thing on the plane over my dead body!"

She smacks me right on the butt and I yelp just like I did when I was twelve. "Don't you go using profanity in my house, young lady. God's listening!"

I turn to my grandmother and tilt my chin. "If God's paying any mind, I can promise you he's on my side."

We both look down at the bed where the enormous pink suitcase adorned with huge yellow letters spelling "Bright Eyed and Bushy Tailed" stares up at us.

"Bunny spent all week cross-stitching that for you. She's just about worked herself blind." She crosses her arms and shoots me a victorious look as she throws out the ulti-mate challenge. "Do you want to hurt her feelings?"

Dammit. She knows she's got me. If I've learned

anything in my thirty-one years it's that you never, *ever*, disrespect your elders—especially the ones who apparently think you'll always be four years old dreaming of your cotillion.

I sigh in resignation and unzip the monstrosity. It *is* rather spacious inside. "Fine. But I hope she knows no taxi within a hundred miles of the airport is gonna pick me up with that thing. I'll look like a mental patient while I'm *walking* into Manhattan." Let's see how Bunny feels when my corpse is found stuffed in the ridiculous suitcase three weeks from now.

Cookie turns me to her and takes both my cheeks in her hands. She's wearing one of her favorite floral-print blouses with an apron over it that says, "Gimme Some Sugar" in sparkly pink letters. She waits until I meet her eyes before speaking, her tone low and sincere. "We're all gonna miss you, that's all. No shame in what you come from, Poppy darlin'." She glances back down to the suitcase and shifts her cherry-painted lips to the side. "Well, you get my meaning."

And I do. I truly do. I love where I'm from almost as much as I love Cookie herself, and I'd do just about anything for her. Being proud of my roots is not a hardship. But last I checked we weren't living on Tara and Rhett Butler damn sure wasn't knocking on my door. Bobby Lee Collinsworth, on the other hand, can't seem to stop. I feel my heartburn kick in again at the thought, but I muster up a smile because I know she needs it. "I know, Cookie. And it's just New York, not New Zealand. I'll be back so often y'all will be sick of me."

A wistful smile curves her lips and I feel myself beginning to tear up. She must notice because she releases me and steps back. "Well, supper's not gonna fix itself. You come on down and I'll put you to work."

I manage a return smile and nod. "Be right there."

Cooking with my grandmother while I've been staying here these past two weeks has been a secret pleasure. We wake with the proverbial rooster and prepare scrumptious plates of crepes with fresh cream and wild berries or fluffy omelets with Gruyère and chives with stacks of bacon and sausage from a farm just outside Savannah. And always, *always*, a giant platter of flaky scratch biscuits with home-made preserves. Guests at the historic Violette Inn awake to the scents of freshly ground coffee and buttery baked goods right out of the oven. It's all part of the tradition Cookie's own mother began and one her daughter is sure to maintain until she outlives us all.

I look around the room where I've been staying, its buttercup yellow walls and maple four-poster bed as familiar to me as my own reflection. I'll probably miss the B & B more than the apartment I just gave up. But it's all part of a bigger plan.

"No fair." Another voice comes from the doorway and I don't need to look to know it's my sister. "If you start crying, I'm gonna start crying, and then before you know it, every damn person in the place will be blubbering like it's a funeral procession."

I cough out a laugh through the lump in my throat.

I reckon I shouldn't be surprised at my tears since moving means leaving my entire family behind—not that I haven't thought about selling a member or two over the years but who hasn't? And I know I'm being a bit impulsive, but my gut keeps telling me I need to get my ass out of here and shake things up—spread my wings.

So, when a long weekend visit to my friend Katelyn in the Big Apple turned into an impromptu interview with the publisher of *Warbey's Home Living* magazine—yeah, *that* magazine—I took it as a sign. I'm turning over a new leaf and New York had better watch out for Poppy James!

But it doesn't make saying goodbye any easier.

I sharpen my expression. "I'm a badass modern woman and we don't shed tears. We strike fear in the hearts of mere mortals and make *them* cry."

Iris whoops, her curly blond locks dancing in time to her movements. "Damn straight!" She comes closer and drops onto the bed. "Now, let's practice again."

I grimace and she shoots me a scolding look. "If you show up with that accent, the only job you're gonna get is in the mailroom or at a strip club wearing nothing but your cowboy boots and a smile."

My eyes dart to the door and I shush my sister. "If Cookie hears you, she'll skin both our hides."

Iris rolls her eyes. "Cookie thinks you should bring a basket of homemade biscuits and a jar of her apple butter to a job interview. She doesn't understand how cutthroat the publishing industry is—especially in New York."

My hand goes to my hip. "And how exactly do you know? You've never even been there."

"I have a TV, Poppy. And I've seen *The Devil Wears Prada*. Meryl Streep would chew your Southern ass up and spit you out before you had a chance to whip out your résumé." She raises an eyebrow and her resemblance to Cookie is uncanny. "You'd best take me seriously or you're gonna be tucking your tail between your legs and coming home before you know it!" Her tone turns ominous. "And we both know what that means."

The heartburn is back. "Fine." I sigh. Maybe she's right, and it never hurts to be prepared. I straighten my spine and clear my throat. "I had the most delectable Brussels sprout tacos last night. They truly were perfection." My voice comes out without a trace of my Georgia accent. Iris raises her pointy little chin and gives me an impressed nod before I continue. "Cancel my one o'clock. My chi is unbalanced and demanding hot yoga. I'll return as soon as balance has been restored."

Iris laughs and I drop on the bed next to her, letting myself fall back on the ruffled duvet. She shoves the empty suitcase to the floor and mimics my pose. "You're gonna do great."

"Your lips to God's ear."

She flips over and props herself up on her elbows so she can look at me straight on. "You're not some inexperienced hack, Poppy. You've been working your tail off for ten years. Nobody knows magazine design like you, and you've got the success stories to back it." She narrows her eyes. "Do I need to pull out Mama and Cookie's scrapbooks to remind you?"

I groan. "Please, no." Then I bolt upright. "Crap. I'd better find those and hide them before anybody shows up tonight."

"Two steps ahead of you, sis. I already stashed them in

the linen closet." She tilts her chin with meaning. "Under the plaid sheets."

I look back at my little sister. The plaid sheets have always been deemed tacky and are only to be used in emergencies. The scrapbooks are safe. "What am I gonna do without you, Rissy?"

She sits up too and pats my thigh. "I guess I'll just have to visit, now won't I?"

"Whenever you want. I mean it." I feel the tears threatening again as my throat gets tight. "I'd best get downstairs and help with supper."

We both stand and Iris rights the suitcase before her hands freeze. "Oh my good lord." Her eyes are fixed on the yellow print. "Somebody's gone and lost their damn mind."

Her gaze shifts to me and we speak simultaneously. "Bunny."

An hour later I'm elbow deep in Cookie's secret fried chicken dry mix—which I'm ninety-nine percent certain is the same one from *The Joy of Cooking*—when a knock sounds at the back door of the historic townhouse. I look at my hands, knowing there's no way I can manage the knob, so I call out, "Come on in!" and immediately wish I hadn't.

Neatly combed tawny hair over a classically handsome face greets me, complete with a gleaming white smile and a genuine cleft chin Superman himself would envy. "Well, good evening, Poppy. How is the girl of the hour?"

I force a polite smile and wish for some Tums. "Hi, Bobby Lee. I'm doing well, how are you?"

He lets himself the rest of the way in and I only have myself to blame.

"I can't complain. Left the office early so I could make

the most of your last night in town." His smile grows and I can't help but notice it has a distinct trace of indulgence in it.

"That's awful sweet of you, Bobby Lee, but you didn't have to do that." *Really, you didn't* I tack on silently as I arrange the dredging station on the counter for the mounds of chicken pieces I prepared.

I know they say New York has some of the best food on the planet, but I'm not leaving Savannah without some homemade fried chicken. For all I know, the only way I might be able to get it up north is by visiting the Colonel, and that's like eating fish sticks and pretending it's a fresh-caught seafood dinner.

He produces a bouquet of red roses from behind his back and my responding gulp is audible. "It wouldn't be a party without flowers." I smile weakly as he goes on, "And I can't have you forgetting about me, now can I?" Good grief. He's laying it on so thick, I reckon Katelyn is getting his meaning all the way from Manhattan.

I hold up both flour-covered hands and look pointedly at them, taking a calming breath so I don't lose my shit. "Uh, I can't..." But before I can figure out what to say, the door opens again and the kitchen shrinks ten sizes.

Bunny clasps her hands together over her mouth and practically floats into the room. "Oh, Bobby Lee! You are so thoughtful. Those roses are just beautiful." She turns to me with stars in her eyes. "Aren't they just gorgeous, Poppy?"

All I can do is nod as I stand in the middle of the kitchen, my white hands held aloft. "Yes, ma'am."

Bobby Lee bends down and kisses her cheek. "Hi, Mama." She grasps his arm and hugs it to her large bosom like a child's favorite blankie. He smiles down at her and laps it up like he thinks he's Jason freaking Momoa in a pastel blue polo and chinos. I fight an eyeroll.

But Bunny's not done. "I see you've got your hands full, dear, so I'll just put these in some water for you." She plucks the bouquet from Bobby Lee's hand and heads directly for the side cabinet where Cookie keeps the vases. Bunny knows this kitchen even better than I do. "We'll be sure to wrap them up in newspapers and a bag of water for you to take with you in the morning."

I turn to the sink and bite my tongue, unable to control the eyeroll this time. I flip the tap with more force than necessary, but I can't help myself. She really thinks I'm gonna take a bouquet of roses on an airplane? Let's set aside for a moment the fact that everyone knows what red roses mean yet I'm the only one who thinks it's all kinds of inappropriate for my *ex*-boyfriend to waltz in here with what looks like two dozen of the wretched things. My list of items to remember to bring as I move my entire life to another state is long—my ID, my phone, my credit card, my stupid suitcase, and let's not forget my vibrator or my favorite boots. But there's not a rose on that list, red or otherwise.

I know what they're doing, the two of them, and it's not going to work. But I channel Cookie and don't say what I want to say—what I've been wanting to say for months now. "Thanks, Bunny. And thank you for the flowers, Bobby Lee."

Bobby Lee leans in and kisses my cheek, the sharp scent of his hair product reaching me before his dry lips. I hear Bunny sigh from behind me and throw her a stiff smile over my shoulder. "And the suitcase was so... unexpected. You shouldn't have." Lord, I mean that from the bottom of my heart. I don't tell her I'm taping over my bright eyes and bushy tail as soon as humanly possible, and instead reach for a white linen dish towel to dry my hands.

"Oh, it was my pleasure, dear. I got the idea from *Warbey's Home Living*."

The towel drops from my hand and I barely notice when Bobby Lee retrieves it for me.

"Of course the article showed it with a different design, but as soon as the idea popped in my head I knew you'd love it!" Her round cheeks are pink with pleasure.

Kill me now.

But death doesn't come, so I choose to take this as a sign that I'm doing the right thing by moving. Katelyn and Athena Lennox, the publisher from the dinner in NYC, are on a mission to overhaul *Warbey's Home Living* and bring it firmly into the twenty-first century. And I'm drooling at the chance to be a part of it, no matter how small.

What I haven't told my family—apart from Iris—is that I don't *technically* have a job in New York yet. They might be under the impression I secured a position with Warbey Publishing, and I may not have said anything to dissuade them from that assumption. But, in my defense, Cookie, Bunny, and my mama were all talking about me having Bobby Lee's babies when the subject came up and I couldn't help myself. I felt the walls closing in and I saw myself scrubbing Bobby Lee's drawers with a baby on one hip and Bunny standing beside me beaming and acting like her son's underpants were made of gold.

So I lied.

There. I said it.

And I don't regret it one bit, because I'm going out there to follow my dream.

And if I can save one poor girl from her ex-boyfriend's mama cross-stitching an insane design on her personal items, I'll count it as a win.

TWO

"A smart woman never leaves the house without two things:
red lipstick and a can of pepper spray."
– Cookie Rutledge

I'M at a bit of a loss. Athena Lennox, badass publisher-at-large, sits across the conference room table waiting for an answer to her question about a color story I proposed. It's not that I don't have a response at the ready—I'm confident the vibrant violet theme is on the nose. No. The problem is the huge mouthful of what I was *told* was iced tea pooling in my mouth like a partially dissolved aspirin on my tongue. In a word, it's revolting.

I put up a finger in the universal gesture for "give me one frickin' minute while I try not to spit my drink on your flawless silk blouse" and breathe through my nose. But there's nothing I can do but force the vile concoction down my throat in one painful gulp. So I do, setting off a violent coughing fit that has me sounding like a chain smoker sucking on his last cigarette.

"Are you okay?" Athena shifts back the tiniest bit in her chair—not that I can blame her.

My finger goes up again, this time communicating I need a minute to either continue dying or get control of myself. A good thump to my chest helps out and I'm finally able to speak. Or, more accurately, croak.

"Sorry." I just know my fair skin is red enough to match my damn hair. "I thought this was iced tea. It surprised me." I push the plastic cup as far away as possible.

Athena's eyebrows spike. "It is." From what I've learned so far, my new sort-of boss has that thing every woman wants. And I'm not talking about the posh job, the killer boobs, or the devoted husband. Athena Lennox has *her shit together*. I've decided she's my new idol.

And, as I have no desire to look any more idiotic in front of her than I already do, I bring the conversation back to topics I've got a firm grasp of.

"Ultraviolet is the unofficial color of the year, so we'd be crazy not to take advantage of it for the first issue. With our own spin, of course. We don't want to trend too young." I slide another page layout in front of her with a stunning mix of violets and grays. "The combination is appealing to both men and women."

Athena nods as she leans forward, bringing her reading glasses to rest on her nose before examining the page design. I want to bite my nails, but I promised myself I wouldn't do that anymore, and I'm actually to the point where I might be able to get a manicure one day. We're waiting for photography and copy, but I'm hoping Athena can still envision the design as being right in line with the brand identity we've worked out over the past couple weeks.

"I love it. Get the latest copy from Katlyn and Naveed and let's take it for a test drive." She removes the glasses and leans back again, holding the temples between her fingers. Her every movement is so natural and confident.

I remember to straighten my back and check my accent.

"Terrific! We'll get it finalized, then."

I've been working with everyone remotely from Savannah for the last few weeks, so I'm up to speed on the project and I'm familiar with most team members—as much as you can be over email and the occasional Face-Time call. But it's always different in person. Back there, I'd be wearing my jeans or shorts and bare feet while I video-conferenced at my desk. From the waist up, I was a slick, Iris-approved executive. From the waist down, I was Daisy-freakin'-Duke. But now that I'm in New York, shit is getting real.

Let me repeat that. I'm in New York. I'm in *New York!* The Big Apple. Gotham. Empire City. The place where *Moonstruck* was filmed and toilet paper was invented (you don't believe me, look it up). The city that never sleeps—a fact I know to be true from the drunk person belting out "Dancing with a Stranger" last night on the sidewalk outside Katelyn's apartment.

But finally being here means I feel like I'm "on" all the time. I was brought in for this exceptional opportunity and I need to get it right. Iris's voice constantly echoes in my head. *Don't even think about putting on those flip flops, Poppy. Throw away that ponytail holder, Poppy. Stop saying y'all, Poppy. Try the green juice, Poppy. It's supposed to be chewy, Poppy.* It's exhausting trying to hold up this high-class persona. Not to mention I've almost bitten a hole straight through my tongue keeping myself from responding, "Yes, ma'am" and "Yes, sir" to every person who speaks to me.

Except when it's just me and Katelyn, that is.

The first time she heard my new "Northern" accent on a video call, I thought she was gonna fall out of her chair. Luckily, she's an excellent friend and didn't call me out in front of everybody. But that doesn't mean I didn't hear all about it later on.

"What the hell was that all about? 'I don't believe so, Athena, but I'll verify.'" Her imitation of me was spot on, I hate to say.

"Hush up, will you?" I had half a mind to hang up on her.

Katelyn laughed. "The Poppy I know would have thrown at least a couple 'I reckon's and a good-old-fashioned 'Later, y'all!' in there somewhere. It's not like they don't know you're from Georgia."

I stood and padded to the door to make sure Cookie wasn't anywhere in earshot. The coast was clear, but I still closed my door. "Look, I'll already be the new girl, not to mention one of the youngest people at this level. The last thing I need is for people to have any reason to not take me seriously."

The first time I was made project leader on a rebrand for a regional publication, I dealt with a few designers who didn't appreciate reporting to a woman half their age. I worked my ass off and eventually won the grudging respect of two of them, but some people will just never accept anything but what their own outdated thinking dictates. And now that I'm entering the piranha-infested jungle swamp that is New York's magazine publishing industry, I'll need all the armor I can wear.

"Oh, come on. Your work speaks for itself. And you forget Athena and Natalie already met the *real* you."

I bit my lip. "I was kinda banking on them maybe being too drunk to remember."

She snickered and I couldn't help but laugh at myself.

Kate and I have an interesting relationship. It's one of those where we don't see or talk to each other for ages but when we finally do, we fall right back into conversation like we'd never been apart. We met in college when we both decided to do summer internships in the Appalachian Mountains working in disadvantaged communities. We clicked from day one and have stayed in touch on and off since, despite living eight hundred miles apart. It was pure chance that had me looking her up in New York last month when I decided to escape there on a whim.

"All right. I'll keep your dirty little secret for now, but I happen to love your accent."

"Aw, shucks, Kate." I purposely drew out the drawl. "I reckon I ain't never had a compliment so dang sweet."

The sound of her laugh hit my ears just before the dial tone. The bitch hung up on me!

But I've stuck to my guns and I'm working this new, improved Poppy. My New York Poppy. Kind of like Clark Kent and Superman. Nobody ever gives Superman a hard time, but plenty of people treat Clark like a nobody from Smallville. And I can't afford to be a nobody.

I still can't believe I got this gig at Warbey. It's the stuff of dreams for a design junkie like me. Okay, so maybe it's not official, but I'm getting paid so that counts for something. Now we just have to finish the research and this prototype so Athena can present it to the board of directors at Warbey. With any luck, they'll approve the transition from stale homemaker's magazine (that gives women crazy-ass ideas like cross-stitching crazy shit on perfectly good luggage) to a fresh, stylish guide for women and men looking to strike a balance in their lives and do it with a flourish. Goodbye to *Warbey's Home Living* and hello to *Work.Home.Life. WHL*.

It's not like they don't have other publications at Warbey, but *Warbey's Home Living* used to be their flagship magazine. Every woman in twentieth-century America had a subscription to the damn thing. But it's been the twenty-first century for going on twenty years now and it's high time for an overhaul before the circulation numbers finish circling the drain. There are only so many Bunnys in this world who still consider greeting your husband at the door with a cocktail and his favorite slippers as the way to please a man. From what I can tell, today's man would much rather come home to a nice blow job. The cocktail is optional.

Not that the new, improved *WHL* will be giving out that kind of advice, but it's downright naïve to ignore sex in this day and age. Athena's team has been busting their asses to come up with a winning variety of content. We've all offered our own suggestions, of course—you know, since it's fun—but the look of the new magazine is my job. If we pull this off, I'll be the creative director of a real live national publication. I've been pinching myself so often I'm likely to have a nice collection of bruises.

"Honey, I'm home!" I close the door behind me and crane my neck to see if Katelyn's home yet. As far as New York apartments go, hers is huge, I'm told. But it still feels a bit like a shoebox to me. She's lucky because her grandma lived here for ages so it's one of the few rent-controlled apartments in the neighborhood. There's hardly room for a kitchen table, and the kitchen itself is about half the size of my old one in Savannah, but I can't complain.

Kate has been nice enough to let me stay here as long as I need, and her guest bed is a pillowy heaven. I'm dreading shopping for my own place, but I need to do it soon. As in, tomorrow. Ugh. I'm not taking advantage of Kate's hospitality any longer than strictly necessary. You know what they say about houseguests: they're like fish. After three days they start to stink.

I can hear the shower running, so I wander to the kitchen to grab a snack while I wait for Kate to finish. It took me forever to get back to her place from work because the sidewalks and subway were jammed like you'd expect on a Friday at rush hour. I didn't dare descend to the 7th Avenue station until seven o'clock or I'd have likely been crushed to death or had a panic attack from the swarm of warm bodies.

But I'm here now and it's my first Friday in New York. I secretly hope Katelyn has plans for us tonight. The last time I was here, we had a blast, but I know that was just because I was on a short vacation of sorts. I have to assume tequila shots aren't Kate's norm on a Thursday night. But I still want to go out. I want to see the city at night again and go dancing or something. Anything to celebrate my new life—my new freedom!

I shove a handful of raisins in my mouth just as Katelyn emerges from the bathroom—in her pajamas. Now, I've watched *Sex and the City* so I know there are plenty of night clubs here with weird-ass themes. Yet I'm guessing none of them call for sleep attire. Sigh.

"How old are you?"

Katelyn gasps and brings a hand to her boobs.

"Crap! You scared me."

"You're really not helping your case by clutching your pearls, Kate." I grin at her and throw a few more raisins in my mouth.

She scowls at me. "Give me a break. I'm still not used to having anybody here."

I feel guilty for a hot second before I remember I'll probably be living in my own shoebox with six roommates come next week. I was warned everybody here has roommates and lives in a hellhole. But I still know it's time for me to find a place of my own.

But, more importantly, it's time to go dancing.

"Tell me you're not going to bed." I gesture up and down her frame, indicating her matching cotton shorts and cami. "It's like seven thirty."

She strides past me and I don't miss her slight chin raise as she grabs her laptop from the counter. "I have work to do. The story assignments aren't going to make themselves. And if I have any hope of catching up with you or Zach—" Her words skid to a stop before she stalks past me again on her way to the couch. "Anyway, I need to buckle down and catch up this weekend."

My grin is huge now, and I suppress the urge to sing a version of "Kate and Zach Sittin' in a Tree." She's got a new boyfriend, but she's staying pretty tight-lipped about it.

I watch her again as her brow furrows at something on her laptop and she chews on her lip. I guess I hadn't realized just how stressed she was, but it shouldn't surprise me. She's got a gazillion people under her at Warbey and she ditched her old job to take a chance on this new magazine. I set down my box of raisins and go over to the couch.

"Can I do anything to help?" I plop down beside Kate and rest my head on her shoulder.

She turns, one corner of her mouth lifting. "No. But thanks." She sighs and rests her head against mine, her straight blond bob getting caught up in my crazy red mess of hair. "Sorry to flake on you your first weekend here."

"It's okay. I should probably spend tonight calling everyone back home to assure them I haven't been murdered or kidnapped yet."

"Has Bobby Lee called?"

I cough out a laugh and straighten to look at her. "Surprisingly, no."

"Wow. I think I underestimated him. Of course, you know, he could be on his way here right now to throw you over his shoulder and drag you back to Savannah."

I straighten and fake a shudder, but I don't have to work too hard at it.

"Okay, that settles it. I'm going out. I can't be here when he comes knockin'." I jump up from the couch.

"I'll just tell him you found your own place when he shows up at the door." She grins at me. "If he asks for the address I'll say cardboard boxes don't get house numbers around here."

It's my turn to laugh, but I'm not joking about going out. It's my first Friday in the Big Apple and I'm not spending it in my pjs reassuring Cookie and Mama that I'm following their advice and walking around double-fisting pepper spray. I mean, really, how much trouble can a girl get into going dancing?

"HERE YOU GO." One of those mini glass bottles of Coke appears on the speckled countertop before me with a thud, the condensation beading and dripping down the slim container.

I grasp it and bring it to my lips where I greedily suck the contents down my dry throat, not stopping to thank the waitress or caring that I just paid four dollars for the lousy thing. Cookie would be utterly appalled by every aspect of my behavior, but she's not here. Here being the broiler pit of Satan that is New York City in midsummer. Who knew?

Dropping the empty bottle back to the counter, I gasp in a breath and pull at my top for the eightieth time in the last hour and a half. It must be all the tall buildings; they don't allow for any breeze. Combine that with the congested traffic and the sidewalks that absorb the sun's rays by day only to spit them back out at night, and I'm beginning to feel like Georgia might not be the hottest spot on earth anymore.

I know I should have been drinking water all night, but

it's not as easy as it sounds. The lines are long and there's not a drinking fountain or vending machine in sight. I guess I should have stopped at the bodega down the street from Kate's apartment, but it was hard enough getting out of there in the first place.

It seems Katelyn thought I was kidding when I said I was going out on my own for a night on the town. So, when I emerged from the bathroom with fresh makeup and my favorite sparkly top, I got her panic eyes.

"You can't go out by yourself." Kate's hands dropped from her laptop to the couch cushions.

I smiled and continued to the kitchen to grab my purse. "Uh, why not, Mama? I swear I finished my homework."

"Not funny."

Not wanting to make her feel bad, I reined in my sarcasm. "I won't go far, and I promise I'll take a taxi home."

She scoffed. "Yeah, Poppy. Be sure to tell the guy who roofies you to tip well."

I zipped my purse and leaned against the counter to face her. "I'll be fine. I'm not even planning on drinking. I just want to go out."

Kate bit her lip and looked down to her laptop again before setting it aside and standing. "Haven't you ever heard of the buddy system? It was invented for single women in New York." She scurries toward her room. "I'm coming with you."

She was like a mama bear protecting her cub from the poachers—and the sleazy dudes of Midtown.

"Kate, no." I moved to cut her off. "You said yourself

you need to catch up on work. I refuse to be an inconvenience or get in the way of your badass-ness."

The corner of her mouth lifted. "Is that a technical term?"

"Yeah."

She tilted her head. "You know you could never be an inconvenience, right?"

I smiled and smushed her in a hug, further cementing my resolve to find my own place before I got Kate fired or gave her an ulcer.

"And *you* know I've got two cans of pepper spray in my purse and dead-to-nuts aim with these boots, right?"

It took a bit of convincing, but she finally relented once I downloaded a locator app on my phone and promised not to talk to any boys.

And I've kept my promise, not that it's been too hard. For one, I haven't found a single place that might have a dance floor—apart from a small jazz club I'd need a week's rent to pay cover entry for. Second, there's something seriously wrong with the men here. Or, at least the men I've encountered tonight. Half of them are prettier than me and the other half look directly through me. It's a whole lotta weird.

The only attention I've gotten was from a homeless guy who called me Daphne and asked if he could see my underwear. I politely declined and got my ass out of there.

Despite the heat, I've noticed everyone is dressed like they're on their way to the office, making me wonder exactly how late things get started around here. As far as I can tell, it might be past my bedtime.

So, I've been walking. Past the clusters of narrow

restaurants and newsstands, past the slick suits drinking at the whiskey bar with their two-hundred-dollar haircuts and freshly-shaved chins. And right on by the twenty-some-things dressed in black pants and ponytails hoofing their way down to the subway for their shifts at one restaurant or another. The city is alive. And it's frenetic.

I swear, the sidewalks are a perpetual starting line of the Boston Marathon, people on all sides trying to push their way to the front of the pack for a breakaway. And I'm that racer who forgot to train and chugged a bottle of wine the night before the big race. It's enough to make a girl downright claustrophobic.

I reckon New York will take a lot of getting used to.

I run the back of my hand over my forehead, knowing I'm well past wiping away any makeup that may have lingered. It's probably time to call it a night. I was a damn fool to think I could just wander down the street and happen upon a casual dance club. This is Manhattan, for cryin' out loud!

The waitress is busy with someone else so I drop a five on the counter and slide off my stool, ready to find my way back to Katelyn's. But when the door of the diner shuts behind me, I realize I have no freakin' idea where I am. Oops.

A quick look at my phone's GPS shows I'm a good two miles from the apartment. How did I go so far? The streets are still lined with cars and a couple taxi drivers are yelling back and forth at each other in a language I can't identify. I squeeze past a group of laughing women and step out of the way before I'm plowed down by a rogue duo who appear to be late for their scuba lessons. What else could explain the neoprene?

I know I should get a taxi like I promised Kate, but the walk back will do me good—and save me a few more bucks for my apartment hunt. The map has me walking up four more blocks before turning left at a broad brick building with three closed garage bays and a large darkened window covered in dust. The street traffic here is thinner and the cross-street looks more like an alley to me than the kind of well-lit, overpopulated street a first-timer like me should traverse at night, so I stop at the corner and hesitate. I'm sure I've seen this in more than one horror movie. If I go up another couple blocks and cut over, I'll only add a few more minutes to my route.

I shove my phone in the back pocket of my jeans, wishing yet again that I'd worn a skirt so I could at least get a breeze up in there. But a deep, stony rumble freezes me before I can take a step.

"Stop. Right. There."

THREE

WHY MY FEET OBEY, I have no damn clue, except for some possible primal instinct that assumes the voice I heard is that of God. Or Samuel L. Jackson. You know, because they've both been known to hang out in dim Manhattan alleyways.

"Just stop!" The tone shifts from a growl to a bellow and I turn to it before I can think better.

The breath I've been holding whooshes out as I realize the voice is coming from the other side of the dark, dirty window of the building. This guy isn't talking to *me*. In fact, considering I know about three people in this city, and the only person who's deigned to speak to me tonight thought I was the real-life incarnation of Daphne from *Scooby Doo*, I want to laugh at myself for assuming he was.

My boot pivots on the pavement to take me back to the sidewalk, but not before the window is flooded with light from inside. A large form steps out behind the glass and I find my back plastered to the brick alleyway wall beside the window. What the hell am I doing?

"You know I don't deal with this shit. Talk to Elle." The voice comes again, and it's so close I swear I can almost feel this dude's breath on my neck. I wouldn't be surprised to discover he just finished dining on a plateful of razor blades with the rough way his words are climbing out of his throat. One thing is for sure. I'm glad I'm not on the other end of that phone call 'cuz *somebody's* got their panties in a serious bunch.

Sweat runs down the back of my neck and soaks into the fabric of my top. The brick bites into my spine when I push off the wall the tiniest bit so I don't ruin the silk—okay fine, the polyester blend.

It's not like I have any reason to hide in the first place; last I checked this is a free country and I can walk by a damn window if I please. Iris would be rolling her eyes if she saw me now. What ever happened to the badass woman who makes grown men cry? I'll be damned if I'm gonna cower under the voice of some random guy who's not even talking to me.

The figure moves away from the window and I crane my neck as curiosity gets the better of me. The window is one of those old ones with over a dozen individual leaded panes. The top row stands open which explains why the man's voice feels so close. I briefly question the wisdom of leaving your windows open at night in New York City but dismiss that thought immediately when he speaks again. I'd dare anybody to mess with that voice.

"Yeah. Fine. I gotta go."

His back is to me and I watch as he pulls his phone from his ear and drops it on a nearby table with a crack. He straightens and brings a hand behind his neck to grip his t-shirt and then it's gone, leaving a huge swath of muscled, inked skin and a dryness in my throat even the hottest of weather couldn't duplicate.

The caked-on grime fanning out from the grilles of the window panes impedes my view, but one thing is crystal clear.

King Kong wasn't a myth. There is a real live beast living in New York City.

And I've just discovered his lair.

"WHAT'S HE DOING NOW?"

I have officially entered the stalker zone and there is no going back. Iris is literally on the other end of the line eating popcorn and listening to me describe every move this guy makes. I'm doing my best to be subtle, but I'm a bit surprised he hasn't drawn a crowd, to be honest. If the window faced the main street he could sell tickets.

What started off as me sneaking a peek to make sure the dude was human sort of... evolved... into a straight-out creeperfest hosted by yours truly. Lord knows what they put in the water up here, but we don't grow men like that back home. He's easily six-foot-five with a crown of tangled midnight hair and a finely hewn body of muscle and tattoos. While he's roughly the *size* of King Kong, he's not covered in a fur pelt, thank God. I have yet to get a good look at his face, but there is *plenty* to feast my eyes on elsewhere.

"Huh?" I bite my lip as the guy lets out a grunt over the music coming from inside. He's partial to classic rock if the soundtrack so far is anything to go by.

"Poppy! Focus!"

His arms halt their circular movements as he straightens again and takes a few steps closer to the wall in front of him where two heavy ropes are anchored. It was about the time he started doing these battle-rope exercises that my thumbs dialed Iris. And all three of us have been working up quite a sweat over the past twenty minutes as he's run through his workout and I've followed his every move. At first, I had no damn clue what he was doing, but Iris cleared it up once I sent her a picture.

What? The guy was unfurling these giant ropes the circumference of my biceps and it was within the realm of possibility that he had a nefarious purpose. I'm determined to be a good citizen of my new city.

Anyway, she told me what the ropes were called, and I've been narrating his workout since.

"Um," I tilt my head and follow the line of a winding black and red tattoo until it meets with his gym shorts over his left butt cheek. I can't even begin to examine below his exposed skin just yet or my head might explode. "He's kind of crossing the ropes back and forth now. Do you think I should get a tattoo?"

"You've been in New York for like five minutes. I'd hold off a few more days."

"Yeah, you're probably right." I watch as the hulking man's muscles bunch and release with every movement. Led Zepplin blares from the speakers and sweat pours over his skin like he's just risen from the ocean. Good God above, who *is* this guy?

The room is some kind of open warehouse space with a few shop tables scattered throughout the part I can see. Maybe an old firehouse or garage? A good portion of the interior is blocked from view, but I'm pretty sure he's alone.

I glance around me, but nobody is paying any mind. People continue to pass on the sidewalk, although the crowd here is much sparser than before, and I'm still off to the side where the streetlights don't quite reach.

"So, what else have you been doing on your first big night on the town? And where's Katelyn anyway?"

We honestly hadn't gotten past the topic of mysterious muscle-bound hotties.

"She had to stay in and work, so I went out on my own."

"Nice! Good for you, sis." She crunches another bite of popcorn.

"Yeah, well, I'm trying." I shrug and shift my weight to one hip. "Did I tell you Mama called last night to check on me *again*?"

"No. Not that it surprises me. Are she and Daddy having fun on their trip?"

I snicker. "I think she was drunk."

Iris snorts out a laugh. Mama's been known to have a

Mimosa now and then but I've never once seen her tipsy. Now, Cookie, on the other hand...

"I guess that's what an all-inclusive vacation gets you."

I'm fixing to give her a recap when the first few notes of the next song hit our ears and Iris starts laughing. "Is your big dude listening to 'Cherry Pie'?"

The lyrics of the ridiculous Warrant song blast from the window behind me.

"Sorry, Popps, but I can't let you lust after a guy who has this song on his playlist."

I gasp. "What are you talkin' about? This is one of the greatest works of the twentieth century. You should see how hard I'm jamming to this song."

A chime sounds in my ear and Iris has switched to FaceTime. I hit accept and start headbanging, my hair flying around me and coming loose from the impromptu ponytail I shoved it in at the diner.

She starts shouting the lyrics and I'm having trouble properly rocking out while one hand tries to hold the phone steady. I bend my knees and go low, sticking my ass in the air as my shoulders shimmy and my boots rock against the pavement.

My heart is light as air right now. Who needs a club when I can dance my ass off and act like an idiot with my sister? I don't even care if anyone is looking anymore. Let them look, because I'm in New York City having a blast and letting my freak flag fly—even if I'm technically by myself. And even if I'm doing it while tethered to home. It's a start, and I'll take it.

"Work it, bitch!" Iris cackles.

So I toss my head and shoulders back and mouth the

words into the phone like a bonafide rock star at Madison Square Garden. My hair clings to my face and neck and sweat beads at my temples but the heat no longer bothers me.

"Bobby Lee would lose his shit if he saw you like this."

I move to a one-hand air guitar and pant. "Bobby Lee can kiss my lily-white Southern ass for all I care!"

"You best watch your mouth, young lady. God's listenin'." Her Cookie impression is spot on.

"Not now, Cookie. I gotta finish my song." I resume shredding the bridge and Iris takes over on drums. We're utterly ridiculous and it's sublime.

When we hit the chorus again, I throw my free hand in the air and swing my hips. "I swear, it's so good to talk face to face."

Iris adjusts her phone so she can pull popcorn out of her hair. "Well, I'm glad my face makes you happy." She sticks her tongue out.

I shake my ass in appreciation and she spills her drink on herself. "You'd think with the sheer number of people here you couldn't feel lonely, but they walk around in these self-contained little bubbles." I scrape back a couple strands of sweaty hair from my cheek. "I guess I'm just gonna have to fight the federation with my mad air-guitar skills."

"And your ass shaking," she adds as the song starts winding down.

I laugh and smack my own ass, holding the phone out so she doesn't miss it. "Never underestimate the power of a nice ass to bring people together."

Iris opens her mouth to deliver what I'm sure will be a smart-ass reply but instead I just get an, "Oh, shit! Hide!"

"Wha—" I start, but she's dropped the phone and all I hear is her cursing.

That and the creak of what I suspect might be a very old, very dirty window opening behind me. My eyes go wide and I freeze with my palm on my buttcheek.

"Can I help you?" A familiar growl comes from behind me, followed by the clearing of a few stray razor blades from a throat.

It's highly possible King Kong has just gotten an up-close-and-personal view of my ass.

I rack my brain but cannot think of a single thing to get me out of this, so I lower my phone and run a quick hand over my hair before finally turning around. Genius strikes at the last second and I open my mouth.

"No hablo ingles." Ha! Brilliant!

I try fixing a perplexed expression to my face and hope he thinks I just have a sunburn instead of the serious case of humiliation coloring my face red as... well, a cherry. But as soon as my eyes hit the sweat-soaked t-shirt and travel up—and up—to meet his face, I know I'm not fooling anyone.

And that's when I choke on my own saliva.

Because the most intense set of brown eyes this side of Joe Manganiello are drilling right through me, wiping whatever I had been thinking or planning right from my brain and down to the subway tracks below.

I try swallowing, but I just cough again. Nope. I got nothin'.

He's not smiling, but he's not frowning either. His lips rest in a naturally sensuous line, like he's posing for a sculptor who specializes in super-hot Greek gods. Even with the dim light, I can clearly see his full bottom lip and a jaw that hasn't seen a razor in several days—you know, because he ate them all. Everything on him is damp with sweat, and I'm downright grateful that he thought to throw his shirt back on before speaking to me.

One thick eyebrow makes an almost imperceptible shift upward and his eyes hold mine. "You sure about that?" Then they drop to do a quick sweep of my body and all my nerve ending snap to attention.

At this point, I have no idea what he's even referring to. When I don't respond, he wets his bottom lip and turns his head to the side, revealing a mean scar on his crooked nose and part of a tattoo climbing into the hair behind his ear.

I tuck my hair behind my own ears with nervous fingers. I'm not sure whether to turn tail and run or stand my ground and pretend I wasn't just spying on this giant's super-human workout. I send up a silent prayer in the hopes he didn't notice.

The last few notes of "Cherry Pie" fade from inside and then the music switches to Queen. When I still don't respond, he reaches to close the window. My heart skitters in my chest, more from our strange encounter than the headbanging session.

He's just going to leave without another word? Why did he even open the window in the first place then? Damn, I must be a pretty good actress after all. But there's no time to congratulate myself.

"Can't say I've met too many redheaded Latinas."

And before I can stop my stupid mouth, it opens and throws me right under the bus. "Guess you need to get around more."

There's no need to face-palm, however. Iris is clearly

doing it for us both. "Smooth, Poppy," her voice comes loud and clear from the phone dangling at my side. "Real smooth."

And, if I'm not mistaken, I glimpse a tiny upturn to the corner of King Kong's mouth before the lock clicks shut and he steps out of view, leaving me alone again in the semi-darkness.

It's time to get the hell back to Kate's place where I can die in privacy. I don't dare chance another glance in the window, instead hanging up on my sister and letting my boots take me back through the crowds and on to the apartment. But I have to admit, a small part of me wonders if he might have taken even the tiniest glimpse as I retreated. Is it wrong that I kinda wanted him to?

"God don't like ugly, y'all. That's why He invented karma."
– Cookie Rutledge

"I DON'T CARE what anybody says. Macaroni and cheese is *not* meant to be low fat, low cal or low anything."

Naveed, the feature's editor who's been pulled over to work on the new *WHL* project, grins as he twirls a pen between his well-manicured fingers. Despite my best efforts at ditching my accent and polishing my appearance, I fear I've let the façade slip a tad with a couple people this past week—Naveed being one, and a marketing executive I referred to as "ma'am" being another. It's hard holding up this image for eight hours straight, so it was bound to happen at some point.

I stopped by Naveed's office on my way to get lunch and got a little sidetracked at the mention of cheese. One of the lifestyle writers emailed a piece on Geoffrey Sang, an up-and-coming new chef in town, and I need to get it into the layout of our prototype. Along with the offensive recipe he included for a healthy weeknight twist on mac and cheese.

Obviously, I have no say. My job is to make sure the recipe *looks* good, not tastes good, even if it does feel like sacrilege.

"Lots of young professionals want healthy options they can whip up in thirty minutes or less. We need to remember our core demographic." Naveed eyes me. "As you well know."

I've gotten on with Naveed since our very first meeting. He's friendly, smart, and works just the right combination of confidence and self-deprecation. And he wears yummy cologne so it's enjoyable sitting near him.

"Of course I do, but nobody is going to trust our food section if we push a recipe that doesn't impress." Ugh.

He turns in his chair, the light catching his cropped dark hair and freaking flawless bone structure. "This is Geoffrey Sang we're talking about. You could be black-balled just for suggesting one of his recipes might not be perfect."

I put my hand up. "Okay. But you better believe I'm trying that recipe before it ever goes to print. If it tastes like I think it will, I'll chain myself to the front doors of this building before I let the first issue run with it."

"I'll have to trust your judgment. I don't do carbs." He smooths a hand over his wrinkle-free dress shirt.

Choke!

"There are so very many things wrong with that statement."

He waves the pen in the air in front of him. "You think all this happens naturally? And besides, I save my cheat calories for when I want drinks with a hot date, not some sad evening of... cheese, alone in my kitchen." His lip curls and it's only his wink that keeps me from scowling at him.

"Well." I straighten and reply with feigned superiority. "Some of us are channeling our carbs into our careers, not dating."

He laughs. "Then you've been dating the wrong guys."

I immediately slump. Because he's not wrong. And because Mr. Tall-Dark-and-Growly didn't, in fact, follow me home and beg to take my body last Friday.

It looks like I'll have to live vicariously through other people's sex lives. The last guy I dated was Bobby Lee and he wanted to "wait." For what, I'm not entirely sure. He implied it was marriage, but I got the feeling it was more like Bunny's permission he was waiting on. Turns out we're both old-fashioned in our own way—he doesn't believe in sex before marriage and I don't believe in allowing his mama in the bedroom. Go figure.

But it's a moot point, really, 'cuz there's no way I'm ever marrying Bobby Lee Collinsworth. And he never fooled me anyway. I knew he was sleeping with Courtney Swayne-Thompson back when he was in high school because that girl couldn't keep her mouth shut if you shoved a cat-head biscuit in it. They were all a few years older than me, but the gossip mill runs fast and hard back home, so everybody knows everyone else's business.

That's why I've always been careful to keep my shit wrapped up tight. I kissed my virginity goodbye my sopho-more year of college, but I was damn careful not to do it with anyone from Savannah. Marc Jardina took my v-card and gave me a few orgasms in return over the six months we dated, but the only people to know about that were my college friends, not one of whom was interested in spreading my business around like chicken feed for the clucking hens. And roosters. I swear the men are worse than the women half the time.

"Anyway!" Naveed snaps forward in his chair as if he's just remembered we're at work instead of chatting about our love lives over happy hour. "I've got something to show you, Little Miss Georgia Peach 2010." I sigh and let go of any illusions I had that Naveed was going to forget my slip-up from the other day. You ask somebody about their kin one damn time and suddenly you're a retired pageant queen blessing everybody's freakin' heart. Good God.

But I can't dwell on my ruined reputation with Naveed long when I hear his next words.

"I had the most brilliant idea for that local artisan spotlight you mentioned. I thought you might want to see."

"Absolutely." I lean in when he slides his iPad across the desk toward me.

Being a designer, I'm always interested in following the arts in any form. When we were brainstorming about the magazine, I threw out the idea of featuring different urban artisans each month, and it went over like hotcakes. Big cities are full of artists embracing traditional media and crafts—it's all part of our attempt to recapture a simpler time in our history. That, and rich people pay a shitload for that stuff so they can boast about owning a one-of-a-kind, handmade trinket or wastebasket or whatever.

Naveed opens a new browser window and taps a few

times. "So, this guy does these commissioned iron furniture pieces as well as some general retail items. He's also done a few sculptures. His last piece sold for some ridiculous sum of money." He scrolls and stops on an image.

On the screen is an intricate swirl of black and rust-colored arms curving around a central sphere like planets embracing the sun. It's beautiful and painstakingly detailed.

"Wow. That's gorgeous."

I reach out a finger and continue scrolling down, revealing several chair designs and a set of stools I'd sell my mama for.

"That right there would ensure I'd never leave my apartment." Naveed points out a black chair that looks like it's sole purpose for existence is to hug the human body. I nod in agreement and continue scrolling to a photograph of the artist and my breath catches in my lungs.

The photo is a bit blurry, but I'd know that stare—and that nose—anywhere.

"Oh my God." I can feel my ears get hot.

"What?" Naveed looks up.

I point to the screen without taking my eyes off the brown orbs staring back at me. "I know that guy."

He looks from the iPad to me and back again.

"Not possible. You just moved here." Is that a hint of petulance in Naveed's voice?

I can feel the heat climb up my neck at the memory of Friday's encounter and I focus on the toes of my glossy heels before he can spot my discomfort.

"I, uh, ran into him. The other night."

Naveed is silent for only a second before he exclaims,

"This is perfect!" Either I'm missing his sarcasm by a mile or he is genuinely pleased at my news.

I cough and look up at him again. "How so?"

His mouth is set in a satisfied smile showcasing a deep dimple and a chin as smooth as a baby's butt. "The divo is not taking interviews." He pulls his hand back to inspect his nails. "In fact, I was ready to call in a favor to try and get a one-on-one." His dark eyes snap back up and his steady gaze lends a dramatic overtone to his next words. "Let's just say it's not one I'm anxious to use."

I'll probably find that funny later, but I'm still too discombobulated to find humor in the situation.

Naveed holds the iPad up and jabs King Kong with a finger. "This guy is *hot*."

Ha! He doesn't have to tell me. The image of a broad sweat-slicked back is permanently burned into the back of my eyeballs. I cough again, but Naveed doesn't seem to notice or care that I'm squirming in my drawers over here.

I hum a non-response as I figure out what to say. It's not like I can tell the features editor of the magazine that I practically pole danced in front of this man and then acted like a complete moron. My one job is to project a professional, no-bullshit image, not act like a college kid on spring break.

"I don't *really* know him." Naveed cocks his head and I stumble on, not daring to meet his eyes. "I mean, I just met him briefly. The one time. I don't..." A smile starts spreading over his lips and I might hate him a little. "I don't even know his name."

He's wearing a full-on smirk now.

"Honey, please. If I had to count the times." He sets the

iPad back down and brushes nonexistent lint from his jacket sleeves.

I gasp. "No! No, that's not what I meant." The red is back, and you could fry an egg on my forehead. "Jeez. I didn't... you know."

Naveed's eyes drop back down to the iPad screen and mine can't help but follow when I hear him sigh dramatically.

"I wouldn't blame you if you had."

Bambi in the headlights ain't got nothin' on me.

"Can I go now?"

He reaches a hand across the desk and pats my arm, although he's still smiling like a jerk.

"I'm just teasing. But, really, we should use any in we can to nail this guy down."

Naveed chokes on a laugh when my jaw drops. "Seriously?"

He tosses his hands up. "Sorry. Bad choice of words."

"Can't we just go with some old lady who makes wind-chimes or something?" I'm not above begging.

"Are you joking?" Naveed practically squeaks. "This interview would be a total coup! It's appeal like this that will reach the broadest market. Come on, Pop-Tart. You're charming as hell. If anyone can get this guy to cave, it's you."

My teeth grind at his nickname, but it's like he knows my kryptonite. The last thing I want is to let the team down and not pull my weight. My mind skips back to how hard Kate worked all weekend while I flitted about and went sightseeing, and I can feel the inevitable coming. I'll suck up my pride and take one for the team. Besides, it's not like this furniture guy will remember me anyway. Yeah, let's stick with that.

"Fine."

Naveed hoots and rubs his hands together ala Cruella DeVille, only better dressed.

"But don't be surprised if I get the door slammed in my face." I pin him down with a wicked index finger.

"We've got a ringer," Naveed sings to himself, sending my teeth grating again.

How do I get myself into these things?

WHEN I LEAVE Naveed's office, I'm no longer hungry. Instead, my gut is filled with a cocktail of dread with a splash of lingering butterflies from the memory of a certain furniture-maker's penetrating gaze.

I stop in the restroom on the writers' floor and, like any normal woman, use the opportunity for a bit of self-reflection.

But I barely get past the initial evaluation of my current predicament when the outer door opens and the clack of heels sounds across the tile floor.

"Hey, I meant to congratulate you on the Grammercy Park piece. I see features editor in your future," the first voice says with a teasing tone.

"Thanks," a second one replies. "But don't jinx me."

They've stopped by the sinks and I try not to eavesdrop but it's impossible not to.

"You don't believe in that woo woo garbage any more than I do."

"Maybe not, but better to be safe than sorry. I could end up working on that new disaster of the *Ladies' Book* rebrand."

I slap a hand over my mouth to smother my gasp. What the hell? Who doesn't check under the stalls before talking shit? With that in mind, I sink to a new level and draw my knees up to my chest so my feet don't show should they think better of their careless gossiping. Damn, this is uncomfortable.

"You don't know it'll be a disaster." Okay, I don't hate this one.

"Have you seen the executives they have lined up? Please. Katelyn Perry at least has some built-in credibility, but who in the hell is this chick they brought in for creative? She's younger than my daughter, and I swear I saw her curtsey at security the other day."

The other woman laughs. "Now you're just making shit up."

Yeah! I haven't curtseyed since my fourth-grade performance as Shephard Number Two in the Nativity play. And even then, it was meant to be ironic. I'm sure I just dropped a pen or something when I was passing security. I have half a mind to stomp my way out of this stall and give this twat a piece of my mind. But my brain is having trouble thinking of the right comeback—and I'm apparently a giant coward.

"I'm not." The first woman returns the laugh. "Okay, I might be slightly exaggerating but you know I'm friends with Jen Baylor in the art department. She's paid her dues and then some. It must be nepotism."

I grit my teeth.

"Or she's sleeping with the right person. I hear Art Hillard is due for a fourth wife." Okay, I officially hate them both.

"God, if she can stand looking at that wrinkly set of balls, she deserves the job."

They both laugh their stupid asses off at that one and I can hear two stall doors close as they finally get down to the business of peeing.

I hold my breath and wait for them to finish. It isn't until I hear the outer door close behind them that I finally uncurl my body from its fetal position and get the hell out of there.

They think I'm not cut out for this job? I'll freaking show them.

I hightail it back to the elevator and to my office where I smooth down my hair and adjust my position in my chair before clicking on my new email from Naveed.

Here's the number for his studio. Good luck, ringer!

Damn straight!

My hands are sweating and I'd much rather be doing anything else right now, but I know I need to woman up so I punch in the number on my phone.

"Hello." I practice as I wait for someone to pick up. Too low. "Hello!" I practically screech. Ugh. Too shrill. I can do this.

"Hello, this is Jonathan." A slightly muffled, bored voice sounds on the other end of the line. It's a man, but it's not *my* man. Crap. You know what I mean. Why I thought the beast would answer his own phone is beyond me.

"Hello!" Dammit! I went with the screech. "Ahem. This is Poppy James with Warbey Publishing. How are you today?"

I can hear him sigh on the other end and know this will be an uphill battle. "It's a busy day. How may I help you?"

"We're putting together a series on urban artisans for—"

"Didn't I already speak to someone about this the other day?"

I figure I have maybe ten more seconds before this guy hangs up on me.

"Yes. I believe you did. One of our features writers spoke with someone in your office."

"Well, I'll tell you what I told him. Mr. McKinley doesn't do interviews."

I'm quick to respond. "Yes. I was told this, but I'm hoping he can make an exception."

He does a poor job of holding back his laugh. "And why would he do that? Listen, if you're calling about a chair or a commission, I can help you, but an interview? No."

This is going nowhere fast. I can't let the call end without at least a chance.

I put on my best New York Poppy attitude and try matching his cool tone. "Jonathan, was it?"

"Uh, yes." That's more like it.

"Jonathan, I can assure you Mr. McKinley would benefit greatly from the kind of exposure we're offering." My mind dashes back to the kind of exposure he offered *me* the other night and a flush crawls up my neck again. And then those eyes and that mouth. I mean, wow. An idea strikes and I go with it. "We're talking a possible cover of a national publication. You can't *buy* this kind of publicity. But if he's not interested, I'm sure we can find an alternate—"

"Hold, please."

Yes! I'll ignore the fact that I just kinda promised something I have no business promising. Never mind the prototype cover already features a stunning photo of JoJo Ames —self-made millionaire starlet and entrepreneur. Things are likely to change by the first issue's release in January, right? At least I used the word "possible." Ack.

Thirty seconds pass and my thumb creeps up to my mouth where I start gnawing on the nail. Screw manicures; I've got bigger things to worry about.

Tick, tick, tick. The seconds pass and I'm pretty sure he forgot about me when the line is picked up again.

"Can you be here this evening at six-thirty to meet with his agent?"

I bolt upright in my chair.

"Absolutely!"

"Your name again?"

"Poppy James. And, thank you. I'll see you at six-thirty."

Dropping the phone back down to my desk, I bite my lip to hold back a squeal. I did it! I actually did it! Never mind the interview itself is not a done deal, but I snagged a meeting. New York Poppy is kicking ass and taking names. Those assholes from the restroom can shove it!

I glance down at my gray skirt suit and yellow blouse, suddenly glad I dropped the money on it even though $300 is a ridiculous sum to pay for something that's not even leather. I may have my finger on the pulse of what's new and hot in the design world, but that doesn't mean my personal taste runs the way of hot-shot New York socialites. I'd rather kick it in my jeans and boots any day. But it's like Cookie always says, "You don't need be a racehorse to know how to win." Nevertheless, I'm sticking with my plan to dress the part. Iris and I went on a shopping spree on Broughton Street before I left, and I've had less painful migraines.

But I could kiss Iris right now. I look sharp and put together, and my heels only pinch when I walk. Now I need to call Naveed with the good news and tell him any plans he had for after work are officially canceled.

'Cuz we've got a date with this magazine's future.

FIVE

*"Best stick to your strengths or you just might find yourself
riding backwards on a horse where the view ain't nearly so
nice."*
— Cookie Rutledge

BY THE TIME Naveed and I find a taxi and get our asses down to 10th Street, I'm a mess. Luckily, it's just on the inside. My hair is up in a tight chignon that took me about an hour to accomplish and my makeup says, "Step aside 'cuz I'm fixin' to kick your ass!" Add that to the killer outfit and I definitely look the part. Too bad my insides feel like I'm about to drop off the backside of a rollercoaster at Six Flags.

On the seat next to me, Naveed maintains his air of snappy confidence and types into his phone.

How can he be so damn relaxed? Needing a distraction, I decide to be nosy.

"Anything interesting?"

He glances at me, his mouth curved up and showing off that killer dimple on his left cheek.

"Just digging up some dirt on our man here." He turns the screen so I can see a news headline that reads "Tenneson/McKinley Lawsuit Settled for Undisclosed Sum." I can't see the date or any details, just a grainy photo of several individuals leaving a courthouse. "You can never be too prepared."

I groan inwardly at my stupidity in not doing the very same thing. I need to know more about this guy to make a convincing argument as to why he should give us the time of day. This right here is one of the many reasons I stay behind the scenes in the creative zone.

But it's too late. The taxi comes to a stop and the driver barks out the fare. Before I can react, Naveed whips out a credit card and swipes it on the meter while simultaneously opening the door. I barely have time to jump out before the taxi is pulling away and I'm left on the sidewalk to adjust my skirt back down to a socially acceptable length.

"After you, my dear." He fakes a small bow and gestures for me to go ahead of him. There's no turning back now.

The scene is way too familiar as the brick building looms before me. In the light of day, I can see the garage doors need paint and the windows aren't the only thing needing a scrub down. A set of double doors I missed the last time stand to the left of the garage doors and have two windows covered in newsprint. For someone who hangs out in this kind of dive, this guy sure is a bit self-important.

I try first one knob and then the other but they're both

locked. One deep breath and I summon my self-confidence and knock firmly on the glass before turning to Naveed with a fake-ass smile.

He gives me a nod of assurance and I want to hug him —and smack him for getting me into this.

Before I can cross that line, though, the door swings open and we're greeted by Charlize Theron's twin sister.

"Welcome. Come in, come in. I apologize for the mess." She steps back and gestures around her.

My lips lock in a toothless smile and I reach out a hand. "Hello. Poppy James from Warbey. This is my colleague, Naveed Shah."

Her handshake is firm, her skin dry, and I just hope she dismisses my damp palm as a consequence of the weather.

"Elle Valentine." Of course this is her name. Because with those long legs and gorgeous face, you need additional encouragement for men to fall in love with you. Sigh. "I'm sorry to keep you waiting. My assistant has run off somewhere." I can only assume she's referring to Jonathan and I find myself a bit relieved I won't be dealing with him again today.

"A pleasure to meet you, Ms. Valentine," Naveed practically oozes natural charm and ease.

"Please, call me Elle." Her smile is open.

The space is even bigger than I imagined. The sound of our footsteps on the concrete floor echoes up and around the tall ceilings in this section of the building where metal beams crisscross and industrial lights dangle from huge black fixtures. Accordion metal partitions divide the space, hiding our view of the majority of the area, so I can't see the battling ropes or the side window where I conducted my peeping Tom routine. There is very little natural light due to the lack of windows here, and bright fluorescents leave me feeling over-exposed.

Elle leads us past a set of high white partitions to a large makeshift office to the left of the entryway. I want to check out more of the building, but common courtesy —and the mission at hand—keep me from sneaking a peek.

"Have a seat." She indicates two designer leather chairs sitting across from a sleek glass and iron desk before stepping to the other side and taking a seat in her own chair.

"Thank you for seeing us... Elle," I say as I sit and smooth my skirt over my lap.

She waves me off with a smile and a casual sway of her straight honeyed tresses. "I understand you're interested in Angus for the cover of your premier edition."

Naveed coughs and I want to sink to the floor, but I summon New York Poppy instead.

"It's a distinct possibility, provided the interview goes well, that is." I want to swell with pride at the even control of my voice.

I can feel Naveed's eyeballs searing into my temple.

"Well, he certainly has the face for it." Elle emits a light chuckle and Naveed finally snaps out of it, thank God.

"That he does, Elle. The focus on artisans is aimed at capturing a wide audience, but aesthetics are always the first thing to get the reader's attention, am I right?" His return chuckle is more than convincing.

I could kiss Naveed for playing into my scheme, knowing it's undoubtedly painful for him to put hotness above good writing. Or maybe not. I mean, the man does dress better than anyone I've seen so far in New York. Either way, I owe him for not killing me on the spot.

Elle leans back in her chair and crosses her impossibly long legs. "A cover would certainly bring him to a new echelon, and it would mean more clients. I'm always telling Angus he doesn't use his... assets to his own benefit enough."

The two of them laugh conspiratorially and I have to force myself to join in, suddenly feeling a bit like a smarmy pimp negotiating some exploitative promo for a shy virgin.

But the brute of a man I met the other night is no virgin, and from the sound of his phone conversation, he's no pushover either. I'm sure he can stand on his own two feet without needing protection from anyone, much less his willowy gazelle of an agent. I need to remember I'm here with one goal in mind: make this magazine a success.

If I don't do every damn thing I can to get this publication off the ground, it'll be my own damn fault when I go crawling back to Savannah with my tail between my legs and a smug Bobby Lee Collinsworth to greet me at the airport.

"So, Elle, if you can see your way to smoothing the path for an exclusive with Mr. McKinley, I can assure you we'd be *extremely* grateful."

Elle re-crosses her legs and studies me with a steady gaze. I force myself not to blink under her examination. I'm not exactly sure, but the way I worded that last statement kinda sounded like I might be promising yet another thing I have zero business promising. What the hell am I doing?

Naveed is scratching his chin, something that tells me I'm fully justified in my panic. I need to back up, restate, undo whatever I just did. I open my mouth to begin my retreat, but another voice fills the room instead of mine.

"Making arrangements to sell my soul?"

Double damn!

Elle stands, a stiff smile spreading her lips. "Angus. I didn't realize you were here."

"I wasn't. But I am now."

Naveed stands and I'm the only one left who hasn't turned to face the man I now know to be Angus McKinley, urban blacksmith and sexy beast of the East Village.

Would it really be so bad to call it quits and go back to Georgia?

Despite any preferences I may have on the matter, I'm being forced to face the music as Naveed lightly kicks my foot and I gird myself as I stand and turn. It's possible I'm wearing the same expression I had the time Cookie caught Iris and me leafing through our granddaddy's *Hustler* stash under the bathroom sink, but there's no helping it.

My eyes take in first one bicep and then another, although they're covered by a long sleeve button down this time. I forgot how damn tall the man is, so I'm feeling at an even bigger disadvantage as my gaze sweeps up to take in his scowling face. The whiskered chin and slash of thick eyebrows are the same as I remember, as well as the deep scar across the right side of his nose.

But gone is the neutral expression from before. His mouth is set in an angry twist while his nostrils flare and those flashing eyes are filled with fire. It's a wonder I don't shrivel up into a pile of smoking bones on the concrete floor with the look he's giving me. The beast has transformed from King Kong into a fire-breathing dragon. One that doesn't appear to recognize me, thank God.

Naveed steps forward with a hand extended, which is a good thing since my throat has closed in on itself to the point where I'm lucky I'm still breathing.

"Mr. McKinley, it's a pleasure to meet you."

But Naveed may as well be a tiny gnat for all the attention Angus McKinley pays him. The dragon only has eyes for me. I whimper inwardly as I begin to leak sweat from every pore.

Until my new favorite person on the planet rescues me and puts me firmly in her debt for all eternity.

"Stop terrifying the neighborhood, Angus," Elle scolds with a playful air that impresses the ever-loving shit out of me. She strides over and pets his arm like she's soothing a riled-up stallion.

His expression doesn't change, and his eyes don't stray from me, but the tension in the air eases just enough to allow me to suck in a reviving—if not shaky—breath.

Elle continues stroking his arm as she speaks, "Angus, this is Ms. James and Mr. Shah from Warbey."

He doesn't move a muscle apart from the rise and fall of his chest and I make a concerted effort to block out any image of the tattoos I know to rest beneath the cotton of his shirt. I need to get my act together and salvage whatever I can of this mess.

I force my spine to straighten and I channel Dixie Carter and all the Golden Girls put together. "Mr. McKinley, we were just discussing how we could benefit your business with an article in our forthcoming publication this winter." My voice isn't wavering even a tiny bit so I push on before all my nerve evaporates. "We believe the men and women of our readership are exactly the kind of target—" My resurrected confidence spoke too soon, however, as he cuts me off.

"I don't do interviews." He finally rips his gaze from me and fixes that stare on Elle who, I might note, is not presently sweating like a whore in church. "Made that more than clear."

Elle smiles—*she smiles*—back at him and pats his arm. "Relax. We're just talking."

He stares her down for another few beats and then shakes off her hand before turning to stalk from the room without another word.

Naveed clears his throat as I stand, wishing I had a bath towel to mop up the puddles of sweat that have probably ruined my new suit. Appearing utterly unaffected, Elle leans her hip against the front of her desk and crosses her arms.

"I'll talk to him. Email me your proposal and a contract and I'll be in touch by the end of the week."

"I THOUGHT you said you knew him!" Naveed perches both hands on his hips like a true Kardashian.

"I never said that!" Okay, well I did, but I explained myself quite clearly, I thought.

We're standing on the sidewalk outside Angus McKinley's studio whisper-yelling at each other. I need a stiff drink right the hell now.

"I figured that was how you got the meeting in the first place." Naveed leans in until I can see the flecks of gold in his dark irises. He has really long eyelashes for a dude.

I throw my hands in the air and back up a step. "Well, it wasn't, okay?"

"So you got it by promising his agent a cover story?"

"Yes. No. I don't know!" My eyes go to the sky looking for help I don't deserve. "I don't have a damn clue, to be perfectly honest." I balance on one foot while I reach down and remove one of my heels before I lose circulation and need to amputate my pinky toe. The other one comes off after it and I practically sigh with relief as my bare toes grip the sidewalk. "God, that's heaven."

"Focus, Miss Peach," Naveed hisses. "What are we going to do when Elle gets us the interview and JoJo Ames appears on the cover instead?"

"Jeez Louise, Naveed, I haven't thought that far ahead." In truth, I haven't thought at all—and I'm beyond caring if my South shows its mouth.

Naveed whips out his phone and starts typing with his thumbs while I strip off my suit jacket and fan myself to get my mind rolling. If the contract doesn't promise a cover, then technically I didn't do anything wrong. But will Elle still be interested if a cover isn't part of the deal? It's clear she wants exposure for her client, as any good agent would, but she's shrewd so she won't be a pushover.

"Are you sure there aren't any other reclusive artists we could call on and woo out of their lairs?"

He doesn't even look up from his phone as he hooks a thumb to the brick building. "Not one as fine as that."

I sink my ass down to the curb, not caring how dirty my

skirt gets anymore. A passerby hits me in the head with her huge purse and I give up. "I'm sorry, Naveed. I thought I could... I don't know what I thought."

He looks down at me for a few seconds and then sighs, dropping his phone to his side. "Don't worry your adorable little melon about it." He leans against a signpost and takes me in. "It's not like I helped much."

My mouth curls in a defeated smile. "That right there is the problem."

"Harsh."

"No." My smile is a touch more genuine at that. "It's my 'adorable little melon' that's the trouble. Nobody is gonna take me seriously if y'all see me as some airhead hick playing at the publishing game on some kind of whim. I know what I'm doing. Well, usually—" I huff. "When it comes to *design*, I know what I'm doing." I could tell him about his bitchy writer colleagues, but it's too embarrassing.

Naveed crosses his arms and frowns. "The fact that you're here in New York told me from day one that you know your shit. Athena Lennox doesn't hire charity cases and she sure as shit doesn't keep slackers around."

Well, that's a relief, I suppose. And I know that deep down, but I've got so much riding on this.

"Is that why you only have a Southern accent when you're talking to yourself—or yelling at me on the sidewalk?"

I groan and cover my face.

Naveed laughs. "Why do you think I keep calling you Miss Georgia Peach 2010? The day we met you were having a full conversation with yourself while reviewing layouts. I was ready to pull up a chair just so I could see how the story ended. Riveting stuff."

"Pull out the shotgun and just get it over with, will you?"

"Hey." When I don't respond, he nudges me with his foot. "Hey. I understand where you're coming from. Believe me." I look up and he's gesturing up and down his designer suit as he looks at me. "I'm a thirty-six-year-old gay Pakistani man in a position usually held by fifty-year-old straight white folks with pedigrees the Queen's corgis would envy. There was a time when I tried playing the part, but it doesn't work. You can't do your best work when you're worried about what everybody else is going to think. Now," He straightens his lapels that are already crisp as an origami swan. "Do I look like I give one single fuck if someone doesn't get me?"

I can't help the smile pulling at the corners of my mouth as Naveed runs a hand over the side of his close-cropped hair like he's posing for a cologne ad. "I'll have you know my mama would skin your hide for cursin' in front of a lady like that." I let loose with all the Georgia I have.

He drops the act and grins at me, holding out a hand. "Now, that's more like it."

I take it and let him pull me up next to him.

"I guess I got in a little over my head with this Angus guy, huh?"

He pretends to consider it. "Eh, maybe just a bit. Let Uncle Naveed take care of it."

I scrunch my nose. "Now you're just being creepy."

He smiles and the dimple makes an appearance. He is

one pretty man, I gotta say. "Leave it to me. You focus on being a creative genius and leave the interviews to us pros."

I want to do just that, but I feel responsible—and I don't know if I can rest until I'm sure the magazine will be a success. I clearly ruffled the beast's feathers and I like to clean up my own messes.

The question remains, how in the hell am I gonna do that?

SIX

*"God never liked a liar, unless it was a woman
complimenting her mother-in-law's cookin'."*
– Cookie Rutledge

NEEDLESS TO SAY, my evening plan involves some intense internet stalking of one Angus McKinley. But I need to properly prepare first.

Kate is thankfully off with her boy toy so I'm in no danger of being discovered and I can play my stalking playlist as loud as I want—not that I technically have one, per se. Now all I need are snacks, drinks, a comfy seat, and a notebook for keeping track of pertinent details. Yes, this is serious business. If something I can find will help us secure an interview, I'd be an idiot not to at least do a bit of snooping.

As soon as I'm settled on the couch with a glass of

Moscato, potato chips (don't judge me), and my laptop, I'm ready to begin the hunt. I try unsuccessfully to block out the mental image of his angry snarl and press forward.

"Okay, Mr. McKinley, let's see what you got."

The initial search brings up a couple articles and about a hundred social media profiles, most of which I can immediately dismiss based on age, profession, or location. A couple executives, a pastor, a chef, and several random dudes. It takes a little bit of digging, but I uncover the website Naveed showed me earlier listed under McKinley Forge and Design. I admit I get a bit distracted gazing at all the pretty things I want in my future home, but I purposely avoid stopping for too long at the man's photo. He's sort of like a bad rash—super annoying and impossible to ignore.

The website has very little personal information on the artist himself, so I go back to my friend Google and type in the headline I remember from earlier.

"Tenneson/McKinley Lawsuit Settled for Undisclosed Sum"

Aha! There it is. I sip my wine and start scrolling.

Shipping magnate Dan Tenneson has paid an undisclosed sum of money to settle a lawsuit filed against his family by his former son-in-law stemming from an incident last year.

Angus McKinley, Sr., 56—formerly married to Tenneson's daughter, Margaret Tenneson-Pile, 54—suffered life-threatening injuries after a fall last June from a second-story balcony at the Tenneson home in Norfolk County, Massachusetts. McKinley remains paralyzed from the neck down.

Tenneson, 78—the Boston-based owner of Ten Fleet and whose estimated net worth is just over four billion dollars—declined to comment on the lawsuit's settlement. Bert Dunlaven, a New York attorney representing Mr. Tenneson, issued a statement on Wednesday stating, "Mr. Tenneson and his family are happy to put this ugly episode behind them and get back to the business of shipping. While his deepest sympathy extends to Mr. McKinley, my client admits to no wrongdoing and wishes his former son-in-law only the best."

No response to inquiries for comment from the McKinley family has been received as of the time of printing.

Notably, at the time of the incident, McKinley and Tenneson-Pile's son, Angus McKinley Jr., 35, unsuccessfully pursued criminal charges.

There were no witnesses to the incident and no other parties were injured.

How awful. Suddenly the growly blacksmith's persistent bad mood makes a little more sense. I scroll back to the top to find the date. The article was printed almost three years ago. I do another quick search for Angus McKinley and Dan Tenneson and discover something even worse.

"Paralyzed Man Succumbs to Injuries Following Tenneson Settlement"

I close my laptop, unable to bring myself to read any more. So much for a fun evening of internet stalking. My stomach hurts so I pour the Moscato down the sink, put away the chips, and turn off my music. Serves me right for digging into someone's private life for my own gain. I send a little apology up to the heavens and decide my night would be better spent doing laundry.

I VOW NOT to pester Naveed about his communications with Elle Valentine, knowing that he likely sent a contract without the cover promise. Instead, I choose to focus on doing my actual job and finding an apartment.

If there's one thing I learn from my apartment hunt it's that you can't have a weak stomach or a strong gag reflex if you hope to explore all your options in Manhattan. I don't want to get in over my head so I'm trying to be conservative with my monthly rent. Thankfully, the fees I banked from my last big freelance project with *Bells Magazine* mean I'm not forced to take the fifth-floor walk-up above a seafood shop—even if it's super close to a subway stop and a sex toy emporium that promises to meet all my self-pleasuring needs. Not that I'm into animal-shaped butt plugs, but it's a free country, y'all.

Since I'm still a contract employee until the magazine gets full approval, I don't have as much proof of income to work with. Which is why I thought I'd end up in a shithole with a dozen strange roommates—especially since renting my own place involves a broker's fee plus first and last month's rent.

But luck is finally on my side because my broker calls on Thursday with a renovated one-bedroom in my price range and I sign that lease faster than my granddaddy could load a shotgun. It's a forty-five-minute walk from Kate's place but only a fraction of that if I take the subway, and it's even closer to work. The neighborhood is one of the safest in Manhattan, something I know will keep all of Savannah from caravanning up to NYC to personally deliver more pepper spray.

It feels good to accomplish something on my own. I get to move in next week, so I'll be arranging a reunion with all my worldly possessions as soon as possible. I suspect Iris plans on using that as an excuse to come see me, and I admit I miss her already so I won't complain.

By Friday morning, Naveed still hasn't called so I've all but lost hope on the McKinley piece. But I don't know if Naveed has called in his favor yet or not. Either way, I'm glad I've changed my focus to perfecting our prototype for the board meeting that will decide our magazine's fate. Even if I do still feel responsible for screwing things up for Naveed.

I'm more than pleased with the branding identity we've achieved on the magazine, and the content is going to be fresh and engaging. Katelyn is in charge of content and Athena runs point on everything from marketing to circulation, but if the product doesn't look perfect, it's going nowhere fast. I've put together a bold aesthetic with standout typography, transparency play, and careful attention to white spaces. It's freakin' beautiful, if I do say so myself. And Warbey has some amazing designers, photographers, and web designers so I'll have a crack team when this thing gets approved.

I close my laptop and gather up the power cord so I can take it back to Katelyn's. She's cleared her calendar tonight so we're going out for dinner and drinks, and I need to shake off this raincloud over my head so I don't ruin our night.

My phone rings and when I see it's Naveed, I mentally cross every appendage I own.

"Tell me it's good news." I lean against my desk.

"I wish I could, but the super model said it's a no."

"Dammit. What exactly did she say?" I don't know if I actually want to know since the reason very well could be my big mouth, but I can't help asking.

"She was cagey when I pressed her. Seemed set on just delivering the canned 'thanks but no thanks' response."

I slump back down in my chair. "Well, thanks for trying, Naveed."

"Oh, you think I'm done?" His tone lightens.

A smile pulls at my mouth. "Uh, no?"

"Not by a long shot, Miss Peach. Watch me do my magic."

"That sounds both intriguing and a little scary."

"That's more like it. I'll talk to you Monday."

We say our goodbyes and I'm feeling a little more optimistic—just what I need to start my girls' night out.

"SO, what's this about you going to a meeting with Naveed?"

How I thought I could hide my little mishap from Kate, I don't know. She's Naveed's boss, for cryin' out loud.

I sip my cocktail and look everywhere but at her.

"For what it's worth, I think he'd make a great cover."

"Dude would make a great billboard in Times Square." I roll my eyes and Kate grins at me as she stirs her drink.

We snagged a high table at a pub near Sutton Place because Kate insisted I show her my new apartment building, and now we're on our second drink of the night. I'm surprised it took her this long to bring it up.

"Seriously, though, we could probably make a go of it for one of the later issues."

I scrunch my nose. "Yeah, I may have burned that bridge unless Naveed can work miracles. And, besides, the guy is practically a recluse." I summon up my most grumpy expression and mimic the big beast. "I don't do interviews, dammit!"

Kate hums her response and studies me in silence from behind her drink.

"What?"

She shrugs but it doesn't come off quite as casual as I think she intended. "You have an awful lot invested in this for someone who's in a completely different department."

I open my mouth to respond but nothing snappy comes out, so I deflect. "Do you have to pee? I think I have to pee." I make a move to hop down from my stool.

Kate grabs my arm and grins like a monster. "All right, all right, I'll shut up about it."

I draw in a breath and then give up. "Oh, God." My forehead drops to my hands. "You'd have to meet this guy to understand. He looks at you and you're like... uhng. And then his voice, I mean... gah. Even his eyebrows, it's like... I don't even know!" I risk a glance and Kate's biting her lip to keep herself from laughing in my face.

I consider for a brief moment that I may have romanticized some of it in my head since reading that news story but... nope—my gut still drops to my toes when I imagine being in the same room as him. I throw my hands out. "Seriously, this man can say more with an eyebrow than Nora Roberts can say with a whole damn book. And all of it is downright filthy—at least that's how it is in my head. And Naveed's too, I'm pretty sure."

She finally gathers herself enough to speak. "Well, he sounds... delightful." She's a damn Cheshire cat. "You should ask him out."

My jaw drops. "Did you not hear what I just said?"

Kate nods. "Yup. You think he's hot and you want him to talk dirty to you."

I have no words, so I throw my napkin at her.

She dodges it and laughs. "Relax, I'm just joking."

I scowl at her and shift in my seat, ignoring the stab of disappointment that comes from God knows where.

"If it were a discreet roll in the sheets, I'd say go for it, but nothing about that tongue-tied, lovesick show you just put on says casual and discreet to me." She grins. "Probably best to keep your nose clean and admire him from afar."

I nod in agreement, trying not to let her see the pout I feel coming on. Then I slip off the stool and retreat to the ladies', muttering to myself the whole way. The bar is noisy with voices raised over the music—some mix of alt-rock and R&B that has me scratching my head. There's a line at the restroom so I settle in for a wait, relieved I don't really have to go so much as I just needed a minute.

I don't know why Kate's assessment of me and Angus McKinley bothers me. I mean, even the thought is preposterous—I know this. He would chew me up and spit me out in five seconds flat, not that I wouldn't thank him for the pleasure. But it's just plain crazy. And Katelyn is absolutely right. It would only end in professional and personal disaster.

My phone vibrates in my back pocket and I pull it out. Bobby Lee's name appears on the screen, so I press decline. I'm not feeling patient enough to talk to him just now. But it vibrates again before I have a chance to put it away and there's a text from him.

BOBBY LEE

Please pick up, Poppy.

Well, shit. What if something's seriously wrong?

I glance around and see there's a back door just at the end of the hall, so I ditch the line and make my way there, hoping it's quieter than the pub. I push through the door and find myself on the sidewalk where a couple is smoking and chatting while passersby go about their business on the steamy sidewalks.

Bobby Lee picks up on the first ring.

"How's my girl?" His voice is like a toothpaste commercial.

I respond through clenched teeth. "I'm just fine, Bobby Lee. How are you?"

"Much better now that I hear your voice."

"That's kind of you." If I didn't know word of this conversation would get back to every damn person I know by morning, I'd cut the bullshit and ask him what the hell he wants. "So, are you just calling to say hello or..."

He chuckles lightly and I press my forehead against the cement of the building. "Getting right to the point? I see the Big Apple is making an impression already."

"Yes, well, I reckon things do move faster up here." Come on, Bobby Lee, get on with it already.

"Well, it's no wonder I prefer it down here, then." When I don't respond, he continues. "Mama sends her best."

I force a smile into my tone and hope he can't hear my molars grinding. "Well, you tell her I said hello, will you?"

"She's worried you're not eating well up there." Another chuckle.

"They have food up here, same as Georgia. I'm gettin' along fine."

"Of course you are. You've always been a resourceful girl, Poppy." And dammit if that doesn't sound patronizing as hell. Time to switch topics.

"How are things at the firm?" Bobby Lee works with his daddy at one of our local accounting firms, engaging in the age-old tradition of nepotism. He's poised to take over when his daddy retires in a couple months, and Bunny is beside herself with pride, of course. Bobby Lee was what we like to refer to as a happy surprise and what other people call a late-in-life baby—while others might just use the term, "Oh shit." At any rate, being born to a couple who thought they couldn't have children practically made him the second coming in Bunny and Vern's eyes, a treatment he still enjoys.

Okay, well now I'm just being kind of a bitch. I know Bobby Lee is smart and he works hard, so who am I to begrudge him a good job and a proud mama? I just can't buy into the whole golden-boy-on-a-pedestal thing, especially when that pedestal is handmade by Bunny herself out of the bones of lesser men.

"Work is going real well. Second quarter numbers looked even better than last year's."

"I'm happy to hear that." Time to wrap this up.

"So, listen, Poppy." Uh oh, here it comes. "You've been gone goin' on two weeks now…"

If he thinks I'm filling in that blank for him, he's in for a long-ass wait.

"Don't you think it's time for at least a visit back home, if not a… longer stay?"

What in Idris Elba's britches is he talking about?

"Bobby Lee, I have a job."

He has the nerve to chuckle again and I wanna reach my hand through the phone and strangle him till he cries. "Plenty of jobs around here. Just look at all the design jobs you scrounged up without needing to leave Savannah."

My jaw threatens to unhinge itself and hit the sidewalk. Is he insane?

"Look, all I'm sayin' is that everyone here misses you and now that you've had a chance to sow your oats, so to speak, you can come on home. Hold your head high."

I seriously can't believe I ever dated this guy.

I finally find my voice. "Bobby Lee, I'm not *sowing* anything. I'm building a career with a well-respected publishing company and I'm kicking ass."

"No need to curse, Poppy." The censure in his voice is glaring.

That's it. Manners be damned. I mentally apologize to

Cookie and prepare to tell Bobby Lee Collinsworth what's what.

"I can say anything I damn well please, Bobby Lee. I'm a grown woman with a mind of my own and I'm not accountable to you or anyone else. I'm not coming home now or anytime soon, and when I eventually do it's likely to be for a visit and nothing more, no matter what you think I should or shouldn't be doing with my life. You forget, I'm not your girlfriend anymore and haven't been for some time."

"I can see you're upset and it seems I've hit a nerve. We can certainly talk about this later once you've—"

"If the words 'calm down' leave your mouth next I swear to God I'm hanging up on you and deleting your contact info."

He clears his throat. "Fine. We'll table this for now, but can I just say one more thing?"

My jaw sets. "Fine." If it will get him off the phone.

"We both know this break we're taking ain't gonna last. I know you need time to spread your wings before you settle down and I can be patient because I know it's important to you."

Of all the... "Bobby—"

"I'm not done yet. Look, you take the time you need, that's all I'm sayin'."

"Bob—"

"I'll wait. You know you're the most important thing in the world to me, Poppy."

"Bobby L—"

"Okay, now you can talk."

My head is spinning and I might be in danger of

passing out. I open my mouth again and the words come tumbling out.

"I'm dating a blacksmith named Angus McKinley and we're madly in love!"

Well, damn. It's gonna take Cookie a whole *month* at church to save my lying soul.

SEVEN

"Keep it simple, stupid. Creation only took God seven days, so I don't wanna hear your excuse." – Cookie Rutledge

SATURDAY BEGINS WITH COFFEE, a map of the city, and my phone on Do Not Disturb. I've been up since the butt crack of dawn when I declined my first call of the day from Iris. There is no way I'm wasting today fielding calls or explaining myself or eating crow. I plan on spending the day walking around town and doing all the touristy things before I become an official, jaded New Yorker and am required to shake my head at the fanny-packed Midwestern interlopers. Times Square, Rockefeller Center, the Empire State Building, Central Park—I'm doing it all and I'm taking a boatload of pictures to send back home once I've worked my shit out.

Kate's already gone, which impresses the hell out of me given the four cocktails we each had last night. When I returned from my phone call from hell, I declared it was time for shots, but Kate maintained a more level head and, instead, ordered us another round of pear mojitos. I woke up with only the smallest of headaches, thanks in no small part to the water and ibuprofen by my bedside. Thank you, Katelyn.

I can't even think about the mess I left down in Savannah, so I'm focusing on my New York day. And since I'm not working, I'm also dressing the part with cut-offs and a classic "I (heart) NY" tank top I picked up on my trip here last month along with matching red Converse on my feet. And while I don't own a fanny pack, I'm bringing a small backpack with a couple huge bottles of water so I don't pass out from dehydration. My lunch plan is a street dog in the park and I can't friggin' wait. If I happen upon some real sweet tea, it'll be the cherry on my sundae. Bring it on, NYC!

By mid-afternoon, I've all but forgotten about Bobby Lee and am lost in the hedge maze that is Strand Bookstore. This place is nuts. I'm beginning to suspect they intentionally make it this way so you'll be forced to stay and spend all your money. I've already picked out a coffee table book on New York artists for my new apartment and a couple paperbacks from my favorite romance authors. Next up is the cookbook section where I plan to treat myself to something local.

I've been cooking for Kate and me a lot of nights in lieu of rent since she won't let me pay a dime. And it's a good thing because Kate's a disaster in the kitchen, something she's managed to hide from me all these years. I had to wipe cobwebs out of her sauté pan, for God's sake.

An employee leads me to the right section and I start pulling books from New York chefs to check out my options, careful to bypass Geoffrey Sang in the event he's peddling more low-fat blasphemy.

One cookbook catches my attention.

The Art of Macaroni and Cheese

Somebody ain't right, that's for damn sure.

What is it with this city and their mac and cheese obsession?

"What's that?"

I realize I've spoken out loud. An older woman perusing the section nearby looks at me expectantly.

"Oh, sorry." I hold up the book for her inspection. "I was just talking about this cookbook."

She nods politely and I should probably take this as a sign our conversation is done, but I haven't talked to a damn soul all day apart from general pleasantries while handing over cash. When I smiled at some guy in the park he looked like I'd just asked him for a pint of his best blood. So I'm latching onto my one chance for human connection today. And, besides, she started it.

"I mean, how can there possibly be an entire book on mac and cheese?"

She shrugs but says nothing, suddenly finding something fascinating in another aisle.

I ignore the unspoken rule of hushed voices and raise mine a touch. "It ain't rocket science."

A man in a sport coat furrows his brow at me as he passes by and I quiet back down.

"I mean, why mess with a good thing, y'all? Make a

roux, add in milk and cheese, throw in some salt and pepper, and mix it with macaroni. Voi-freakin'-la."

I shove the book back in its spot and give up on my mission, but not before covering the spine with a book on Italian cuisine.

"There." I turn to go and almost run right into a mannequin. But, of course, it's not really a mannequin. We're in a bookstore, for goodness sake.

"Ms. James, I thought that was you."

Elle Valentine stands before me wearing a green halter maxi dress and sky-high strappy sandals. The woman doesn't even have tan lines on her shoulders. Not that I have too much time to investigate because right behind her is the last man on earth I need to see right now and the one man who can set my stomach dropping with nothing more than a growl.

Frack. My. Life.

Despite what's going on in my belly, I can't screw this up again. I give myself a mental slap and paste on a smile as I take him in without looking directly at his face. He's wearing jeans and a navy blue t-shirt, the arm holes straining around his biceps. His dusting of arm hair does nothing to hide the muscular forearms I want to run my fingers over.

I force myself to blink. "Ms. Valentine." My voice is almost convincing when I continue, "Mr. McKinley, it's a pleasure seeing you again." I resist the urge to pull on my shorts or smooth my halo of frizzed-out hair I earned from my day of walking the streets in the humidity. I can only imagine what they're thinking looking at me like this. Give a girl some warning, would you?

Despite my best efforts, my eyes dart up to glance at Angus McKinley's face and, yup, he's still stupid-hot. And he's studying me with a frown.

"You as well." Elle smiles at me, unlike her compatriot. Would it kill him to crack a damn smile now and then? "What brings you here?"

I hold up my loot, only realizing way too late that I just flashed them a cover of *Alphas Do It Best: The Sinner's Collection*, complete with a shirtless man-chest and a nice happy trail. Good God, why couldn't I have put the art book on top? My face immediately heats and I try conjuring up a massive city-wide blackout with no success.

Elle rescues me and reaffirms her position as my new best friend by putting a hand on Angus's arm and attempting to draw his attention away from my flaming face. "I dragged Angus here to buy a copy of a new furniture book. One of his chairs is featured."

I nod and smile, making the appropriate noises, but I'm all but pinned in place under his grumpy gaze. Intense much? What is he looking at anyway?

I don't have time to let him keep intimidating me, though. The chances of randomly running into these two is a gazillion to one, so I need to use this to my advantage.

I clear my throat, making sure New York Poppy is the one doing the talking. "Well, it must be fate that brought us here. I'm still hoping we can make that interview happen. It would be nice to continue the momentum from the furniture book, don't you agree?"

One brow lowers and he watches me some more, those ridiculously penetrating brown orbs searing into me. Gah!

For the first time, Elle doesn't look directly at me when she speaks. "Yes, well..."

King Kong finally lets his eyes fall to the side, having finished with whatever assessment he was making.

He speaks in a deep rumble. "I'm sure you'll find someone else." And, with that, he turns and stalks away, dismissing me like a cat would a person eager for snuggles.

"I'm... sorry." Elle smiles weakly and follows in his wake, her perfect butt swaying back and forth as she goes after her moody boyfriend.

She deserves better than him, not that it's any of my business.

I look at my stack of books, not really feeling in the mood for the romance novels anymore. It's official, I screwed the pooch and screwed him good.

I slump my way to the checkout and buy my art book before pulling out my phone and turning off the Do Not Disturb. The sooner I face the music, the sooner I can put all my messes behind me and move on.

"Dammit, sis, why have you been holding out on me?" This is the first thing out of Iris's mouth.

I'm standing outside Strand with one hand on the back of my neck and the other holding the phone.

"Oh, God," I groan.

"I swear, you're the only person I know who would move to New York City and fall in love with a blacksmith... although, I will say I was almost ready to forgive that big sweaty guy for his bad taste in music. That man was scorchin'."

I laugh because I can't do anything else. "Well, you're in luck then because that big sweaty guy *is* the blacksmith."

"Shut the front door!"

"Believe me, I wish I could."

She misses my sarcasm completely. "Details! I can't believe you have a hot new boyfriend and you hid him from me."

"I hate to burst your bubble, Rissy, but we're not dating. In fact, we've hardly even spoken. And I'm pretty sure he's dating Charlize Theron. Oh, and he *hates* me."

"Huh? But Bobby Lee—"

"Called and all but told me to come home and have his babies."

"Oh." She blows out a breath. "So you don't have a hot new boyfriend?"

"That would be a no."

"Well, that sucks."

I have to agree with her on that. "But you know Bobby Lee can never find out. As far as he's concerned I've been swept off my feet by one Angus McKinley."

"Believe me, my lips are sealed. I'd be the first to object at the wedding if he ever got you to the altar."

"And that's why I love you."

Iris sighs. "But you gotta know he's not just gonna take this lying down, Poppy." I might whimper a bit at that, but it's because I know she's right. "I mean, Bunny doesn't know yet, but it's only a matter of time. And she's not above gettin' on a plane to defend her son's honor *and* save you from a Yankee."

I bite my lip and stomp my foot on the sidewalk. "Dammit all!" My heartburn threatens to kick in, but I'm through letting Bobby Lee influence me in any way, shape, or form. "Since when is a girl not allowed to pick her own blasted boyfriend? Even if he *is* a giant brute who snarls and broods and hates my guts. If I wanna date a sweaty blacksmith, I'll damn well date a sweaty blacksmith!"

I pivot on my rubber soles, intent on getting on with the rest of my friggin' glorious day as a New York tourist.

"Damn straight!" Iris shouts in my ear.

But my feet stick like molasses to the sidewalk and I hardly hear her as my eyes hit a set of muscled arms folded over a broad chest. I don't even need to look up to know I'll find a mouth set in a straight line and shrewd brown eyes picking up everything in their domain. But I do anyway, and my instincts are only confirmed. Except, looky there— both eyebrows are arched this time. I'm truly unsure if things could get any worse.

"Iris, I'm gonna have to call you back."

IT GOES without saying that I turned tail and ran after that fiasco. I believe I muttered something along the lines of, "Sorry. Just rehearsing for a play," as I made my exit—in order to complete my full and utter humiliation.

I didn't get another look at his face to confirm it, but I'm pretty sure he didn't buy my load of bullshit. I can only pray Elle wasn't a witness, but I was too intent on getting the hell out of there to check.

One upside to embarrassing the shit out of yourself is that it's exhausting as hell, so I practically fall into bed when I get back to Kate's. My sleep is fitful and my dreams are filled with chase scenes where I'm running away from dinosaurs and giant hamburgers. I can only assume the dinosaurs are a metaphor for my own bad choices. The hamburgers must be because I skipped supper.

I spend Sunday scoping out some cheap odds and ends for my new place and returning calls and texts from home. I let Mama in on the fake-boyfriend secret since she's on her cruise and won't have reason to talk to Bunny for weeks. Otherwise I'd be asking her to lie for me and I learned way back that that shit doesn't fly the time I expected her to cover for me when I pretended to be sick so I wouldn't have to dance at my ballet recital. The woman practically shoved me out on stage and I swear hers was the biggest smile in the crowd even though her daughter spent the entire routine scowling at her and missing almost every step. While Mama doesn't necessarily think Bobby Lee is a bad choice, she trusts me to know my own mind and that's good enough for me.

Cookie is another issue altogether, so I just go with the tried and true, "I don't really feel like talking about it," and it works like a charm. She's happy to chat about my adventures at work and around town, and she laughs like I knew she would when I tell her New Yorkers think oxtails are gourmet.

By the time I hang up the phone for the final time, I'm missing home like crazy and wishing I were back in the yellow bedroom at the Violette Inn or fixing supper with Cookie while she gossips about her weekly ladies' lunch and tells me I need to eat more.

It's not that I don't think I can cut it in New York; I know I can—just behind the scenes instead of sticking my foot in my mouth with local celebrities and super models.

Our prototype is gonna blow the socks off the board, I can just feel it.

But I miss being comfortable in my surroundings. I miss daily hugs and knowing the guy I buy coffee from and chatting about *The Good Place* with the checkout girl at the market. I miss having a slice of sidewalk to myself. I miss the smell of magnolias and the Spanish moss dripping off the old live oaks. I miss the breeze off the Savannah River and the cemeteries that make me feel like I'm part of history in the making. I took a chance in coming here—a leap of faith, and I can't give up on that now. I just need to figure out a way to merge old Poppy with New York Poppy, and try not to lose my soul in the process.

EIGHT

"When you find yourself in a pickle, just dill."
– Cookie Rutledge

"WELL, WELL, WELL." Naveed leans against my door jamb wearing an electric blue button-down and grey trousers that look like they were tailor-made for him—and they probably were.

It's nice of him to come all this way. My temporary office is tucked back in a hallway off the main executive offices and takes a few extra minutes to reach. You have to really want to see me to come hunt me down here. Once the magazine is approved, I'll move down to the ninth floor where the new design team will be, but most of its future members are still busy working on *Warbey's Home Living* and reporting to its creative director who's retiring in two months. Athena and company thought it best we don't ruffle any feathers that don't need ruffling for the time being.

And given my anxiety about people questioning my qualifications, I'm happy to gain my footing before I storm in and take over as the department head. Of course, the fact that I can play music and take my heels off in my hidden quarters makes them even better.

Naveed is studying me with his head cocked to the side, not allowing me to get a good read on him so I circle a finger in the air. "What does this mean?"

He clicks his tongue once and shifts his lips to the side. "I'm not sure yet."

"Oookay." I pretend to ignore him and type on my laptop but I'm really just typing gibberish into the search bar.

Obviously I haven't played into whatever scenario he was hoping for because he caves right away. "I just got an interesting phone call from one Jonathan Abernathy at McKinley Forge and Design."

My gibberish turns to exclamation marks and one long spacebar as I pretend I'm not panicking. "Oh?"

Naveed slinks up to my desk and shuts my laptop right on my fingers. My eyes dart up to his face.

"Cut the crap, sister, and tell me how you worked that miracle."

This time I'm speechless because I truly don't know what in the world he means.

"Don't play coy with me, Miss Peach."

"I... I'm not. I swear I don't know what you're talking about." I pull my fingers out of the computer trap and rest my hands flat on my desk.

"You got the interview."

"I did?"

"Yes! Wait, how do you not know that?"

I open my mouth and stammer again before regaining the power of speech. "That's great. I'm so happy for you. For us."

He narrows his eyes at me. "I'll get the details out of you eventually." He taps the top of my laptop. "But for now, we've got some prep work to do."

"I'm sure you do. And, really, I'm ecstatic. I know you'll do an amazing job." I lean back in my chair and pretend this news doesn't make my heart rate kick up a few notches.

"What are you talking about?"

"Well, the interview. Wait, what are you talking about?" Am I in the Twilight Zone? Is he on drugs? Can he get me some? Wait, no—terrible idea.

"The interview, little miss thing. We need to prep you so you can ask the right questions."

I'm sure my expression is equal parts befuddlement and horror. "Wh... what do you mean prep *me*? I'm not going."

He laughs and I can't for the life of me figure out what I'm missing. "You sure as shit are. You're the one doing the interview."

Noooo! "No. No. Why? That doesn't make any sense." My voice squeaks.

"I don't make the rules, I just follow them. Well, some-times." Naveed crosses his arms and I want to throat punch him to get that smug grin off his face. "Angus McKinley, heir to the smoldering crown of Scottish-American hotness, wants you to be the one to interview him or he's not playing."

I open my mouth but the only thing to come out is a whimper which, let's face it, pretty much sums it all up.

If I thought it would be easy to talk my way out of this, I obviously underestimated the other players, specifically Naveed and Angus McKinley. Naveed's response to every one of my protests is an elaborate mime production involving feigned deafness followed by a dramatic interpretation of me conducting an interview with the big blacksmith. There's lots of chest beating and eyelash fluttering— I'm assuming I'm the eyelash character.

At any rate, when he finally decides to use his voice again, it's to tell me he's already arranged the time and Angus McKinley is expecting me tomorrow afternoon. Then I'm drilled on the rules of conducting an interview where I'm told in no uncertain terms to never let my eyes waver from my subject, something I'll never ever *ever* accomplish in this lifetime or the next. In fact, I'm pretty sure if you look Angus McKinley in the eye for more than five seconds you disintegrate into a pile of ash.

"Now, remember, if you don't actively listen to his answers, you won't know which question to ask next. Do not, under any circumstances, let him think you're focusing on your next question instead of the answer he's giving."

I honestly can't believe I've agreed to this—not that I have much of a choice. It's in the best interest of the magazine. In theory, that is. In practice, I might show up and find that I'm the butt of a practical joke and will soon be appearing on a hidden-camera reality show. Anything is in the realm of possibility based on the nature of all my previous encounters with Angus McKinley.

"Eyes on me!" Naveed snaps his fingers and my gaze shoots back to him. "That's better. Now, what's your first question."

"Um..." I glance down at the pad of paper in front of me where I've jotted down a list of potential questions Naveed suggested, but he snaps his fingers again and I don't get a chance to pick one. "What made you want to become a blacksmith?"

Naveed's mouth splits in a melodramatic yawn. "Bor-rrring. Try again."

He tuts when I try glancing down again and I growl a little at him.

"That's good. Use your frustration."

I roll my eyes at him but try again. "What is your favorite piece you've ever designed?"

Naveed nods in approval and then drops his voice a dozen octaves. "Well, Ms. James, I'd have to say it's the bed of nails I sleep on every night."

The corner of my mouth hitches without my permission and I hold Naveed's gaze.

"Is that right? And have you always slept on a bed of nails or did you have to work up from a crib of screws as a baby?"

Naveed's mouth turns down and he drops both hands to the armrests of his chair. "Nope. Not that I don't appreciate the nice follow-up question, but you'll only put him on the defensive if you ask about his family or past. He made it clear he won't talk about it. Just his work, remember?"

I sigh, but only because I'm frustrated I messed up again. Honestly, I'm thrilled I won't have to ask Mr. McKinley anything about the awful events I glimpsed in those articles the other night. I'd feel like I was trying to open a door I have absolutely no business behind. And even more terrifying is the thought that he might actually answer.

I'm not the type of person who can emotionally detach from heartbreaking circumstances for the sake of professionalism. If I were a real writer and doing an article on orphaned babies, I'd end up with a houseful of poopy diapers in no time flat. Which is why I'm a designer and not a writer. Or a doctor. Or a social worker. Or about ten thousand other things.

"Right." I stretch my neck from side to side like I just finished a grueling workout. My eyes go back to Naveed. "Um, what's the difference in your creative process for furniture design versus your sculptures?"

Naveed smiles and nods again and I'm disproportionately pleased at his approval. He drops his voice again and says, "I usually design my sculptures in the nude while the furniture requires more of a white t-shirt and ripped Diesel jeans vibe."

I slam my hand to the desk. "How do you expect me to take this seriously when you're acting ridiculous?"

He tries straightening his features. "Sorry. Couldn't resist." He clears his throat and takes it down only a couple octaves this time before diving into a more appropriate answer. We continue in this vein for another hour until Naveed checks his watch.

"Ah." He springs up from his chair across the desk from me. "I need to fly. Didn't realize it was so late."

Part of me is relieved and the rest of me panics. I'm so not ready.

Reading my mind, Naveed leans in and stills. "You've got this, ringer." He waits until I nod and then backs up toward the door. "I'll check in on you between meetings tomorrow. And, don't forget to dress to kill." A quick wink and he's gone.

I don't know what to do with myself now that he's left and the reality of the situation is bearing down on me. So I take a breath and think about what Cookie would do.

Then I swipe up my purse and head out shopping.

JONATHAN ABERNATHY IS NOT what I expected. From his haughtiness and his bored attitude on the phone, I expected a bespectacled millennial with an intimate knowledge of both hair product and esoteric barbs. So when the chubby forty-something man in running shoes and a beige sweater vest opens the studio door, I'm a bit taken aback.

"Ms. James, I presume?" He doesn't wait for me to respond before stepping aside and continuing in a bland tone. "Come in. He's waiting for you."

I glance at my phone and see that, yes, I'm ten minutes early. But he's waiting for me? Eeek. Cue sweat glands. So much for my carefully-applied makeup and killer sangria lipstick.

"Thank you," I croak as I follow him through the makeshift entry, my purse perched on my shoulder in a death grip.

Jonathan trudges ahead of me, motioning unenthusiastically to each side as we walk. "Offices are that way. Retail studio is down there." The space has even more partitions than I realized, creating a series of makeshift hallways and work areas.

I scurry in my four-inch ankle-strap sandals to keep up with him. My outfit met Naveed's approval when he checked me out earlier at the office, so I know I have that going for me. I'm decked out in a silver lace pencil skirt and a rose-pink capped-sleeve blouse with a floppy bow at the neck—something I carefully planned due to my tendency to heat to my core around my interviewee. No more suit jackets for me. The shoes were a splurge, but they were the most comfortable ones I could find and the bow in back makes me happy.

I smooth a hand over my hair to make sure my updo is secure as we pass by a wide heavy-looking door.

"That's the forge. Don't go in there." Jonathan spares me a quick backward glare before continuing ahead of me and finally pausing at the opening to a huge open space with a lower ceiling. I recognize it as the room where I caught my first glimpse of Angus McKinley less than two weeks ago. My throat dries and all I can do is offer Jonathan an unsteady nod.

I'm about to approach a man who, not forty-eight hours ago, got a good glimpse of my dirty romance books and heard me yammer on about my right to date a giant sweaty blacksmith. Odds are there aren't too many of those in town. But I need to shove that shit down deep if I'm ever gonna to make it through the next hour. I'm counting on New York Poppy and the bitch better not let me down. I straighten my spine, smooth down my skirt and prepare to kick this interview's ass.

Without another word, Jonathan retreats and I take a deep breath as I enter the room, infusing each step with forced confidence.

What I'm not quite prepared for when I glance around, however, is the sight of Angus McKinley and his hot bod in *exactly* the clothes Naveed described when he was screwing with me in our mock interview. Tight white t-shirt, ripped jeans that hug his hips like he was born wearing them, and rips that sure as hell didn't come from anything but the way God intended—through physical motion and good-old-fashioned friction.

Is it hot in here?

He's wheeling a shop table against the wall and his back is to me, which is just as well since I realize I've halted in my stride. I pick it up again and he turns at the click of my heels against the sealed concrete floor. I raise my chin to focus on his right ear as I approach.

No matter what Naveed said, I just can't meet his eyes. I'm too afraid of what I'll see in them. The possibilities are limitless: boredom, impatience, scrutiny, amusement (at my expense, of course)—I'm not sure which one would be the worst. So the ear it is. But it's a mistake too because I catch a glimpse of that tattoo curling behind the pink shell of his ear and dipping below the neckline of his shirt. And now I'm looking at his shoulder and the way the fabric strains.

Crap. Get yourself together, Poppy.

I force a cordial smile. "It's lovely to see you again, Mr. McKinley." I extend my hand. "Thank you for taking the time to meet with me."

But he doesn't shake my hand. Instead, he rakes his eyes over me and grunts one single word: "No."

I blink, sure I've misheard him. Despite my plan for self-preservation, my eyes fly to his. What stares back at me is worse than any of the things I could have anticipated.

Ice.

His eyes are ice cold. And there is none of the usual intensity there, whether it be rage or interest. It's like a fire has gone out and I feel an actual shiver run down my spine.

"I'm sorry?"

He shakes his head once, making the dark mess of hair on top move and I can feel his voice scratch at my skin. "This is a mistake."

"I... don't understand, Mr. McKinley."

But he's already turned his back and returned his attention to the table like I'm no longer in the room. I glance around for any sign of Jonathan, which is how I know I'm truly desperate, but he's nowhere to be seen.

I watch Angus McKinley's back for a few more seconds before something in my gut starts to heat up and the coldness that had washed over me begins to clear. But it's not embarrassment or warm fuzzies or the heat from the forge we passed by. It's hot molten anger.

I force the words out through a tight jaw. "Excuse me, but I was told you were expecting me for an interview."

He acts like he didn't hear me.

I don't think so!

"In fact, I was under the distinct impression it was *you* who requested *me* in particular, so I don't see what the issue is."

My voice is firm and my accent is spot on. Iris would give me a gold frickin' star.

At that, he finally turns to face me again and I have to force myself from swallowing my tongue at the look on his face. He's a coiled spring.

His eyes rake me again from head to toe, but it's not sexual or suggestive in the least. It's as dispassionate as a farmer assessing a cow at auction—or probably more so. "I didn't ask for... you."

Ouch.

I feel like he just punched me in the gut and stole the breath from my lungs.

But he's not done yet. "Like I said, this is a mistake." He reiterates his point before turning again in beast-speak for "you're dismissed."

A mistake? A *mistake?*

I do not think so. I can feel the heat of my anger rise up from my gut and populate every cell in my body, starting with my lungs and shooting out to the tips of my fingers and the ends of my neatly piled hair. I busted my balls rehearsing for this stupid interview. I tossed and turned all night worrying I'd forget something or deliver less-than perfect questions. Not to mention the $250 I dropped on this ridiculous outfit and these stupid freaking heels, and it's a mistake?

I'll show him a mistake.

... But I can't.

I draw in a deep breath and pray for calm. This isn't about my pride or my schedule or my hurt feelings. This is about the magazine. This is exactly why I need New York Poppy—to save me from myself and the impression I'll make if I don't watch my step. I release the breath in a long slow stream and try visualizing puppies.

"I'm sorry." I want to choke on the words, but I push on. "I'm not familiar with the usual parameters in conducting an interview with... a creative mind such as yours."

Read: batshit crazy asshole.

"If you require certain accommodations—say, a bowl full of purple M&Ms or the blood of a virgin..." Shit. I didn't mean to say that last part out loud. I hurry on, "I'm sure we can reschedule with another individual from the magazine with whom you'd be more comfortable."

There. I ended it on a more professional note and even used proper grammar. Now I'm getting the hell out of dodge and away from this entitled douchebag. Naveed can sort things out from here.

I turn on my heel to leave and get about five feet before his voice stops me. "They don't make purple M&Ms."

Out of everything I said, this is what he latches onto? I mouth a few expletives into the air before pasting a fake-ass smile on my face and turning once again. This time I choose to focus on a spot on the wall behind him.

"Indeed. The choice of color is entirely up to you." Damn, New York Poppy is throwing down.

He takes a step closer and I resist the urge to back up. I'll eat my hat before I'll let him think he can intimidate me.

Almost as if he's reading my mind he narrows the gap by a few more feet. Even out of the corner of my eye, I can make out the individual whiskers on his jaw as he opens his mouth to speak again.

"I'm more partial to... cherry pie."

NINE

"No need to put up with anybody's bull when you got the
pointy end of a boot in your favor."
— Cookie Rutledge

MY EYES FLY to his and I gasp before I can tamp it down. All traces of cold have been consumed by a volcano waiting to erupt behind his eyes.

Did he just…?

But then right at the edges I see something else—something that neutralizes any power his hot gaze could wield. It's the amusement I was so afraid of in the first place.

I clench my teeth and form my hands into fists where they rest along my hips.

He's toying with me. There may not be hidden cameras or his model girlfriend hanging out around the corner laughing at me, but this man is clearly toying with me.

But I'm no plaything, that's for damn certain. I may

have embarrassed myself in front of him, but I came here today as a professional with a job to do and he just wasted my time and money—not to mention my pride. It's like I'm back to square one here in New York. I'm nothing but a young country bumpkin undeserving of respect and credit for my contributions.

I think we're done here.

"Good day, Mr. McKinley," I hiss out through my teeth and turn to go, just like Scarlett O'Hara would.

He puts a staying hand on my elbow and his callused fingers all but burn my bare skin. I yank out of his grip even though it's not restraining in the least—my instincts protecting me from the waves of energy this man exudes.

"Wait." The rumble is back.

I whip my head around and will ice into my voice. "You've had your fun at my expense. And it's been great, really, but if you don't mind I have a job to get back to." And a bus to jump in front of, but that part goes without saying.

My strides are sure and strong, but I refuse to run. He doesn't get one more piece of me. As soon as I pass back through the threshold, though, I pick up my pace. Tears threaten but I won't shed them here. Unfortunately, they do a number on my vision because I take a wrong turn and need to backtrack to find the entryway again.

"No, no, no," I chant to myself while my heels click against the floor, my steps getting shorter. I blink back the tears and, thank God, they obey.

The industrial lights flicker above as I turn down what I'm finally sure is the right way, but the space is blocked by none other than the hulking blacksmith with his tangle of black hair and that damn t-shirt and jeans.

Just as I decide in favor of the pepper spray over my new shoes as weapons in my forthcoming assault on the man, he brings both hands in front of his chest in surrender.

"Please, Ms. James. I didn't..." He stops talking like he's done.

I swear this man has yet to speak a complete sentence.

But I've got enough words for both of us.

"You didn't what, Mr. McKinley? You didn't learn the manners God gave to a dog? Now, if you don't step aside you might just find yourself on the learning end of a lesson you're not likely to forget anytime soon." Lord, I wish I had my boots so I could kick one where the sun don't shine. Instead I grind the spiked heel of my right shoe into the floor so he knows I mean business.

I figure I've made my point when both his eyebrows reach for his hairline and his full bottom lip drops a fraction in surprise. It seems I've accomplished the impossible and conjured an expression other than brooding dragon beast of the city. Well, what do you know?

It isn't until I've stalked past him and gulped in the humid city air on the streets that I realize I didn't check my accent back there in that hallway. And more than that, refined New York Poppy was nowhere to be seen. But Poppy James of Savannah, Georgia kicked even bigger ass.

IF NAVEED IS MAD, he doesn't show it. After I spend twenty minutes walking the edge off my anger, I call him with a brief and probably inadequate explanation, but I think he can sense I'm not in the right headspace to chat. There's work left to do at the office so I head back there, planning on tiptoeing past any humans and sequestering myself for a few hours. At least it will get my mind off Angus Dickhead McKinley and that joke of an interview. I wouldn't let him be featured in our amazing magazine if my life depended on it!

Tomorrow will be a new day. I'll officially be back in my design wheelhouse, Naveed can move on and find a fabulous alternative for the urban artisan spot, JoJo can stay on the cover—which is just as well since it saves me the bother of a redesign—and, best of all, my apartment will officially be ready.

This is one time where I'm glad for the anonymity New York offers. I scan my card and slide right past security in the lobby and no one pays me any mind on the elevator. A glance around at the women and men shows that I fit right in with my fancy duds and designer handbag. Who cares if I had to blow more money on the outfit than I technically should? Even with my walking, I don't have a blister, so these shoes were totally worth it.

I sneak by the executive offices without stopping to speak to anyone and am almost home free as I turn the last corner in the maze to my private domain when I spot Naveed coming from the direction of my office.

He looks... guilty.

I stop. "Naveed?"

He keeps walking and when he gets within a few feet

he wrinkles his nose just like Iris when she's been caught red-handed with my turquoise hand-stitched boots.

"Sorry," is all he says—not sounding sorry at all—as he keeps walking past me and turns a corner.

I swear, that man confounds me. I consider going after him, but curiosity gets the better of me and my feet take me to my office with careful steps. At this point, there could be anything waiting for me in there—flowers, a pit bull, a homeless stripper—or...

NO!

Just as I take my last step it dawns on me that freaking Bobby Lee Collinsworth is undoubtedly waiting for me like the turd on my dog-crap sandwich of a day.

But when my eyes hit the room, I realize it's infinitely worse.

Because Bobby Lee is nowhere to be found. Angus McKinley, on the other hand, is leaning his firm backside against my desk, set jaw and penetrating eyes fixed directly on me like I'm a plate of ribs he's fixing to eat with his bare hands. Not that I'd ever accuse him of having table manners anyway.

"What the devil are *you* doing here?" It's out before I can help it.

I am gonna skin Naveed alive for this. What part of "disaster" and "infuriating suckhole" did he not understand?

But Angus McKinley throws his hands out in front of him again and drops his eyes to my shoes.

"I come in peace," he grinds out without moving from my desk.

I sidestep him to get to the other side of the desk,

needing something solid between us. It causes him to rise to his full height and turn. I fuss with setting my purse in my drawer to buy myself some time and avoid looking at him. This office is way too small for him. I wonder if he had to duck his head to get through the doorway.

"I want to... apologize." The word sounds like it took a bit more effort to expel than he would have liked.

But it hits its mark because my purse is forgotten and my eyes swing up to his face again. I'm sure my open mouth reflects every bit of surprise I feel.

"Um, okay," I manage. Then I wrestle my manners in place. He may be a bit of a heathen and an ass, but Cookie would kick my butt if I didn't offer a seat to someone calling on me to apologize. "You want a seat?"

He spares the chairs across from my desk the briefest of glances before shaking his head once. Which is probably just as well since he might send it crumbling to the ground if he did squeeze his big bod in one.

But he does take a step back, as if he realizes the difference in our heights now that I'm sitting makes his presence even more intimidating.

He draws in a deep breath and, Jesus help me, I can't keep my eyes from dropping to his expansive chest. The white t-shirt strains with his inhale and my scalp begins to sweat. Dammit!

When he finally lets it out, he says the last thing on God's green earth I expect to hear.

"I thought you had a twin."

My head cocks hard to the side ala every damn cartoon character ever. "Huh?" Wow, it's a good thing I'm no longer worried about my impression with this guy.

He runs a thumb and forefinger over his scruff and I must have the hearing of a hound dog because I can hear the scrape from across the desk. It registers in the very depths of my panties.

"Only that day in Elle's office." His finger makes the smallest of motions from its spot on his jaw to the air. "With the hair." He pauses and drops his hand back to his thigh. "And the shark thing."

Uh, somebody's lost the plot. I can only assume he's talking about the difference in my professional persona versus the train wreck he met the other times, but I have no idea what the shark thing is about.

"The shark thing?"

He just nods.

"Um, okay."

"But the bookstore... cleared things up."

This guy talks like he's paying tax on every word he speaks. And that damn inscrutable expression doesn't help either.

But my mind races back to the sidewalk outside Strand and I want Dorothy's tornado to pick me up and swing on by Savannah to drop me on its way to Kansas. My ears burn and I remember I need to search in my desk for something super important.

What I really need is to get this guy out of my office, and the only way I can see to do that is by letting him get on with what he came for.

"So, you're sorry you thought I had a twin?"

And he comes right out with it. "No. I'm sorry I acted like an asshole."

Ah. It seems we're being brutally honest here. It's about

damn time. I forget my desk and my embarrassment, letting my eyes settle on his again. He runs his tongue over his bottom teeth like he's chewing on his next words, so I fill in the space.

"Can I ask you a question?" I set both hands on my desk top.

He gives one short nod.

"Why did you agree to the interview?" I put a hand in the air because I'm not finished, not that he was racing to answer or anything. "I mean, after Elle officially turned us down. You were scot-free."

His nostrils flare and I'm worried I pissed him off all over again, but then one corner of his mouth lifts the teensiest bit. If I hadn't been studying his face like it was the answer to a final exam in biology I wouldn't have caught it at all. But there it was.

"Curiosity," he finally says—or, more accurately, grunts.

"Curiosity," I repeat, not even putting any question in my tone. I'm like a parrot with the way I keep repeating every damn word he says.

Another barely-there nod.

Since I seem to have his attention and he shows no sign of leaving, I prop an elbow on my desk and decide to go for broke.

"You do know I'm not actually a writer, don't you?"

A repeat of the chin dip of affirmation.

"Is that why you kicked me out when I came over today?"

"No."

My brows draw together.

"So, you're just... moody?"

Another twitch of his lip.

"Definitely no."

A short laugh escapes my throat. "You sure about that?"

"I only have one mood."

His economy of words and movements might say that, but his eyebrows and lip quirks say something else.

"If you say so." I shrug and lean forward. "Where do we go from here? I doubt you want to give me that interview. Last time I tried to interview you, you barked at me and then made fun of me."

Is that a wince I see? One mood, my ass.

"I guess my one mood is an asshole."

I bark out another laugh despite myself.

His hand comes to the back of his neck and a furrow forms on his brow. "I'll do the interview."

My eyes go wide and I cross my arms on the desk. "With me?"

The curt nod again.

I gesture to the floor under my desk. "I'm still wearing the shoes, you know."

"I'm aware." His eyes narrow the slightest bit and I'm starting to feel like he has the ability to see through not just my desk but my clothes.

I squirm in my seat and try wrestling New York Poppy back to the surface. When my spine is straight, I open my drawer back up and pull my pad of paper from my bag. Then I clear my throat.

"Okay, Mr. McKinley," I begin, but he cuts me off.

"Mac."

"Mac?" Again with the parrot.

"Call me Mac."

I stare at him, words failing me. Mac? What happened to Angus? Or Mr. McKinley? I distinctly remember Elle calling him Angus.

I muster a weak smile, but there is no way I can call him Mac. It's way too... familiar.

"Before we begin, I want to make sure you understand that while there will be photos taken at another date, there's no cover in the contract you signed."

"Thank Christ."

Oookay. This whole thing is beyond strange. I look down at my pad and quickly scan the questions, desperate for solid footing. Everything he says throws me and confuses the ever-loving crap out of me.

Screw it. I slide the papers aside.

"Question number one: What's your favorite rock band?"

Yep. There's no mistaking it this time when his lips quirk and amusement makes its way into those brown eyes. But, for once, it's not at my expense.

TEN

"Men wearing smiles are the same ones who know the power
of a well-timed, expensive gift."
– Cookie Rutledge

IF I THOUGHT I could throw a few questions at Angus
"Mac" McKinley and magically produce everything
needed for a riveting magazine article from his answers, I
was dead wrong. This interviewing thing is *hard*. Especially since he only speaks enough words to fill out a
quarter column of copy. Now, if I could interview his lips
or his eyebrows, or that damn tick in his left cheek, I might
have more material, but they don't translate very well to
paper. This article is gonna need a hell of a lot more details
to inform it.

I sigh as I hit send on my email to Naveed with the
paltry contents of my notes.

When I was in the moment, I could swear I felt real

substance and authenticity in his answers, but I realize now it's a lot like interpreting a conversation with the real King Kong, in the sense that it would make much better TV. Especially with the growly bits.

Suffice it to say, by the time I shook his hand goodbye, I was not only a tiny bit smitten with the man, but I was also feeling almost protective of his laconic nature. I'm now of the opinion that he'd come off as disingenuous if he used more words. But none of this helps create a magazine article that gets down to the root of the brilliant and broody blacksmith.

And brilliant he is, I have no doubt. I've spent the last half hour poring over an Instagram account he mentioned Elle set up for him. While I'm sure he's not the one to post, it doesn't stop me from reading every single word and zooming in on the photos. I'm dying to see the man at work, especially when a shot pops up of him in a shadowed room full of tools, flames, and steam. He wears a leather apron of sorts with dark-rimmed frames over his eyes and a t-shirt much like the one he wore today. His sweat-slicked biceps gleam in the orange light as he grips a hammer that conjures images of Thor himself. This is undoubtedly the forge I was warned against by Jonathan.

The part of me that craves another excuse to be around him can't wait for the photo shoot, but I know I'm being ridiculous. I have every right to be there as the creative director, but I'd just fade into the background as the photographer does her thing. Mac won't even notice me if I'm not doing something to humiliate myself, and that is very much not in my current plans, thank you very much.

Which brings me to my upcoming move and Iris's

imminent arrival in New York. The James girls can't seem to help but get into trouble. She's scheduled to arrive in two days with a U-Haul trailer—if she can get out of Savannah without somebody hiring a chaperone, that is. She claimed she could get a friend to help her load my stuff from the storage unit without Cookie finding out, but I'm not counting my chickens just yet.

I sigh and close the app, knowing there's no good reason to look at the pictures anymore now that my part is done and the notes have been sent to Naveed. My desk phone rings and I roll my eyes, figuring it's the man in question calling to complain about the brevity.

But I'm proven wrong again when the receptionist's voice sounds in my ear. "Ms. James, I have a Mr. McKinley on the line for you. Would you like me to put him through or send him to your voicemail?"

I smooth my hair as if anyone can see me and bite my lip while I consider my options. Oh, who am I kidding? "Put him through, please."

I drop the phone back in its cradle and practically jump out of my seat when it rings again.

"This is Poppy James." I feign ignorance and a breezy tone.

"It's Mac." Oh, sweet lord, his voice is even deeper over the phone.

"Oh!" I'm an awful actress. "Did you forget something?" Wow, talk about bad manners.

"I want to show you something."

Oh, if he only knew how badly I wanted to see something. I bite my knuckle at my inner brazenness and roll my eyes at myself.

"What's that?" I will every ounce of flirtiness out of my tone and almost succeed. The man has a super model girlfriend, for glory's sake.

But if I thought he'd actually answer, I've clearly forgotten who I'm dealing with.

"Meet me at my studio tonight at nine."

"Tonight?"

"You got other plans?"

The nerve! I'm tempted to make something up, but it's no use lying to myself.

"Fine. I'll see you at nine, Mr. McKinley."

"Mac," he replies and then hangs up before I can rebut.

I'm thinking I won't need to wait for Iris to get to town. I'm in a world of trouble all on my own.

"HELLO?" I knock on the newsprint-covered window for a second time.

Maybe he thought better of it but didn't have my cell number to cancel. Or maybe Elle stripped naked in front of him and he can't remember my name or who I am. Yeah, that's probably more likely.

It's not like I spent any time getting ready for our meeting or whatever this is. It only took four outfit changes to find the right combination of professionalism and after-hours casual. And since I'm not sure what he wants to show me, I didn't want to risk catching myself on fire. So I went with skinny jeans and the blouse from earlier, but I paired them with my tan cowhide boots in case he decides to be an ass again and needs kicking. Okay, not really, but the boots help with my confidence so they're just right for a night like this.

But it looks like the outfit's been wasted. I turn to go just as the door swings open and I'm hit with a gust of air from the sheer force of it. I stumble back and Mac—Angus—Mr. McKinley—Mac (grrrr) reaches out to steady me with a hand on my arm. So much for the self-confidence. But my brain doesn't register anything much apart from his warm callused hand on my skin. Heat radiates from the spot where our skin meets and I look down to make sure I haven't caught my damn self on fire.

Mac mistakes my look for one of reproach and quickly releases his grip.

"Sorry."

"Oh, no need." I push my hair behind my ear. That's another thing I debated when I was getting ready. My hair went down and up and down again before I threw in the towel and left it hanging around my face. Now I'm second guessing that too as my skin warms at his misinterpretation of my movements.

I try a small smile and it sticks. "Thanks."

He nods one of his clipped chin dips and holds the door for me. When I follow him in, I immediately notice how different the place looks without the overhead lights. Only a dim light down the make-shift hall illuminates the space and we're left in near darkness as he closes the door behind us.

My back is to him, but I know exactly where he is and how close his body is to mine by the energy he puts off.

Either he's his own nuclear power plant or my body runs on some wavelength shared by just the two of us.

Which is batshit loco.

Still, awareness sings down my spine as he steps closer, his front less than a foot from my back. I have the crazy urge to lean back, knowing I'll find the firm support of his broad chest and strong hands.

But I don't, of course. I close my eyes tight and will myself to get my act together before stepping forward so I'm out of temptation's way.

I clear my throat. "So, what is it you wanted to show me?" I turn and smile brightly, breaking whatever tension there was.

As usual, his expression is indiscernible, especially in the dark, but I see him extend his hand to gesture down the hall. "Here."

I go where he directs on shaky knees until we're in the same room from earlier today—the same room from the night I first laid eyes on him. The battling ropes lay rolled in the corner and a single light shines from a black lamp on the shop table, but I'm not looking at the lamp or the table or the ropes.

Instead, my eyes are drawn to a chair resting on the sealed concrete floor a few feet from the light source. Its design is deceptively simple, but it's nothing short of beautiful. Ribbons of wrought iron fold back on themselves to create a curved seat that rises in the back only to fold again and curve down to the floor to act as the back legs of the chair.

"Wow." I breathe the word out like it came from my

toes. My boots slide against the floor as I creep closer and reach out a finger to the metal. I pull my hand back at the last second and shift my eyes to Mac. He's watching me.

"May I?"

I get another nod, but it's slower and deeper this time.

I know I'm smiling like a loon when I trace the cold iron and let my hand smooth down the back of the chair.

"It's beautiful."

"Good. It's yours."

I snatch my hand back like the iron is still red hot and almost choke on my saliva as I stare back at him.

"I couldn't. I couldn't possibly." My head is shaking like he just told me Mrs. Wilkes stopped serving fried chicken on Fridays.

Mac's eyebrows inch together. "Of course you can."

"No." Still shaking.

His lips tighten in a straight line like I'm annoying him and so I roll my eyes.

"You can't just go giving me a gazillion dollar chair. You don't even know me."

He releases the tension in his mouth and his lower lip goes back to its normal fullness, not that I notice or anything.

"That's easily fixed." His shoulders give an almost imperceptible shrug and it takes concerted effort not to let my jaw drop to the ground.

"What does that mean?"

"It means we'll get to know each other," he grinds out like his statement is both obvious and final.

I open my mouth to respond but I'm just a goldfish sucking on water that's not there.

If I'm not mistaken, Angus "Mac" McKinley just asked me out on a date.

"Right," he says, like that's all settled. "Send your address to Jonathan and it'll get delivered tomorrow."

"I can't," I practically shout, finally finding my voice.

He starts doing the tight jaw and mouth thing again so I jump in and the yammering begins. "I mean, I get the keys to my place tomorrow but I'm not moving in until Thursday. That is, if my sister can get up here without a damn police escort from Georgia. You'd think all of them would realize it's the twenty-first century and a woman can, in fact, pull a trailer, but you try reasoning with a bunch of folks who still think a woman wearing long pants in church is a cardinal sin deserving of an extra stint in purgatory. Anyway..." I trail off, knowing I've officially sealed my impression as a lunatic in this guy's eyes.

But when I look him over I see that Mac's jaw isn't the only thing that's unclenched at my word vomit. If I'm not mistaken, his shoulders have loosened as well and he's now resting with his legs shoulder-width apart and that damn eyebrow raised again. I'd be mad at the self-satisfied aura he's exuding if I weren't so damn turned on by it. I need to bite something.

I tuck my hair behind my ear again and his eyes narrow like something he doesn't like just occurred to him.

"Where're you staying now?" His voice drops even deeper and I can feel it in my gut.

I shoo him off, feigning a relaxed vibe. "Oh, I'm crashing at a friend's place. I just moved here from Savannah."

This earns me another of his slower nods. I'm beginning to understand the difference between the two. The curt one means, "Okay" or "Yeah, and don't bother asking again" while the slow one means he's thinking on something and is probably gonna blow your mind with what comes out of his mouth next.

And, yup, I must be brilliant because he confirms this with his next words.

"I'll bring it myself on Thursday, then take you out."

Holy mother of David Beckham's backside.

When I don't respond, because, let's face it, my brain is still trying to process what just happened, he does one of his quick nods and starts walking back to the front of the studio. My eyes glue themselves to his ass in those jeans and I have to scurry to keep up with him when I realize he's leaving and my boots are still nailed to the floor.

Without another word, we make our way to the front doors where he holds one open for me and I find myself back out on the sidewalk. New York has been buzzing on as usual while I've been lost in the Narnia of Mac's building. The sound of chatter, car horns, and sirens are an assault, breaking whatever spell I was under.

Mac whistles and a cab stops at the curb in point-two seconds—without him even needing to raise a hand, of course. He opens the door for me and I know I should say something. I should tell him I'm not the kind of girl who dates gorillas. I'm not the kind of girl who can have a fling with a guy while he's dating Charlize Theron. I'm not the kind of girl who can handle the emotions he's stirring in me or pretend having a meal and owning a piece of furniture he created with his hands is no big deal.

But I don't say any of those things.

Instead, I let him pay for my cab and shut the door with nothing more than a gravelly, "Thursday."

Then I faint dead away in the cab. Not really, but would you blame me if I had?

ELEVEN

"Who needs enemies when you've got a perfectly good sister."
– Cookie Rutledge

MY NEW APARTMENT IS AMAZING. Small, but amazing. A bit noisy, but amazing. Kind of expensive but... okay, it's tiny and the kitchen feels like a dollhouse kitchen, but it's *mine*. The first thing I do when I pick up my keys is get my butt over to my new place and bask in the glory of having my very own New York apartment. This involves cranking up Spotify on my phone and dancing to "Hotel Key" by Old Dominion in every room—all four of them.

The queen-size bed I'm having delivered on Friday will allow just enough room for my old walnut dresser and bedside table in the cozy bedroom. And, while I don't have a bathtub, the owners installed an amazing rainfall shower-head in the newly tiled shower and a bench seat perfect for propping a leg on while shaving. What more does a girl need?

I'll figure out some way to fit all my cookware and food in the available cabinet space, and my hands are already itching to cook my first meal on the gas stove. The newly refinished oak floors gleam and the whole place is almost spotless, I'm pleased to see. My dance marathon continues in the living room/dining area while I mentally plan how to arrange my kitchen table and couch to create two distinct spaces. I don't know how I'll do it, but I know it'll be fab.

Now all I need is my stuff. Iris left this morning and is stopping in Virginia to stay with a college friend tonight before making the final leg tomorrow to Manhattan. I scheduled the afternoon off so we can unpack the trailer and get everything moved in. As far as furniture goes, there really isn't much besides my small couch, kitchen table and chairs, and a couple more pieces, but I'm keeping my fingers crossed for a cold snap to magically hit anyway so we don't expire from the combination of exertion and heat. I thought about trying to recruit some help, but I don't really know anyone well enough to beg a moving-sized favor. Those are usually reserved for people you're either related to, sleeping with, or have some serious blackmail material on. Kate said she could help and she'd ask Zach, but the James girls are badasses and we can handle it ourselves.

Badass though I may be, I'm still a complete coward as well. When I left McKinley Forge and Design last night, it was with the knowledge that Mac fully expects me to contact Jonathan and hand over my new address—something I have yet to do. Part of the reason is that I don't feel comfortable accepting his gift, no matter how stunning it is. The other part is that I'm a big fat baby and can't handle the notion of that man coming over to "take me out." I haven't let myself even begin to fathom what a date with Angus McKinley might entail. So I'm stalling.

But if even a tenth of my impression of Mac is accurate, he's not a man to let a little thing like a missing address get in his way. Which scares the ever-loving crap out of me. Do I really want to further an association with a man as over-whelming as I know him to be? It not only sounds like a hell of a lot of work, it also promises to make me feel on shakier ground than I am already. One life upheaval at a time is enough—I don't need to be concerned with nailing anything other than this job.

I walk over to my living room windows and look out at my new view. I can see over part of a small courtyard from a building behind mine and straight into the window of an apartment across the way. I'll be adding curtains to my list of things to buy so I can walk around in my underwear if the mood strikes. And it often does. The only thing better than dancing to a favorite playlist in your apartment is doing it half-naked. Everybody knows that.

"Hotel Key" switches over to "All on Me" by Devin Dawson and I'm swaying at the window with my arms wrapped around myself. The song reminds me so much of home it almost hurts. I used to listen to it so often even Cookie knew all the words by the time I left Savannah. I can almost smell her orange-blossom perfume and the lobelia that would be blooming just about now around some of the city's famous squares and the Violette Inn's back garden. We'd buy lavender shortbread cookies from

Back in the Day and Mama would make sweet tea and we'd all sit out in the back garden planning menus and re-telling the same stories about Granddaddy Rutledge—God rest his soul—while the summer air stuck to our skin and the honeybees sang.

Hearing the buzz of a bee over the cacophony of the city streets and crowds would be an impossibility here, as would relaxing out back in a tranquil garden with Cookie or Mama. But I can find my own moments here. And somebody in this city is bound to have a good lavender short-bread and a real sweet tea, right?

My phone rings, breaking through the music. Since I had to leave early to get my apartment keys, I asked reception to forward my calls for the afternoon. Nevertheless, my heart takes off in a sprint at the possibility it could be Mac. But, really, it's probably a robocall offering me enough credit to buy half of Manhattan and throwing in an all-expense paid cruise to a war-torn nation while they're at it.

"Hello?" My voice is tentative at best.

"Ms. James?"

"Yes?" I almost phrase it as a question because this is no robocall and I'm pretty sure I recognize that voice.

"Jonathan Abernathy. Mr. McKinley needs your address for delivery of an item you..." He trails off and I bite my lip hoping he just decides to hang up. I hear typing and an annoyed huff before he continues. "Hold please."

The phone goes silent before I even have a chance to speak. Without my music, the street sounds seep through the windows and fill the empty space around me. I don't know if I'll ever get used to the constant din. Maybe if I got one of those nature sound machines, like the ones with whales singing? Oh, or maybe the rainforest would be better. But, no, that would just make me need to pee.

"Ms. James," Jonathan all but spits out, like I'm inconveniencing him by my mere existence.

"I'm here."

"Your address, please."

"I..." I begin, but I don't know what to say. If I give him the address, Mac will undoubtedly show up on my doorstep, chair in hand and God knows what else planned.

Jonathan sighs in exasperation, not that I blame him entirely. I mean, how hard is it to say your address? But he's still kind of a jerk.

"Look, do you want your free chair or not? If not, I know plenty of people who—"

I cut him off with, "Fine," because even though I know I shouldn't accept the chair, something in me doesn't want anybody else to have it either. I rattle off my address before he wishes me a good day in a tone that reads more like he's wishing me an afternoon in line at the DMV with the unwashed hordes.

Why would Mac have someone so rude working for him?

I laugh at my own question. Proper manners are clearly not a priority in Angus McKinley's world, so Jonathan's winning attributes must lie elsewhere. His rudeness probably keeps the riffraff out, so maybe that's it. Mac is free to carry on alone as the beast of his domain while Jonathan and his bad attitude guard the gates and Elle smooths the way for normal humans.

The thought of Elle has my stomach plummeting. Does she know Mac takes women "out"? At the feeling in my belly, my resolve strengthens. I'll just have to explain to him that I don't date, that I'm working on my career and don't have time for...

Good grief. Men like Mac probably don't date anyway. They just drop in women's apartments and destroy their beds before vanishing into thin air to go forge manly things in blazing fire.

All the more reason to tell him I'm not interested. I'll simply explain myself and say thanks but no thanks to both the chair and the taking-me-out thing and move on with my life.

Easy peasy.

Yeah, not even *I* believe that crock of shit.

"OH MY GOD, I've missed you so much!" Iris shrieks.

We practically collide as we bound toward one another, smiling like a couple of crazies. I wrap my arms around her and squeeze way too hard, but I can't help myself. We haven't seen each other in almost three weeks, the longest stretch I reckon we've ever gone. We both went to college in Savannah and, apart from trips here and there, it's where we've lived since we were born. Even when we were both busy with our own lives and our own jobs, we always made time for family—always.

I pull back and take her face in my hands to look her over. Her blond tresses have gotten longer and she's wearing them straight. She also got an eyebrow piercing, something that makes me laugh.

"Good lord, look at you! What inspired this?"

She doesn't need to ask what I'm talking about. "You ran off to New York. I had to rebel in some way too."

I shake my head and let go of her. "Like you've ever toed the line, Rissy."

She sticks her tongue out to the side and smiles at me before gesturing back to her SUV with the U-Haul trailer attached. "We better find a place for this sucker before I get towed."

A car horn blares from behind us, making me wince. Iris is double parked outside my new building and I can't believe it hadn't occurred to me until this very moment to figure out what the heck to do with the vehicle and trailer. There's zero parking in Manhattan as far as I've been able to see. I bite my lip and think on it, but nothing comes to mind.

Reading my thoughts, Iris jumps back in the driver's seat. "Come on. We'll drive around the block while we figure it out." I follow as I pull my phone out and call Kate. She's lived here long enough to know what to do.

By the time I reach Katelyn and get an answer, Iris has driven around the block three times, doling out princess waves to people as we pass and making a general fool of herself. Despite my worry about the trailer, I can't help laughing at her. Kate tells me to park in front of a fire hydrant while we unload, so I pass the info on to Iris so we can both keep an eye out for a hydrant.

"But make sure someone stays with the car at all times or your belongings will go conveniently missing," Kate advises. When her words are met with complete silence, she figures out real quick we don't have a third.

"Oh no. I would come and be your lookout, but I got called into a meeting that starts in ten minutes. I'm so sorry, Poppy. Do you want me to call Zach?"

I chew on my thumbnail as Iris turns the corner onto my street again.

"I see a hydrant!" She points to a spot down a ways from my building.

I don't see the hydrant but it's only because my eyes have caught on something else—a tall denim and t-shirt clad man climbing out of a black pick-up truck right in front of my building. Without thinking, I duck down in the passenger seat and squeak, "It's okay, Kate. We'll figure it out," then hang up the phone.

"What the hell are you doin'?" Iris gives me the side-eye before effortlessly gliding into what I assume is the parking spot in front of the fire hydrant and putting the SUV in park. She turns toward me with her eyebrows at her hairline.

"Um..." I begin. "I forgot to tell you somebody might be stopping by."

Her eyes shoot directly to Mac as if he were a living, breathing homing beacon. "Holy balls!" She squints. "Is that... him?"

"If by him you mean the hot blacksmith who moon-lights as the witness to my every humiliating misstep as a New Yorker, then yes, that's him," I croak.

"Ooooh my." She blinks and then brings her eyes back to me. "He's even bigger in person."

I give her an *uh-doi* look from my crouched position.

"He's going to the building." Her eyes flash back to me. "Wait, why does he get to double park and we don't?"

Does she need a repeat of the *uh-doi?*

Iris pulls on my arm and ignores my recoil. "What are you doing? Let's go meet the hottie!" She opens her door and I go into panic mode.

"No," I try to protest but she's pulling my door open and yanking on my arm. "Iris, I can't!"

"Of course you can! You are such a big liar." She shakes her head at me. "You said he hated you."

I grip my seatbelt for dear life. "Turns out I was wrong." Now he just wants to give me furniture and eat me for lunch.

Her shit-eating grin is annoying as all get-out. "You have two seconds to get your sexy little butt out of that car or I'm calling him over to haul you out himself."

I gasp and grip the seatbelt even tighter. "You wouldn't!" But I've met her before and she so would.

She turns her head and cups a hand around her mouth, drawing in a huge breath.

"No! Fine! I'll go! Just hush your mouth."

The grin is back, and I gingerly unfasten the seatbelt before slinking out of the car and running a hand over my hair.

"How do I look?"

"Like a hot mess," she responds without hesitation. "But emphasis on the hot."

I meant to dress to kill, but then got all up in my own head. I didn't need to look sexy or cool to send Mac away so why bother? But now I'm regretting my decision to wear a ponytail, cut-offs, and my threadbare t-shirt that says "Kiss my grits." I squeeze my eyes shut. Nothing I can do about it now.

Iris practically frog marches me over to where I can now see Mac buzzing my empty apartment. I don't know that I'd ever tire of the back view of that man—or the front for that matter.

He's in his uniform of thigh-hugging denim and t-shirt, this time a dark gray one, and he's wearing work boots that have suffered countless scuffs and scratches. He's got his keys in one hand while the other pushes my button (ha!), his eyes trained on his boots.

"Why in heavens would you be avoiding *that?*" Iris whispers in my ear and I smack her hands off my shoulders.

Mac still hasn't seen us but I'm too close to run away now, even without my jailer behind me, so I figure the sooner I start this the sooner he'll leave and I can breathe again.

I take a deep inhale and force a casual tone. "Hi." I follow this with a wave only slightly less corny than Iris's princess wave.

His eyes lift from his boots and to the side and my womb pulses like a heartbeat. I vaguely hear a whispered "Whoa" from behind me but all my senses are focused in one direction. Exactly why was it a bad idea for Mac to be here? I honestly can't remember.

TWELVE

"Speechlessness is God's way of saving you from your own self." – Cookie Rutledge

"POPPY." The word is low and gruff and in that moment I'm thanking my mama for giving me a name with so many Ps in it—because when it leaves his mouth it looks like his lush bottom lip is kissing my damn name.

I swear if Iris weren't pressing herself against my back I might go and mount the beast right there on my sidewalk. But she is, so I grasp her arm and pull her to my side with a jerk, almost causing her to fall on her face. "This is my sister, Iris. Iris, this is Angus McKinley."

"Mac," he corrects with a chin dip.

"Mac," Iris repeats. Thank you! At least I'm not the only one who repeats his words back to him.

"We're, uh, moving my stuff in." I gesture awkwardly between the building and the SUV.

Mac's eyes narrow. "Who's we?"

Iris is still standing there staring so I respond for both of us. "Me and Iris."

He makes a noise in his throat and Iris's eyes all but bug out of her face. Then he raises an index finger and pulls a phone from his pocket. Iris is squeezing my elbow so hard I'm gonna need a sling tomorrow, but I send her a silent look telling her to calm the hell down while I try listening to Mac's conversation.

It pretty much consists of a couple "yeah"s and my address. Who is he inviting over? Iris hasn't even seen the place yet for goodness sake.

His eyes finally come back to us and Iris strikes an overly casual pose.

"Leave the trailer. Let's get the chair up."

My mouth twists to the side and I brace. "Um, about that."

Mac freezes and lifts that damn single brow again. I want to lick it, which I know is all sorts of weird.

"I know you came all this way, but I've been thinking on it and I don't feel right taking the chair. I mean, at least let me pay for it. How much does it cost?" I reach for my phone so I can maybe PayPal him my firstborn or something.

His eyes have narrowed again and both hands rest naturally at his thighs while his left cheek does that tick thing. "Thirty-five hundred."

"Thirty-five..." I shove my phone back in my pocket faster than Cookie can spot a store-bought cake. "That may be a tad over budget for me."

"What chair?" Iris asks, helpful as ever.

It's just the excuse Mac is looking for because he strides to his truck without hesitation and hoists himself up and into the bed as gracefully as if he grew up scaling mountains in the Alps or whatever. He unhooks some straps and then yanks a drop cloth off the remarkable piece of furniture.

Iris forgets all about her initial Mac-induced shock as she approaches the truck bed. "Pretty. Did you make this?"

Mac does another one of his nods. "Been waiting for the right owner." His eyes dart back to me and I'm stunned speechless.

He thinks *I'm* that owner. Gah!

Without another word, he slides the chair to the end of the tailgate and hops down off the truck where he hoists it up in his arms. The movements cause his biceps to bulge and test the seams of his shirt while his back muscles visibly ripple beneath the fabric.

Iris's eyes widen again and she mouths, "I'll cut you if you don't hit that," just as Mac asks, "Can you get the door?"

I haul ass, telling myself I'm only doing it because I'm afraid he might drop the chair and ruin it. But I know I'm lying.

"I'll stay with the truck," Iris says to Mac's back while miming dirty hand signals to me.

I roll my eyes at her and follow him in.

"I'm on the third floor."

He's already on his way up the stairs and I'm treated to a close-up view of his thighs stretching the denim to its limit while his butt works in those jeans. Let me tell you, his gym or his studio or wherever the hell he does all his workouts should be named a holy place if they produced the other-worldly eye candy climbing up my stairs. There's not a flat inch of... anything in sight and I would bet Cookie's Anna Weatherley teacup collection that he's got those two back dimples above his muscular buttcheeks.

When we reach the third floor, he glances back at me and all the blood in my body rushes to my face because I've been caught red-handed—or red-cheeked in this case—staring at his backside. And there goes that eyebrow, confirming what I already know. Thankfully, he doesn't mention it.

"What number?"

"Oh, 3-A." I point to the left and will my face to cool down a few degrees as I hurry ahead of him to unlock my door and hold it open.

It's a squeeze getting through with the chair and his bulk so I shouldn't be surprised when his bicep brushes against my breast on his way in. He doesn't appear to notice, but when I look down at my shirt I've got one erect nipple waving hello from just above the word Grits. Fabulous.

"Where do you want it?"

I cross my arms and let the door close.

"Anywhere is fine. I'm not real sure where anything is going yet."

Mac lowers the chair down in front of the window like he's simply setting down an empty box and straightens again. His gaze sweeps me from head to toe and I squirm inside like a kid who might pee his pants.

"Listen, Mac," I begin and then pause as his eyes dart back to mine, the irises going almost liquid as a hum sounds from his chest. At first it doesn't compute, but then I realize it's a sound of pleasure, and I'm pretty sure it's because I called him *Mac* for the first time ever.

My mouth is Sahara dry but I forge on. "I don't have the kind of money you're talking about, which I'm sure you knew before you hauled that chair up here. I just... it's way too generous. You don't even know—" I stop before I can finish my sentence, vividly recalling his response the last time I said those words.

"I already told you it's yours."

I chew on my lip, trying to figure out where to go from here.

His hands grip his hips on either side. "Look, if it makes you feel any better, I wasn't going to sell it."

My mouth gapes. "That makes it even worse! You were saving it for something special."

He gives me one of the slow nods this time.

As soon as the meaning of that nod registers, my entire body threatens to burst into flame—and not the embarrassment kind. The fully turned on, mama's-gettin'-lucky-tonight-so-send-the-kids-to-Grandma kind of heat. Is it possible to orgasm from just a head nod?

I'm so flustered I don't know what to do with any of my appendages. They all feel like they belong to somebody else and I just have them on loan today.

But I don't have to stand there silently offering my body up to him for too long because a buzzing sound indicates he has a call. His eyes don't stray from me for a millisecond as he brings his phone to his ear.

"Down in a sec."

It's back in his pocket and he's walking toward me, his

eyes locked on mine, pinning me in place. There is nowhere in the world I can think of that would beat this spot on my bare wood floor right this minute.

Mac's hand comes up when we're just a couple feet apart and his long fingers reach toward my face where he runs one along my hairline and then tucks a wayward strand of hair behind my ear. His touch is incredibly gentle for someone so imposing and I shiver at the sensation of his skin on mine. He lets his finger trace behind the shell of my ear and then down the column of my neck, only lifting it when he reaches the cotton of my t-shirt.

"We'll get your stuff moved. Then I'm taking you out." Our close proximity means he only needs to breathe the words for me to hear them, but they catch on the rough edges of his vocals chords nonetheless.

My own voice is a barely audible croak. "Okay."

OKAY? *Okay?*

No! Not okay!

I was supposed to tell him all those things about not being available to date or go "out," not roll over like a freakin' hound dog in a damn sunbeam.

But by the time I regained my better sense, Mac was already on his way back down the stairs. There was nothing I could do but follow.

When we reached the street again, a guy in coveralls was flirting with Iris but got straight to work with Mac unloading the U-Haul and SUV. When Iris or I tried helping out, all we got was a stern look from Mac and a friendly "we got this" from the other guy, so we stood lookout instead until every last thing was in my apartment. It took all of about thirty minutes before they finished and coveralls guy was asking for Iris's phone number.

Now I'm standing in the middle of my living room with an appraising eye toward my furniture. I'll need to add a rug to my list, but I like the configuration we have so far with the sofa facing the windows and acting as a divider to the living space. Mac's chair has a place of honor sitting at an angle with a view of the entire apartment. I rub the spot on my neck where Mac's finger drew a soft line and feel... things... tighten all over.

"Everybody back home is gonna lose their collective shit when they see this." Iris's voice cuts into my private moment.

I glance over and see her leaning against the kitchen table holding out her phone. Since I'm several feet away, I can't get a perfect view, but it looks like a picture of Mac and Alec, the coveralls guy, carrying my dresser into the front of the building. If memory serves, and, oh, how I know it does, just about every one of Mac's muscles was on display during that maneuver. I might need to crank up the A/C.

"You can't show them that." I shake my head and go to take her phone.

She holds it away from me. "Why not? You want Bobby Lee off your back, don't you?"

"Yeah, but not this way." I give up and lean against the table next to her. "I don't like lying."

"But why? You're so good at it." She gives me a shoulder shove and I scowl at her.

"It was enough that I said it in the first place. I don't want to rub Bobby Lee's nose in it—especially since it isn't true."

"Now you're just lying to *yourself*." Iris points to the floor. "That man wants to plow you like last year's crops."

I half laugh and cover my face. "Iris!"

"What? He does, and don't even try to pretend you don't know it."

I stumble over to the sofa and fall onto it, my eyes to the ceiling. "Fine. It's pretty clear he wants to sleep with me. But I'm not doing it!"

"Why the hell not? I'd let that Yankee doodle my dandy anytime he wanted." She follows and stands over me with her hands fixed on her hips.

"Have you seen him?!" I ignore her last comment and throw my arms out in defeat. "He'll wreck me for every other man I ever meet. Five years from now, some perfectly nice guy might get down on one knee to propose to me and all I'll be thinking about are the orgasms King Kong gave me!"

She scrunches her face up. "First, you gotta stop calling him that—it makes him sound like a filthy gorilla. And second, that's like saying no to a hot fudge sundae from your favorite ice cream place when they're going out of business. It don't hold water. If somebody offers you the hot fudge, you take it and run with it."

"Even if the hot fudge might already belong to someone else?"

"That's crazy. Hot fudge doesn't belong to anybody."

"Exactly my point!" I scratch my head. "Well, kind of."

"If you're trying to say he's not 'boyfriend material',"
Iris says with air quotes, "I'm not gonna argue with you. I
can't see that guy buying you flowers and cooking up his
famous ramen noodle surprise to impress you. But why
can't you hang out a few times and let him have his dirty
way with you?"

"Reasons, okay! Not the least of which is Elle, his probably supermodel-slash-agent-with-benefits or whatever.
And besides, Mac is not hot fudge. He could seriously ruin
me." I cover my face again.

Iris pauses and then gasps. "Wait, do you like him? I
mean *like* him, like him?"

I groan from behind my hands. "He's grown on me,
okay?" And it's true. From his dedication to his craft and
the hidden passion for creating things of beauty to his
cryptic panty-melting declarations and his disregard for
anyone who expects him to change who he is, I'm
completely hooked.

"Damn, he could grow on me any day."

I lower my hands and give Iris the stink-face. "Ew."

She cackles and shoves my legs aside so she can sit on
the sofa.

"Well, you better get your ass in gear because he's
gonna be back any minute now. It can't take that long to
find a parking spot."

My heart knocks against my ribcage. When they
finished unloading everything, Mac sent Alec to drive Iris's
SUV and the U-Haul to his building while he went to find
a spot nearby for his truck.

"You have to help me get out of this date or whatever it is," I plead with her.

"Why would I do that?"

I bat my eyelashes. "Because you're my sister and you love me."

"That's exactly why I'm making you *go* on this date." She points in my face.

"Iris!" I shove her.

"Poppy!" She shoves back. It's like we're still little tweens back at Mama and Daddy's house outside Savannah.

"You just got in town and it's your first time in New York. No matter what kind of brat you're being, I'm not leaving you for some guy who could easily scratch his itch with any freakin' girl on this island."

Iris sighs and pulls me in for a hug. "You're not just any freakin' girl on this island, and you're gonna be fine." She squeezes me. "I'll be fine too. Katelyn will be home to keep me company. Go out with the hot blacksmith tonight and then tomorrow your bed will be here and we can have an official celebration complete with champagne, a night on the town, and a good-old-fashioned pajama party."

I lean into her hug and try to form a response but there's a swift knock at the door and I realize my time is up.

Iris practically throws me to the other side of the sofa and sprints for the door.

I reckon my number is officially up.

THIRTEEN

*"Stepping outta your comfort zone is best done wearin' the
right shoes."*
– Cookie Rutledge

IF I EVER HAD ANY delusions that I might beg off on this date, they're blown to smithereens when the door opens and I'm stunned absolutely stupid by the sight of Mac wearing a fresh t-shirt covered by a blue button down with the sleeves rolled up to expose his corded forearms.

It takes Iris acting as a buffer for me to finally excuse myself to go tear into a box of clothes in my new bedroom for anything that might make me look even marginally well-suited to accompany Mac somewhere. A denim skirt paired with flat sandals and a baby-doll top will have to do because everything is either in a mess on the floor or packed in another box. I can't do anything about my hair or makeup since I haven't brought my toiletries over from Katelyn's yet, so au natural will have to do.

I trek back out with my small purse across my shoulder and hand over all my keys to Iris. "I already ordered you an Uber to Katelyn's and these will get you in if she's not home yet." I rattle off the apartment number and instructions to get in the building while all three of us descend the steps. My eyes stay trained on Iris so I don't hyperventilate, but I can *feel* Mac behind me on the steps.

We file out onto the sidewalk and the Uber is already waiting. Mac stows her suitcase in the trunk while Iris almost skips toward the car with little more than a wave. "Y'all have fun! And, Mac, we'll be having words if you don't bring her home after midnight!" She disappears into the car and I begin formulating my tenth round of plans for her imminent demise.

Mac doesn't even appear to notice, however, as he rejoins me, takes my hand in his, and begins leading us down the sidewalk, utterly blowing my mind in the process.

Angus "Mac" McKinley is a *hand holder*.

I'm beginning to question everything I know about humankind.

"Can you walk in those?" He dips his chin to indicate my sandals.

"Y... yeah," I stammer, still recovering from the explosion of my frontal lobe. And now all I can focus on is the feel of his rough hand enveloping my much smaller one. His skin is warm and dry and the pad of his thumb where it rests against the side of my wrist has revealed a heretofore unknown path straight to my uterus.

We walk the next two blocks in silence until I can't stand it anymore.

"So, where are you taking me?" It's only six-thirty so we're clearly not going clubbing. Even the notion of Mac in a dance club makes me want to laugh.

Half of me expects him to respond, "To bed," while the other half thinks maybe he'll go with, "Does it matter?" But his actual response is a bit more practical.

"Dinner."

"Do you have a daily word limit?" I blurt.

Mac turns his head to me and even from my view way down here, I sense a definite lift to the corner of his mouth.

Since he doesn't respond, I figure it's my turn again. "I thought no one in this town ate supper before ten."

He looks my way again. "Then we shouldn't have trouble getting a table."

I nod. "Brilliant. I like the way you think."

I'm not sure if I imagine it, but I think he gives my hand a small squeeze at that.

My steps speed to keep up with him and when I look at our feet I see I'm taking about four steps to his one. I'm embarrassed to admit I'm actually getting winded.

"Do you mind if we slow down just a little."

He immediately slows his steps to a crawl and takes a sweeping glance down my entire body to my feet.

"Short legs." I point to my knees in explanation.

His eyes linger on the skin of my thighs exposed by my short skirt and I swear I hear a hum from his chest. *Great balls of lady town fire!*

When his eyes finally come back up to meet mine, the look in them would leave me entirely unsurprised should he beat his chest, then hoist my body over his shoulder and keep on walking.

Slow down, big guy!

"Where are we going for dinner?" I let my gaze fall to the side and we resume a more reasonable pace. But I can't ignore the contact of our skin and the brush of his thumb across my wrist.

"You like sushi?"

My brain threatens to explode again at the word sushi. I figured Mac just ate whatever he hunted down and killed each morning. But sushi?

"I love sushi." I don't even have to hesitate in my answer. I'd sell Iris for a good spicy salmon roll.

Mac gives me a short nod of approval and veers right at the next intersection.

I let myself look around and see the usual suits hurrying down the sidewalks and people disappearing into apartment buildings and corner shops. Several moms speed by us with trendy strollers and hair pulled back in slick ponytails. And all I can think is how they're all missing out.

My eyes come back to Mac and I inspect his stubbled jaw and crooked nose. I can't see the scar from this side, but I want to ask what caused it. I want to know a lot of things about this man that I have no business asking. So I decide to start easy.

"Have you ever been to Japan? I hear Tokyo is even more crowded than here."

"Never been," Mac answers. "Never been much of anywhere, really."

I don't know why this surprises me. The man seems to

prefer a degree of solitude one doesn't generally see in world travelers.

I shrug. "Me either. New York is my biggest adventure so far."

We come to a stop at a nondescript storefront and Mac pulls a glass door open for me. The inside is small with a few tables scattered across the commercial flooring and photos of Japanese tourist attractions covering the walls. Mac holds two fingers up to the hostess and we're seated immediately at a table in the corner.

"Have you lived here your whole life?" I continue my get-to-know-you quiz once we're seated with our menus.

He looks down at his while he answers. "Sort of."

I'm not sure if I should take his non-answer as a sign the topic is off limits. His past was forbidden territory during our interview but surely it's not unexpected to talk about your past on a date, is it?

"Then maybe you can point me in the direction of a place that serves sweet tea."

His eyes flick up from his menu. "Shouldn't be too hard to find."

I throw my hands out. "I know! Yet the best I've been able to do is McDonalds."

I'm confident I don't imagine the confusion in his eyes, but there's no time to explain because our waitress arrives to take our drink order. We both ask for water, me because I can't afford to cloud my judgement with anything approaching alcohol, and Mac for reasons I don't know.

She asks if we're ready to order and I nod, not because I've perused the entire menu, but because I know what I like and I sense Mac does too.

Gulp.

He proceeds to order what I'm pretty sure is just a bunch of raw fish without the benefit of rice or fancy crap. It's only then it occurs to me that a body like his, regardless of genetics, probably requires a fastidious diet and a whole lot of self-control. Which is right on par with what I've gleaned about Mac so far. I'm guessing this is a man who can take control to the next level.

All the more reason this date is a terrible idea. But I'm here and physically buzzing from pretty much everything he's laying down, so that ship has sailed.

"How long have you been here?" Mac rests both fore-arms on the table, letting them stretch across the surface in front of him. We might need to ask for a bigger table.

I tuck my hands in my lap. "Almost three weeks."

He narrows his eyes. "So, the night outside my studio..." His rough voice trails off.

"Was my first weekend in town," I finish for him with a self-deprecating smile. "I'll bet you couldn't tell at all."

His tongue swipes across his bottom lip and I'm sure it's an unconscious gesture but, *dayum.*

Apropos of just about nothing, he says, "You like dancing."

I open my mouth to answer and then bite down on my lip for a second when I realize it wasn't a question. His eyes focus in on the movement so I immediately release my grip. "You could say that." Just like you could say the sky is blue or Sam Hunt is okay looking. "How about you?" I ask, just so I can see his reaction.

He sends me the single brow arch and I laugh out loud,

not even caring that the sound carries through the entire restaurant.

But my smile dies on my lips at his next words.

"You're fuckin' gorgeous."

My head straightens and my breath locks in my lungs. Nobody has ever talked to me like that in my entire life and I know I should probably be put off by his bluntness but I *so* am not. In fact, half of me is ready to yell, "Check, please!" and go see if he can break my sofa.

His eyes are daring mine to break contact and my entire body has turned electric. So, of course, that's when the waitress returns with our dinner.

I clear my throat and thank her before gripping my water glass and chugging the entire contents. When I glance back at Mac, he's opening his chopsticks but that damn corner of his mouth is turned up again.

We eat mostly in silence but it's surprisingly not awkward. He's a pro with his chopsticks, something that may be difficult for a lot of men with hands his size, but considering the delicate work he can perform with said hands, it just makes sense.

My spicy salmon roll is freakin' delicious and I'm pretty sure I moan more than once while eating. Mac basically inhales his fish and polishes off three refills of water before paying our bill and ushering me back out to the sidewalk.

Now is my opportunity to thank him for dinner and grab an Uber back to Katelyn's. Even if he makes my entire body sing and gives me beautiful furniture and moves me into my apartment and thinks I'm "fuckin' gorgeous," the fact remains that I'm not a wham-bam-thank-you-ma'am girl and I don't like breaking the girl code, even if Elle could probably get any guy she wants.

Not to mention, I should be focusing on doing everything I can to ensure this magazine gets the green light from the board less than two weeks from now or I might be stuck working as a staff designer on some two-bit publication. And that is so not the reason I moved my ass to New York.

I need to be smart and keep my eye on the ball, not get swept up by hormones that can't see past the here and now. Those bitches just see a hot man who tells me I'm pretty and they're ready to roll.

Mac signals a cab and I try formulating the right words to tell him I can't go back to his lair and sleep with him, but it turns out I'm wasting my time when he casually asks, "What's your friend's address?"

I rattle off Katelyn's address as an odd numbness spreads through me. What is wrong with me? This is exactly what I was hoping for, isn't it?

Mac hands the driver a wad of cash and repeats the information while I stand with my hands limply at my sides. Then he opens the back door and steps right up into my space, causing me to stagger back so I'm almost pressed up against the taxi.

I swallow hard and look up at him. With my flat sandals and shorter than average stature, there's a good foot of height difference between us. I feel a sudden panic and an overwhelming need to drink in every detail of his face. This might be the last time I see him, apart from the internet stalking I'll undoubtedly do from now until eternity, and I haven't even gotten a chance to ask about his scar or investigate his neck tattoo!

"Mac." His name comes out without my permission and with a tone of longing I certainly didn't intend. His response is to dip his head down and raise both hands to my face. But only the pads of his thumbs make contact, tracing the line of my jaw on either side and sending a shiver through me.

"Go spend time with your sister." The deep timbre of his voice does nothing to help my current condition.

His thumbs stroke back toward my chin and I forget I even have a sister.

"I'll call you." I watch his lips form the words right before he lowers his head down all the way and captures my lips with his.

His kiss is hard and assertive, just like him.

He takes my breath with the first bruising contact of his mouth on mine, drawing my upper lip between his and sliding the tip of his wet tongue across it as my own lips finally catch on that full lower curve that's been driving me nuts. His skin there is soft and pliant in contrast to the scruff of his trimmed beard scraping against my chin. But I don't care if I have beard burn for the rest of my life because my sex thrums and my body screams to get closer.

He doesn't embrace me or even try to feel me up, unfortunately. This kiss is all about lips and tongue and the firm press of his thumbs holding my face exactly where he wants it.

The delicious assault on my senses continues while his mouth slants for another taste and my hands finally reach up to rest on his firm chest. Even through the double layers of cotton I can feel the warmth of his skin and the contraction of his pecs at my touch.

When he finally releases me, I'm a puddle of goo and have only remained upright due to my grip on Mac's shirt and the frame of the taxi pressing into my back.

He's not even the least bit winded when he guides me down to a seated position and leans into the cab. His whiskers brush against the side of my face and his warm breath tickles my ear as he gets real close.

"Oh, and, Poppy," he grinds out.

"Yeah," I pant.

"I don't hate you." He pulls back and I just stare.

"Okay."

He closes the taxi door and I collapse against the seat wondering if that man has ever made an exit that wasn't completely earthshattering.

My guess is a big fat no.

FOURTEEN

FRIDAY IS SPENT DOING last-minute adjustments before the latest version of the prototype is sent to Athena for review. We still don't have Mac's article—we haven't even taken the photos—but we'll fit it in before the final mock-up runs through each department next week.

I'm thrilled at the aesthetic we've achieved, and I'm confident it's fresh and appealing enough to capture a wide readership. We need to strike a careful balance since we're overhauling one of the country's oldest magazines, but I think even the old subscribers will find the new content and look engaging enough to subscribe—especially with the marketing plan our team has in the works to entice them.

Even if I weren't working for the publication, I know

I'd be a subscriber. Who doesn't need time-saving tricks paired with weekend getaway ideas, quick recipes, the lowdown on the latest gadgets, and some hot eye candy all in one place? I have a wild hair to get Bunny's reaction to the new *WHL* and see if she'd be willing to give it a go. She'd make an excellent case study for her ever-shrinking demographic—the classic Southern housewife who still puts her face on before her husband wakes up and considers a new recipe from Paula Deen "news."

And there I go being hateful again. I suspect it has to do with the package I found waiting for me last night when I got back to Katelyn's after my womb-imploding date with Mac.

I thought Iris was going to disown me when I walked in the door well before dark—until I described the entire date in detail. Then she looked about as swoony as I'm sure I did.

But the high didn't last long when I spotted a gift-wrapped package on the counter done up so fancy it could only have been from Bunny or Martha Stewart herself.

"What is that?" My lip had a definite curl to it.

Iris followed my gaze over to the offending box and her mouth turned down. "Oh, that. Bunny dropped it off before I left and asked me to bring it to you. I forgot about it till I opened my suitcase."

I approached it like it was a bomb and plucked the card off the top where it was secured by sparkly gold ribbon. Inside the envelope was a card with a print of the Waving Girl statue, a famous Savannah landmark overlooking the Savannah river. Inside was a handwritten note in Bunny's familiar rounded script.

Dearest Poppy,

I hope this note finds you well. I thought you could use a little something to remind you of home and all of us here who are desperately missing you. Take good care of yourself and come see us sooner rather than later.

All My Love,
Bunny Collinsworth

Because I know so many Bunnys.

Iris came and read over my shoulder and I handed the card over so I could unwrap the package. It was a shame to ruin it, given that I'm sure the elaborate wrapping cost more than the contents of the box, but there wasn't much I could do.

"Oh, good God," Iris groaned when I pulled out the first item. It was a framed photo of Bobby Lee and me from way back when we were kids. He was giving me bunny ears and I was lifting up my Sunday dress so you could see my damn bloomers. The frame was inscribed with the words "Home is where the heart is" in fancy script.

I know Iris was on fire because she saw it for what it was—blatant manipulation. But there's a reason Bunny wins more arguments than she loses; she's damn good at it. Despite myself, I got a little teary. Not because seeing myself flashing Bobby Lee when he was six and I was three made me suddenly realize I was helplessly in love with the man. But because I remembered some genuinely great times with Bobby Lee—times when he was sweet and considerate and wanted nothing but for me to be happy. And I miss that. I truly do. I was lucky to have him as my boyfriend for the year that we dated, even if he turned out to be the wrong man for me.

I handed the photo off to Iris and pulled out the next item. It was a bag of my favorite cheddar jalapeno cookies. I knew for a fact that Bunny had to wait in line to buy that for me, something she'd know I knew.

"Oooh," Iris said, snatching the bag from me and ripping it open. "I haven't had one of these in forever."

After that came a pair of sea-glass-adorned hairclips and a hand-embroidered tea towel with my name on it.

Then, at the very bottom of the box was another photo, this one not in a frame but laying loose. I knew what picture it was before I even pulled it out. It was from the summer I turned sixteen when I started getting paid for working at the Violette Inn. Cookie, Mama, Bunny, Iris, and I were standing in front of the inn, all five of us linking arms, dressed in fancy duds for a night out. I was looking particularly proud because I was using my first paycheck to treat everyone to dessert on the rooftop terrace of Churchill's Pub with my hard-earned money. Unfortunately, my wide-eyed teenage self didn't realize my check wouldn't even cover half the bill. But Cookie slipped me some cash under the table so I could save face, whispering that I could pay her back later—something she pretended to forget all about when I eventually did try paying her.

Iris rested her chin on my shoulder. "Aww. I remember that night. Didn't Cookie get drunk and hit on our waiter?"

I laughed. "I don't think she even had one drink that night. But the other part is probably true."

I set the photo down next to the other items on the counter and ran my eyes lovingly over each gift. Then I changed into my pajamas and listened as Iris caught me up on everything going down in her life since I left. But when we finally settled down to sleep in Katelyn's guest bed together, it was with two photos resting on the nightstand next to my pillow.

Well played, Bunny Collinsworth.

NAVEED STOPS by my office just before five and invites himself out for drinks with Iris and me. I haven't seen him since Tuesday and I'm happy to have him school us newbies on the best places for happy hour. He chooses a vintage-inspired pub about six blocks from work and Iris agrees to meet us, claiming she's mastered the subway system and wants to show off her new skills.

As we walk to the bar, I listen as Naveed tells me about a guy he's been "talking to" online and I do my best to pretend I'm not completely distracted. But inside I feel like I'm slowly dying.

Mac didn't call.

I'm aware of all the various rules about how much time you should wait before calling after a date, but none of them are helpful in this case. Because a) Mac does not strike me as a person who plays by the rules. In fact, he strikes me as the kind of person who'd burn the whole damn rulebook after scowling at it in a super sexy way. And

b) it's Friday evening and Mac does not have my cell phone number.

I've been kicking myself all day long for not clearing my Mac-induced haze for long enough last night to give him my digits, but it's no use. This means if I want to talk to him before Monday, I'll have to be the one to call and, most likely, need to deal with Jonathan in the process. Ugh.

When we arrive at the bar, Iris is already standing outside. I introduce her to Naveed and we all go inside where Iris and I look for a spot to park our trio and Naveed grabs us our first round of drinks.

And, because she's my sister, Iris immediately knows something's wrong.

"Spill it."

"Spill what?" I feign innocence as I tuck back a strand of hair that's fallen out of my updo.

"The reason your face looks like that."

"Rude." I look her over to see if I can throw an insult her way but she looks adorable as usual, with her shiny blond hair and her slim bod decked out in a trendy floral romper and heeled sandals.

"Quick. Before your friend gets back." She cocks her head to the bar.

I crane my neck and see that Naveed is already being served by the bartender.

"Fine. He didn't call." I sigh.

"Who? Mac?"

"No. Donald Trump. Of course Mac."

Her brow knits. "It hasn't even been twenty-four hours."

I know she's right, but I explain my thought process,

ending with, "I'm obviously a horrible kisser and he's decided Elle the supermodel is a much better option."

"Chill please. He'll call." She leans against the wood-paneled wall.

I open my mouth to argue about the cell number again but she cuts me off.

"You really think a man like that can't find a way to get your number? He probably just had a busy day banging on fiery things."

The mental image of Mac doing just that fills my mind and I suddenly feel a bit woozy.

"How can you sound so sure?"

Her hand hits her hip. "Easy, dummy. He has my car."

"Oh." I'd completely forgotten about that.

"And besides," Iris holds up her phone. "I have Alec's number. I can just text him for Mac's if you want."

"No!" I lunge for her phone just as Naveed approaches with three drinks.

"Oooh. Girl fight." He waggles his dark brows.

Iris bares her teeth and growls like a tiger.

"I like her," Naveed says to me, handing over my drink.

"Good. You can have her." I scowl at Iris but it bounces right off her.

"Whatever. You'd miss me too much."

She's absolutely right, of course.

"Why the jello wrestling over the phone?" Naveed asks, bringing his drink straw to his mouth.

"Poppy doesn't want me to hunt down this hot guy's number."

I don't want Naveed knowing anything about Mac and me. He may be one of the only people in my professional life who's seen the real me, but even so, it can't look good if I'm seen getting involved with someone we have business with. And anyway, Mac and I aren't involved. In fact, I should be happy he didn't call. It makes things simpler.

"All I heard was hot guy. Tell me more."

I give Iris the universal girl face for "Abort!" and, thankfully, she receives it loud and clear.

She waves a dismissive hand. "Just some dude who helped us out yesterday."

"Oh." Naveed seems deflated so I bring up the subject of his new guy and before long he's regaling us with stories of some of his wilder online conquests.

After a bit, we're able to snag a high bar table from a departing couple and we settle ourselves in. I'm beyond relieved to get off my feet, promising myself to relegate these heels to the nope bin as soon as we get home.

In the middle of Naveed's introductory lesson on how to shop in Manhattan Iris slides her phone across the table with a sly smile. When I look down I see she has three new text messages from a clearly eager Alec.

ALEC

Hey beautiful. Returned the trailer.

Mac wants your girl's number.

You want to meet up for a drink tomorrow?

It's all I can do not to take a victory lap around the bar. I will my face to remain expressionless in case Naveed is watching me. But I don't need to worry because when I glance his way he's got his nose in his own phone looking for a link for Iris. I shoot her a subtle nod and she grins like a lunatic as she types a response to Alec.

Five minutes later, my phone vibrates with an incoming call. I shoot Iris a wide-eyed look of panic and quickly excuse myself. It takes what feels like an eternity to weave my way through the happy hour crowd and out to the sidewalk where I can hopefully hear.

"Hello?"

"It's Mac."

A sappy smile overtakes my face and I give myself an eyeroll when I realize I'm literally twirling my hair between my fingers like a lovesick teenager.

"Hi."

"Your bed get delivered?"

Hearing him just say the word bed makes something go bump in my panties.

"It did. First thing this morning, in fact. I'm looking forward to testing it out tonight." Oh my good lord baby Cheez-its. I can't believe I just said that.

Mac makes that humming sound.

If I don't bring things around, I'll be combusting with pent-up sexual frustration out here on the freakin' sidewalk for all to see.

"Yeah, Iris and I are having drinks in Midtown and then we're packing my suitcases to finish moving me in. I'm an official New Yorker."

"How long is she in town?"

"Um, just through the weekend." *Why? Do you want to check out my bed?* I tack on silently.

"Wanted to see you again. Will she mind if I borrow

you?" His voice is like a shot of liquor without the benefit of ice.

I can't exactly tell him that if she had her way I reckon Iris would personally deliver me to him with a big red bow.

"Um, I don't think so." I peer back into the bar. Iris is laughing at something Naveed is saying and a nagging feeling pulls at my stomach. "Are you... sure this is a good idea?"

"Absolutely. Why?"

"I just..." *I just don't know if I can handle how intense you are and I'm afraid you'll ravish me and then ditch me for the next supermodel who happens by. Oh, and I'm being an idiot and mixing business with pleasure.*

"You don't want to see me?" He manages to make it sound completely inconsequential.

"No!" I jump in to reassure, not that he needs it. "I do. I'm just..." I sigh in frustration. "Has anybody ever told you that you're intense?"

I hear an amused chuffing sound. "Maybe."

"Well, you're kind of a lot, Mac. I'm just not used to that, I guess." I decide to go for broke. "And, frankly, I'm a bit worried about my job."

I can feel the change in him, even over the phone.

"Explain."

"Gee, Poppy, that's a bummer. Do you mind telling me about it?" I mimic his voice because I've clearly lost my mind.

I hear the gravelly humming again but he doesn't say anything.

"Look, you know I'm new to this job. I can't afford to do anything to jeopardize it and I'm afraid developing a...

personal connection to the subject of a feature might be frowned upon." Not to mention, my heart has an aversion to bulldozers.

"I'm gonna be straight up with you."

I bite my lip to keep myself from laughing hysterically. Like the guy could ever be accused of sugar-coating anything.

"There wouldn't be an article without the *personal connection* part." He says the words like he's making air quotes that offend him somehow. "The only reason they got their interview is because I'm into you and, as far as I'm concerned, it's none of their business if I want to take you out, kiss your fuckin' perfect mouth, or do any of the hundred other things I've got planned. So the only question that really matters is, do you want to see me?"

My jaw is unhinged by this point so it's a damn miracle I manage to form intelligible speech, not that my strangled "Uh-huh" is all that impressive.

FIFTEEN

IT'S safe to say Bobby Lee has been sulking, something I'm both annoyed by and feeling the teensiest bit guilty about. He hasn't so much as sent me a text since we hung up last weekend after my Angus McKinley mic drop. Regardless, I have no doubt he and Bunny have been strategizing about how to get me to ditch my fake boyfriend and fancy new job and run on home to marry Bobby Lee before things get out of hand and/or I grow a year older into spinsterhood.

The part I refuse to let myself consider is the possibility that, up to this point, one or both of them have been operating under the assumption I wouldn't cut it at the new job and it was only a matter of time before I'd come running back home.

Just the notion gives me worse heartburn than my normal Bobby Lee indigestion, especially since I won't know for a couple weeks yet if the magazine is a go or not. If Athena Lennox gets turned down, then anyone who doubted me may be proven right. I need all the cheerleaders I can gather in my corner, and the naysayers can skedaddle.

And, even though Bobby Lee hasn't reached out, I'd bet my turquoise-stitched boots Bunny's care package was sent off with his blessing. They're not giving up, regardless of the state of my job or my made-up love life.

Which, it turns out, may not be so made up after all. Well, the love part, yeah, but it's looking like I may be on the brink of my first honest-to-goodness affair. It sounds so damn cosmopolitan, something New York Poppy would most definitely approve of.

I pull my brush through my hair even harder at the thought of said affair, ripping out a couple tangles in the wet mass around my shoulders and hardly even noticing as the pain stings my nose.

Iris is still asleep on her side of my new bed and I'm scrambling to get ready because Mac will be here to pick me up in twenty minutes. It's only ten after seven on Saturday morning, which is apparently a perfectly logical time for a date in his world.

He didn't say what we were doing, except to suggest I dress comfortably and wear closed-toed shoes (as only a man could ask). I didn't think to press him because his declaration about doing "any of the hundred other things" to me was still swirling in my brain with all the possibilities it suggested. Possibilities I'm now very eager to explore.

Magazine, schmagazine. Bulldozer, schmulldozer. I dare any woman with a working clitoris and legs to walk away from that speech with a "Meh, no thanks."

The one thing I did manage to insist on, however, was that I be back in time to hang out with Iris this afternoon and evening. I haven't lost my mind completely.

After a few rounds with the blow dryer and a light dusting of make-up, I slip into my shoes and face the full-length mirror resting against the wall. I'm wearing a couple layered tank tops tied in a knot at my waist paired with cut-offs and my red Converse. I considered going with something nicer, but I really have no idea what Mac's definition of comfortable is, and if we're lighting things on fire, the last thing I want is excess material floating about waiting to light me up like a campfire marshmallow. Thank the good lord Iris is still asleep or she'd never let me out of the house in this.

With that in mind, I decide to meet Mac downstairs and slip out my apartment door.

My apartment. It feels so good to say that.

Leaving Katelyn's last night was bittersweet, but I think she's secretly gonna be happy to have her own space back. Three women sharing one and a half baths, even for thirty-six hours, was getting old. Not to mention I'm guessing she's dying to bring Zach home without having to worry about the red-headed third wheel hanging around and cramping her style.

I bound down the stairs, looking forward to the morning air and trying to calm the swarm of butterflies in my stomach. As soon as I fling the building's door open, the butterflies morph into a flock of miniature parrots flapping their wings while they discuss the sight before me.

If I had to imagine the conversation, it would probably go something like this:

Mini Parrot #1: "Damn, girl, you better jump on that."

Mini Parrot #2: "No joke! Ask him to do a little twirl so I can see that tailfeather."

Mini Parrot #3: "Get out of my way! I'm gonna sit on that man's shoulder."

Mini Parrot #4: "Screw that! I'm gonna sit on that man's *face!*"

Apparently, parrots are pervs, not that I can really argue. But, honestly, how am I not used to this by now?

Mac is jaywalking toward me, a pair of dark sunglasses pushed up into his mess of black hair and his uniform of work boots, denim, and t-shirt—this one army green—hugging his hard body like they don't ever want to let go. Not that I blame them. He practically glides as he walks without a trace of self-consciousness or pretense, the fabric of his clothes straining with each movement. I want to straddle his thigh and ride it like a circus pony. I mean, this dude is ridiculous with his degree of absolute solidity, not to mention his towering height.

I'm so busy checking out his body that I don't notice until too late that he's been tracking my eyes, something I know by the slight upward tilt of the left side of his mouth and the set of parentheses etched between his lush eyebrows.

My teeth sink into my bottom lip and I don't even try to pretend he hasn't struck me stupid.

"Morning," he says, not slowing his stride until he's

right up in my business where he ducks his head down and lands a quick kiss on my mouth, causing me to gasp and my teeth to release my lip at the warm contact.

His mouth leaves mine before the kiss can fully register, but he remains close enough that I can smell soap and leather and feel his innate energy vibrating off his skin and jumping the small gap between us.

Instead of responding to his greeting, I let out a little sigh and consider burrowing into his chest just to see how it would feel.

"You eat yet?" His voice rumbles at the question and I want to sigh again as I realize this is very much a part of who Mac is—making sure I'm taken care of. I don't really know how to feel about that. Do people in torrid sexual affairs worry themselves about those things?

I nod, choosing not to reveal that my breakfast consisted of a handful of Teddy Grahams and a hastily chugged cup of coffee. I'm guessing he wouldn't consider that a meal.

"Absolutely. I'm fully nourished and ready to go."

He eyes me for a second, as if gauging how truthful I'm being, before returning my nod and taking my hand just like he did the other night.

"Where are we going anyway?" I ask as I let him lead me up the sidewalk.

"Been thinking about that article and I want to show you something."

This surprises me. The article is completely out of my hands now and Naveed has taken over. He did a bit of grumbling after reading what I'd compiled, but said he'd be able to round it out when he met Mac for the photo shoot.

Technically, as the creative director, I can be there too, but Naveed and the photographer will have it well in hand.

"Oh." I pause and then continue, "You remember the part about me not being a writer, right?"

He dips his chin.

"So, my part of the interview is over. I mean, I can tell Naveed about whatever it is you want me to see but it might be better for you to show him yourself."

Now, why in heavens am I trying to end this date before it's even begun? Coward!

"Nah." He steers me south at the next intersection.

"Nah?" My tennis shoes slap the sidewalk as I try to keep up. "Hey, can we slow down a bit?"

Mac stops short. "Sorry. I'm not used to..."

I nod and squeeze his hand. "It's okay. I could probably use the exercise, but it's Saturday and all."

His nose scrunches up a little, making the scar pucker even more than usual. It's a face I haven't seen on him yet—it's so expressive and almost silly—and it makes me want to smile, so I do.

"What does the day of the week have to do with not exercising?"

I shrug. "It's the weekend, not to mention the Sabbath."

"You Jewish?"

"No."

His head cocks a tiny bit before he shakes it and starts us moving again at a slower pace.

"Anyway, what did you mean by 'nah'? You don't want Naveed to see this... whatever it is?" I admit I'm more than a little curious.

"You'll see."

And that's all I get until we reach the Lexington Avenue/53rd Street station. We're about to descend the stairs when Mac's eye catches on something and he veers to the side, pushing my back up against the half wall of the station entrance.

"Wait here."

I do as he asks, not quite sure why I don't just follow, yet allowing him space to do whatever he's got in mind. He crosses the street and disappears into a building where I lose sight of his butt in those jeans. Damn.

My eyes wander the early-morning crowds full of a mix of casually-dressed groups and yummy mummies and daddies strolling the sidewalks. Just about everyone carries some version of a Starbucks coffee cup and my stomach groans at me about the cookies I scarfed back at my apartment.

Just as I'm considering crossing the street after Mac to try hunting down a bottle of water, he emerges carrying a large plastic cup with a straw poking out the top. This surprises me for two reasons. First, it seems unlike him to grab a drink for himself without asking me if I want one. And, second, I never would have pegged Mac as a coke guy.

The mystery is solved, however, when he reaches me, eyes traveling my body like he's doing a safety check, and holds the drink out to me.

My eyes pop. "For me?"

"Yeah." He extends his other hand and I see a small bag of almonds caught between his fingers.

I take the cup in both hands—the damn thing is so ginormous it takes both to keep my grip—and smile up at him.

"Thanks." I bring the straw to my mouth and he watches intently as I draw the liquid up the plastic tube.

"I remember you mentioning iced tea."

His words register at the same time the cold wetness hits my tongue and every part of me locks up.

Mac bought me iced tea.

He remembered me talking about how I loved it, he didn't believe that I had a good breakfast, and he interrupted our outing to take care of me.

By buying me a bag of nuts and some tea.

A King Kong sized portion of tea without a lick of sugar in it and no polite way for me do anything but smile and choke that shit down.

It's simultaneously horrendous and so freaking romantic I want to cry.

Mac McKinley is sweet.

Unlike this awful tea, but who the hell cares?

I smile up at him like he's Paul McCartney and I'm a sixteen-year-old virgin. Which is ridiculous for many reasons, not the least of which being that dude's an old man now and *ew*. Mac tosses his chin toward the subway station stairs.

"WHAT IS THIS PLACE?"

I've managed to ditch my tea after feigning a full stomach and pretending the caffeine is too much for me. Mac has my hand again and is leading me through the double wood doors of what appears to be an old garage.

He doesn't respond because there's no need when we cross the threshold and I see that it is indeed just that. And it's full of guys dressed in blue coveralls, t-shirts, and a varying assortment of colored snapbacks or bandanas. Most of them have their heads ducked under the hoods of one of the six or so cars parked in the space while a few others are gathered around an older gray-haired man talking and gesturing to a laptop screen on a cart.

Mac starts toward the older man whose face lights up in a huge grin when he catches sight of him. Well, I'll be darned.

He snatches up a red shop towel and makes a half-hearted attempt at wiping up his hands before he tucks it in his back pocket and extends a hand to Mac.

"Long time no see, Mac."

Mac drops my hand and accepts the man's handshake. "Javier." Then he tips his head my way. "This is Poppy James. She's writing an article for a magazine."

Javier's eyes widen and his smile falters just a touch before he readjusts his expression and holds his hand in the air like he's surrendering. "I would shake your hand, sweetheart, but I don't want you getting grease all over you."

I nod. "It's nice to meet you, Javier." I still don't know what we're doing here or why Javier's giving off a wary vibe, but I can roll with it.

"You got a minute to show her around the shop?"

Javier's bushy eyebrows shoot for his hairline and a hopefulness lights his blue eyes, eradicating any trace of hesitance. "You writing about the shop?"

I open my mouth, no doubt wearing a panicked look, but Mac steps in. "Haven't told her anything about it yet."

Javier nods, still grinning, and I grit my teeth in a forced version of my smile. What the hell is Mac doing? Why is he telling this guy I'm writing an article about his shop when he knows quite clearly I'm not? And furthermore, who the hell does an interview wearing cutoffs and Converse freaking tennis shoes? Talk about another blow to my professional image. I'm gonna kill him.

But manners dictate I play along since Javier seems so damn happy about the whole situation. He turns and gestures excitedly to the men, many of whom have stopped their work and trained curious eyes on me and Mac. It's only then I realize they're not men at all. Well, some of them are, but I spot a few who can't be older than fifteen, with the oldest one maybe just under twenty or so.

"We have visitors, gentlemen. Say hello to Ms. James and Mr. McKinley."

We get a few Mac-style nods, hand flicks, and a couple "hey"s. I even rate one whistle and a drawn-out "Helloooo there" which Javier nips in the bud with a, "Cut the shit, Robinson," to the grinning Romeo. I can't help smiling back. He's awfully cute but he's also about sixteen. I have no doubt the kid has teenage girls lined up around the block.

Javier walks us between two cars while the boys get back to work. "The program takes applicants between fourteen and nineteen, most of whom have been referred by teachers, social workers, and the occasional neighborhood *abuela*. The ones who express an interest in cars get sent to me."

"What program is this?" I ask, interest rising despite my

vow to give Mac a piece of my mind about this whole article sham.

Javier glances at Mac and back to me again, blinking. "Mac's program."

A tense grumble comes from behind me. "Not my program."

Javier's lips curve as he shakes his head. "Whatever you say, man."

I can't help it. My head swings around and up to Mac's face. His mouth is turned down and the lines in his forehead are particularly pronounced. "Well, well, well." I can't help my drawn-out teasing tone, especially when I see it makes that spot on his left cheek tick.

"It's a community program." Mac walks forward, forcing both Javier and me to move along so we don't become his roadkill.

"Don't let him fool you, sweetheart. He and his pops started the whole thing up about a decade ago." I freeze at the reference to the man I assume to be Mac's father, but I do my best to hide it. "Hundreds of kids have gone through the program, coming out the other end with jobs in respectable trades, earning a great living for their families and staying out of trouble."

My eyes stray to Mac again, but his expression is closed. Is he thinking about his father? All I know is I need to forget I ever read anything about Mac's family. Everything in me says he'd be furious to know I went snooping into his business, especially given his refusal to answer questions about his past or personal life when he agreed to the interview contract.

And speaking of the interview... "You want me to include the program in the article." It's not a question.

Mac nods, but his expression doesn't clear.

I laugh despite his face. "Then you're gonna have to own up to your part in it, I hate to tell you."

I recognize what I'm pretty sure is a glower at this point.

"We can't very well say, 'Hey, y'all, check out this kick-ass blacksmith and, by the way, here are some kids working on cars.'"

He narrows his eyes and lets out a breath that I interpret to be a silent, "Shut up, smartass."

But Javier interrupts before he can get a word out. "Oh, there are several other trades too. Carpentry, plumbing, electrical work. The kids go on to qualify for some excellent apprenticeships."

I smile at Javier's enthusiasm and turn back around to take in the shop again. A couple of the boys are laughing at something one of them said while the percussion of pneumatic tools reverberates off the walls.

It sounds like a phenomenal project, one surely deserving of a front-page article in any publication. But that doesn't mean it's going to happen. Never mind the fact that I have zero say in the content of *WHL*, but this isn't the kind of subject that gets a feature article. Like it or not, it's just not... sexy enough.

Good God, I hate myself not just for thinking that but for knowing the truth of it in the first place.

"Mac." I turn to look up at him again and his burning golden-brown eyes are sweeping my face. My stomach turns to mush and I almost forget where I was going with this.

"I think you should switch the article's focus to this." He flicks his eyes to the side to indicate the shop.

Oh, Mac.

You big giant softie of a metropolitan-trampling mutant gorilla.

All I can do is take a breath and send him my best smile while Javier leads us to an old Chevy and proceeds to take us through how the group plans to refurbish and sell the hunk of junk.

Could I get Naveed to mention the program in the article? I'm sure I could. But I don't think Mac understands what that might mean. He'd be opening himself up to questions about his family just to win a small mention tucked away in a brief paragraph near the end of the feature on him. He'll still be front and center—he and his amazing pieces of work. It's a done deal, and there's nothing I could do about it... even if I wanted to.

So I listen to Javier and delay the inevitable. It's the least I can do to give these men and boys their moment for as long as I can.

SIXTEEN

"YOU EVER HEARD the saying 'Keeping your business tight'?"

I play with the knot on my shirt and eye Mac from my seat beside him.

"A variation of it, sure."

"I'm not surprised. It seems to be your mantra."

The corner of his mouth turns down as the subway car rattles and screeches on the tracks. We're lucky we got seats as the crowd has gotten thicker on our journey back to my neighborhood.

"You ever heard the saying 'live and learn'?"

His expression tells me not to delve any further, but I

can't help the slight harrumphing sound from escaping my throat.

We left the garage after the tour from Javier and a chat with a couple of the boys. They were gregarious and playful, belying the implications of the backgrounds Javier indicated as the basis for the program. Most of these kids have either been in trouble with the law or come from families where one or more parent is behind bars. It's such a stark contrast to the way I grew up that I have trouble wrapping my brain around it. I mean, I know I was sheltered, but I hate to think I'm so far out of touch.

Mac remained silent through most of our visit, not that it was surprising, but I can't help wondering if it's due more to the mention of his daddy than his general modus operandi.

"You know, it wouldn't kill you to at least acknowledge that you are, in fact, human."

Mac turns his body to fully face me, sending a jolt of electricity down my spine. I hadn't meant to activate some alpha switch or something. But if I thought his move would be followed by some profound confession or declaration, I was wrong.

When I finally get the nerve to peek at him, he's just studying me again. Good lord, how can I possibly be that interesting?

Just when I think I'm gonna combust from the pressure of his stare, he switches tacks.

"You miss home?"

Dammit! How does he do that?

I know right away he already knows the answer, but I decide to try keeping my cards close to the vest for once.

"Now, what makes you think that?"

He doesn't play. "You're mindful of your time with your sister. You curl into yourself when you get caught in a crowd. You look like you're in pain when you put on that shark act even though you suck at it and I can tell you hate it. And your smile is fuckin' beautiful when you're thinking about anything that reminds you of life before this cesspool of a city."

I swallow hard and try not to let my face show how thoroughly he just gutted me.

"I..." Come on, Poppy. Don't let him think he can just sum you up and fit you in a little box. Bastard. "I'll have you know I love my job—and my new apartment. And I'm making friends left and right. Don't act like you know me, Angus McKinley, just because we've spent a few hours together. I happen to talk a lot when I'm nervous and even I don't know what I'm saying half the time."

I grit my teeth.

"And if you hate this cesspool so much, why the hell are you living here?" Sanctimonious jerk.

His jaw locks. Yeah, how about that, Mac?!

"You're not the only one who can make assumptions, I'm just too polite to tell you what I think about you."

"Don't hold back on my account."

The subway car jerks and I barely keep myself from being thrown in Mac's lap.

"Ha! I'm not falling for that. Despite what you think about little old backwater Poppy, I wasn't born yesterday, you big oaf."

This makes his lips twitch and his jaw release.

"I'm not tryin' to be funny here, Mac. I'm good and

pissed." Because maybe he hit the nail on the head a little too closely? Possible, but it was still an arrogant move.

"I can see that. You done?"

My mouth pops open in a gasp and I spring up from my seat.

Before I can take even one step, Mac has my elbow in his grip and he's pulling me back down.

"Get your hand off of me!"

My gaze darts around the passenger car looking to see which good Samaritan I'll have to thank later for extracting me from this unfortunate situation. But nobody is even looking our way. I turn my shoulders to get a full view but nope. Everyone is minding their own frickin' business.

I look back at Mac's hand around my arm and then up at his face. I must admit, his grip is so light it wouldn't take anything for me to get my arm back. But it's the principle of the thing.

"Unbelievable," I mutter, just as the subway slows in a screech of brakes for our stop. People rise from their seats and shuffle toward the doors. Mac stands and pulls me up with him, but I finally shake my arm free.

"Please, people, don't worry about me!" I raise my voice, but the only person to acknowledge me is a middle-aged woman with a hair net and a paperback tucked under her arm. All she does is shrug and then check Mac out from head to toe.

Oh, for Pete's sake.

Mac steps in behind me, practically molding his front to my back and I can feel a rumbling vibration that sure as hell isn't coming from the train. If I didn't know better, I'd say Mac is laughing at me. But before I can think too much of it, another crush of passengers pushes in from both sides and the air immediately becomes thick. How in the hell can so many people fit on one train car?

A young guy in front of me stumbles and starts falling back toward me, but Mac's hands catch him and bring him upright again before he can touch me. I'm breathing a bit too hard now. What in the hell is taking so long for these doors to open? I exhale and I'm trying to slow my breathing when I feel the warmth of Mac's breath in my ear.

"We'll be out in fifteen seconds, honey."

I close my eyes and lean back into his hard chest, letting him take over. Before I know it, he's shifting me forward, arms locked around me and hands holding both of mine across my stomach. I open my eyes in time to not trip over the threshold of the train car and practically sing when we're released from the throng and I can finally breath again, even if it's the smelly sub-level air of the Lexington Street station.

It doesn't even occur to me until after Mac drops me off and Iris is grilling me about my morning that he called me "honey."

I saw you called. What's up?

MY PHONE RINGS and I bite my lip when I see it's Mac.

"Mac, I'm walking to a meeting." I sidestep two executives from legal, smiling and sending a wave to the one I've met.

"Wanted to make sure you were coming to the photo thing."

I roll my eyes but only because I secretly think it's cute. Yeah, I said cute.

"Yes, I'm coming. We'll be there at three. You could have just texted, you know." I stop at the elevators and press the down button.

"I don't text."

Why does this not surprise me?

"Everybody texts." I feel a need to point out the obvious. "My grandmother texts. The only person I know who doesn't text is my Uncle Hugh and that's just because he thinks cell phones are government tools to spy on us." I glance around quickly to make sure nobody heard that last one. Can't be too careful.

He obviously doesn't feel this deserves a response because I get none.

"Anyway, I'll see you in a bit, okay?"

"Later."

That's all he says before he hangs up.

Our last date or non-date or whatever you want to call it is still knocking around in my head every spare minute I have. Suffice it to say, any ill feelings I had flew out the window after Mac ushered me out that subway car and walked me home with his arm around me. Good lord, the memory of his strong body around mine will probably be enough to keep me warm through the entire New York winter to come. I'll save a boatload on my heating bill.

He didn't kiss me, though, when he left me at my door. I'm unsure if it was due to my temper on the train, my almost passing out from the crowd, or Iris's smug smile as she flung the apartment door open when she heard our footsteps. I kind of wanted to kill her.

There's a lot to unpack from that date with Mac, the least of which is the fact that he still hasn't told me one personal thing about himself, while I seem to have revealed enough about me to allow him to make a ridiculously infuriating and accurate observation about my innermost thoughts.

I don't like the idea of being so vulnerable to someone who can't reciprocate. Which is why it's better if Mac and I just don't pursue whatever this is between us. I mean, if he still wants to jump in bed with me, I'm sure I can wrap my brain around that somehow, but having all my personal business out there between us means it would be more than just a roll in the hay—for me, at least.

And there's still the issue of Elle, although I know I'm only using that as an excuse. It's safe to say at this point that there's no way Mac and Elle are dating. And I'm pretty sure they're not sleeping together either. I can't see her putting up with a guy who's so closed off, not to mention Mac hasn't kept her name out of conversation—which any player knows is the number one rule of manwhoring.

But she'll surely be at the shoot today where I can spend my time overanalyzing every interaction she and Mac have. I'm not gonna lie to myself and say I'm going for professional reasons. I mean, yes, as the creative director, I want the shoot to be amazing, but the photographer has a wonderful eye and she's acquainted herself with Mac's work and is excited to do the shoot.

I'm strictly there for spying and the eye candy.

Really freaking smart, I know.

My meeting drags on since it's one of those dotting the i's ones that nobody in their right mind enjoys, and I manage to get a few more things done before catching up with Naveed to grab a cab to Mac's studio. Mirren, the photographer, is meeting us there, having gone over an hour earlier to set up with her crew.

"Look at you all dressed in red," Naveed says as his eyes sweep my outfit. Yes, I went for a power color today and it's no mistake. If I'm going to be in a room with Mac and Elle freakin' Valentine, I need all the advantages I can get. Not that I'm trying to impress anybody or anything.

"And look at you, a vision in charcoal," I volley back to a sharp-looking Naveed in another of his designer suits. "Tell me to shove off if I'm being too nosy, but how in the heck do you afford to dress like you do, Naveed?"

He pretends to be offended, but he's clearly not. "I eat a lot of broccoli, sweets, and not the kind from Gomi, sadly."

I'm not sure if I believe him, but I let it go and he hails a taxi. We pile in and are off to 10th Street, traffic swirling around us.

"Did you get the links I sent you on the youth program?" I ask.

I'd debated giving Naveed the information on the charity out of my fears for Mac. And yes, I understand the irony of me wanting to protect his privacy while at the same time resenting it when it comes to our personal relationship/non-relationship. But there it is.

What finally decided it for me was the memory of Robinson, my Romeo, saying he credited the program with him not being in jail with one of his best friends. I knew this was important to more people than just Mac. And, besides, he asked me to.

"I did. And thank God. Between you and me, doll, I had my work cut out for me on this one before I got ahold of that charity gig. Does the man even speak?"

Defensiveness on Mac's behalf stiffens my spine before I force myself to calm the hell down. "When he needs to."

Naveed grins at me. "I know it's not professional, but I never really claimed to be one." He turns in his seat like he's about to drop a secret on me. "I honestly don't know how I'm going to send this copy in for approval without adding at least four paragraphs about the man's pectorals. I'm dying to know what he does to get those."

I almost blurt out that Mac has a thing for ropes but I catch myself at the last second. Dummy.

The taxi drops us off and Jonathan greets us at the door when we knock. He's in a short-sleeved button down the color of dirt and is wearing the same sour expression as he steps aside to let us in.

"Down there," is all he says, pointing to the retail studio I have yet to see.

The hall is silent except for the clack of my heels and Naveed's dress shoes on the floor until we get to the door and Naveed swings it open. The first voice I hear is Elle's and I look down at my tight red dress, thanking Bergdorf's for having a sale.

When we step in, I notice three things immediately.

Elle is running this show.

Mirren despises Elle with the power of a thousand suns.

And Mac is so over this already that I reckon he regrets ever setting eyes on me in the first place.

"Don't you think the light is better over here?" Elle waves her hand through the air, her silky white blouse fluttering at the movement.

Mirren visibly grinds her teeth and I send Naveed panic eyes.

"On it," he replies from the corner of his mouth before plastering on a smile so big we all might go blind from the sparkle.

"Ms. Valentine, what a pleasure to see you again!"

Elle is momentarily distracted from her mission, but it's long enough for Mirren to redirect her staff to her desired set-up.

I pull my lips between my teeth so I don't smile.

My eyes survey the room, stopping on the artfully placed chairs, tables, and smaller decorative pieces in the room. I recognize most of them from the website, but they're even more impressive in person. It's no wonder he can afford this place.

Mac hasn't noticed me yet, but I think it's because he's attempting to block out the entire world around him as he scratches a pencil on the pad of paper in front of him. He sits on a stool pulled up to a small worktable and is wearing his usual jeans, but this time it's with a dress shirt, the first few buttons undone to reveal a dark blue t-shirt underneath.

I release my lips only to run my tongue over the bottom one. I can't help but stare. It's obvious he—or someone here—has taken some care with his hair since it doesn't have its usual appearance of just having survived a hurricane, and while his face isn't clean-shaven, it's been trimmed so the scruff looks quite intentional.

"Whooo Mama," I breathe out.

"Are you sure you wouldn't be more comfortable waiting in Ms. Valentine's office?"

I jump at the voice, cursing myself for not noticing Jonathan's approach.

"Oh. No." I attempt a smile and check my accent. "I'm quite fine where I am."

He pauses a beat and I raise a brow, hoping I come off as intimidating.

"Mr. McKinley doesn't like... people." He meets me in a stare-down.

Part of me wants to laugh. The other part of me is pissed.

"Well, then it's a good thing he *personally* invited me." I can't help it. This guy is too much.

He finally blinks, then shifts his eyes first to Elle, then to Mac, then back to me before turning and leaving the room without another word.

Jesus. Mac isn't the only one skilled at silent communication around here.

"Ms. James!" Elle's voice echoes off the walls as she strides toward me, a welcoming smile beaming from behind her red lipstick.

See, now this is the kind of greeting a girl deserves.

I see Mac's head snap up at my name and a trill of pleasure races through me.

"Ms. Valentine," I respond, pretending not to watch Mac in my peripheral vision.

Elle reaches me and we shake hands.

"I've already told you. Please, call me Elle."

I smile back. "Of course. And call me Poppy." I catch myself before I tack on some comment about Poppy being better than the various other names I've been called before. Totally smooth.

"Has anyone ever told you you look stunning in red, Poppy?" She laughs before I can answer. "Of course! It goes right along with your name. How charming."

Either Elle has been sampling the sauce already, or she's just in an exceptionally good mood. Either way, I'm grateful.

I'm about to compliment her on her outfit, as any woman worth her salt would naturally do in response, when Mac approaches.

I think for a split second that he's going to lean down and kiss me, a thought which sends all my blood racing for the hills. It occurs to me we never explicitly talked about my wish to keep my professional and personal lives completely separate.

But I don't have to worry. He just nods with a quick, "Ms. James." His eyes, however, send a completely different greeting. One that, if I'm not mistaken, is something along the lines of, "Tell these people to get the hell out of here."

Naveed is gonna have a hell of a time with Mac, I can tell already.

"I was thinking we should shoot Angus in the corner piece." Elle points to a curved affair nestled in the studio's corner. "It's going up for auction next month at a fundraiser so it will be the last chance to capture him in a shot with it."

My eyes swing to Mac. "You're doing an auction?"

"He does several throughout the year. The man does love his charities." Elle fills me in.

"So I hear."

Elle blinks and then her gaze turns the slightest bit assessing.

Shit!

"Well," I say a bit too loud. "I know Mirren already has several shots in mind and she'll work her magic."

"Of course." Elle's tone is definitely distracted now.

"Mr. McKinley, if you would?" Naveed calls from the other side of the room where he stands with Mirren and her assistant by a low-sitting chaise.

I swear I hear Mac growl before he turns and crosses the space to Naveed.

Elle turns to watch him walk away, making it ridiculously awkward if I pretend I don't notice the giant gorilla in the room.

Then my heart ceases beating when her next words are, "So, how long have you and Angus been screwing?"

SEVENTEEN

"Women who wear red lipstick always have more fun."
– Cookie Rutledge

CONSIDER me a cartoon character falling off a cliff right about now, my extended, slow-motion "Nooooooooooooo" echoing off the canyon walls.

"You should see your face," Elle says. And then she smiles. The woman actually *smiles*. "I wasn't sure until just now, but your face says it all."

I couldn't find my voice in a paper sack with both hands.

She laughs and puts a hand on my arm at my guppy impression. "I think it's perfect."

My head jerks back. "You do?" Then I remember exactly what she's referring to and I hurry on. "I mean, we're not..." My eyes dart between Elle and Mac.

She shrugs. "Maybe not yet, but I know he fancies you."

Fancies me? I'm pretty sure no one in the history of time has ever accused Mac McKinley of *fancying* anything.

"Don't look so shocked. He's only a man. He has needs just like any other man."

There is no good response to this. I just know it. So I smile nervously instead.

"I'll admit, there was a time when I thought about... trying him on for size, but we're much better as friends. Besides, he's a disaster at dinner parties." She chuckles.

"I can imagine," I finally eek out.

"I also don't have the patience for a project, if you know what I mean."

My shoulders tense. I'm not sure I like her—or anyone —making implications like that about Mac.

"I can't say that I do." I know my tone gives away my irritation, something that doesn't go undetected.

Her hand is on my arm again. "Oh, wow. I'll bet that sounded awful. It's not what I meant at all, Poppy. I love Angus like my own family, but he does come with a lot of baggage. Not that any of it is his fault. Quite the opposite, actually." She sighs. "I can be a selfish bitch at times, I'll admit."

My eyes seek out Mac without me meaning to. He's got his hands propped on his hips and is giving Naveed and Mirren a few of his short nods. I can see the tension in his neck and it makes me want to walk right over there and soothe it with my fingers—or my lips. Instead, I take a breath and bring my gaze back to Elle. She's watching me with her brilliant blue eyes.

Despite my fondness of her, a thread of resentment winds through me at the knowledge that she knows Mac —*really* knows him, in a way I'm pretty certain he would never let me. She knows his past, his struggles, his entire story, and all I know is that he talks with his eyebrows, has a protective streak, and likes classic rock. So it doesn't matter that he and Elle aren't romantically or sexually involved. She has a piece of him I'll never have.

"Oh, Poppy, I didn't mean to make you sad. Look what I've done." Her perfectly manicured fingers squeeze my arm in reassurance. "He's all bluster at first, that's all. Before you know it, he'll be spilling all his dirty laundry and you won't even know what to do with the big lug." She smiles again at me and I muster a return one.

"I wish I could say more, but it's his story to tell. The part I *can* say is that I promised his dad I'd look out for Angus, and from what I can tell, you'll be good for him."

I speak before I think. "Is that why you call him Angus?"

Her brows draw together.

"You call him Angus instead of Mac. Is that what his dad called him?"

Her expression turns almost soft. "No. Angus, Sr. called him *a sheòid*. It means *my warrior*."

At those words, I can practically feel my heart cracking open another inch—putting me that much closer to inevitable heartbreak.

Elle releases me and takes a step back. "Well, I'm so glad he finally agreed to the interview. I was certain it was a lost cause, and I believe I have you to thank."

A small smile touches my lips. "To tell the truth, I don't have a clue what changed his mind."

Elle tuts. "Don't be so modest. I told you he's smitten."

Another term I wouldn't associate with Mac. Is it because I don't actually know the first thing about him?

My response is a blush I wish I could erase.

"I have to tell you I'm so grateful. Sometimes the man makes it impossible for me to do my job." She winks at me, her long eyelashes brushing her cheek.

"How so?"

"Don't get me wrong, his work is superb, but it doesn't sell itself. You're part of the game so you know better than most that it's all about exposure." Her eyes travel to Mac and mine follow. His posture is the picture of closed off as Naveed tosses questions at him.

A quiet chuckle bubbles up my throat. "You need to ask for a raise."

Elle's laugh bounces off the walls, making it hard to quell my own responding laughter. And when Mac turns, sending us his classic broody frown, it's really no use even trying.

"LOKI'S BALLS, it's like drawing blood from a stone. Thank God the photos are stunning." Naveed loosens his tie and then rolls down his window. It seems we chose a taxi without air conditioning.

I snicker at Naveed's assessment.

"I take back everything I may have said behind your back about your initial interview."

This earns him an elbow to the kidneys. "Jerk."

"Joking. I didn't say a word—out loud, at least. But I think I have enough, especially with some of Elle's input and the bit about the charity angle. Although he was silent as ever about its origins. No worries, though, I can do some digging."

I shift on the vinyl seat and refrain from begging him not to. Instead, I steer him away. "Well, it's not a cover feature, so I'm sure all the beautiful furniture and his process will be riveting enough."

Naveed blows out a breath as the cab driver takes a sharp turn that has me gripping the seat for dear life. "Remind me to buy you dinner for making that small miracle possible."

I breathe in a lungful of much-needed oxygen at the memory of Mac standing in his forge before the orange and gold glow of the fire. While he didn't actually make anything or even wield his hammer for his gathered audience, he did agree to setting the scene and being photographed in his element.

Gone was the button-down and it was just Mac. T-shirt, jeans, boots, and his stoic expression. Mirren could hardly contain herself, nor could Naveed or I. Although, I think I did a damn good job of covering up the effect the whole picture had on me. I feel a sudden urge to fan myself and it's not due to the lack of air conditioning.

But Naveed's assumption it was my doing is misplaced. All I did was nod in encouragement when it was suggested. Who knew Mac would actually allow it?

"Speaking of, what kind of stick does Jonathan have up his ass? I thought he was going to kick us all out when we dared trespass on the forge." He tilts his head to me and waggles his brows. "But that whole scene has me feeling decidedly medieval."

This makes me laugh because I know exactly what he means. Against the backdrop of fire and steel, Jonathan looked like he might try to behead the entire Warbey contingent when we moved the party to the forge. Besides running around barking at everyone not to touch anything, he focused on shooting daggers at me in particular, like I ever did anything to him. I kind of missed the bored yet rude Jonathan.

But Mac and Elle both appeared to ignore him, so I tried to do the same. I figured if Mac really didn't want us in there, we wouldn't be in there. He doesn't need a bouncer.

"I'm not sure," I respond. "But Mac must like him for a reason."

Naveed turns in his seat. "Mac, is it?"

Dammit!

I do my best to cover. "Didn't you hear him telling everyone to call him that?"

His tongue pokes the inside of his cheek and it takes him a moment to respond while I will my blood to stay away from my face. "I must have missed that."

Gah.

"Well, let me know when the article is done and I'll get right on the layout," I say, telling him something he already knows. But it seems to do the trick because he lets my previous comment go and moves on to the next topic.

I have got to watch my big damn mouth!

On a scale of one to ten, how bad was it?

MY PHONE RINGS and I grin like a baby who's just discovered feet.

"Hello? Who is this?" I decide to play with him.

I'm rewarded with a chest rumble I can feel in my sex.

"You busy tonight?"

"Why, do you have something else you want to show me?"

Oh my God. My sass has risen to a level five hundred.

Thankfully, he doesn't directly answer.

"That depends."

"On what?" I continue to play. Cookie and Bunny would be appalled that this guy keeps asking me out with no notice whatsoever, but they'd forgive him if they met him, I'm sure.

"On if you're gonna wear that red dress."

Oooooh my.

Needless to say, I'm not changing.

An hour later, Mac is at my door. I feel a little silly wearing this get-up, complete with heels, to answer my door at eight-thirty on a Wednesday night, but the hungry look in Mac's eyes when he sees me wearing it makes any doubt go flying out the window.

As does his wordless entry into my apartment which is

followed up by my back hitting the entry wall and Mac's mouth crashing down on mine.

Talk about fire! Who needs a forge?

Unlike our other kisses, this one involves hands and skin and teeth and tongues. And it is exquisite. When his tongue glides past my lips to sweep against mine I lose the ability to stand. Luckily, Mac has his thighs pressed against my hips to hold me up as his upper half has to practically fold itself over to align our mouths.

With my legs not doing anything to help, he must figure I'm at his mercy—which I totally am—so he reaches one arm under my butt and boosts me up so he doesn't have to give himself scoliosis to kiss me.

My squeak of surprise is lost in his mouth, though, as he continues to lick and bite at me while my hands bury themselves in his thick hair, giving me my first bit of unobstructed access to the glorious mess that it is. The strands are silky and lush, to many a woman's great envy, and the skin beneath is hot. I let the fingers of one hand roam to his neck as I kiss him back with everything in me.

His lips, his tongue, the scrape of his stubble against my chin and cheeks—it's all too much. I break free of his kiss to draw in a ragged breath and his mouth trails down my chin to my neck, making me moan. Hell, I don't even know if he closed my front door, but I'm too caught up on our hot make-out session to open my eyes or care.

Mac's hand drops from where it was holding the back of my neck and he brings it between us where the back of it grazes my breast over the red fabric of my dress. The contact sends me panting and gripping his t-shirt. When he lifts his head at the sounds I'm making, I finally open my eyes again to see that his pupils have all but overtaken his brown irises and his nostrils are flared like the snarling dragon I've suspected he is.

Whatever he sees in my expression prompts him to spin on his heel and stalk past my kitchen and table and on to the living room where my sofa sits, inviting us to use and abuse it. All the while, he's carrying me with one hand under my butt, the other between my shoulder blades and my feet dangling about two feet above the ground. Until he sits his fine ass on the sofa, that is, and brings my legs around to straddle him.

And, that, ladies and gentlemen, is how I get my first feel of the other beast living in Manhattan.

I don't even have time to fully react, though, because Mac's mouth is back worshipping mine again as I savor his taste of mint, spice, and sweetness, a combination that is apparently the perfect recipe for horniness. I'm losing my damn mind as our tongues tangle and my hands go on an exploratory vacation across his chest, his back, his shoulders. There are so many ridges and bumps, the man has an entire mountain range under that t-shirt. And, because he's wearing short sleeves, I get skin-on-skin contact as my fingers skate along his biceps and down to his corded forearms.

I arch into Mac as both his hands drop to my butt where it's perched on his lap. He squeezes and pulls me into him, causing my dress to ride up even more than it already has to the point where I'm sure my panties are now on display. His movement seats his rock-hard member firmly against me and I can't help it when I grind down on him a little.

He lets out one of his growly sounds and his grip on my ass tightens, kneading my flesh over my dress and making stars explode behind my eyelids.

This man's touch, his taste, his heat—it's all more addictive than hot fudge and I'm seriously considering quitting my new job just so I can dedicate all my time to being a complete glutton.

One of Mac's hands leaves my butt and works its way between us, a true feat given how I've plastered myself to his chest. When his thumb sweeps over my right nipple I release his mouth again, my head falling back while I focus on the sensation. He circles it again, bringing the peak to an aching point and then dipping his head down to cover it with his mouth. I can hear the scrape of his whiskers against the silky fabric of my dress and they may as well be brushing against the inside of my thighs for how sharply I react. I feel him capture the bud between his teeth and bite down just hard enough for the pleasure to shoot down my spine and right to my core. If he can do this to me with two layers of fabric between his mouth and my nipple, I'm scared to think how he'll undo me when we're naked.

Because we're getting naked. There ain't no two ways about that.

I'm not sure if it's because he hadn't planned on attacking me right away when I opened the door or if it's because he suddenly remembers he has urgent business to attend to, but Mac cuts things short about two minutes after he does those magical things to my breast.

One minute he's practically giving me an orgasm with his teeth and the next he has me on my feet and he's stalking to my door with a raging hard-on and hair looking like it was styled by Albert Einstein himself.

He doesn't take me out for a drink, he doesn't tell me his deep dark secrets, and he doesn't show me anything, apart from his deadly kissing skills.

He just departs as quickly and silently as he came, leaving me a keyed-up, sweaty, well-dressed mess. Is it possible to actually die from sexual frustration?

I put a hand out to the wall to steady myself while I look down at my clothes. My dress is still riding up around my hips and there's a damp spot over my right nipple. As I try regaining my breath I realize I'm missing one of my heels, which could explain why it's hard standing straight, but really, I know the real reason.

Once I'm confident I won't fall over, I bend my knee and remove my other shoe, dropping it on the floor.

And, even though I'm now alone in my apartment, I open my mouth and say the one word I can think of to sum up what just happened.

"Wow."

It's not lost on me that it's the only word that's been uttered since Mac knocked on my door. Maybe he's right. Sometimes you just don't need words at all.

EIGHTEEN

*"Try all you like, but there's never been a woman who could
keep a secret from herself."*
– Cookie Rutledge

I'VE BEEN AVOIDING KATELYN. And Cookie. And definitely Bunny and Bobby Lee. I think part of it is I'm trying to cut down on my lying, but the other part most likely has to do with the fact that I don't have a clue how to interpret the feelings Mac has rising in me.

Iris is the only one who even comes close to knowing what's actually going on and even she doesn't have the full story. Hell, *I* don't have the full story and I'm the one living it!

Suffice it to say, Mac is confusing as shit.

He practically eats me alive with his eyes and mouth and tongue one minute and the next he's completely AWOL. Even my cute texts aren't getting a response.

If I were stupid, I'd say he's just not attracted to me, but I've never been stupid. I know what those smoldering looks and that rock-hard monster in his pants mean and it's a far cry from *meh*. Mac wants me. Which is a damn good thing because I've never wanted someone so badly in my entire life.

My vibrator is going through batteries like a colicky baby's bouncy chair at four a.m. and it's doing a piss poor job at finishing what Mac started.

He's got me going crazy wondering what in the actual hell is going on here and why we're not setting my bed on fire right this damn minute. But, if I've learned anything about Mac thus far, it's that he's very deliberate in his actions. So something is going on that I'm clearly not privy to.

I pick up my phone, letting my thumbs work over it for a few minutes before I finally settle on something I hope might work.

> I got the photos back. You want to see them?

Previous unsent versions included "I'm ordering sushi tonight. And eating it naked," "Was that a hammer in your pants or were you just happy to see me?" and "Goddammit, Mac, I'm super horny, you big giant bastard!"

I think I made the right choice.

My phone remains silent, not that I expected anything else.

I sigh and lean back in my chair, eyes going back to my computer screen where Mac's broody countenance stares back at me. The photos turned out beautiful, not that there was any doubt. Mirren had given us a peek during the shoot, but the finished products are nothing short of breathtaking. Unbelievably, she was able to capture the essence of his quiet intensity not to mention the shadowed outline of all those muscles hiding under his clothes.

I take a minute to read over the article one more time, not that there's any need. I devoured it the moment Naveed sent it over, my chest loosening when I saw that he didn't dive too deeply into the charity or its origins. Hopefully, the provided link and the few sentences about it will be enough to garner some attention and donations while still allowing Mac his privacy.

I just wish I knew what deserved such lengths to protect.

Knowing there's nothing left to tweak, I shut down my computer and start gathering my things. I'm finally biting the bullet and stopping by Kate's office on my way out. She definitely suspects something, but she hasn't called me out on it yet—something that has me wondering if Zach's been keeping her too busy to fully turn on her friend-bullshit-meter to its full power.

Before I can move an inch, though, my cellphone rings. I snatch it up, pinning all my hopes and future orgasms on what I hope to see on the screen.

But it's not Mac. It's Bobby Lee.

Crap, crap, double crap!

This is a sign that I've been selfish. It's God or karma or whatever coming to kick me in the ass for ignoring all the people in my life just so I can get my rocks off. So I scrunch my nose up and answer.

"Hey, Bobby Lee." I even manage to sound cheerful.

"Well, hello yourself, Poppy." He's sounding even more cheerful than me, which immediately makes me suspicious. His ignoring me had all the earmarks of sulking.

I rack my brain trying to stay one step ahead of him.

"I heard Mama sent you a package."

Dammit! Did I forget to send Bunny a thank you note? No. I'm sure I sent one. And, anyway, me forgetting would be more likely to prompt a call from Cookie, not Bobby Lee. Back to square one.

"She did and it was lovely."

"I reckon you've already gone through the entire bag of cookies if I know you." I can hear the smile in his voice. He does know me, so of course the cookies are gone. Hell, they were gone before Iris and I hit the sack that night.

"Why, Bobby Lee, didn't Bunny ever tell you it's not polite to ask a lady about how much she's eating?" I'm totally pushing it now.

He chuckles. "I do apologize. But I think I can make it up to you."

"How's that?" I'm almost afraid to ask. Strike that. I'm terrified.

My fear proves entirely warranted at the next words out of his mouth.

"By personally delivering another batch."

I RACE up the stairs two at a time—quite a feat given the kitten heels I'm wearing. I'm unsure how my urgency is gonna make this situation any better, but something in me says the longer Bobby Lee is left roaming the streets of New York on his own the worse things will be for me. Hell, he's likely to get a wild hair and take a trip to Tiffany's just to surprise me.

My heartburn digs at my chest as I round the corner and finally set eyes on the man of the hour.

Bobby Lee is standing in my doorway, shoulder leaning on the jamb and one of those leather satchels lying on the ground at his feet. He's the picture of clean-cut, handsome businessman, complete with carefully combed tawny hair and not a wrinkle in his dress shirt. He's also wearing a warm smile aimed right at me.

Dammit, Bobby Lee, why do you have to make this so hard?

"Hey there." My voice is a bit quieter than I intended when I greet him with a tiny wave and a smile.

He shakes his head, his own smile getting bigger. "Aren't you a sight for sore eyes, Poppy James." Then he pushes off the door jamb and approaches.

What used to be completely natural between us is now painfully awkward as he dips in to kiss my cheek and I, for some unknown reason, decide to go for a handshake. I don't miss the hurt look on his face at my blunder.

"Sorry." I force out a laugh and an eyeroll. "I don't know what's wrong with me." Then I go in for a hug and I can feel whatever tension I caused release from his posture.

"Well, I reckon they do things a bit different up here."

I want to respond that we're not on Mars, but then I remind myself of all the things that really are so much different here.

There's not much else I can do so I unlock my door and

invite him in. He ambles around the small space, taking it in from the newly-curtained windows to the tiny kitchen to the beautiful chair from Mac I haven't been able to bring myself to sit in yet. I decide to let him be the first to speak while I drop my things on the kitchen counter and reach into the fridge.

"You want some tea?" Dammit, I was supposed to let him talk first. I don't want to make this too easy on him since he's the one who traveled eight hundred miles to show up unannounced on my doorstep.

"Sure."

I pull out the pitcher of liquid gold and set it on the counter while I forage for two glasses. I finally broke down the other night and made a batch of sweet tea myself. It's not quite as good as Mama's or Cookie's but it's a far sight better than the horrifying colored water they serve up here.

When he still doesn't bring up the elephant in the room, I decide I've had enough and set the two glasses on my table with a thunk. "So, what brings you to town?"

He saunters over nice and slow, eyes never leaving me.

"Well, let's see." He brings a hand up to his chin like he's thinking real hard on it. I try not to roll my eyes. "I was sitting in my office yesterday and I got to thinking about my daddy retiring this fall. We're throwing him a big party, if you haven't heard. Complete with a zydeco band and everything." He winks at me and I can't help the smile that curves my lips.

"Lord knows it wouldn't be a Collinsworth party without accordions and fiddles." His daddy is nuts.

"Anyway, it had me thinking, as these things do, about

what a great life he's had up to now and how I'm ready to follow in his footsteps."

My heartburn kicks up a notch and I put a hand to my chest, as if that can somehow quell the pain.

I deliberately misunderstand his meaning. "Well, he couldn't leave the firm in better hands, Bobby Lee. I know you'll make him proud."

He nods and keeps his eyes on me as he slowly side-steps the table and begins his final approach.

Alert! Alert!

"I reckon you know there's only one thing that would make him prouder."

Where is a damn fire alarm pull when you need one? In the absence of that, I put my hand out in front of me.

"Bobby Lee, I thought we discussed this already."

He stills his steps.

"I think I've been more than patient, Poppy."

My lip curls. I can't help it. The nerve of this guy!

"And I think *I've* been more than clear."

He smiles at that and I want to punch him in his perfectly symmetrical face. On a scale of one to take-me-now, asking someone to marry you by telling them you've put in your quota of patience and your daddy wants you to wrap shit up, Bobby Lee is at a firm minus twelve.

"I do love your pluck, Poppy. I always have. But—"

He doesn't get the rest out as a heavy knocking sounds at my door. I honestly don't care if it's a serial killer as long as it gets me out of this conversation. Needless to say I all but sprint for the door.

My stomach falls out of my torso and onto the floor when I fling the door open and see Mac on the other side wearing a sweaty t-shirt, dark athletic shorts, and a sheen of perspiration that tells me ran his tight ass here.

"Honestly, Poppy, it could be anyone. Aren't you going to at least ask who it..." Bobby Lee's words trail off as he simultaneously realizes they're useless and gets his first view of Mac.

Now, Bobby Lee is not a slight man at all. He's got the kind of muscles one gets from jogging and frequenting the gym, and he's taller than the average man. But he has absolutely nothing on Angus McKinley, especially a tensed-up Angus McKinley like the one standing on the other side of my door letting his eyes ping-pong between me and Bobby Lee while he quickly assesses the situation.

I don't even get a word in before Mac's eyes hit mine and he sends me a short nod and a "Sorry" before turning on his heel.

But I'm in full-on crisis mode so my survival instincts kick in faster than Mac can lumber his big bod down the stairs. Both my hands dart out and grab onto a hard bicep with everything I've got.

"Hey, darlin'! What took you so long?" I infuse my words with all the pep and familiarity I can muster.

Mac turns his head to eye me over his shoulder and that single eyebrow pops. He does not know how dead sexy that look is on him. He can't possibly or he'd have a whole warehouse full of free stuff women would foist on him every time he flashed them that look. Hell, I'm ready to hand over my panties right now and I'm in the middle of a damn crisis.

"Never mind. You're here now," I continue, pulling on his arm and silently begging him to play along. The reality that I have no idea of Mac's purpose in knocking on my door does not matter one bit at this point. I can figure that out later. One emergency at a time is all I can handle. "Come on in." I pull again and he finally turns and lets me guide him through the doorway, although not far enough that I can close the door just yet. "There's someone I'd like you to meet."

Mac spares Bobby Lee another glance and then his eyes are back on me. I can feel my face threatening to burn but I tamp that shit down and turn back to Bobby Lee.

He looks... hurt. My stomach clenches. I don't want to be the one to tell him Santa ain't real, but come on, he's a grown man and he refuses to listen to reason. He just thinks he can declare the way things are gonna be and they'll magically be that way. Which is a bit ironic since that's essentially how Mac appears to operate his entire world.

Despite the distress sitting behind his eyes, Bobby Lee musters a polite smile and steps forward, hand extended. Bunny would be proud. "Bobby Lee Collinsworth."

"Angus McKinley." Mac accepts his hand and they shake briefly. It doesn't escape my attention that Bobby Lee flexes his hand after Mac releases it. Good gravy.

"Bobby Lee paid me a surprise visit all the way from Savannah. Isn't that nice?" I stroke Mac's arm just like I remember watching Elle do that first time I saw them together. I'm laying it on so thick it'll take weeks to scrape all this bullshit off the floor.

Mac doesn't respond, of course. I try and fail to pull him further into the apartment.

"Took the first flight up this morning to see my girl."

I don't miss his careful choice of words. He may be hurt, but he's fighting back. My fingers constrict around Mac's arm without me even realizing it and before I can blink he's got my hand in his and he's bringing it against his sweaty chest where Bobby Lee would have to be blind to miss it. I want to reach up and kiss the hell out of him.

Mac still doesn't speak; our proximity and his thumb stroking the back of my hand say everything that needs to be said. I struggle to keep my smile stable as Bobby Lee takes it all in.

"Well, it's always good to see my friends from home." He's not the only one good at choosing words.

Bobby Lee's smile is stiff but it doesn't waver. "Of course, I should have checked first to make sure you didn't have plans, but then it wouldn't have been a surprise, now would it?" He gestures our way. "How about we all go out for supper together?"

How about we all go watch an open-heart surgery? It's liable to be more fun.

"Gonna have a word with Poppy," Mac finally says as he pulls me out into the hallway and closes my apartment door behind us.

I have eleventy billion questions and even more explanations but not nearly enough time, so I prioritize. "I'm sorry. He just showed up out of the blue and I can't exactly kick him out—you'd have to know our mamas to fully understand—but then you showed up like a freaking knight in shining armor or whatever and I think he bought it. Oh God, I hope he bought it."

I put my free hand to the back of my neck and glance behind me to make sure Bobby Lee didn't follow us out.

"Not that it's really a lie—I mean, we did make out a couple times, but I know we're not, you know, a *thing*." My eyes jump back to his face which I can't read, per usual. "Actually, I have no idea what it is we've got going on, if anything, especially since you ghosted me and stopped returning my texts."

I take a step back and narrow my eyes, but he's still got ahold of my hand. "Speaking of which, I think you owe me an apology. If you don't want to see me, you can just be a man and tell me so, not go slink off into your lair and pretend you don't own a phone."

I realize at this point that I'm not prioritizing at all, but instead just spewing out every damn thought in my head as it comes. Too late now.

"What *are* you doing here anyway?"

Mac's tongue peeks out to wet the corner of his lips. "Yes, we are."

I shake my head in a slow sway back and forth. "Yes, we are *what*?" I don't speak beast.

"A thing." The words come from chest deep.

My eyebrows jump. "We are?"

I get the slow nod this time and it does fantastic things to my entire body. But then I catch ahold of myself.

"Wait. We don't have time for this right now. Bobby Lee isn't gonna just stand in there while we iron whatever this is out."

"You want me to get rid of him?" Mac's jaw goes tight while his grip on my hand firms.

I shake my head. "No, I wasn't lying when I said he's a friend—or about our mamas."

Mac studies me for another second. "Right." Then he

steers me back to my door and opens it for me, allowing me to go in front of him. All the while, he keeps ahold of my hand.

Bobby Lee is right where we left him, an expectant look in place. I send him a nervous smile but Mac is the one to speak.

"Can't make it for dinner, but I'll pick Poppy up after."

I try not to let my eyes pop out of my head. Which becomes even more difficult when Mac turns me to him and lays a hot wet kiss on my mouth before shooting Bobby Lee a casual man wave and walking out the door.

Holeeey crap.

NINETEEN

"Patience is a virtue. Unless you're dealing with a truly stupid man."
– Cookie Rutledge

I CONSIDER INVITING somebody I know to act as a buffer at dinner until I realize I hardly know anybody. Kate and Naveed aren't options because Bobby Lee will surely use the opportunity to do reconnaissance on Mac and neither one of them know about our *thing*. So I'm left to fend for myself. One of these days, I need to fix my life.

I take Bobby Lee for Thai since it's easy to find a place, and his mood picks up. Maybe he was just hungry. A girl can hope, right? We chat about the business and his parents and he tells me about Cookie's latest run-in with the tourist board over Violette Inn's listing in the new brochure. Before I know it, I'm laughing and having a great time, just like the old days. I remind him of the time he and my cousin got their hands on a batch of moonshine and Iris and I had to drag their drunk asses into the garage at the back of his parents' property so they didn't get a whoopin' come morning. He has the decency to look sheepish at that one and assures me he hasn't been able to even look at moonshine since.

The one thing we don't talk about is his reason for being here, and I thank my lucky stars he's letting it rest.

By the time we pay our bill—dutch, much to Bobby Lee's consternation—I've almost forgotten why I'm mad at him. Until he reminds me.

"I don't suppose you'd let me sleep on your sofa, would you?"

I turn to look at him as we walk side-by-side down the sidewalk.

He throws a hand up. "I have a hotel reservation, don't worry. I just think I'll feel better knowing you're safe in the next room."

If I thought for one minute this actually had anything to do with my personal safety—a notion that's preposterous in itself—I might not respond how I do.

"I've been here a month and I'm doing just fine on my own, thank you very much."

"Don't get so bent out of shape. I'm just looking out for you."

Looking out for me, my ass. He's just trying to make sure I'm not sleeping with Mac!

I stop in my tracks and he has to back up a few steps. "You never felt the need to stay at my place when I was living in Savannah," I throw back at him.

His hands come to his hips. "Back in Savannah, you didn't need protecting."

According to him, I apparently didn't need orgasms either—not that this is the time to bring up his antiquated wait-until-marriage sex policy. But with the way he's acting, maybe it'll do us some good if I clear the air by declaring to all the citizens of New York that I'm no virgin and my maidenhood doesn't require protecting. But perhaps that's a bit off topic.

"And I still don't. Nobody is breaking into my apartment, Bobby Lee. You watch too much TV." I shake my head and start walking again.

"Sometimes we need protecting from ourselves, Poppy!" he calls out after me.

The nerve!

I'm good and pissed now so I snatch my phone from my purse and hit Mac's contact. He picks up on the first ring.

"Hey."

"Hi, Mac. We're done with dinner and I'm ready for you to pick me up. Bobby Lee is gonna stay at my place tonight and save some money on a hotel."

Bobby Lee is shooting me daggers and I don't give a good goddamn.

"Right. Be there in twenty."

Mac hangs up and I stalk down the sidewalk, not even waiting to see if Bobby Lee is following.

I DON'T CONSIDER the implications of Mac coming to pick me up until I'm packing an overnight bag and avoiding Bobby Lee's pacing in my living room. Not only am I spending the night at Mac's place, I'm spending the night *with Mac*. The thought has my knees going weak and my hands reaching for two more pairs of undies. I haven't the first clue what to pack so I throw in a variety of potential sleepwear in addition to a change of clothes for tomorrow. I've got an oversized t-shirt and stretchy shorts, a silky nightie Iris insisted on buying me over the weekend, and a pair of long-sleeved flannel pajamas Cookie got for me when I told her I was moving up north.

The other thing I didn't give enough thought to is the fact that Bobby Lee is likely to call Bunny the minute I walk out that door. Word of my scandalous night at my lover's place will have made the rounds by breakfast. Unless Bobby Lee's pride gets in the way of him sharing—and, oh, how I hope it does. I mean, really, it's my own damn business if I want to spend the night with a man I'm maybe dating. Hell, most everybody already thinks I'm in love as it is, so what's the big deal?

I huff and zip the bag closed just as a familiar knock hits the door. My heart slams against my ribs and I race to answer it before Bobby Lee can.

Mac's thick hair is damp from a shower and is haphazardly swept back from his face. He's wearing a fresh pair of gym shorts and a t-shirt and an expression full of possession and hunger. It looks damn good on him.

"Come on in," I tell him and he doesn't wait to be asked twice before stepping up into my space and dropping a hard kiss on my mouth. Yum.

I blink a few times and then get my wits about me again.

"Bobby Lee, I put fresh sheets on the bed and I'm leaving a key on the counter for you." I look over my shoulder to see him with his butt leaning against the back of my sofa and his arms crossed. I ignore whatever his posture is supposed to be communicating. I've said everything I need to say. Well, except what's required of me if I don't want Mama shaking her head in shame. "Help yourself to anything and call if you need me. I'll be back first thing."

Mac doesn't bother saying anything. He just takes my bag and ushers me out the door.

By the time the taxi drops us off at Mac's studio, I've practically chewed a hole through my bottom lip and my foot has tapped out the entire soundtrack to *Hamilton* on the floorboard.

For once, I haven't been jabbering, instead just letting my mind race while Mac holds my hand on his hard thigh and traces patterns on the back with his thumb. I'm so caught up in my head that it doesn't really hit me until Mac unlocks the front doors that we're at his studio, not an apartment building.

"What are we doing here?" I finally ask.

"I live here."

I gawk at him. "You *live* here?"

"Yeah. Got a place upstairs."

My mouth drops open. "How big is this place?"

"I'll show you."

He locks the door behind us, then picks up my bag and catches my hand before striding down the makeshift hall.

We pass Elle's office, the forge, the retail studio, and move on to the room where I first laid eyes on him doing his battling ropes and stealing my breath. There's a door on the far side of the room which I'd previously just assumed was a closet or something, but when Mac crosses us to it and swings it open, I realize it leads to a staircase.

The stairs turn on a landing and an entryway opens to reveal a spacious living area complete with two couches, a huge television, an open-plan kitchen full of stainless steel, and a large table with enough chairs to seat close to a dozen people. And that's just the part I can see from where we stand.

I bark out a laugh and Mac's head turns sharply at the sound. I can't help it. His gaze flits from me to his "place" and back again.

"What's funny?"

My chest shakes as I try to get ahold of myself and I grip his arm with my free hand. "I'm sorry. It's not funny." I laugh again, belying my statement. "It's just... this set-up is pretty much exactly what the magazine would feature as an entertainer's paradise." I pat his arm a couple times. "And you, Mac, are the last person I can see having a dinner party for ten of your closest friends or hosting an Oscar's watch party." I let my hand sweep the giant room and his eyes follow.

His shoulders tick up in a pseudo-shrug. "I like big spaces."

This sends me off into another fit of laughter.

The man has one of the nicest apartments in Manhattan and he acts like he just invited me into his garage.

I gather myself again. "All I can say is the furniture business must be *booming*." I let my eyes go wide in an exaggerated fashion as I sweep the room one more time. I can tell right away he didn't hire a decorator, but instead, chose pieces he found pleasing to the eye while still putting comfort above all else. His sofas are made from buttery cognac leather and the rug beneath them begs to be rolled on where it covers the weathered hardwood floor beneath. The kitchen has a huge stainless-steel island that doubles as a bar and the counters behind hold the usual appliances plus what appears to be the most complicated blender in existence. Mac is definitely a protein shake kind of guy, so it makes sense.

"Glad you find it amusing." He sends me one of his smoldering looks while his lips quirk to tell me he's not offended.

"I find it beautiful is more like it." I smile at him and his eyes drop to my mouth. Eek. I pull my hand free of his and take a few steps forward, unable to remain under his gaze without squirming or exploding into a quivering mass of shattered nerves. I'm in Mac's lair and I'm pretty sure I know what happens to small animals who wander into the den of the beast.

They get eaten.

But, as usual, Mac surprises the heck out of me when he walks forward, drops my bag on the couch and makes his way to the kitchen.

"Want a drink?"

"Sure," I answer, less because I need a drink and more because it will give me something to do with my hands.

"I got wine, beer, and water."

"Wine would be great."

He nods and pulls a bottle of white from his fridge.

"I would never have pegged you as a wine guy," I tease.

"I'm not," he says to the counter where he's uncorking the bottle.

"Oh." What does that mean? Does he keep it around for his various women? God, why doesn't he communicate and put me out of my misery? I consider asking him straight out, but I hate being the only one of us who doesn't hold onto information like it's the last Oreo.

Mac slides the glass across the island, so I walk over and take a seat on one of the barstools. He reaches back into the fridge and pulls out a water. Of course, he's not drinking. That would put us too close to a level playing field. With that in mind, I don't sip my wine but spin the glass with nervous fingers on the stainless-steel surface instead.

He watches me for a few moments, taking a long swallow of his water. My eyes are immediately drawn to the bob of his Adam's apple as the muscles of his throat work the liquid down. Despite the comfortable temperature of his apartment, I can feel a sheen a sweat forming on my lower back.

When he finally brings the bottle back to the counter, eyes never leaving mine, he leans forward to prop his elbows on the surface. Then he blows my mind as only he can do.

"I read sci-fi novels."

My head jerks. "I'm sorry, you... what?"

He looks down at his water for a second and then back to me. "I was sixteen and getting into all sorts of shit, driving everyone I knew up the damn wall. My pops comes into my room one night and throws this book at me—almost hits me in the face." His finger flips up, pointing toward his face. "Tells me if I want to be a little shit that's my prerogative but to at least do him a favor and not be a *dumb* little shit." He shrugs and continues, "Being the punk-ass kid I was, I told him what he could do with his book. But seeing as he then sold our TV and took my set of truck keys, I got bored. Picked up the book. It was *Hitchhiker's Guide to the Galaxy*. That was all it took to get me hooked."

I find my voice but it comes out rusty. "And you stopped being a little shit?"

A grin curves the corners of his mouth and it does things to me. "Didn't say that. But I figure maybe I wasn't such an idiot after that."

I can't help the smile from spreading across my face. "Why are you telling me this?"

Mac's grin drops and he leans forward on his elbows, his teeth grazing his bottom lip as he chooses his words. "Because you give me you without even meaning to and every damn piece of it is a gift. And I'm a selfish bastard so I take it without giving anything back."

My throat is too dry to swallow.

"And because even though I know I should stay away, I can't."

Cue full-body collapse. I hope he has a mop in this giant apartment 'cuz it's the only way he's getting me off the floor.

"Mac." I'm surprised the word is even audible with how tightly my throat is constricting.

"I didn't ignore you because I wanted to."

I nod, even though I know I don't fully understand—I

know there's a warehouse-sized storage unit of things he keeps hidden inside himself.

"And I sure as hell didn't leave you in your apartment looking like a man's dying dream because I wanted to either."

I nod again, this time getting what he's saying.

"I just didn't want to be the one doing all the taking anymore."

I remove my fingers from the wine glass and slide off my stool. My feet take me right around the island and directly to him where I let my palm slide over his t-shirt from his stomach to his chest as he turns to me. There's no way I can do this on my own, so I'm relieved as hell when he dips his head down and meets my mouth halfway.

TWENTY

"Live in the present 'cuz no amount of wishing will bring it back tomorrow."
– Cookie Rutledge

I HONESTLY NEVER THOUGHT OF myself as a wanton kind of girl. Sure, I enjoy sex, and who doesn't love a good orgasm, but the complete lack of control over my own body comes as something of a surprise. Although, maybe it shouldn't.

Mac doesn't waste any time letting me do my little seduction routine and instead takes control of our kiss right away. His hands are on my ass as he turns us so my back hits the island and then my feet are off the floor and my butt lands on the metal surface. I'm still wearing my work clothes, so when he pulls me to the edge of the counter to nestle his hips between my thighs, my skirt gets in the way.

But Mac's mouth doesn't leave mine. Instead I can feel

his growl of frustration against my tongue and it makes me want to strip naked and climb into him. With an efficiency I'll only properly appreciate later, he hoists me up again, shoves the fabric up with one swipe of his big paw and sets my butt back down again. I yelp in surprise when the bare skin of my thighs hits the cold stainless-steel. But when Mac's hands settle on the tops of my thighs and both thumbs skim from my knees up along my inner thighs to my panties, the cold races away and is replaced by nothing but molten fire. The hard-earned rough pads of his fingers ruin me for smooth hands of white-collar guys for the rest of my life.

I squirm and my head falls back, opening my neck to his seeking lips and tongue. I fist his hair and probably pull a little too hard, but I'm no longer in control of my own senses or actions—or anything for that matter. It's spectacular.

Mac's hands slide back toward my knees and I whimper a little until he pulls my hips into him and the firm evidence of his arousal presses hard against my panties. I moan at the contact and Mac's head snaps up so he's looking down at me. I focus enough to see the tension lining his jaw and cheeks and mouth, but it's his eyes that steal the breath from my lungs. There's probably a fine line between the look this man might get when he wants to murder someone and when he wants to screw their brains out. I'm banking on this being the latter. His expression is fueled by an inferno behind his eyes, one that would probably render his forge completely unnecessary were he to work out how to source it.

And it's all focused on me.

His lips are wet from our kisses and I want to lick them and then mount them. Like I said... *wanton.*

But this is clearly Mac's show and I'm more than happy to see what happens next. What I don't expect is for me to lose his hands.

He releases me and steps back, letting his eyes roam from my sex-hair to my bruised lips and on down to where I know my nipples are straining the fabric of my top. I can see his chest rise and fall with labored breaths when his eyes drop lower still to the apex of my thighs where only the thin cotton of my panties covers me.

So I do the only thing reasonable for a wanton girl in this moment and I let my knees fall to the sides, opening my thighs wider for his eyes.

I seriously don't know what's gotten into me. I mean, I've been known to be playful in the sack and try out new things. If sex isn't fun, then why bother? But fun is the absolute last word I'd use to label my encounter with Mac. Intense, yes. Arousing, hell yes. And so absolutely imperative. As in, my body and soul are telling me if I don't get this man inside me, my entire existence might be in peril.

Mac appears to be of the same mind when he groans a ragged breath and plucks me off the counter like I'm a lunch sack and he's off to work.

"Mac!" I wrap my arms around him and hold on for dear life.

He doesn't slow down. He stalks straight past his sofas and on by the giant dining table to a door at the far side of the room. It bangs against the wall as he throws it open and flips on the light, and then I'm airborne for a second before his bed cushions my fall and he's pulling off my shoes.

Thump. Thump.

They both hit the floor and his lips are tracing along the inside of my knee while large hands smooth over the skin of my outer thighs and on up to my hips.

The tickle of his scruff has my hips lifting off the bed but he pushes them back down with a grunt I interpret as, "stay." Normally, I don't like being bossed around, but I know for a fact I'd be missing out on a whole lot of amazing if I bother making a fuss. If Mac wants to be the boss in bed, I can work with that. Especially when he's paying his employee in orgasms. Wait, that makes me sound like a hooker. But my brain can only do so much when his tongue is licking a path up my inner thigh.

My hand flies to his hair again, whether to pull him off because my skin is so agonizingly sensitized to his touch or to urge him on, I'm not sure.

"Mac," I moan into the cool air of the room.

He must take that as a sign because his hands sneak up under my bunched-up skirt and his fingers hook into the sides of my panties. He brings his head up and watches as he slides my undies down my thighs.

Despite my newly-found lust-driven self, I have to fight the urge not to bring my knees together. I've never had anybody stare so openly and hungrily at my lady town before. It's always been more of a means to an end rather than a headlining feature of its own, if you know what I mean.

But by the ticking of Mac's jaw I'd say it's this year's Broadway smash hit, a notion that's reaffirmed when my panties join my shoes on the floor and Mac buries his face between my thighs.

I can't let myself think too hard on exactly where Mac acquired his skills between the sheets. If I do, I might either cry or go on a killing spree of all the women in his past. Or, perhaps I should buy them flowers. Anyway, I settle for just reveling in everything he's doing to me.

When my orgasm hits, I see the face of God—or maybe it's just Morgan Freeman, but whoever it is, he's in complete agreement with me when I call out his name. I'm surprised I haven't pulled out a giant tuft of Mac's hair, but I see I have messed it up to the point where he'll need a good shower if he ever hopes to go out in public again.

My chest rises and falls in quick pants as Mac lifts his head and sends me a searing look from between my legs. The snapshot is utterly salacious and I commit it to memory immediately, filing it in my mental scrapbook of dirtiest moments.

"Lift up." Mac's command is pure gravel, and aftershocks from my orgasm pulse through my sex at his tone.

I do what he says because I'm not an idiot. Doing what he wants leads to orgasms, just as I suspected, so I'm quick to comply. Mac unzips my skirt and pulls it down my legs, leaving me in just my flimsy blouse and bra.

This is clearly unsatisfactory to him because next he grabs my hand and pulls me up to sitting where he carefully lifts my top over my head and tosses it to the side. His forefinger traces along the lace of my bra cup and I swear my breasts physically swell at his touch. A new shiver runs across my skin and I suck in a breath.

"Fuckin' beautiful."

The breath catches at his words and my eyes fly up to Mac's face. He's watching the movement of his finger as it skims up only to slide the strap of my bra off my shoulder. He repeats it on the other side, him watching me and me watching him. His expression is one of complete adulation, as if he's never seen or touched a woman's skin before. As if his face wasn't just between my thighs. I'm dumbstruck.

There have been any number of times in my life when I've been called beautiful. I'm not being boastful; I just know I did better than average in the DNA lottery. My boyfriend back in eighth grade told me I was beautiful in my favorite dress. Bobby Lee said on our very first date that I was beautiful, and Cookie and Mama and Daddy tell me all the time that I'm beautiful.

But I've never felt it bone deep like I do when Mac says it. And it's not because he used the f-word to modify it. It's because he doesn't say anything he doesn't mean, and the expression on his face tells me it's one of life's simple truths for him. Poppy James is "fuckin' beautiful" to Mac McKinley and that's all there is to say.

"Mac." All *I* seem to be able to say, on the other hand, is the man's damn name.

His eyes flick up to mine at the sound of my voice and it's a wonder I don't drop dead on the spot from their shimmering intensity. Without another word, one of Mac's hands snakes behind my back and my bra falls from my breasts like a soft sigh.

"Lie back." His voice is smoke and need.

My hand comes up to cup his cheek and his whiskers scrape my palm. I run my thumb over the corner of his mouth and on up toward the scar that mars the side of his nose. The skin there is pink and angry, standing in contrast to the surrounding flesh. On any other man, it might be the kind of imperfection you avoid looking at. On Mac it's part of what makes him so exquisite.

"I want to see you." My words are imbued with more meaning than he likely recognizes, but that's okay. For now.

He hums in his chest and then his hand is behind his neck and he's pulling off his shirt.

If ever there was a moment for cursing in my life, it's right now. Because there are no other words to describe the sight of Mac's body in its full glory looming over me. It's a fucking miracle.

My eyes don't know where to start their optical feast. Dark hair dusts over hewn muscle and tanned skin while colorful ink runs the width of his broad chest and dots other planes along his arms, shoulders, and stomach. The man is a work of art in more ways than one.

"Lie back," he tells me again, this time with a hint of impatience around the edges.

I shake my head, not pulling my eyes from his skin. "I want to touch you."

"Want that too, but I'm not done."

I glance up and scowl at him, then slide my hand up his arm, ignoring his words. I've seen this particular tattoo peeking out from the arm of his t-shirts, but I've never been able to study it up close. It's a dagger engulfed in flame, the meaning of which escapes me. My fingers trace his collarbone next and sweep down to skim over the largest of his tattoos, a brilliantly-colored fire-breathing dragon over his pectorals. My intention is to continue exploring all his tattoos with my fingers, but my lips decide they want in on the action and I bend forward to taste the hollow just above his clavicle.

He hisses and his thumb grazes one of my nipples before he circles it and then captures the peak between his thumb and forefinger. I moan into his chest and, before I know it, he's gotten his way and I'm flat on my back again, a giant Mac hovering over my naked body.

My mouth loses contact with his skin when he pins me with his hips and goes up on an elbow, one hand still working my breast while the fingers of the other trace the skin at my hairline and tuck a strand of wild hair behind my ear.

His eyes study my features and I can see questions behind them, making me wonder if they mirror my own.

What are you doing to me?

How am I feeling so much?

Are you going to break me?

But he doesn't voice them so I can't know.

I pull him down to me for a kiss, letting my lips and tongue speak for me against his wet mouth. My fingers dig into the warm flesh and hard muscles of his back and shoulders while his erection presses down onto my naked sex through the material of his shorts. I circle his hips with my legs and push up into him.

He releases my mouth and groans my name against my jaw, and then his mouth is on my breast—licking, sucking, biting—yet all his movements are controlled. Mine, on the other hand, are that of the wanton woman we talked about. I'm thrashing and scraping my fingernails over his scalp and shoulder while I grind shamelessly up into his hardness.

Finally, he rises onto his knees like a warrior on the brink of battle, but he doesn't stay still for long. He leans his long body to the side to reach into his bedside table where he extracts a box of condoms. An unopened box of condoms, I don't fail to note, as I file that away for later.

He wastes no time, in classic Mac fashion, and I get only the briefest glimpse of gray boxer briefs before his shorts and briefs join the rest of our clothes on the floor and he's rolling a condom over his thick length and settling himself back between my thighs. Part of me feels a pout coming on that I didn't even get to touch him, but the other part of me tells everyone to shut up because the real show is about to begin.

He positions himself at my entrance and I gasp as he starts to press inside. It's safe to say it's been a while for me, but even if that weren't so, Mac would take some serious getting used to. Suffice it to say he's very proportionate.

He draws his hips back and pushes forward again, stretching me with a beautiful burn. I close my eyes and tilt my head back into the mattress.

"Open," Mac rasps, pulling back and thrusting forward again until he's almost fully inside me.

My inner walls tremble and my eyes fly open to see him watching me with eyes on fire. His jaw is clenched tight as he maintains a grip on his control and holds my gaze. Our eyes are locked together when he withdraws almost completely and powers forward so he's fully seated inside me. I gasp and clench around him, my back arching.

"You okay?" he asks on what's almost a wheeze. Glad I'm not the only one.

I just nod because I can't speak. I'm so full yet it's still not enough. It's exquisite and torturous and mind-blowing all at once, but it's nothing compared to what I feel when he reassures himself I'm truly okay and begins setting a rhythm.

With each stroke, he gives and takes, the effort forming a sheen of sweat between us where our bodies glide against one another, bare skin to bare skin. He's attuned to every shift of my body, every sound I make, constantly adjusting his movements to drive me higher into this stratosphere of pleasure he's building.

I'm unaware of how my hands get to the places on his body where they squeeze and caress and scratch, driven completely by instinct and the mindlessness of the storm between us. It's as if I finally understand my body's purpose and it's to absorb pleasure and sensual power through every pore of my skin where it meets Mac's. He's a god and a man and a wizard and an orgasm fairy all in one. And he's mine. At least for now.

By the time he's shifted my body for the fourth time, I've lost all connection between my brain and my muscles and I'm pretty much just a vessel of nerve endings. Mac stands at the side of the bed with my ankles held to his shoulders as he drives into me at a brutal pace. I've already come twice and there's no way I can handle any more, but I'm too overwhelmed to form the words to tell him I'm toast. Instead, I lay with my arms tossed above my head and my back keenly arched while I watch Mac's face and revel in the wonderfully dirty things he's doing to me. He's the picture of tortured restraint, powering forward with beautiful strokes into me, lighting my core and ruining me in the best of ways.

Sweat drips down his face and chest as he watches where our bodies connect. It might be the sexiest thing I've ever seen. He thrusts forward, hitting the most secret and sensitive points in my entire being with each stroke. I'm mesmerized by the bunching and shifting of all two million muscles before my eyes and promise myself to get my hands back on his skin once I can move again.

Aaaand... it looks like I'm not toast after all because a new wave crashes over me and I'm whimpering and panting his name while my inner walls pulse around him, my hips rising off the bed and my toes curling by his neck. It takes what feels like forever to come down from my new high.

I have no idea how long we've been at it, but two things are clear: I'm gonna sleep like a baby tonight, and I'm throwing my vibrator away the minute I get home.

Mac's eyes find mine again in the dim light and his teeth clench with his final strokes before he roars a delicious manly growl and reaches his climax, eventually stilling inside me.

The only sound to fill the air then is our labored breathing. Mac lets go of my ankles and falls forward to the bed on his elbows, careful not to crush me. My thighs naturally fall apart to accommodate him and then I wrap him up with my arms around his neck and my legs circling his hips.

It occurs to me that if I don't move, we may be able to just stay like this forever. It's one of my better ideas, I must admit.

TWENTY-ONE

"God made men and women different for a reason; what else would we have to talk about?"
– Cookie Rutledge

"SO, WHAT DOES THIS ONE MEAN?" I run my finger along the tattoo that snakes behind Mac's ear—the same one that's been taunting and winking at me since the very first time we spoke.

He's lying on his back with his elbows cocked and his hands behind his head while I use his chest as a very hard, yet very warm pillow. Honestly, I've never given underarm hair a single thought, except to be annoyed that I have to waste time shaving my own—until about point-two seconds after Mac pulled his t-shirt over his head tonight and I realized exactly how manly and sexy I find it to be. I've been sneaking peeks at his since he positioned us this way after our glorious and exhausting sexathon, but I'm finally shifting my focus to his tattoos.

Mac spouts out an unintelligible mush of words I assume are Gaelic by the general cadence. Then he switches from word salad to normal English. "No man can serve two masters."

"Ah," I respond as my finger reaches the end of the inked text at his shoulder and lingers there on the warm skin. "Very deep."

I still can't believe I get to touch him like this. I mean, I know parts of him have literally been inside of me, but he's possibly the most beautiful human specimen I've ever seen. In fact, I'm thinking about taking up sculpting as I sit here admiring him.

He grunts and shifts his chin down to see me better. "Don't be fooled." He catches my hand and guides my finger over to his right shoulder. "This one back here says, 'So long and thanks for all the fish.'"

My chin digs into his chest when I laugh. "I'm so afraid to ask."

His mouth slides into an almost-full grin. "Remember the book?"

I laugh again. "Let me guess, your first tattoo?"

His answer is a brow quirk and I consider my previous instinct to lean forward and run my tongue over it. Instead, I choose normal human behavior.

"Isn't that book kind of... a comedy?"

"Yeah." The added *so what* is silent.

"Hmm."

His brows come down. "You don't think I have a sense of humor?"

"Uh, it's not the *first* attribute that comes to mind." Hello, orgasm whisperer.

Mac's response is to pull on a strand of my hair that I'm sure looks like Sideshow Bob from *The Simpsons* at this point. If I'm not mistaken, Mac is being playful. Who knew?

I grin and hope it's adequately sassy. My post-coital haze has taken my inhibitions down to zero. "So, Mac, about this sci-fi thing... does that mean you're a Trekkie?"

"What if I am?" He asks with a straight face.

Aside from it blowing my mind, it wouldn't matter much at all, per se. In the interest of keeping the current lines of communication open, I'm careful with my next words.

"Well, that would make my day since I'm a total Trekkie too." In other words, I lie. I mean, seriously, I just don't get it. Apart from the hotness that is Chris Pine, I'm lost.

"You lie like it's your job." Mac completely calls me out.

I gasp and poke him in the ribs. This no inhibitions thing is fun. "I do not."

He grunts but doesn't try to remove my hand. "Name one conversation we've had where you didn't lie."

I open my mouth to respond and come up empty. "Well, that's not fair. We really haven't talked all that much when you think about it."

His lips twitch again. "And that's better somehow?"

I send him a scowl. "Anyway, it's just because you hardly talk at all so I have to fill in the silence with *something*."

"I talk. When I have something to say."

Stop the presses, y'all!

"With your eyebrows, maybe."

The thick sexy slashes spike at that. "My eyebrows?"

"Yes. Your eyebrows are as prolific as William freakin' Shakespeare."

"They write plays?" Now who's being sassy?

"You know what I mean." I resettle myself so my chin rests on my hands where they're folded on his chest. How did I get here? Sigh.

"I'm afraid I don't."

"See! Right there." I whip a hand out and point to his face. "Your left eyebrow just said, 'You're certifiable, Poppy James.'"

"It said all that?" He lifts his head to rake me with his eyes and then his voice drops especially low. "What is the right one saying?"

"Oh. Oh. No." I pretend to back away. "That's too dirty to say out loud."

Mac flips me on my back in one smooth motion and I forget all about being a smartass. It's only later that I find out he's not a Trekkie at all, but he does have an entire bookshelf crammed with sci-fi paperbacks and a collection of vinyl records, and I'm totally down with that.

AFTER A BREAKFAST of egg white omelets and a few additional personal Mac tidbits I hoard to myself like a crotchety old miser, it's time to face the music—the music being one of those incessant old Rick Astley songs that get stuck in your head until you want to claw your own ears off. Namely, a worn-out tune by the name of Bobby Lee Collinsworth.

But when I go to get dressed and attempt an awkward goodbye with Mac, he's having nothing of it. Instead, I find myself naked and in the shower with Mac soaping up every inch of my body and tracing it all with his mouth just to make sure he got everything. He's thorough like that.

Then, of course, I have to make sure he's clean, a process that's cut short when he decides I've done enough and pins me to his shower wall to do me like a bad habit. Suffice it to say, we're both super clean by the time I'm allowed to get dressed. Mac throws on jeans and a t-shirt and walks me out to grab a taxi.

And that's how I find myself climbing my apartment building's stairs with Mac on my heels and Bobby Lee waiting inside. How in the world did I get here?

"Morning!" I greet the entryway wall. If I know Bobby Lee, he's been up since the crack of dawn, so there's no reason to keep my voice down. And, yup, there he is, hair still damp from the shower and pressed chinos and a dress shirt covering his tall frame. He has a newspaper spread before him on the table and a cup of coffee that I'm guessing has been refilled more than once.

He wipes his lips with a paper napkin and rises. "Morning, Poppy. Angus." He doesn't extend a hand to Mac, nor does Mac make an attempt from where he stands pressed up against my back. This is even more awkward than I thought it would be.

I rock on my Converse soles and Bobby Lee shoves his

hands in his front pockets, neither of us knowing what to say. And it's not like I can count on Mac to break the tension. Hell, his middle name is probably Tension, a moniker he wears proudly, no doubt.

"So..." I finally say, ever so helpfully.

Bobby Lee smiles painfully. "So..."

Good God. Where is the Kool-Aid man when you need him?

I finally crack. "You have breakfast yet? I can make you something. Or maybe we can pop around the corner and grab a bite. Somewhere around here is bound to have a half-decent biscuit, right?" At this I turn to Mac for confirmation—or maybe to hand out a distress signal. But he's not looking at me. His eyes are on Bobby Lee.

Crap. I'm thinking we might just have ourselves a good old-fashioned pissing contest on our hands.

"No, Poppy, darlin'. I already ate."

Mac's hand winds around my waist and settles on my belly at Bobby Lee's endearment. And I know I was the one to use Mac as my buffer with Bobby Lee in the first place, but I've got a better handle on it now. So I gently move Mac's hand and, in a minor miracle, he lets me.

"Okay. Well..." It's not like I can ask Bobby Lee to come hang out for the day. I have work and two meetings scheduled. But, like it or not, Bobby Lee is family, and you don't kick family out unless they do something unforgivable like not replacing the toilet paper roll. Last I checked, caring about somebody is not a crime worthy of being cast out.

I take a few steps closer and Bobby Lee is watching my face. "Listen, I've got a few meetings scheduled, but I'm sure I can get away for lunch or something. What do you say?"

One side of his mouth turns up, but it's a poor excuse for a smile. His eyes dart to Mac where I know he's still standing there like a sentry behind me.

"That's all right. You go do your thing. I'm gonna head on home."

"Already?" It's a weak protest, but there it is.

"Yeah, I reckon I finished what I came for."

Oh, Bobby Lee. Dammit.

"Walk me out?" He bends and picks up his leather satchel I didn't notice at the leg of the table.

"Of course." I turn and walk to the door, biting my lip as I go and not daring to look at Mac.

The two men exchange polite farewells behind me but I just keep on walking until I'm back out on the sidewalk.

I hear Bobby Lee's shoes scuffing the concrete behind me. "You're happy." His words take me by surprise, but my response comes easily.

"Yeah, I am." I turn to face him and I have to look up because he's still on the steps.

"And *he* makes you happy?" Bobby Lee's eyes shift up toward my apartment.

I nod since answering that question with words would take approximately thirty-two years and nobody's got time for that.

He sighs and drops down the rest of the steps until we're toe to toe. "Well, I reckon that's all that's really important, then."

Dammit, Bobby Lee. "Are you *trying* to make me cry?"

He coughs out a laugh. "No, but I'd be lying if I said it

wouldn't do my heart some good to know you shed a tear or two over me."

"Bobby Lee." I don't say anything else. I just hug him and hold on tight for a few seconds.

"You just make sure he knows the minute he does something to hurt you, I'm coming right back up to show him how us Southern boys throw down."

It takes everything in me not to laugh at the mental picture he's painting, not to mention the fact that the phrase "throw down" just came out of his preppy proper mouth. So I nod, not letting myself consider his words too carefully or I might admit that Mac hurting me is probably a foregone conclusion.

But I shove that down, and as soon as I lose sight of Bobby Lee's cab, I run back up to my apartment to get ready for work and take advantage of any time I can get with Mac.

"WELL, THIS IS IT." Athena brings her hands together on the conference table before her. The surface is littered with printouts, photographs, and probably a dozen empty coffee cups.

"How in the hell are we supposed to enjoy Labor Day weekend with this looming over our heads?" Kate's brows are drawn together and she's got a pencil stuck in her hair.

"That's easy," Natalie, another of the executives, chimes in. "Lots and lots of wine."

This makes us all smile and eases some of the tension in the air. It's the end of the day on Friday and the next time we see each other after the long weekend, the presentation will be over. Athena is pitching the new *WHL* to the board of directors Tuesday morning and there's nothing left we can do.

Everybody has worked their asses off, so there's no room for regret, but it's still scary when jobs are essentially on the line. Well, at least mine is.

And it's been impossible to ignore the whispers in the hallway and the sidelong glances that have come our way as the presentation draws nearer. But we'll show them all.

I take a deep breath. "We've got nothing to worry about. Our vision is fresh, the look is clean, and our team is the best out there." If I say it enough times, it has to be true, right? "They'd be crazy to turn us down."

"Absolutely," Kate affirms.

"That's what I'm talking about," Natalie raises a pretend glass to me.

"They'll be eating out of my hand." Athena's confident smirk settles over us all.

And that's all we can do. Hope for the best.

Suffice it to say, I'm more than ready for a drink by the time I pack up my things and leave the office. I heard Kate on the phone with Zach, so I don't want to butt into her date night, but there's no way I'm hanging out at my apartment alone tonight.

My stomach, my heart, and my hoo-ha want to pick up the phone and call Mac, but after last night, the last thing I want to do is come off as too needy. I didn't force him to take me to his place and ravish me, but my claiming him in front of Bobby Lee was kind of ballsy, so maybe it's best to leave the ball in his court for now.

So I call Iris instead.

"Please tell me you've sealed the deal with Mac by now!"

Why bother with a polite greeting when you can be obnoxious instead?

"Hello, Iris. How are you?" I pick my way past a gaggle of prep-school girls in plaid uniforms who are using the sidewalk as their own personal catwalk.

"Same old, same old. Manny is a dick and Mama wants me to go stay at the house the rest of the time she and Daddy are gone because she heard burglars have been casing the neighborhood. I feel so loved and cherished that she wants to offer me up as human bait."

I can't stop my snicker. Manny, her boss, is indeed a dick, and it's good to know that not much has changed at home, even if our parents are still away on their marathon vacation.

"Now tell me, have we proven once and for all the truth of the old saying about the size of a man's feet?"

"Ummmm."

"I knew it! He's got to be a size sixteen. Can you even walk after that?"

"Rissy!" I snort laugh. "Oh my God."

"I notice you haven't answered."

I turn the corner at a noodle joint. "It's not like I whipped out a tape measure. Jeez, woman."

I'm pretty sure she's dancing at this point. "Yeah, but at least give me an approximation."

"I'm not giving you a damn thing. This is not why I called."

I can hear her pout over the line. "Fine, then what did you call about if it's not to gossip about Mac and his enormous penis."

I almost trip over my heels. "Please tell me you're not at work with that mouth."

"Relax. I'm at Mama and Daddy's making sure no ax murderers are hiding in the closets."

"Thank God." The fact that she hasn't mentioned Bobby Lee tells me the gossip train is still parked at the station—or Bobby Lee missed his flight. Either way, I'm not bringing it up. "So, I'm really just calling to say hi. And because I have to talk to someone or I'm gonna go nuts. The presentation is all ready and it's pretty much in the board's hands now. I'll know next week if I'm going to be Poppy James, creative director of the fabulous *WHL*, or Poppy James, staff designer and coffee wench for a random publication out of someone's creepy basement."

"No way! Nuh uh. You guys are gonna get the go-ahead. I just know it."

"You really think so?" I know it's silly to look to Iris for reassurance on something she's never even laid eyes on, but it still helps.

"I know so."

"Well, I can always come home if it crashes and burns, I guess." I'm waiting at a cross walk with half of Manhattan, so I refuse to let the lump in my throat have its way.

"Popps, as much as I miss you, it ain't your time. Maybe one day you'll come home to stay, but not until you've kicked ass all over New York."

I smile at that, the lump shrinking a little. "Thanks, Rissy."

"And besides, they don't grow men like Mac down here."

Seeing as I've said this exact thing a time or seven, this doesn't require a response so I ignore it. "Man, what I really need is a drink and a dance club."

"Since you're obviously ignoring my attempts to talk about your red-hot stallion, you should go out with Kate and have some girl time."

"Eh, she's got a date. It might just be me, Netflix, and a bottle of wine."

"No! You're in New York City! Call Naveed. I'm pretty sure it's a rule that every single girl in New York needs a gay best friend."

I get pushed along with the throng when the signal turns green. "I don't have nearly enough eyerolls to respond to that comment."

"Ha. Ha." Her response is flat. "I'm only trying to help, and Naveed is fun."

"I know." I pull on my hair in frustration. "But if I have drinks with Naveed, I'm bound to slip up and say something about Mac and me, and I can't have anyone at work knowing about... whatever it is between us. Not yet." And, besides, it would be just like me to get drunk and gush about Mac only to have him never call me again.

"I still don't understand why not. It's not like it's some kind of HR issue. Mac doesn't even work there."

"I know, I know, but just trust me. Nepotism, friendly favors, mixing business with pleasure... it's all fine and good back home, but it's a different world up here. I can't even begin to tell you the shit I hear in the office bathroom. You should see how fast they can tear you down up here.

"I saw the security guard walking someone out last week for stealing binder clips, Iris. *Binder clips!* Not to mention yesterday when some woman in twelve-inch heels asked me to get her coffee just because I happened to be standing beside her outside the elevators. She assumed I was the receptionist. My God, with the look she gave me, I was two seconds away from saying, 'Yes, ma'am, how many sugars?'

"I'm not gonna be that green young thing who can't take her job seriously enough to keep it in her panties. My first assignment and I go hopping into bed with the subject of an interview? Please. Besides, you're the one who told me to dress for the job I want and you were right." I'm out of breath by the time I finish.

"Okay, okay. Point taken. But just remember, even that boss of yours you admire so much, that Athena woman? I'll bet my ass she's got a sex life and doesn't apologize for it. Just sayin'."

"And when I'm established here and have a laundry list of successful projects under my belt—and don't get mistaken for a college student—I'll gladly shout about my sex life and maybe even do it with my full-on accent and my cowboy boots. But until then, I'm keeping a low profile."

"Whatever you say, Poppy."

I realize I've been all but stalking down the sidewalk when my toes cry out in protest. Damn, that was stupid. I look around, but it's rush hour and there is no hope of catching a cab. I'll just have to walk the rest of the way home or grab the subway. Even the thought of that has me feeling slightly ill, though. My mind immediately goes to the last time I was on an overcrowded subway car with Mac surrounding me and calling me honey. My limbs get rubbery at the memory.

I sigh and slow my steps. "Sorry to dump all that on you."

"Hey, I'm your sister. It's in the job description."

"Well, you're an excellent employee. Make sure you tell Manny I said so."

She snorts. "Yeah, I'll get right on that."

"I guess I should go. I need to figure out a way home during rush hour."

"Well, if you're not going out with Kate or Naveed, you should just give in and call Mac. I'm sure you two could think of something to do that won't involve going out in public and risking your career."

Smartass.

"I don't know. He's a little hot and cold." Although, last night was definitely hot. "I'm leaving the ball in his court right now."

"Because you seduced him and then ran away? Please don't tell me that's what happened."

"I didn't seduce him and I didn't run away."

"Thank God for small favors."

I close one eye and get it over with. "But Bobby Lee might have shown up at my doorstep at the same time as Mac and I might have stroked Mac like a pony and pretended he was my boyfriend so Bobby Lee would get off my back. And it might have ended up with Mac taking me home with him so I wouldn't have to deal with the whole disaster that is Bobby Lee but I *would* have to deal with a very naked and very hot Mac McKinley." I suck in a breath while the line goes completely silent.

"Iris?" I eek out in a whisper.

But all I get back is a giant whoop of laughter I can hear echoing off the walls of my folks' house back in Savannah.

TWENTY-TWO

*"When you don't know where you stand, sometimes it helps
to just take a seat and wait."*
– Cookie Rutledge

IN ALL FAIRNESS, Mac didn't say he was going to call today. By the time I said goodbye to Bobby Lee, got changed, and Mac put me in a cab to work this morning, I was running so late there wasn't much time to say anything at all. I hate feeling like I don't know where I stand. On the one hand, we had sex—very hot, very intimate sex. And Mac shared something personal with me. And he had both an unopened bottle of wine and an unopened box of condoms I could conceivably convince myself were purchased with me in mind. On the other hand, Elle's ominous statements and the messy past I don't know the first thing about throw up some pretty freaking huge red flags.

In my limited experience, it's normal to share things about yourself and your past with someone you're dating. Not so much with someone you're screwing.

So, that might be my answer right there.

But I can't forget his earnest expression when he told me he didn't want to be the one doing all the taking. That has to mean something, right?

Gah! I can run this around in circles in my head all I want, but it will always come down to one thing: I can't make someone feel something they don't want to.

The best thing I can do is figure out my own feelings about Mac and let him decide for himself what he wants from me. If he says, "Thanks for the hot sex," and walks away, I can't be angry at him for that.

But I can still be sad. And I will be. Hell, just the thought of it is making me want to cry, and I hardly even know the guy.

Guess I've got *my* feelings all figured out, so at least I can cross one thing off my list.

I push a sweaty strand of hair off my face and limp around the corner onto my block, cursing myself for the tenth time for forgetting a change of shoes in my hurry this morning. But wine will surely dull the pain. I just hope I remembered to stock up.

"What happened?"

I nearly jump out of my cursed heels at the sound of Mac's troubled voice. My head pops up to find him bearing down on me on the sidewalk and I can't help myself. I break out into what's probably the goofiest grin this side of Japanese anime. And I don't give one flying frack.

He stops in front of me but his hands stay at his sides as

his eyes sweep me, assessing for injury. It makes my smile even stupider.

"Nothing," I reply. "Just forgot sensible shoes."

His chest rumbles and he bends at the waist without another word, sweeping me up in a fireman's hold and whipping us around to head back the way he came.

"Mac!" I achieve a pitch invented for canine ears only. "What are you doing?"

He doesn't respond, of course.

I smack his back but then get distracted by the way his muscles contract when he walks. Pretty soon, the hand that was meant to be scolding him is feeling him up, stroking the muscles on either side of his spine and heading downtown to Upper Assville. This was one area I didn't get to adequately explore last night due to his habit of moving me where he wants me and always needing to have his eyes on me. But I need to bookmark this for later.

"Ride it like you stole it, girl!" comes a shout from across the street and I can't bring myself to look for its source. What am I doing?

Luckily, Mac needs to set me down so I can unlock my building's door, something that sparks a question I've been meaning to ask.

"How have you been getting in my building all this time?"

His response is a half shrug and a frown as he tilts his head to look at my throbbing feet.

"Mac!"

I get his eyes on mine and he just says, "I'm good with my hands."

And if that just doesn't say everything...

I shove the door open and move to the stairs but he's on me again and, yup, I'm up and over his shoulder and he's jogging up the stairs. Yes, I said jogging.

I don't bother scolding him again because we're at my door before I know it. Mac takes the key from me, opens my door, and holds his hand out. I give him a look and take the proffered keys, but his hand doesn't go down.

"Shoes."

I roll my eyes and bend first one leg and then the other until I have both shoes in hand and hold them out to him. Mac takes them and we enter my apartment—where he proceeds to stalk over to the windows, open one, and throw my shoes out into the alley below.

"I can't believe you just did that!"

"I can't believe you wear those things," he replies as calm as can be and then walks to my kitchen to pull two glasses down from the cabinet (without having to rummage around at all, of course). I watch, speechless, as he pretends like he didn't just throw my hundred-dollar shoes out the window and reaches into the fridge for my pitcher of sweet tea. He fills both glasses with ice and tops that off with the tea before setting one down on the counter in front of me and taking a Mac-sized swallow from the other. A move which is immediately followed by him dumping the rest of the contents of his glass down my sink.

"What. The fuck. Is that?"

I perch my fists on my hips, pissed off I'm now at an even bigger disadvantage without my heels.

"Tea. What did you think it was?"

"That." He points at the pitcher. "Is not tea."

I roll my eyes. "Yes it is." And to prove the point, I grab

my glass from the counter and bring it to my lips. The sweet, icy concoction hits my tongue and it's pure heaven on earth. I pull in a mouthful, moaning at the rich flavor and letting it slide down my parched throat. I don't stop until the ice cubes gather at my lips and I've swallowed every last drop. "Ahh. Damn, that's good." I drop the glass back down to the counter and glance up at Mac.

His jawbone could crack nuts, but he still manages to open his mouth far enough to growl, "Jesus." And then he's coming toward me again, wicked smolder firmly in place.

I guess Mac likes sweet tea. Even if he doesn't like drinking it himself.

"SO THAT'S why Cookie says it's not bragging when she tells people Savannah's the best town south of the Mason-Dixon line. If Sherman himself couldn't bear to burn any of that beauty, it must mean something."

Mac runs the back of his hand over my nipple while I shovel Chinese takeout into my face. It was his idea to eat naked and I was so starving I didn't brook much of an argument. I did draw the line at sitting cross-legged with my lady town on display while I fumble with my chopsticks, though. Having a sheet there to catch any flying bites of hot food is basic common sense. Likewise, he's got a sheet draped carelessly across his lap. His back is to my headboard and he's picking at some bland steamed affair in between letting his hands roam my body. I'm sharing stories from back home while trying not to shiver at his touch or peek underneath the sheet. Again.

He doesn't respond much, but I can tell he's listening from his sporadic hums and small upturns of his lips. So I keep talking.

"She'll brag to just about anyone about her beloved town and that inn. Of course, I brag about the inn too. I can't help it. It's the most charming spot on earth."

"You grow up in it?" He asks, lifting his gaze from my bare breasts and meeting my eyes.

"The inn? Kind of. I mean Mama and Daddy's place is just at the outskirts of town where they could get more property, but I've probably spent just as many nights at the Violette. My great granddaddy owned the building before passing it down. It's really two townhouses put together, one for family and one for guests."

Mac nods and brings a snap pea to his mouth. I watch him chew, the memory of what he did not thirty minutes ago with that mouth making me shiver with renewed arousal. The man is skilled. At many things.

I open my mouth to say one more thing about the inn, but something else comes out instead. "Don't you get sick of eating all that healthy stuff?"

He pauses mid-chew and looks at me before swallowing. Then he snags his glass of water from the bedside table and takes a sip. "Never really thought about it."

My jaw drops open. "How is that possible?" I swing a hand out toward my bedroom window. "This city has about six million restaurants and probably twice as many bakeries and dessert places. You never think to yourself, *man, a big cheeseburger sounds great just about now?*"

"That shit's not good for you."

I look at him like he just gave me whiplash. "That ain't even close to being the point." As if to prove it, I shove another bite of kung pao chicken in my face.

He watches my mouth and I curse myself for focusing so much on being a smartass that I forgot to try maintaining a sexy vibe.

Mac sets his takeout container on the table with his water and pulls me by my hips so I have to straddle him to avoid tipping over the side of the bed. I keep my grip on my dinner, though, and grab a piece of chicken with the chopsticks.

"Here." I hold it out to him. "Try it. I'll make you a convert."

He leans forward and snaps his teeth over the bite of chicken, making all parts south clench. He chews it while holding my eyes and I can feel the effect my squirming is having on him.

"It's not that I don't like it. I'm just careful with my body."

I raise a brow and deliberately take my time running my eyes over his bare chest. "And, let me be the first to tell you, it's very much appreciated."

He smirks and his hips twitch, making my eyes want to roll back into my head.

I decide to venture a bit further down this road while the opportunity presents itself. "Have you always looked like this?" I lean forward and set my own meal down so I can give Mac all my focus.

"No. Not until my late twenties, I guess."

"So you were a total slob until then?" I shake my head. "Shame."

He pinches my ass and I yelp. He's being playful again and I freaking love it.

"My pops was in an accident. Made me re-evaluate some things."

My insides still and I try not to let it show. But when I do some counting in my head, the timing doesn't reconcile with the article I read. I distinctly remember that incident with his father being from three or four years ago, not ten or more. I don't want anything to get in the way of Mac opening up to me so I just wait for him to continue.

He doesn't.

I decide to take a chance.

"What kind of accident?"

"Car accident." Mac swipes a hand down his face and I'm afraid for a second I went too far. But then his eyes come back to mine. "He was helping me haul some stuff for a job I was doing over in Jersey where we lived. Roads were icy and a car came too fast in the other direction. Truck flipped. I got thrown free and he rolled six times before it was done." He brings a finger up to the angry scar along the side of his nose, the one I've seen a hundred times when I close my eyes. "I got a souvenir. My pops got... more."

My hand comes up before I know what I'm doing and my fingers tremble as they settle over the warm skin of his hand at his face. "Mac."

He turns his hand so his fingers weave with mine. "It's okay, Poppy."

I can't believe he's comforting me instead of the other

way around. It's clear from the faraway look he blinks away that he was right back in the moment of the accident.

Any normal person would ask the logical follow-up question. *Is your dad okay?* But I already know the answer, even though I wish I didn't.

So I do the only thing I can and lean forward to place my lips on his.

MAC SPENDS THE NIGHT, making this our second sleepover in as many nights and making this a definite *thing*. Add to that the sharing he did last night and I'm flying high on a flight to relationship central. Now I've just got to remember not to get too far ahead of myself.

Which is pretty freaking hard to do when Mac decides the thing our Saturday needs is more together time and a trip to Chelsea Market, where I told him I've never been. From what I know of Mac, it's the furthest thing from his scene, so he's clearly doing it just for me.

To make me happy.

That in and of itself is enough to have me skipping across the sky on a unicorn pooping out rainbows. Yeah, sorry. Gross.

He doesn't even give me a hard time when I insist on stopping at every one of the six bakeries just to make sure I didn't miss anything. And I pretend I don't notice the gawks and flirty looks coming his way from every third woman we pass. The others are obviously getting really good sex at home or they're blind.

We're each carrying a shopping bag in one hand and holding hands with the other like one of those blissfully disgusting couples people live to hate. I'm talking his ear off about the magazine when he stops without warning. I almost drop my bag as my body goes flying back where our hands are still connected.

I'm about to ask if he's okay when I see he's clearly not. Four weeks ago, I would have been at a loss to determine the meaning of his current expression, but now I spot it for what I'm sure it is—a mix of anger and panic. So I follow his eyeline and see his attention is caught on a slick-suited woman waiting for her coffee order and talking on a cell phone. She looks to be in her late fifties with perfectly coifed dark hair and a posture that smacks of good breeding.

"Mac." I squeeze his hand but I'm not sure he even feels it. I'm about to say something—anything—when the woman turns and does a double take before taking her phone from her ear and carefully returning it to her purse. She watches Mac, who stands next to me like the tension rolling off him is freezing him in place.

Then her gaze slides to me and she plucks her coffee off the counter and practically glides over to where we stand in the middle of the busy concourse.

"Darling, isn't this a lovely surprise?"

She's probably five-foot-ten in her heels, but Mac still has more than half a head on her. I'm utterly shocked when she gets close and tilts her head, clearly offering her cheek for a kiss. Who the hell is this, and why would she think in a million years that Mac is a cheek kisser?

He proves me right when he doesn't move a muscle to comply.

"Mother." The word escapes through clenched teeth.

I swallow a cough. This is Mac's mama? This news requires a next-level inspection, which I attempt to be real subtle about. There's no doubt she's beautiful, with delicate features and stunning gray eyes. I don't know that I've ever seen makeup this flawless, and if she's had work done, I can't tell. But no amount of makeup or surgery can hide the hint of disappointment when Mac doesn't kiss her.

I'm feeling at a bit of a loss because I don't know the first thing about this woman, except for the fact that she makes Mac upset. Which, let's face it, is enough to make me hate her on sight.

She sighs a beleaguered sigh and I want to take Mac home and feed him carbs. But there's no moving this mountain.

"You didn't return my calls. Elle said she'd pass on my message as well, but I see she must have forgotten." She reaches out to pat the hand that's holding the shopping bag and I can see Mac curl it into a fist in response. Either she doesn't notice or she pretends not to. "Sterling and I were so looking forward to getting together while we're in town. It's been too long, don't you agree?"

Mac still doesn't move or respond. What happened to the guy who has no qualms with walking away from a conversation he hates? Come on, Mac, let's go!

I squeeze his hand again and it seems to kickstart his brain.

"We have to go," he finally says and starts moving again, pulling me with him. His feet are unusually clumsy.

But the woman has the nerve to step in front of me. I'll give her this, her sense of self-preservation is keen given that she chose me instead of the big guy.

I paste on an uncomfortable smile. "Excuse me." But she grabs my arm in a grip way too firm for a lady so skinny.

"You must be Mac's... friend." She smiles and it's as tight as Ryan Reynolds' ass—but in a bad way.

Mac strikes like a rattlesnake and wedges himself between us, looking down his nose at her.

His voice is pure caged lion. "I said we had to go. Now get your hand off her."

His mother releases a tense, humorless laugh but only tightens her grip. Her features turn pinched and what I mistook for beauty reveals itself as just a pretense for the vitriol lying underneath. "I'm just trying to meet your friend. Since when can't a mother know her own son's girlfriend?"

My eyes are darting so fast between the two of them I'm afraid I'm gonna strain something. And I really wish she'd let go of me. I'm gonna have a frickin' bruise from this witch.

Mac's nostrils flare and his face darkens even further, but he doesn't answer her. Instead, he curls his fingers around her wrist and starts squeezing.

She yelps like she's been slapped and releases my arm. Which is complete bullshit because Mac has grabbed my arm more than once and he never uses a fraction of the power I know he's capable of.

As soon as my arm is free, he stalks toward the exit, me scampering after him to keep up and not dislocate my damn shoulder.

His mother's voice slams into our backs just before we reach the exit.

"You're heartless, just like he was!"

Mac doesn't look back. He doesn't stop walking. And he doesn't say another word the entire way home.

I don't see him again for a week.

"The best and worst thing about family is there's no escaping it."
– Cookie Rutledge

THE CHAMPAGNE CORKS pop and the room fills with cheers and whoops.

WHL is officially approved and I am a real, live, bonafide creative director of a national publication. I can't stop repeating it in my head—maybe one of these times I'll start to believe it.

Naveed hands me a glass and I take it with a smile, then clink mine with his.

"Here's to the future, Miss Peach." He grins at me, giving me the dimple, and I can't help smiling in return.

The official announcement was just made and our crew of *WHL* faithfuls has gathered for an impromptu celebration in one of the conference rooms on Athena's floor.

Looking around, I'm amazed at what the small group of us have accomplished in such a short time. But this is only the beginning.

There's endless work ahead as we form teams and shuffle offices and then get to work on the first few issues. My stomach is swirling with excitement and nerves as the reality tries to settle in. I'm heading an entire department, complete with directors, editors, and staff designers. Thus far, it's been a complete skeleton crew, but pretty soon things are going to get nuts.

And I'm happy. I'm so freaking happy.

Really.

Okay, I'm miserable. But I *want* to be happy, so that has to count for something.

I mentally curse Mac's mother for the thousandth time this week. Because she's the one I hold responsible for Mac going off the grid and making it impossible for me to fully immerse myself in this incredible life victory.

The first thing I did when Kate marched into my office to tell me the good news was, of course, hug the crap out of her. Then I texted Iris because the girl wouldn't stop blowing up my phone this week and I needed to throw her a bone.

But when my finger hovered above Mac's contact, a knot immediately settled in the pit of my stomach and I called his mom some filthy names before shoving the phone back in my purse and heading to the celebration.

"We're cutting out early for happy hour." Naveed tilts his head to the door. "Come on, Pop-Tart."

I narrow my eyes at him. He knows how much I despise that nickname. As usual, he ignores me.

"I don't know, Naveed." I shift uncomfortably in my heels. "Now that the reality is setting in, there's so much work to be done."

He puts a hand to the small of my back and nods, steering me toward the door. "Yes, and it can all wait until Monday."

I sidestep and scramble for an excuse. "How about if I meet you there. I just have a couple calls to make."

His lips purse, but he's distracted by a guy from circulation trying to top off his champagne.

"Okay, but you better be there." He points at me and I force a bright smile.

"Who am I to turn down cocktails?"

The amount of work ahead of me is monumental, but it truly can wait until Monday. We have almost four months until the first issue goes live and much of the work for that one is already under our belts. This is a marathon, and it's undoubtedly best to approach it as such, which means not burning myself out in the first mile.

I exchange a few more congratulations and make a point to thank Athena for her hard work championing us to the board, and then I head back to my office.

But it's too quiet and the air is too still. The room has no personality, as I didn't think it was worth wasting the energy on a temporary space, but now the bare walls and bland carpet make me want to wince. I crave vibrancy and life, not this cold, stale box. I vow to myself to make my new office warm and inviting and lousy with color.

I pack up my things and pull out my phone again. There's a congratulatory text from Iris and a new email from Cookie with a link to a nasty review of the inn on Yelp.

Before I can think too much about it, I hit the inn's number.

"Violette Inn, this is Cookie Rutledge speaking. How can I help you today?"

"Is this the world-famous Violette Inn? The one that poisons unsuspecting guests with tainted biscuits?"

She clucks her tongue and launches right in. "Don't even get me started. I told that vile woman my biscuits are not gluten-free, but it didn't stop her from gorging herself on half a dozen of the darn things, did it? I can't be responsible for her gut exploding like an overfilled Macy's Day Parade balloon. I even offered her cornbread, and you know I don't make that in the mornings."

I wanted to sigh at the sound of her voice, even with the exasperated tone.

"I'm mentally composing my rebuttal to the review as we speak."

"I appreciate that, darlin'. Now, enough about that gluttonous ignoramus. Tell me about you."

I play with the zipper on my laptop bag. I can picture her perfectly, pulling up a stool in the kitchen to give me all her attention. "Well, let's see." I pretend to think on it. "Work is going really well. We just got approval on a big project so that's a nice feather in our cap." I have yet to confess that my job here wasn't exactly the sure thing I'd led them all to believe it was. But at least now it's all on the level.

"I'm still waiting for a copy of the first issue of this new version of *Warbey's*. When is it coming out? Did I tell you

Bunny is hording all her back issues, thinking they'll be collector's items?"

Of course she is.

"You'll have to sit tight till January, I'm afraid."

"Well, that's all right. Patience is natural when you reach my age." This makes me want to laugh because Cookie's never exactly been known for her patience, no matter what her age. "You still enjoying the work?"

"I am." I don't tell her about how it's fixing to get ten times crazier.

"Why don't you sound so sure about that?"

My head snaps up. "I do! I am. It's not that."

"Ah, then this has something to do with the reason Bobby Lee is walking around like someone ran over his dog, I reckon."

I groan and close one eye. "Maybe?"

"Listen, sugar, you know I'll never make you talk about things you prefer keepin' to yourself, but I'm always here for you. You just remember that."

My ugly office swims in my vision with the threatening tears.

"I know."

"Then you also know your granddaddy's shotgun is still tucked under my bed gathering dust."

I cough out a laugh. "I do now."

She's silent for a minute, letting me decide where our conversation will head. So, of course, I spill my guts out. Well, mostly anyway.

I tell her about Mac and me. About how he's this magnetic mix of profoundly deliberate acts and guarded secrets and how inspiring his work is and how he treats me like I'm a gift to be cherished in one moment and completely shuts me out the next. And I tell her how I want to save him and lean into him at the same time and how I'm scared that I may have already given him pieces of myself I can't get back.

And Cookie listens as I relate the bizarre encounter with his mother at Chelsea Market and Mac's disappearing act immediately afterward.

All the while, I can feel her soothing presence across the miles that separate us, making me wonder what took me so damn long to confide in her.

When I'm finally done talking, she breaks it down. "It sounds to me like what this boy needs is family."

I swallow as the simple truth of her words settles over me.

"I think you're right, Cookie. But I can't force the man to talk to me. I can't even find him, for glory's sake." I close my eyes as helpless frustration pushes at my chest. "He's not answering his phone, his agent doesn't know where he is, and his assistant won't call me back." Not that I'm surprised by Jonathan giving me the cold shoulder, but still.

She tuts, telling me my negativity won't stand with her. "Well then, you're just gonna have to get creative, aren't you?"

As usual, she's right.

OLD DOMINION'S "Written in the Stars" drifts over the cool air of my living room as I settle in with renewed energy. My fingers tap on the keyboard, typing in the search criteria for the community youth program and its various iterations. I've already combed over the website we included in the *WHL* article, but I'm looking for something else.

I key in "at-risk youth New Jersey blacksmith" and there it is.

A simple click takes me to a description from the early two-thousands.

I don't know why it never occurred to me to ask the very first question I proposed to Naveed on the day we prepped me for my interview with Mac.

What made you want to become a blacksmith?

It seems so glaringly obvious now, but if Mac's head is wrapped up in whatever happened with his family in the past, then the past is where he might have gone.

I pour over the short piece in the small neighborhood paper, then enter the phone number into my phone and press the green button.

My call is answered after several rings.

"Bastion Forge."

"Hi. Um, I'm calling to see if you still run apprenticeship programs for aspiring blacksmiths." I'm determined to fake it till I make it.

I can hear banging in the background and a loud hissing sound. "Uh, you talking about the youth program?"

"Yes. Is that still running?" My heart rate kicks up and I push my laptop aside so I can stand up.

"Nah. Sorry. The last guy who ran that shut it down about... eh... maybe four years ago now."

My heart hammers at his words and I start pacing my

living room. Damn. But the timing lines up perfectly with Mac's dad's second accident. This could still be what I'm looking for.

"Do you know, uh, what happened to the guy? The one running the program?"

"Mac? Yeah, um, he's some big-shot furniture designer now over in Manhattan."

White flares in my vision at the sound of his name, but it's looking like this is another dead end.

"He still comes around every once in a while—he's got some property up here—but I haven't seen him in probably, oh, six months, maybe."

I close my eyes tight and still my steps.

"Um, what did you say your name was?"

"Paul. Why?"

I pull in a deep breath. "Paul, I'm wondering if maybe you can help me out with something."

I'VE NEVER BEEN to New Jersey and I'm beginning to think there's a reason for that. I'm sure there are lovely areas to visit in the garden state—perhaps even ones with actual gardens—but the spot where the bus drops me is not one of them. I clutch my purse to me like the blatant outsider I am and hurry to the first open shop I see. Luckily, it's broad daylight.

The cashier doesn't give me a second glance as I pull out my phone and order an Uber. I buy a coke and watch out the clouded glass of the door until my ride pulls up.

I don't chat with the driver, my nerves causing me to make mincemeat of my nails with my teeth as we wind our way out of the town center, past boarded up and graffitied storefronts, and out onto a decidedly less urban road. The drive only takes about twenty minutes, but it's enough time to finish completely ruining any chance of a manicure in my near future while simultaneously allowing my stomach to eat itself from the inside out.

Gravel crunches under the tires as the car slows to a stop in front of a small single-story house with faded siding and a detached garage. The breath I feel like I've been holding for the last week whooshes from my lungs as I catch sight of a familiar black pick-up parked in front of the garage.

Thank God.

I throw a quick thank you to the driver and get out, still gripping my purse to my chest. Now that I'm here, I have not the first clue what I'm going to say.

But it's too late to second guess myself as the car pulls away, leaving me on the blacktop in front of Mac's dad's house. The house where he grew up, where he read his first sci-fi book and got into trouble as a teenager.

And he's here, somewhere behind that door.

I pull in a fortifying breath and remind myself that I'm Poppy James, slayer of magazine empires and badass modern woman who makes mere mortals cry. My shoulders fall back as I stride right up the front steps and pound on the door like a woman who's owed something. Because I am.

When there's no answer, I try again, this time harder

and louder. Mac is here, dammit, and I'm not leaving until I talk to him, if only for him to tell me to go to hell.

It takes another round of banging before I hear the shift of the deadbolt releasing and the knob turns.

My first glimpse of Mac has me blinking as it hits me in the chest. There's a distinct pallor to his cheeks and dark circles ring the undersides of his eyes. He's both beautiful and heartbreaking at the same time and I feel tears choke my throat when I look at him.

"Poppy?" His voice is rusty with that razor blade edge I remember so well. It's like he hasn't used it in the week since I've seen him.

He doesn't need to say anything else, though, because the man who keeps himself so guarded can't hide the relief in his eyes at seeing me on his doorstep. Intentional or not, he's told me everything I need to know so I don't hesitate when I barrel into him and wrap my arms around his waist.

He doesn't try to push me away, and even if he did, I'd hang onto him like a spider monkey and not let go. I reckon I'm a believer in immersion therapy.

"What are you doing here?" His warm breath fans over my hair.

"You needed me." It's the truth, so I don't beat around the bush.

It takes him a few seconds, but he finally runs a hand down my back and I can feel his shoulders start to release. Only when I'm sure he's not going to run or kick me out do I allow him to pull back. His thumb goes to my chin and he tilts my face up, his eyes scanning every inch like he needs to reassure himself of something.

"How did you get here?"

"Bus. Uber. Your friend Paul." I shrug, not feeling like giving a long explanation. I'd rather just look at him and hug him.

He shakes his head, his brows drawing together, but I don't let him ask another question.

"Are you okay?"

I immediately regret asking when his eyes shutter and he takes a step back.

"Mac?"

"You shouldn't be here. This isn't a nice neighborhood." He assumes his gruff tone, as if it's going to scare me away. "I'll drive you back." He moves to usher me right back out the door but I put a hard hand to his chest.

"Not so fast. I'm not going anywhere until you talk to me."

His jaw sets, but two can play at this game.

"I get that something spooked you and you've been dealing in your own way, but I care about you and I'm not letting you disappear back into your manly fortress of solitude. You need me, whether you want to admit it or not, and I'm not leaving." I pat my purse. "I've got a purse full of snacks so I'm prepared to wait you out, Angus McKinley."

His head shifts back on his neck in surprise. I doubt anyone has ever called him on his defense mechanisms before, but there's a first time for everything.

I stalk right on past him into the house and don't stop until I'm standing in the middle of the living room. The completely *empty* living room.

There's not a lick of furniture in the place. In fact, there's not even carpet or floor coverings of any kind. A glance around the kitchen and a side room confirms that the house is a shell.

"You've been staying here all week?" My voice cracks as it goes high.

He glares at me, but I can take it.

If Cookie were here she'd smack him upside the head, and I can't say I'm not tempted to as well.

"Is there even electricity?" Not that I really need an answer to that question when I breathe in the thick, musty air around us.

He marches up to me and puts a hand between my shoulder blades, using it to try leading me out the door, but I'm having none of it. I duck down and skitter backward.

"Like I said, I'm not going anywhere until you start talking, so if you want me gone, I suggest you work on formulating a damn good opening remark." And, with that, I plonk my ass down on the dirty floor and prepare for battle.

Only I'm not fighting to win. I'm fighting to set him free.

TWENTY-FOUR

"Good luck to anyone who tries arguin' with a Southern woman who knows she's right."
— Cookie Rutledge

MAC SPENDS the first hour pretending I'm not there. In fact, at one point he even snatches his keys and stalks out to his truck like he's gonna leave me here, but he makes it a whole three seconds behind the wheel in the driveway before he climbs back out and slams the door behind him. That's followed by a little bit of driveway pacing—which I enjoy from my vantagepoint behind the dusty front window—and then a healthy slam of the front door behind him as he prowls back into the house.

From there, he stands with stiff shoulders staring out into the overgrown backyard and ignoring my existence.

I entertain myself by surfing the internet and nibbling

on some Chex Mix, all the while humming a few of my favorite songs.

After a while, I get bored, so I turn on some music and open my laptop.

I can feel Mac sneaking glances at me as he continues the silent treatment. He takes brooding to a whole new level, but there's no way I'm giving up.

Like Cookie said, he needs family, and if he doesn't have a blood one to speak of, I can be what he needs.

I'm not saying I expect him to break down and confess all his secrets to me or declare his undying love for me, but he needs to know not everyone is going to disappoint him. Because it's clear he's had more than his fair share of that.

Mac has had his turn of trying to push me away, and now I need to make it clear I'm not that easy to scare.

Okay, fine, I *am* easy to scare, but not when I have my mind set on something—not when it's this important.

"This one's my favorite," I say, acting like we're in the middle of a conversation.

The song is by Old Dominion, of course, and it couldn't be more perfect for where we are right now—where *he* is right now. The lyrics to "One Man Band" pierce the humid air of the room and it's like the song is offering him a choice.

Does he want to go it alone for the rest of his life, or does he want to see what could happen if he opens the door and lets me—someone—anyone—in to try and see how much better it can be when you don't have to bear the load all on your own?

It doesn't work, in case you're wondering. He ignores me, ignores the song, and goes out to the backyard, making sure he lets the back door slam his farewell.

Now, I'm no idiot. I know he could make me leave anytime he wants. He's proven before that he can carry me around like I'm nothing more than ten-pound sack of potatoes which—let me assure you—does wonderful things for a girl's self-image.

We both know he's fighting with himself, not with me. All that remains to be seen is which side of him wins out and how long it'll take.

I scroll down and click send on an email to one of the web designers at Warbey and almost jump out of my skin at the unexpected sound of Mac's voice behind me.

"You always listen to country?"

I think over my answer before I speak. "I listen to a little bit of everything, but I suppose more country than not. If it's got a beat I can dance to, though, I don't discriminate."

I don't need to look at him to know he's remembering the night we met. Good. At least my humiliation is serving a noble purpose.

I hear him inch closer and can't help thinking how ironic it is that this mountain of a man feels the need to approach human interaction like a mouse entering a lion's den. The rules have changed and nothing makes sense because the beast isn't the one doing the terrorizing. He's the one feeling all the terror.

"Old Dominion is definitely my favorite band, though. We saw them in concert last year in Atlanta and I swear Iris had to hold me back from climbing on stage."

He grunts at that and I have to bite my lip so I don't smile. So I'm playing a little dirty—whatever it takes, right?

Another step and he's closer still.

"My mother is a viper and an opportunist," he says with not a spec of a segue in sight.

I'm careful not to let my spine stiffen. I'm unused to the part of the predator, but I reckon that's what I represent right now to Mac. We'll have to work on that, though, because that role doesn't suit me at all. I prefer to think of myself as the plucky go-getter instead.

"She looks for vulnerabilities, angles she can work, and then she infiltrates and she doesn't care who she destroys in the process."

I swallow past the sudden lump in my throat. His mother sounds like a disease instead of a human being. Possibly even a sociopath. I can't say I've ever met one of those before, and I'm not itching to.

"Her husband is under investigation by the federal government. If I had to guess I'd say money laundering. Her back is to the wall and she's getting desperate." His boots scuff the floor as he takes another step closer. "She'll use you to get to me." His words are like a shot in the chest. "And she'll play dirtier than you can possibly imagine."

And now it all makes sense. Mac getting us away from her before she learned my name, him building up this distance between us, him running away to New Jersey.

He wasn't protecting *himself*.

He was protecting *me*.

Of course he was.

I twist at the waist to watch him. "What does she want from you?"

"What everyone from that world wants. Money."

I turn my body so I'm facing him, my legs still crossed on the grimy floor. "No offense, Mac, but she looked like she had plenty of money to me." I don't mention that he's kinda part of that world too, by both association and his income from his business.

He stands in the middle of the floor, his shoulders tense, and shakes his head. "They always do. Keeping up appearances is almost more important than the money itself."

"And she thinks you'll just give her all your money?" I don't even want to think about how much he must have that a woman who looks and dresses like her would come chasing.

He coughs out something approaching a laugh, but it misses the mark by a mile. "I'd give her every dime if I could."

Huh? "I don't understand."

He runs a tired hand over his face. "It's complicated."

"Sounds like it."

When he doesn't say anything else, I try letting the silence settle for a minute. It doesn't last long.

"Is her husband really named *Sterling?*"

His lips quirk and I want to sing with relief. He shakes his head.

"Fuckin' stupid name."

"Fuckin' stupid name," I agree.

He meets my eyes and I can see he's still fighting with himself. "She's gonna find out who you are."

My heart hammers, not because I'm afraid of his mama, but because he's referring to a future—to a moment in time following this awful week and this suffocating house.

I stand and take a step toward him. "Let her."

He watches my face, eyes darting to every corner.

"I've got a closet full of boots and high heels and I ain't afraid to use 'em."

THINGS WEREN'T SUDDENLY all hunky-dory after my declaration that I could kick his mama's ass, but they were at least on their way to being better. About two minutes after that, my stomach growled loud enough to echo around the empty room and Mac took me out to another almost silent lunch at a dive that sold killer tacos.

Then, without discussing it, we drove back into Manhattan, the radio playing the whole way. By the time we hit the Lincoln tunnel, my hand was on his thigh and my fingers threaded with his. And I knew everything was going to be okay.

"I can't believe I forgot to tell you my big news!"

I drop my purse on Mac's kitchen island while he sifts through the pile of mail he picked up on our way in.

"You are looking at the official creative director of the brand new *WHL* magazine." I twist a finger in my cheek for some jaunty emphasis.

He looks up from the mail and arches those lush eyebrows. "Impressive. Congratulations."

"Thank you, sir." I smile at him.

His hands flatten on the counter as he takes in my cheerful expression. "Did you want to..." He doesn't finish.

"Did I want to what?"

He scratches the back of his neck. "Isn't this the kind of thing people like to... I don't know... celebrate?"

I love how he asks this like he's not an actual person. I hide my smile as best I can.

"Yes, I reckon it is."

Mac steps back from the counter and glances around as if searching for something. "Okay. We should probably..." he trails off again.

"Go to a themed restaurant?" I bite my cheek to keep from laughing when he holds his breath. "I totally agree. Preferably one where the staff will sing to me."

He lets out the breath and narrows his eyes at me. "You're fucking with me."

My mouth spreads in a wicked grin. "I am."

"So, you don't want to celebrate. Or you already did." His jaw ticks. "I wasn't here."

I'm not going to let him beat himself up for whatever he thinks he did to me.

"Yes, we celebrated at the office and, no, you didn't miss anything. And, while I might pay good money to see the staff at Benihana try to sing happy birthday to *you*, I have no desire to subject myself to anything of the kind, thank you very much."

This earns me a scowl.

"If you insist on helping me celebrate, though, I'll let you kiss me." I bite my lip and his eyes go straight there. But he doesn't move from behind the island. It's as if he's not giving himself permission to put the last week behind us. So I do it for him and walk right over until my chest is pressed to his torso and my palms are flat on his pecs.

I blink up at him and that's all it takes. His lips crush mine and he's kissing me like it's been a year, not a week. He sucks on my bottom lip and then his tongue is sliding against mine, making me sigh into his mouth. I get his hands on my hips where he flexes his fingers so tight I might have marks tomorrow, but I don't care. He's claiming me, telling me with his lips and tongue and teeth how he missed me—all the things he can't bring himself to say with words. How he hates what separated us and how he's not sure how to navigate what lies ahead. And I hear it all, understand it all, and return every stroke and nip to tell him it's okay and that we'll figure it out together.

We're both panting when we finally pull apart. He squeezes my ass and I lean into him, grabbing onto his biceps so I don't fall over. God, I missed the feel of him beneath my hands, all that taut, hot skin and rock-hard muscle—not to mention the ink I haven't yet traced with my tongue like I've been meaning to.

I burrow into his chest and hear the beating of his heart where my ear presses against his t-shirt. We stay like that for a few minutes, content in the security of one another until our heart rates slow.

"This is the best celebration ever," I murmur into his right pec.

His chest hums. "I'm sure you've had better."

"Not true." I smile against the cotton of his shirt. "Although my high school graduation party might come in at a close second. It's kinda hard to beat an impromptu battle of the bands between a Rascal Flatts cover band and Savannah's top zydeco quartet."

Mac pulls back and looks down his crooked nose at me. "I'm afraid to ask."

I nod. "You should be."

I release him, backing up to hoist myself up onto his

island and then set his mail pile on my lap so he has to touch me while going through it. I hand him the first letter and he rips it open, his eyes still on me and his lips curled in a half-grin. He gives really good grin. It may even be better than his growl. Maybe.

"Don't you ever celebrate anything? Like maybe selling a half-million-dollar chair or something?"

He tosses the letter aside and grabs another one from my lap, completely ignoring my exaggeration of his prices.

"Not really. Never been much of the type."

"Never?" This makes me sad for him.

He does one of his signature half-shrugs. "Barely graduated high school. When I did, my pops and I sat at the kitchen table and had a beer together."

My nose scrunches up at that. "Seriously?"

His eyes come to mine again. "Yeah. It was perfect, actually. It was his way of telling me I was a man, just like him."

I hum, considering that while Mac goes back to the mail.

I want to ask what his mother thought about that, but I'm not sure I want to know. She doesn't strike me as the kind of woman who'd celebrate a graduation with a Bud Light, though.

So, instead, I ask about his dad.

"Were you close to him?"

He doesn't look up from the envelope in his hand when he answers with a simple, "He was my best friend."

My heart constricts. "Can I ask?" I don't finish because I don't want to lie and pretend I don't know how he died, but I still want to know what happened.

His jaw tenses, but it's the only indication that he's bothered by my question.

"Accident. Passed two and a half years ago."

"I'm sorry." I lay a hand on his forearm to stop him from moving. I'm not just extending my sympathies, I'm apologizing for asking the question.

When he looks up at me, his eyes don't look sad, though. They look troubled.

"Promise me you'll tell me immediately if my mother tries to contact you. At work, at home, at the fucking grocery. Promise me you won't talk to her and you'll tell me right away."

My blood races through my veins at the abrupt change in topic.

"I promise." My voice is almost breathless.

He watches me for another second before he nods and goes back to his mail.

But his words from earlier tread through my mind. "*She doesn't care who she destroys in the process.*" It has me thinking Mac wasn't changing the subject at all—he was connecting all sorts of dots instead.

TWENTY-FIVE

*"Secrets are like gas. They all come out one way or another
eventually."*
— Cookie Rutledge

THE NEXT FEW weeks fly by in a whirl of meetings, new
hires, and moving crews creating a whole new *WHL* art
wing on the ninth floor. All our social media accounts are
up and running and the website is already showing sneak
peeks of what's to come in this new era of *WHL*.

My transition into the role of creative director is made a
tiny bit easier by the fact that my predecessor, the creative
director of the outdated *Warbey's Home Living*, announced
his intention to retire even before the magazine was put on
the chopping block. He's just wrapping up the last issue
and then he's off to Maine to run a bed and breakfast with
his wife.

But just because I'm not viewed as a cannibalistic

usurper doesn't mean the art department staff isn't wary. Or bitchy. Or bastardy. I still hear the whispers and I know I'm facing an uphill battle to prove I deserve this position. New York Poppy has been working overtime, strutting around the office in immaculate suits and sky-high heels with perfect freaking grammar, a kill-or-be-killed attitude, and not a trace of Georgia accent to be found.

These people don't know my work first-hand. Yet. But I take it as a positive sign when I stroll past an open laptop two weeks after the official start of *WHL* to see two web designers checking out the work I did on *South by South Journal* last year. That rebrand boosted circulation by forty percent and saved the magazine from going under. I have to remain confident that I'll win these people over.

That doesn't mean, however, that I'm any more comfortable bringing my relationship with Mac out in the open.

It doesn't escape my attention that the prototype copies we have lying around are almost always opened to the spread of him in his forge looking all stupid hot and making me want to publicly claim him as my man—either that or go to his studio over lunch and jump him. I keep telling myself that they can look all they want, as long as he's in *my* bed several nights a week. Or I'm in his. Or we're on one of his couches. Or his kitchen island. You get the point.

We haven't had the "relationship talk," and there's really no need. I'm trying to keep my heart from getting ahead of itself, which is a tall order, but self-preservation is a must. We're not at a place yet where we're inseparable or we keep tabs on each other twenty-four/seven, but we've found a comfortable groove where we both know we mean something to each other and I'm not left wondering if I'm just one of many. It goes without saying that with my incessant talking and oversharing, Mac's in no doubt as to whether I'm seeing anyone else.

Since I went to New Jersey and brought him back to Manhattan, there's been an unspoken cementing of trust between us. Mac has been slowly opening up about himself and his past and I hold each small revelation like it's something precious. But, of course, he does it in his own Mac way.

He chose the cereal aisle of Morton Williams to tell me that he was introduced to blacksmithing when his dad told him he could either choose between that, auto repair, or jail—promising that he'd turn Mac into the cops himself for busting up the window of a car when he was seventeen if he didn't learn to make himself useful. Mac chose blacksmithing because fire and hammering on shit sounded more exciting than power tools—or prison.

It was in the middle of a him putting my bookshelf together in my living room that Mac told me how his dad got his mom pregnant when she was a rich co-ed slumming it in Jersey at a house party with some of her friends. And how she thought it would be exciting to run away and play house with a good-looking working-class son of an immigrant who didn't have two pennies to rub together but was madly in love with her.

And I was making a pitcher of sweet tea in Mac's kitchen when he shared that he went to live with his mother when his parents divorced and that the house filled with expensive furniture and staff was the loneliest place he'd ever been in his life. And that being disowned by his mother when he chose to go live with his dad at fourteen was worth losing any amount of money or opportunity if it meant getting out of that house.

So, yeah, there's no need for a relationship talk between Mac and me. I'm pretty sure I know where I stand, even if I'm still trying to guard my heart.

My cell phone buzzes and I'm not surprised to see a text from Elle.

ELLE

Tell me it's okay to spend $100 on fruit.

I laugh as I plop down in my office chair and toe my heels off. The door is closed so nobody will see me, thank God. I'm tuckered out from keeping up what Mac likes to call my shark persona.

I've come to look forward to Elle's calls and texts in these last few weeks. I've also tried to relax myself around her, to let the accent slide and let some of my... quirkier attributes out to play, but it's still kind of hard when she's so polished and perfect.

When Mac reappeared in Manhattan, she offered me her firstborn child as repayment for finding him. She'd been trying to contact him that entire week and was worried he was going to miss a contractual obligation she'd arranged for some of his work. I declined her offer for the kid but took her up on drinks out instead. We've been chatting on and off since.

That depends. Is it covered in chocolate?

ELLE

No. It's imported ginseng fruit from China.
You'd have to see it to believe it. It literally
has a baby's face on it.

She attaches a picture and I laugh out loud. It really does (look it up if you don't believe me).

I don't think I'll ever forgive you if you
DON'T buy that.

I knew I could count on you! 😏 What are
you doing Saturday?

I chew on my lip as I decide how to respond. I heard Mac play a message from Elle this week about a charity auction on Saturday. It was the same one they referenced weeks ago at the photo shoot. I was sure he'd mention it— maybe even invite me—but he hasn't said a word, and I keep putting off asking about it.

Since we started going out, we really haven't spent all that much time, well, going *out*. Sure, we pop in for a bite to eat at a random sushi restaurant or we grab some groceries at a corner mart, but most of our time spent together is either at his place or mine. And I know it's my own fault —I do.

I don't try to arrange outings or drinks out with my friends because I'm still so afraid of backlash from work if anyone finds out. And I keep telling myself it's no big deal that we stay in—it just means more hot sex for me. And Mac doesn't even like people, anyway.

Well, maybe that's a little harsh. He's just not comfort- able standing around making small talk or pretending to put up with people's bullshit. He says that's what Elle and Jonathan are there for. From anyone else, it would come off as elitist and rude, but from Mac it just sounds practical.

And, besides, he can make people uncomfortable. The fact that he doesn't say much of anything causes other people to come to the conclusion that they did something wrong or it makes them feel like they have to work hard to fill in the silence.

But Mac is who he is. He got to be this way from looking at the game from all angles and deciding that if his words and actions don't come from a genuine place, they serve no purpose. To him it's like lying. And I've got to respect that. As long as he doesn't keep the warmth and goodness lying beneath that exterior hidden from me, it's all good.

I look back at the phone and see that Elle has messaged a follow-up consisting of a bunch of question marks.

It's not like I can go to the charity thing with Mac anyway; there will be photographers and probably more than a few celebrities. I ignore the small voice inside that says it would still be nice to be asked. But I'm being stupid. Mac is probably dreading the event and just assumes I'd dread it as much as him.

I bring my thumbs back to the phone to type my reply.

> Nothing. Why?

> I'm supposed to go to this dreadful club opening in Soho and I need a wing-woman so I don't kill someone.

> Don't go overselling it, Elle.

Please. I'll even let you dance.

She's obviously been paying attention. I'll finally get to fulfill my mission to dance at a real New York City nightclub! That's better than some stupid charity event anyway, right?

Sold!

Thank you! You won't back out on me, right?

Is it possible perfect Elle Valentine has vulnerabilities like the rest of us? That's kind of reassuring.

No way. Cross my heart.

You're the best. Talk later!

I massage the arch of one foot with the toes of my other, making a mental note to wear boots to this dance club on Saturday.

As I look around my new office with its rose quartz walls and ivory leather club chairs, I take fresh stock of my life as a New Yorker. Sure, I miss Savannah and everyone from home, but I've got everything a girl could want here: a swanky new job, a hot boyfriend, a great apartment, and some new friendships to boot. Kate and I have even made a point to do lunch a couple times a week so we don't let things slide like I let happen when I moved out. So maybe Kate and Naveed still don't know about Mac, but I'll tell them soon.

In fact, I make a vow right this minute to tell them the

very next time we get together. I know they'll be happy for me and they can both keep a secret. There. See, I couldn't ask for things to be any better.

My life is officially perfect.

"GOTTA GET GOING," Mac says in a smoky tone against my neck.

I blink my eyelids open and hum, threading my fingers through his hair.

"Did I fall asleep?" I ask on a yawn.

"Mm hm." He nuzzles the corner of my mouth and his whiskers brush against the sensitive skin.

It's Saturday and we were both working last night until the wee hours, me on project assignments and Mac on something he hasn't let me see yet. I'm learning he has a unique process—which is certainly not unusual for an artist —but it rankles a bit when I want to see what he's doing and he won't let me. I have yet to be allowed into the forge while he's working and I'm dying to see the man in action.

I'd be lying if I didn't say I've had a daydream or two where the pottery scene from *Ghost* was reenacted with Mac's sweaty bare chest behind me as he guides my hands in some serious banging. You know, the hammer and anvil kind, you perv.

We met up at my place after breakfast and his workout, but I must have fallen asleep on my couch while I was listening to music and cleaning out my inbox.

I stroke his soft hair and then let my hands wander

down his back. Just as I'm about six inches under his t-shirt hem, he reaches back and stills my hands.

"Would much rather be doing this, believe me, but I've got a thing." He pulls back and I see his eyes are, indeed, hungry.

"A thing?" I pretend I have no idea what he's talking about.

He grunts. "Charity gig. Elle says they need me there."

"Oh?" God, I'm such a fake.

He doesn't offer up anything else so I press forward. "Is this a bachelor auction?"

"No."

"Are you sure? Do I need to clear out my bank account so I can afford item number twelve, the sweaty blacksmith with the strong scowling game?" I reach my lips up to peck his mouth.

I detect a hint of a smile before he responds, "You wouldn't want to go. *I* don't want to go."

My inner pout threatens but I push it back.

"Then why *are* you going?" Elle's got some influence, but not that much.

"Jonathan's been working to expand the community youth projects to all the Burroughs. This auction's for the expansion."

My chin dips and my hands fall to the couch. "Jonathan?"

"Yeah." Mac's left eyebrow looks at me like I'm crazy again.

"The same Jonathan that barely leaves his desk and hates everyone?"

Mac's lips quirk. "He doesn't hate everyone."

"He hates *me*." I cross my arms and Mac sits up on the edge of my couch, still amused.

"No, he doesn't. He likes you."

My mouth drops open and I pull myself to sitting as well. "No. *Elle* likes me. *Jonathan* despises me. I asked him the other day if I could borrow a pen and he handed me a coupon for Office Max."

Mac does a half-shrug. "He was joking."

My eyes narrow. "Does he joke with you?"

He just looks at me.

"Yeah, I didn't think so."

"He doesn't hate you and he doesn't hate people. He's been working on these charities with me for the last few years and I trust him. I don't always like my name attached so he helps me keep a certain... distance."

Yet he didn't keep that distance when it came to the *WHL* article. Of course not. Mac knew as well as I did that the youth program wouldn't make it into a national publication without it being attached to something deemed more interesting—like a hot artist who makes expensive in-demand chairs. Jeez, Mac, you're killing me, always a step ahead.

"But you need to show your pretty face tonight?" I reach out and pinch his cheek as payback for the Jonathan thing.

He doesn't even try to bite my fingers off. "Looks like it."

"Fine." I throw my hair over my shoulder, assuming my best drama queen persona. "I have a life of my own, you know. Places to go, people to dazzle."

"I have no doubt." Mac winks at me and I almost fall off

the couch. This is a new one. I'll have to add it to my list of *Panty-Destroying Looks by Angus McKinley* and decide where it ranks. Probably somewhere below his over-the-shoulder-smolder but just above the single-eyebrow-raise.

I smile stupidly at him as he goes to grab his stuff. I hear a buzzing from the coffee table and look to see who's messaging me, but it's Mac's phone, not mine. And I swear I don't mean to read it, but it's just right there on the lockscreen notification and I can't help it. But I wish I had.

MOTHER

Looking forward to getting to know
Poppy.

I jerk back into my couch cushions and whip my head around to see if Mac is looking my way, but he's in the kitchen with his back to me.

My pulse races as I wrap my head around this and try to decide what to do. If he sees that text, his head will likely explode. Talk about cryptic messages. Jeez Louise. But who knows? Maybe this isn't the first message of its kind and he's just been keeping it from me—handling it quietly on his own. Gah!

Surely, he'd understand if I say I just happened to be sitting here when the message came through. Right? I watch him pull a water from the fridge and grab his keys from the counter, knowing I'm running out of time.

We've been doing so well with him choosing exactly when and where he shares things with me. I don't want to put that progress in jeopardy with a stupid peek at a text from his mom, for Pete's sake. So, I make my decision. He can tell me about it if he wants. No, he *will* tell me about it.

I know it. He'll call in the morning and we'll talk it over, figure out what she's up to.

Mac turns and walks back toward me. He scoops up his phone and slides it into his back pocket before bending to give me a kiss.

His eyes go all hot and he whispers in his low raspy tone, "Have fun dazzling."

I get a little lost in his eyes for a second and then my tongue swipes out to gather the taste of him he left on my lips. The heat in his eyes turns to a full-on inferno and he groans, which makes a laugh bubble up from my chest.

"You have fun too, bachelor number twelve."

He stands and I don't fail to notice the bulge in his pants. Then he turns to the door and I can't help myself.

"Just watch out for the rich old ladies, Mac. I hear they expect the, ahem, *full package* for their money."

He doesn't turn back around or respond, but I do notice his sexy ass tighten a little in what I can only interpret as fear.

TWENTY-SIX

"The only thing that travels faster than gossip is a hungry man to the dinner table."
– Cookie Rutledge

ELLE STRIDES FORWARD and I swear the crowd parts like the freakin' Red Sea for Moses. Only Moses never rocked a Versace slip dress like Elle Valentine. Her honey and bronze hair shines under the colored lights and I can feel the bass in my stomach as we venture farther into the club.

I'm wearing my favorite boots with the turquoise stitching—the ones Iris always tries to steal—and I spent a ridiculous amount of time on my hair and make-up. But it was all worth it because this club is HOT. Male and female dancers perform on elevated platforms while bar staff struts around with lighted trays of shots and throw-back cigarette girls wander the crowd handing out swag.

Elle may not be impressed but I'm completely agog. In fact, that word was made for nights and places like these.

The music is loud so there's no room for conversation as she leads the way to a private bar area and a reserved table for two. God, I want to be her right now. But I'd never make it as an agent so I'll take my fantastic new job instead.

A handsome server approaches before our butts even hit the slick leather stools and Elle raises two fingers as she says something in his ear.

"This is so cool!" I shout from my seat across from her. When she holds a hand up to her ear, I scoot my fancy-ass barstool so I'm sitting next to her instead of across from her.

"I said this is so cool!"

She shakes her head at me and smiles like she thinks I'm ridiculous, which I totally am. My eyes move to the dance floor and I watch the performers on the platforms execute complicated choreographed moves while making it look effortless. My legs are bouncing on the stool and my head moves with the beat.

"I can't stand it anymore! I need to dance!" I shout as I drop back to my feet.

Elle laughs and extends a hand toward the floor, which I take as my sign to do whatever I need to do.

The music is a combination of old-school vinyl and the usual club music, but is has an earthy feel thrown in. I join the throng and shake my ass to the beat, throwing my arms in the air and letting the music take over my body.

The first song ends and blends right over into a remix of an old Mary J. Blige song that has my boots sliding back and forth with my hips. The floor is crowded, but it doesn't bother me in the least. In fact, it energizes me. All these bodies moving to the same rhythm is almost poetic. It occurs to me that if the subways and sidewalks played dance music, I might not be so suffocated by their crowds. But that's probably because we'd all be moving as one instead of a sea of strangers all ricocheting off one another to further their own pace and purpose.

I'm not sure how long I stay on the floor, but by the time I remember Elle and what a lousy friend I am for ditching her in the bar, I'm a sweaty, exhilarated mess. My hair is wild and my dress sticks to my back like superglue, but I don't care.

I crane my neck as I weave through the crowd to get back to the private bar, but I don't see Elle. The reserved sign on our table is gone and it's now occupied by a group of chukka-boot-wearing twenty-somethings drinking glasses of what look like straight-up whiskey.

Glancing around, it becomes clear she's nowhere in the bar. Maybe she went to find me on the dance floor, or maybe she's in the bathroom. I pull out my phone to see if she tried to call or message, but there's only a message from Iris. It's a picture I can't make out with an all caps *WTF?*

I open my app to text Elle, but when I do, the picture from Iris appears—and this time it's large enough to see clearly.

It's a link to a gossip site photo of none other than JoJo Ames, beaming with her raven hair and gorgeous million-dollar smile—the familiar smile she's wearing in the cover photo of the *WHL* prototype. She's wearing a gold cocktail dress and it's the standard paparazzi shot I've seen a hundred times.

Except it's not.

Because she's got her hand on the arm of a tall, devastatingly gorgeous man in a crisp black suit and sexy AF smolder.

A smolder I thought until this very moment was just for me. A smolder that beats even the wink I got when he walked out of my apartment this afternoon. A smolder that tells me I may just be the dumbest rube in all of New York.

I text Elle a quick note to tell her I'm sorry I lost her and I'm feeling sick. Then I hightail it out of the club. The beat I found so mesmerizing and the crowd that drew me in like a magnet thirty minutes ago have suddenly turned overwhelming and migraine-inducing. I gulp in the blessedly cool air of the early autumn night and hurry down the sidewalk, not even knowing which direction I'm headed. I just need to get far enough away so I can think.

I finally find a bare stretch of cinderblock I can lean against and pull my phone out again. My fingers find the link and I devour every word of the short mention on the gossip site, not letting my eyes stray to the photo again until I'm done.

Has JoJo Ames been hiding something from us? Not that we'd blame her if she has. It looks like Hollywood's hot wunderkind starlet has a new beau, and we're all dying to know who the mystery man is. Anyone?

I take a deep breath, then read it again. Okay, this could totally be an innocent mistake. They were just standing near each other at the charity event and someone snapped a picture. That's probably exactly what happened. No need to get all worked up.

I scroll up and scan the photo again, noticing the position of JoJo's hand on Mac's arm. It looks... familiar. Her long, manicured fingers curl around his bicep and she's definitely leaning toward him.

My eyes move to Mac. His body language is unreadable in the still shot, so I can't tell if he's leaning into her or not. What I can tell is he looks absolutely freaking perfect next to a polished megastar like JoJo.

Ugh. This is maddening!

I realize I need to text Iris back before she calls me and catches me freaking out.

> No biggie. Just a stupid paps shot. Don't believe everything you read 😒.

There. That should do it until I figure this mess out. *Think, Poppy, think!*

I thumb back to my text conversations and pick up the one between me and Mac.

> Hey, how's the auction?

Normally I would tease him or say something flirty, but I can't get past the rock in my stomach far enough to be the least bit playful.

I wait, scraping my boots on the sidewalk and ignoring the passing crowds.

Nothing.

Not that that means anything. He's probably still there. I check the time and it's after eleven. Hmm. Well, he must be asleep, then. I briefly consider just going over to his place so we can clear this up here and now, but a tiny nagging thread pulls on my heart. It's doubt niggling away, even though I try banishing it.

No. What I need to do is go home, get a good night's sleep, and just wait for his call in the morning. We'll have a good laugh about it—okay, *I'll* do the laughing; Mac will just do his usual. And then we'll move on and everything will go back to normal.

Great plan. Perfect. Fabulous.

WHEN MY PHONE reads nine a.m. and Mac hasn't called, I chalk it up to him being considerate and letting me sleep in after my night of dazzling.

When it hits ten, I remember that Mac likes to do extra long workouts sometimes and he probably ate a carb or two last night.

When eleven o'clock rolls around I'm officially a basketcase.

I haven't slept for shit because I couldn't seem to turn my brain off, and when I did sleep it was only to have dreams of some faceless woman with ridiculously glossy hair driving Mac away in her convertible while "You're the One That I Want" played in the background.

I finally give in at noon and dial his number. It goes directly to voicemail. I don't leave a message.

Then I break down and scour the internet for any more photos of Mac and JoJo Ames. And I almost choke on my heart that's suddenly decided to crawl up my throat.

TMZ, People, Buzzfeed, Perez Hilton—all of them have shots of JoJo with her mystery man, only he's not such a mystery anymore. Someone got ahold of his name from his auction donation and details about him are cropping up on all the usual sites. Urban blacksmith, Angus McKinley... furniture designer, Angus McKinley... artist and New York studio-owner, Angus McKinley. They're panting for him, comments piling up from readers about how hot he is and how JoJo did well for herself this time around.

My eyes burn and I eventually drop my phone face-down on my bed, unable to read another word.

I worry my lip and develop a serious case of jimmy leg as I figure out what to do. Then I pick the phone back up and call Mac.

It goes to voicemail again, but this time I leave a message.

"Hey, it's me. I saw all the pictures on the internet this morning. I'm just... checking in. I'm worried. Call me back, okay?"

I don't tell him if my worry stems from there possibly being some truth to the online stories or if I'm more worried *for* him and the fact that it's his face and name that are plastered out there. Because I *am* worried for him. This is probably one of his worst nightmares.

And that right there tells me everything I need to know. I thunk myself in the head and fall back to the bed. Idiot!

There's no way on earth Mac would ever involve himself with someone in the public eye. Regardless of his feelings for me, which I know are not insignificant if I'm being honest with myself, he values his privacy way too much to let something (or someone) shiny lure him out of his little bubble he's built.

So why in the hell isn't he calling me back?

I decide to text Elle, and it's only now I realize she

never texted me back from last night. God, I've spent all this time worrying about Mac and I forgot about my freaking friend!

> Hey. Are you okay? Never heard back from you last night.

The three dots appear and I release the breath I was holding.

ELLE

> So sorry! PR nightmare cropped up and I've been dealing with that.

> Does this have anything to do with photos of Mac?

> Damn paparazzi.

I consider asking her more about it but I just need to trust Mac.

> Is Mac okay? I haven't been able to get ahold of him.

> Shit. Someone found his number so his phone has been off. Or it might be under a subway train if I know Angus. Jonathan is with him so just call his cell phone.

Jonathan's mobile contact pops up and I save it to my phone.

> Thanks!

> Are you feeling better? After last night?

I forgot I told her I wasn't feeling well. She's being so good to me while she's in the midst of a work crisis. I make a mental note to get her flowers or maybe some of that Chinese baby fruit.

> All better. Don't worry about me—just go do your job. 🤍

I switch over to the phone and hit Jonathan's contact.

"Jonathan Abernathy."

"Jonathan, hi, it's Poppy."

"Oh. Hi." He sounds just as enthusiastic as ever.

"Hey, I know it's been a crazy night, but I was hoping I could talk to Mac. Elle said he turned off his phone and I could reach him through you."

"Oh, right. Yeah, he's busy right now."

"Oh." I'm not sure how hard to press. I mean, if Jonathan is being his usual difficult self, I reckon I could just go on over there.

There being the studio the paparazzi are probably surrounding. Ugh.

I sigh. "Okay, well can you have him call me as soon as he's free?"

"Sure. Absolutely."

Okay, that's a bit better, I suppose.

"All right. Thanks."

"No problem." He hangs up.

Maybe Mac was right. Maybe Jonathan doesn't hate me.

BY SUPPERTIME I DECIDE THAT, while Jonathan Abernathy might not hate me, God certainly does. Why else would I still have zero word from Mac and, just to make the evening extra special, a message from Bunny telling me how she's just finalized the seating chart for Vern's retirement dinner and saved me a spot next to Bobby Lee at the head table? Add to that a new email from one of the head designers questioning a design theme we already hashed out and it's official that all my lies are catching up to me with the man upstairs.

I measure my words carefully when I go to respond to Jen Baylor—the same woman who'd been mentioned in that eavesdropped bathroom conversation from weeks ago. The same woman who has done everything short of taking out a billboard to let God and country know how she's the one who has the rightful claim to my job. In a super classy twist, she copied everyone in management as well as our entire department on her email. I can't let my current emotions color my response, and I'm afraid that's exactly what will happen if I compose this reply tonight. Lord, how I despise email. There are so many ways to misinterpret a person's tone or say things you would never say to some-one's face.

But work would be a perfect distraction from the broken record I've had playing in my head all day of every single thing Mac has ever said to me, every look he's ever passed my way, and every touch of his skin. If I don't stop thinking about him I'm going to burn all the synapses in my brain and bloody my damn fingernail beds.

I haven't allowed myself to look online again, knowing

I'd just fall down the rabbit hole of internet stalking. So, work it is.

A new email pops up and this time it's from Naveed. Oh, I'd much rather talk to him instead of the dreaded Jen. I click on the message and see that Kate's copied on it as well.

"Poppy, can you do your magic on Angus McKinley and try to get a statement on his relationship with JoJo Ames? It's blowing up Instagram but he's not talking. If we can get ahead of this on the *WHL* social media accounts, it will be a HUGE windfall for us. Imagine an exclusive! We'll have enough followers to ensure our January launch goes through the roof. I see greatness ahead!"

Shit!

Why, oh why, haven't I told Naveed and Kate about Mac yet? It doesn't matter that I totally planned on doing it next week because now they're both expecting me to deliver an exclusive to launch our fledgling magazine into the social media stratosphere. I can't very well respond with, "Hey, funny story, he's actually my boyfriend, not this famous beautiful person's. And, yeah, I've been keeping it from you because I'm an asshole. Wanna braid each other's hair now?"

Why can't Mac just call me back? As soon as I hear his voice I know I'll feel better. He'll tell me about the JoJo nightmare and I'll tease him about being bachelor number twelve and how I told him those women would want their money's worth. And then everything will be back out in the open and, hey, I'll even be honest with him about reading that text from his mother...

That text from his mother.

I don't even stop to think before dialing. The phone picks up on the second ring.

"Jonathan Abernathy." He sounds exhausted, but I can't think about that now.

"Jonathan, it's Poppy again. I need to talk to Mac. It's important."

"Oh, right. Um, he said he'd call you tomorrow or something."

"He... what?"

"Or maybe Tuesday. I'm not sure."

I swallow hard.

I *knew* it!

Mac is running away again. And it's not because of JoJo Ames; it's because of a different socialite altogether—one he feels the need to protect me from, no matter what that might cost.

TWENTY-SEVEN

"Pretty is as pretty does, and don't you forget it."
– Cookie Rutledge

DID I say recently that my life is perfect? Well, scratch that. My life is officially Satan's ashtray after a frat party at Hades U.

I drag my ass into work on Monday and, for reasons clearly due to some truly heinous transgressions in my past life, the design staff is all atwitter about Angus McKinley and JoJo Ames. How fateful it is that they're both being featured in our inaugural issue and how romantic it is and blah, blah, blah.

I want to shout at them that Angus wouldn't touch JoJo Ames with a ten-foot pole, but I can't. Instead, I have to smile and walk on my stupid heels to my office where, yes, Jen Baylor is waiting for me.

Exactly what did past-life Poppy do? Steal baby Jesus's rattle?

I paste on a smile and hold back the curse on my lips because I'm sure Cookie would sense a disturbance in the force all the way from Georgia and come on up to whip me on my butt if I called this woman what I want to (which is *shit-stirring twat terrorist*, by the way).

"Good morning, Jen."

"Morning, Poppy. How was your weekend?"

"Fine, thanks. And yours?" We're so polite I might throw up.

"Good. Listen, I don't know if you saw the email I sent this weekend..."

She waits to see if I'll fill in the rest of that sentence, but I'm letting her talk. I purposely didn't respond to that damn email because I was too pissed to be professional about it. And, yeah, I'm blaming Mac's mama for that too. I just tilt my head and, sure enough, she keeps talking.

"Anyway, some of us were discussing it and we're rethinking the aesthetic on issue two. As I said in the email, we just think it's a bit... tired."

"I see." That's all I say because if she has the nerve to hide behind a mysterious "we" and copy every damn person on the magazine about a complaint she has instead of just coming to me, she can sure as hell express all her thoughts out loud in my office.

"I'm sure the bold layered vibe is fine for some... regional publications, but this is New York, not Kansas, if you know what I mean."

Yes, I think I know exactly what she means. This is the publishing capital of the world and I have no business heading a department here. I'm some nobody from a nobody town and don't let the door hit me in the backside on my way out.

I take a breath. What she really needs is a boot up her ass, but I can't exactly do that.

"I'm sorry you feel that way, Jen, but this design direction is in line with the brand identity the team established with Ms. Lennox's blessing two months ago. More has gone into this than the one meeting we had last week. Fresh ideas and input are valuable, but there's a process."

In other words, don't go above my head and make insinuations when you don't know what the hell you're talking about.

She sends me a saccharine smile as fake as Bunny's hair color. But that's okay because mine's just as fake.

"Well, you're the boss."

Damn right I am.

"Is there anything else?" I boot up my laptop to let her know *I'm* certainly done.

"No." She stands and smooths down her skirt. "I don't think so."

"Okay, well, have a nice morning."

She walks out and I lean back in my chair. Good freaking Monday morning to me.

"HEY!" Katelyn pokes her head in my office two hours later and I sigh in relief.

"Oh, thank God, a friendly face."

Her brow furrows in concern but I wave her off.

"Ignore me. How's it going?"

She drops into one of the chairs across from my desk. "Crazy. You?"

"Same. It's almost like we're starting a new magazine or something," I tease.

"I know, right?" I get her wide eyes and it makes me grin.

"So, what was up with that woman in your department copying everyone—including God himself—on that email this weekend?"

I roll my eyes. "Don't ask. I've got it covered." I lean forward and prop an elbow on the surface. "People will just ignore it, right?"

Her mouth turns down at one corner as she thinks about it. "Yeah, everybody is too busy with their own shit to give it another thought. I just wanted to check in."

"Aw, thanks. We still on for lunch tomorrow?"

"Absolutely."

She doesn't move, so I dip my head and give her the eye. "Was there something else, Katelyn?"

"Ummmm." She picks at the stitching on the chair and is so freaking obvious.

"Spit it out, will you?"

"Fine." She straightens. "I noticed you didn't respond to the email from Naveed last night."

My face drops and she leans forward, her blond hair falling from her shoulder.

"I know, I know, it's my department, not yours, but Naveed called and got the standard 'no comment,' and he said you really had a connection with Mr. McKinley at the photo shoot. I also know how you feel about him from your teenage fantasy swoonfest a few weeks ago..."

"Kate." It might come out as a whine.

"Poppy," she imitates me, sounding way too much like my sister.

God, should I just tell her? I should. I should totally tell her. Ugh, but things are such a mess with Mac right now that it'll sound ridiculous.

"Look, Katelyn—" I begin, but she cuts me off.

"I mean, thank God you didn't go ahead and try sleeping with the man. Can you imagine getting dumped for JoJo Ames? Ouch."

I bite my lip. "Kate, I don't think—"

"Don't get me wrong, he's quite the hottie from what I saw in the photos, but talk about a conflict of interest now that we're covering his relationship with our cover model."

Kill me now.

I smile weakly and mimic swiping my forehead like I barely escaped total professional humiliation by a hair.

"I'll see what I can do." I fix my mouth in a line.

And there I go lying...

Again.

BY THE TIME I give up and head home, it's dark outside and my mood is black enough to match. I walked by the designer staff tables this afternoon to the sight of Jen and two others springing apart from an obvious gossip huddle. Add to that my lying to Kate and the continued silence from Mac and I'm ready for a drink and about twelve hours of sleep. Either that or a plane ticket home.

I'm about to turn the corner to my block when I get a flutter of what feels like hope in my belly. It would be just like Mac to be waiting on my stoop or leaning against my door jamb with his eyebrow raised and his bod looking crazy hot in a pair of jeans and those work boots. He's probably been waiting for me in his quiet way, standing there contemplating his next design or just letting his mind go wherever it usually does in the silence he occupies.

My lips turn up as I try to guess what color t-shirt he'll be wearing, because the man doesn't ever seem to need a coat—of course not, since he is his own furnace. I've just settled on gray when I turn the corner and... nothing.

There's no Mac.

Oh well. I hurry up my steps. He's probably just waiting inside. Hell, he's probably picked my apartment lock and is waiting on my couch or cooking himself some of those boring chicken breasts and steamed veggies he likes to eat.

I'm proud of myself when I'm not even panting on the third set of stairs. I pull out my key in case the door is locked and, yup, he must have locked it for safety.

"Mac?" I close the door behind me and walk through to the kitchen. But the lights are all off.

"Mac?" He's not in the living room so I head back to my bedroom. But I already know I won't find him.

He didn't come. He's not waiting for me. And he still hasn't called. He ran again because of his stupid mother and this money thing I don't understand, and now I'm gonna have to go chasing after him again, reassuring him again, barging my way past his walls again.

I let my bag and purse drop to the floor and kick off my shoes, asking myself one very important question. One I've avoided asking myself all day.

Why am I the one who always has to do the chasing?

Cookie would tell me you don't abandon family when they're troubled. She'd also say just because people don't ask for help doesn't mean they don't need it. But it doesn't feel right now like Mac wants me to be his family—his person. It feels like he'd rather go it on his own and be that one-man band, just like he's been for God knows how long.

Can I really force him?

And, even more important, *should* I?

Because no matter what I know about how good I can be for Mac, the question I maybe should be asking is whether Mac is good for *me*?

I get myself some sweet tea and walk over to my window where I look out on the lighted sliver of courtyard I can see. The apartment across the way has its curtains drawn, but I can see shadows moving inside.

Exactly what did I hope to get from a relationship with Mac? Did I ever think he was going to be my swoony boyfriend who'd take me out to a Broadway show and accompany me to friends' parties? Did I think he might get down on one knee someday and wait at the end of an aisle for me with tears in his eyes? Give me squishy babies and be my biggest cheerleader when I won some prestigious design award? Spend Christmases with my parents and Cookie and Iris and the whole crazy bunch of Savannahians and take me out dancing and grow old with me?

The Mac I know might be able to swing a few of those things, but probably not all of them. Are those the things I want? The things I need?

I learned a long time ago that happiness isn't a magic spell cast by a fairy godmother. You need to grab life by the horns and create your own, but people and connections are vital. And family is the most important, no matter the form it comes in or the unexpected ways it materializes.

I think back to dating Bobby Lee and how he'd take me anywhere that made me happy. He'd show me off and take me dancing and always buy me the biggest Christmas present and tell me how much he loved me.

But I don't think Bobby Lee ever *really* loved me, not like that. He did—and does—in his own way, just like I love him, but I don't think he ever actually even knew me. And maybe I never let him. To him, I'm Poppy James, daughter of Lorna and Jack James, the family friends who've always been around and always will be. Just like Bunny built that pedestal to put him on, Bobby Lee built one for me and tried to pop me on top as his not-quite-virgin bride-to-be. It's what he knows and I fit the bill.

And that's exactly why we're no longer dating—why we'll never ever *ever* get married, no matter how adorable everybody else thinks it would be.

Mac will likely never do all the things Bobby Lee would happily do, yet he's made me feel more vibrant, joyful, and more like myself than I've felt in a long, long time—maybe ever. And when we're together, he's all there. He listens and respects me and wants to protect me from anything out there that could threaten me or make me be something I'm not.

If I didn't know better, I'd say he loves me.

I wipe away the tear that's insisted on dripping down my cheek and heave a huge sigh. The truth of the matter is, I want the same things for him. I want to be that same person for him.

Yeah, I still want Mac—no, I *need* Mac. Even if he's proving to be more high maintenance than a pop princess with a head cold.

So, no, I'm not giving up.

GOOD GOD, Mac was not kidding when he said these people care more about appearances than anything else.

I spent two hours last night plus the hour leading up to my lunch with Kate today looking into Mac's mother's side of the family. Suffice it to say, Sterling Pile is a grade-A douchebag, and that's not just coming from me.

It's right here in print in his college yearbook. Yes, I uncovered a copy while undertaking my new online stalking project. This family is ridiculous.

From what I've discovered thus far, Mac's mother does, indeed, come from money—namely the Tenneson family shipping company kind of money. As I already knew from that article I read weeks ago, her daddy owns Ten Fleet, one of the biggest shipping companies in the world. What I didn't know was that her husband, the aforementioned douchebag, owns a line of exclusive boutique hotels frequented by the rich and famous.

This guy is the definition of money buying a reputation

—or maybe hiding one. I keep finding small mentions of lawsuits here and there that were thrown out or settled before going to court—everything from an assault charge to forgery to a DUI that was thrown out due to procedural error. As far as I can see, the guy comes out the other end of these just as clean and rich as he was to begin with. Entitled jerk—I'm glad he's being investigated by the government.

I also uncover an article probing into some of Ten Fleet's business practices and mentioning Dan Tenneson, Mac's grandfather, although there doesn't appear to be much there.

It isn't until just before lunchtime that I stumble across something on Twitter that has me freezing in my office chair.

@artequalityspeaks: *The rich bitches win again. I hope **@margarettenneson-pile** isn't too disappointed that the suicide didn't take.*

This is followed by a flurry of responses and, by about the fortieth one, I'm able to piece together most of the story. It appears a prestigious Boston art museum had a vacancy on their board a few years back and were deciding between Margaret Tenneson-Pile and another woman named Stacy Showalter. If the tweets are to be believed, Margaret played dirty, to the point where she leaked some false information about Ms. Showalter's son—information that not only cost him his college scholarship but resulted in a mob-mentality rash of harassments that ended in the attempted suicide of her son. Stacy Showalter subsequently removed her name from the running and Margaret Tenneson-Pile was named to the board.

My spine is stick straight as I finish reading, Mac's warnings about his mother surging back into my mind. *"She'll do anything to get what she wants, no matter who she destroys in the process."*

I swallow hard, then decide it's time for my lunch with Kate. My mind needs something that doesn't make me feel like I need a shower. I click the back button and almost close the laptop, but a headline catches my eye. It looks like lunch will have to wait because I've got some more reading to do.

ARMED with my laptop full of eye-opening and nausea-inducing bookmarks, I catch a cab down to Mac's studio just before five. Yeah, you heard me.

All my fingers are crossed that the paparazzi has at least pulled back its forces to chase whatever today's biggest celebrity happening might be, but it really can't wait any longer. I need to talk to Mac and if the mountain won't come to Poppy, Poppy's coming to the mountain.

I'm in luck because there are no cameras in sight when I stalk up to the studio door and bang on it like I'm a rock star and it's my snare drum.

"No comment!" comes Jonathan's voice from inside, so I bang again, hoping he's got his ear up to it.

"It's Poppy! Let me in or so help me God I'll kick the damn door down!"

"Jesus." I hear him mumble from inside, but the door

swings open in the next moment and I'm storming right on in.

"Wait! You can't—"

I don't even pause as I keep walking and cut him off.

"Oh, yes, I can."

I'm wearing heels so I can't stomp the way I really want to, but I'm getting damn good in these things. It'll have to do.

Jonathan scurries into his small office where he'll probably either call the police or his mommy. But he can do whatever the hell he likes as far as I'm concerned.

I turn at the corner of two partitions and that's when I realize the soundtrack that was playing in my head as I killed it in my performance as badass Poppy is, in fact, not in my head. It's coming from a speaker in Mac's open studio.

And it's Old Dominion.

It's all I can do to keep my pace steady and not sprint into the room and launch myself at Mac. Which, it turns out, becomes even harder when I pass through the threshold and there he is, shirt off, muscular arms working, and sweat-slicked back open for my viewing pleasure as he hoists and swings the battling ropes, his grunts of exertion sounding in time to "Shut Me Up."

I bite the knuckle of my index finger because, *come on.* My eyes dart reluctantly to the set of windows I first spied Mac through and I want to throw a sheet over them so nobody else can happen upon my man in all his sexy, sweaty glory. Thank God the paparazzi are nowhere to be found or images of Mac would likely appear in every morning paper, giving heart attacks and spontaneous orgasms to all the women of America.

"There you are!" Elle's voice makes me jump. I was so caught up in Mac I missed her sidling up next to me. "Where've you been?"

I don't—or can't—give her a good answer to that right now so I just shrug.

Mac must sense motion from the corner of his eye because he glances over his shoulder and then does a double take, with perhaps the best over-the-shoulder-smolder I've seen to date. And, yeah, his eyes are hungry, just like that.

He drops the ropes and goes to the table to turn down his music, stretching out his muscles as he walks. His strides take him right in front of me where he stops, eyes on me like Elle isn't even in the room, and says a simple, "Poppy."

Oh, how I love the way this man says my name.

The mini parrots in my belly all blush.

"Hi."

"You two are too adorable," Elle says, and I assume she rolls her eyes but I can't see because I'm watching Mac's lips twitch.

He runs a hand through his sweaty hair.

"Thought maybe I scared you away," he says with a rumble from his chest, leaving me slightly confused.

At what I assume is a perplexed slant to my head, Mac catches my hand and starts pulling me toward the stairs to his apartment.

"Not so fast!" Elle scurries to keep up. "I need that signature page for the Nassar commission."

Mac glances back at her, which I assume is a silent communication for, "fine, whatever," because she follows us up the stairs and proceeds to talk at Mac for a few minutes before taking her leave.

I say "talk at" because Mac spends the entire three minutes watching me tiptoe around his kitchen trying to decide if I'm ready to take a seat or if I'd rather stand during the conversation we're about to have.

By the time Elle leaves with a wink in my direction, I've decided to sit, but only on a barstool, not one of the sofas. Too many things are likely to happen once my ass hits his sofa and we've got some serious discussion ahead of us.

TWENTY-EIGHT

*"Don't ever be ashamed to cry as long as your mascara is
waterproof and your heart's on your sleeve."*
– Cookie Rutledge

"SO," I begin, "what did you mean when you said you
thought you scared me away?"

He keeps his distance—for the moment. "You didn't
come over last night."

My brows draw together. "Well, you never called me
back. And the paparazzi..."

His jaw ticks at the p-word. "Bloodsucking vultures."
But he takes a couple steps closer. "Jonathan told you the
coast was clear, yeah?"

Fracking Jonathan. "Uh, no. Jonathan definitely did not
tell me that."

Mac's eyes narrow.

"The last time I talked to him was Sunday night and he

said you'd call me in a couple days. I figured you freaked out about your mother." I'm laying it all out for him with no sugar to help it go down.

"No. Shit." He runs a hand through his hair. "I guess I should have found a way to call."

You think? I don't have to say the words because my expression speaks for me.

Mac closes the distance between us and brings a thumb to the center of my chin. I shiver at the contact even though I don't want to 'cuz we're not done talking.

"Miscommunication, I guess."

I cross my arms. "Mac, you're generally a perceptive guy, but I'm thinking you need to seriously take another gander at Jonathan's behavior. It's like the man is purposely trying to screw with me."

He shakes his head. "Not him. But somebody else is— or was, I should say."

Now I'm confused. He needs to use more words so I tell him so.

His thumb drops. "Fuck. This is such a mess."

"Can you just start from the beginning?"

"Yeah. No. Fuck."

"I think we've established that." I go for a small smile and his face relaxes.

"Sass," he grumbles, squeezing my knee with his callused hand.

I tap the end of his nose for emphasis and he tries to bite my finger. Playful Mac has arrived, no matter the timing kind of sucks.

"I told Jonathan to tell you I needed a couple days to deal with this JoAnn bullshit."

"JoJo," I correct as I nod, because I guess that *is* kind of what Jonathan said. "Okay, but, Mac, I saw the text from your mother on Saturday. The one with my name in it." I brace, waiting for him to back up or his jaw to turn to stone again. It doesn't.

"Bitch was baiting me."

To hear him call his own mother that name is jarring, not that it isn't deserved. I close my mouth and keep it shut.

"Then this thing with that JoJo person just... happened. Didn't even know who she was. She just grabbed my arm and flashes started going off. My phone was buzzing in my pocket before I could get the hell out of there."

I grab his hand where it rests on my knee. I can only imagine how frustrated he must have been.

"But I got a new text from my mother, this time going on with some bullshit about this JoJo chick. I figured... I don't know. I figured as long as she thought I was involved with someone else—someone with more money—you'd be in the clear."

Of course. That makes perfect sense.

"So you didn't refute the gossip," I finish for him.

He shakes his head, his eyes making sure not to drop mine.

I can't help it. I pull up and plant a soft kiss on his lips. He sighs into my mouth like I've just lifted a five-hundred-pound boulder off him.

When I pull back, my hand is on his cheek and his whiskers are tickling my palm. "But, Mac, you can't keep this charade up forever. I mean, surely, JoJo's people will eventually get around to dispelling the rumor." And, besides, I need my boyfriend back—preferably without JoJo fans chasing me down the New York sidewalks to brand me with a scarlet letter.

He shakes his head again but doesn't knock my hand lose. "According to Elle, they haven't said anything to refute it yet. I can't begin to understand these people. I just want my phone back."

This makes me laugh out loud because it's such a Mac thing to distill it down to the one practical aspect that matters.

"Missed that."

I almost don't catch his words because my laugh is so obnoxious. When I do, though, it hits me right in the heart. He missed my laugh. He missed me.

"Missed you," I say, my thumb swiping his bottom lip. "Don't run away anymore, okay?"

His head shakes again. "I wasn't." Then he pulls my hand from his face and laces our fingers together, drawing our joined hands to his sweaty chest. "I'm sorry. I should have called but I'm not... I'm not used to being accountable to anyone. I saw a solution to a problem and ran with it."

I squeeze his hand. "I know." Then I slide off the stool and look up at him. "But we're gonna solve this problem together."

His brow furrows.

"Your mama is a major freakin' piece of work, Angus McKinley."

His lips twitch.

"But she's also got a huge chink in her armor."

"YOU FOUND ALL this on the internet?" We're sitting on one of his leather sofas and I've got my laptop out.

"Honestly, mostly on Twitter. That place is a wellspring of useless drivel, but damn, do people like to talk."

I think Mac physically shudders at just the notion of ever venturing onto social media.

"Not surprised to read it, but how does this help?"

"Well, the woman's reputation is all she cares about, right?"

He gives a curt nod.

"What if, instead of random Twitter comments by people nobody's ever heard of, her transgressions somehow made their way onto the social media radar of a national magazine publication?"

Mac considers me, his teeth scraping his bottom lip as he realizes what I'm saying.

"Could you... do that?" His voice is low, cautious.

I shrug, trying not to get distracted by his still-naked chest. "Well, *I* can't, but I've been working my ass off for the past few months crafting the aesthetics of our online presence." I brush my shoulder with a smirk. "I know a few people."

He continues looking at me and then shakes his head. "It's no use. People with this kind of money and pedigree are untouchable, believe me."

I throw up a finger. "Aha! I thought you'd say that."

I click a few more tabs on my browser and turn the laptop to Mac again. "Guess who had his offices raided and his assets frozen on Friday? That's right, Sterling Pile. Your mama has got to be panicking—thus her creepy pursuit of you and your gazillions."

"I don't have gazillions. I don't even technically own..." He trails off and scowls at me but he doesn't mean it.

"Whatever." I wave him off. "Then the non-fictional amount you do have. Anyway, no money, no power. She gets the one-two punch of frozen assets and the exposure if her sociopathic shenanigans all over social media."

"Timmm-berrr." I put my arm up in the air and let it fall with a maniacal grin. All I need now is a mustache to twirl the ends of.

Mac stands from the sofa and runs a hand over his face while I clutch the laptop so it doesn't fall to the floor. He doesn't seem as ready as I am to break out the champagne. "She's always got my grandfather to bail her out. It wouldn't be the first time, although she may have burned that bridge." He paces to the end of the other sofa. "Regardless, we... can't."

I look around the room like I'm seeking out someone to agree with me. "Of course we can. It's the only way to get her gone for good."

He paces again to the far side of the rug, his back to me. "You don't understand."

Then explain it to me!

I realize there's only one way through this and it involves me being completely transparent first.

"Mac, I have to tell you something."

He glances back at me, the tension around his eyes pronounced.

I take a breath and let it out. "I know about your dad."

His face goes completely blank and he turns fully toward me again.

"What do you mean?"

"I mean I know about his accident. His lawsuit. His... death." The last word is almost silent.

I can see Mac's Adam's apple bob as he swallows hard. I expect his expression to turn angry. Livid. Hurt. I went snooping into his business and invaded his privacy, even though I knew from the very start he wanted me to stay far away from it.

But it doesn't happen. Instead, he breathes out one word.

"Explain."

"I... I found a couple articles online."

He blinks once. Then twice. "You read an article." It's halfway between a question and a statement.

I nod, my neck muscles barely cooperating. "A couple articles."

"Show me."

I don't even hesitate. I quickly type in the search criteria I remember from weeks ago, and then walk over, practically shoving the laptop at Mac.

He holds it with both hands as his gaze breaks from my face and he scans over the first page before clicking to the next one. I hold my breath and wait.

When his eyes come back up, they're laced with confusion.

"This is your big confession? Two mentions about my pops in a newspaper that don't explain jack shit?"

I open my mouth and then shut it again. "I... uh... yes?" I finally manage.

He closes the laptop and sets it on his coffee table, then turns and disappears into his bedroom.

"Mac! I don't think this is the time for..." I trail off as he reappears and I realize he wasn't wanting me to follow him there so he could ravish me. Instead, he's holding a small piece of paper which he brings with him back to the sofa. He sits, pulling me down next to him on the leather.

He hands me the paper. But it's not just a paper, it's a photograph of a good-looking middle-aged man who bears a striking resemblance to the one sitting next to me. He's got the same dark slash of eyebrows and the thick hair I recognize, only his is gray instead of black. But the damn maddening half-smirk is exactly the same.

Mac's voice comes out in a quiet rasp. "My pops was addicted to pain killers and stole money from my business to fund his habit."

My jaw locks and my nose stings.

"If we retaliate or expose my mother for what she is, it'll expose him too, and that's not happening."

Holy shit. His dad stole from him? The same guy he called his best friend?

I'm beginning to understand exactly how nuts things are around here compared to back home. Stealing? Betrayal? Although, now that I think about it, my daddy hijacked the neighbor's car when he was eighteen and took it for a joyride that ended in a ditch. As far as I can tell, nobody held a grudge past him making appropriate restitutions.

But this is far from the same thing.

I watch Mac's face and silently urge him to continue with a soft touch to his arm.

He leans forward and rests his elbows on his knees, letting his hands fall between them. And then Mac McKinley shares.

And he shares everything.

Angus McKinley, Sr. was not a perfect man. He was careless with money and wasn't one to dole out hugs or compliments. He wasn't savvy or quick with a joke or a particularly good husband. And, while he did involve himself in a youth work program, it was more out of a sense of duty than any personal passion.

But Angus McKinley, Sr. loved his son.

Loved him so much that when he divorced the boy's mother, he let him go with her to have a chance at a better life. And when his angry, bitter son came back to him and started falling through the cracks, he picked his boy's ass up and put him into a trade.

He loved his son so much he worked an extra job to help him start his first forge and wore out three sets of tires hauling ironwork and furniture all over the New York Metropolitan area to make sales for his boy.

He loved him so much that when the pain from the car accident ten years ago made it too difficult to work, instead of leaning on his son, he found his own way through. And when that way turned bad and the opioid dependency slipped out of his grip, he hid the poor decisions he made from his son so he could shoulder it on his own.

He loved his son so much that when he made—and freely admitted to—the biggest mistake of his life and stole from that son, he swallowed all his remaining dignity and begged for help from the very people he swore he'd never allow to make him feel small again.

And when that encounter turned nasty—when his ex-wife, the same one who'd mistreated and ignored their son when motherhood became an inconvenience, pushed him from the second-floor balcony of the family estate—he loved his son so much that he again laid his dignity aside and pursued a lawsuit that would secure the money to pay for his care so his son wouldn't have to lose his business and he wouldn't be a burden.

And when Angus McKinley, Sr. finally died from his injuries, he loved his son so much that he left him a building where his boy could live and work and create beautiful things he loved and never have to lower himself to ask for anything from people who should have loved him but didn't.

By the time Mac is done telling his pops's story, I'm bawling like a baby and Mac has long since pulled his daddy's picture from my hands so I don't ruin it with my blubbering.

My face is buried in his chest, which is still naked from his workout. The hairs on his pecs are soft against my cheek and I'm half mad at myself that I can't even enjoy the bits of underarm hair peeking out from beneath his bulky bicep.

"I think I love your pops." I sniffle into his neck and feel his chest vibrate with what's either one of his hums or a laugh. I'm not sure.

"I can tell you with one-hundred percent certainty, honey, that he would have loved you like his own."

That just sends me off on another crying jag and this time I'm sure Mac is laughing at me. But I don't care. Because Mac had family. He had fierce love like I have. The kind that fights and dies for you. And he lost it.

If that's not a reason to ugly cry, I don't know what is.

By the time my tears subside, they're only replaced by a white-hot anger.

I pull back from his chest and look up at him with fire in my eyes. "Tell me why your mother's not in jail!"

Mac sighs and pushes my mess of hair back from my face. His eyes travel over my splotchy cheeks and red-rimmed eyes and if he finds me hideous, his expression does an excellent job of hiding it.

"Money. Influence. Connections. Monthly payments to Satan."

I scowl at him trying his hand at being funny at a time like this. He just swipes a stray tear from my cheek and looks all tender and shit. Dammit.

"But your pops got a settlement. That's admitting she did something awful."

"A civil settlement," Mac clarifies in a rumbly tone. "Nothing criminal. Not enough evidence to prosecute." He pulls me back into him and the sigh he releases is resigned. "I didn't want any part of that civil suit. In fact, I fought my pops on it. Didn't want a single dime from those assholes. But he didn't ask me. Got lawyers to handle it all and I couldn't do a damn thing about it."

I'm still raring for a fight, but I let him finish talking. "I did my best to take care of him but you never met my pops. He was a stubborn SOB. And once I saw how much that kind of money could do to make him comfortable I shut my fuckin' mouth. I could never get him that kind of care on my own, especially while salvaging my business and the apprenticeship program, which had turned to shit in the process. When he died he left me this whole damn building, already rigged out with the forge and apartment. Put it in a trust so I can't sell it. I wanted to refuse but he knew me too well. It's the only thing he ever asked me to do for him. So I'm trying my best to live up to his memory."

I wedge my hands between his warm back and the sofa to hug him for what he just shared. My heart wants to tell him it loves him but I'm still too mad to get all gooey just yet.

The hug is short and I lean back to see his face again. "That's all kinds of lovely, Mac, and I wanna come back to it, but that's... bullshit!"

His head snaps back and his eyebrow is telling me I've gone and lost my mind again.

"She got away with it!" I point out the obvious.

He nods calmly. It's as if my consuming rage makes it so he can step back and be the rational one.

"Before the civil suit, we thought we had... an advocate."

My brows go up and he continues.

"This guy showed up after my mother... did what she did. Claimed to be a victims' advocate with media ties." He shakes his head. "You have to understand, we had no money. I was putting in a full day at a feed plant and working the forge at night. Neighbors were complaining. It was a mess."

He plays with my hair absently from his seat next to me —or really, behind me, since I'm just about in his lap by this point.

"There was no time to check credentials, not that we would have known where to start, but he wanted to help and we needed it. Pops was in and out of hospitals and I was trying to make ends meet while caring for him. And he hated it. I mean, *hated* it—depending on other people.

"So this guy says he's going to expose the Tenneson/Pile families and bust shit wide open. It'll be in every newspaper. But everyone has a price and they found his. We ended up with a shitty article that used my pops as a case study on how opioid addiction wrecks families. Had to fight for a retraction. Thankfully, we got it. That's actually how we met Elle."

There's too much to unpack in this story. At least now I know why he doesn't do interviews. I'll have to wait until later to fully consider the gravity of him making an exception in my case.

"Wait. That's how you met Elle?" I have to pick one thing at a time or my mind will shut down. I'm still beyond angry that Mac's mother is so damn untouchable. But hopefully not for long. I have half a mind to call on all the women of Savannah to march up here and put that witch in her place—'cuz they could do it, I'm sure.

"Yeah. Elle was working in PR, had encountered the reporter before and offered to help. I don't know, she got charmed by my pops, I guess. Of course, that wasn't hard to do. He might have been past his prime and confined to a wheelchair but he could draw every female eye in the room when he started with his fucking Gaelic." Mac grins at me.

I stifle what threatens to be a giggle. I could totally see that. Hell, if Mac busted out the Gaelic right now, my clothes would probably fall from my body in a tattered heap without me moving a muscle.

He laces his fingers in mine and watches the movement of his thumb over the pulse point on my wrist. It's mesmerizing, but I'm still not done. I need to shake off my Mac haze and concentrate.

"I still don't understand something, though." I look up at him. "Why would your mama do it? Why would she push your father? I mean, what did she have against him other than him asking for money?"

Mac blinks and it's like he's trying and failing to push back something he needs to save for later because it's too big. He swallows and his voice comes out in a rasp. "Because I chose him. And nobody ever puts her second."

I don't think I've ever hated anyone more than I hate fucking Margaret Tenneson-Pile in this moment. And I've never loved anyone more than I love Mac McKinley.

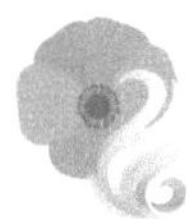

"Don't ever lose sight of what's important or you may lose it altogether."
– Cookie Rutledge

WE DON'T TALK MUCH after that. It's the most I've ever heard Mac say and it's clear he's exhausted. And so am I.

I understand where he's coming from now—why we can't play internet war to catch his mother at her own game and why we need to let this thing ride until the cards fall where they will. I understand a lot of things now. I still want justice and I still have questions, sure, but they can wait.

At least it appears his mother is distracted by JoJo. It should take her a good few weeks of trying to contact the JoJo Ames PR machine before she gives up or confirmation comes to light that JoJo and Mac won't ever get their own couple name. In the meantime, I'm just fine with laying low with my man and pretending the rest of the world doesn't exist.

Mac goes to take a shower and I putter around his apartment, thinking about cooking some dinner but I find nothing inspirational in his fridge.

There's a knock on his door a bit later and my lip curls when I think it's Jonathan, but I hear Elle's voice so I hurry to unlock it.

"Hey," she says, and when she sees my face—which must look a mess—she grabs my arm. "Are you okay?"

"Oh, yeah." I roll my eyes at myself. "I'm just being dramatic, I guess. But, no, I'm fine."

"Okay." She looks skeptical but lets it go. "I think I left my phone in here. I can't find it anywhere."

We both take a peek around and, sure enough, it's laying on the kitchen island. She grabs it and heads for the door, then turns around at the last minute. "He told you, didn't he?"

I want to hold everything from the last hour just between Mac and me, but I nod anyway.

She smiles a sad smile. "Well, at least I can make peace with my promise to Angus, Sr."

I swear, she's trying to make me cry again but I manage a tremulous smile. Then I shoo her away before I turn into a big baby again.

Later, when I'm sprawled on top of Mac in bed, both of us in just our underwear, I think about what Elle said again about his dad—and what Mac said about how his pops would have loved me.

"Tell me something else about your pops, something

that's not caught up in the sadness. What's your favorite memory of him?"

Mac scratches his chin where the scruff is thickest. "Dunno. He wasn't a particularly talkative guy—not all that demonstrative."

"Hmm. You don't say?" I tease and it gets me narrowed eyes.

"He always called me *a sheòid*."

"*My warrior*," I say, tracing his scar with my fingertip.

"Yeah." His thick brows draw together.

"Elle told me."

He doesn't look all that surprised.

"He never called me Mac. Not once. Used to rub him wrong when he heard other people calling me that." His fingers trace circles between my shoulder blades and my nerve endings sing at his touch. "He was a second-generation immigrant with one foot in Scotland and seeing as *Mac* translates to 'son of,' he didn't like it. Said my life was my own to define and I shouldn't be known as just the 'son of' anybody, especially not him." He shakes his head, obviously reliving the memory. "But tell that to a teenager who has to introduce himself by the name Angus. Anguses don't get laid."

I cough out a laugh into his chest. "Trust me, I'm sure the ladies would have made an exception."

One side of his mouth curves up as if to prove me right.

I pull my head up so I can get a full view of his face. "Wait, so if *Mac* means 'son of,' does that mean I can call you MacBitch?"

He looks at me for only a second before his head falls back and he lets out a deep, unrestrained laugh that comes from the bottom of his gut. His perfect mouth spreads in a full-on, blindingly-gorgeous, make-me-need-to-throw-out-these-panties smile. The low joyful sound combined with that smile completely undo me. It's extraordinary and I'm pretty sure I gasp.

Still amused, he finally notices me staring at him like a stunned, lovesick idiot. "What?" The word passes right through the center of his devastating smile.

There are no words so I basically attack him with my mouth, which is a bit of a shame since it covers that smile, but I'm hoping I can get a repeat later. Mac grabs my ass with both hands when I slide my tongue past his lips. He smells of spiced soap and tastes like warm mint with a hint of sweet.

I moan when his fingers edge past the hem of my panties to feel the bare sensitive skin, one finding its way to my wetness and making me squirm on top of him.

He hoists my hip up with his other hand to get better access and I'm willing to go anywhere he takes me. I pull on his hair while his hand works me under my panties and I'm frustrated by the barrier of our underwear.

I break from his mouth. "Naked."

He understands it for the demand it is and quickly shucks his boxer briefs to accommodate me. His sable gaze sears me, the dark ring around his irises almost meeting his lust-enlarged pupils as he resumes his task of pleasuring me.

When my squirming reaches the next level, he takes it upon himself to flip me to my back so he hovers over me, running his whiskers along my collarbone as he nuzzles my neck.

"Mac," I moan, grazing my fingertips across the rigid muscles of his back.

His lips hum along my skin until they reach the top of one of my bra cups. He doesn't hesitate before pulling it down with his teeth and then skimming my turgid nipple before biting down. My shoulders dig into the mattress as my back arches sharply and I cry out. He knows how to drive me completely insane.

I reach behind my back to remove the troublesome bra, but he flicks the closure before I have a chance and swipes the bra aside. My panties are a memory shortly after that and Mac is sliding home with my hips meeting his and welcoming him into me.

It's a perfect storm of desire and fulfillment coming together and it leaves me breathless beneath him.

Mac settles deep and stills for several sweet moments as we revel together in the connection. He kisses my chin and places the softest of kisses on my lips before raising his head and looking down on me with a mix of possession, want, and a sort of contentment I haven't quite seen there before.

He doesn't use any words, but I know in my heart exactly what he's saying.

"WHY THE FUCK would I do that?"

Mac trying to whisper cuss words into a phone is one of the funniest things I've seen in a long time.

We're in the corner of one of the fifth-floor collection

galleries at MoMA the following Saturday, and it's our first real outing together since the stuff with JoJo broke.

Her camp still hasn't denied anything and Mac is letting it ride but, thankfully, the paparazzi seem to have lost all interest in him.

Naveed, however, has not. I told him and Kate that I got the same "no comment" response from Mac's team but Naveed won't let it rest. I honestly think he might be onto me and is just torturing me because he's salty I'm keeping the good stuff from him—Mac being the good stuff, obviously.

I bite my lip to keep from laughing at Mac as he stands with one hand on his hip, his ear to his cellphone with Elle on the other end, and a grumpy scowl that's scaring away every child—and adult—who passes by.

Sometimes I don't know how she puts up with him.

I tug on his arm because I want to go look at my favorite Frida Kahlo with him and he finally pulls the phone away from his ear and shoves it back in his pocket.

"After I show you my favorite, you show me yours." I grin up at him, ignoring his frown and reminding him of our plan. "What did Elle do to torture you this time?"

"She wants to post on my Instagram account that I'm dating JoJo."

I pause. I do *not* like this idea. I mean, yes, it would help keep Margaret sniffing up the wrong tree, but Mac is *my* man, not JoJo's. I find my grip on his arm tightening.

"Finally got rid of the damn photographers and now she wants 'em back." Mac treks in his big boots at my side.

Crap. I haven't asked, but it only makes sense that the

exposure from the mistaken JoJo connection must have been good for sales.

I take a breath. "Come on, bachelor number twelve. Today is a fun day, not a work day."

And thank God for that. Things with Jen Baylor have only escalated in the past few days and I'm about to lose my shit.

But I can ignore it for now because I'm in one of the most amazing museums in the world and I'm about to share some Frida Kahlo with Mac. That's a coalescence of goodness a girl can't pass up.

He lets me lead him to *Fulang-Chang and I*, a self portrait of Frida with one of her pet monkeys. Next to the portrait is a matching mirror which Frida herself intended to hang beside the painting.

"She gave this painting to her best friend so she could look in the mirror and they'd be together." I look at myself in the reflection and wonder if Iris would think I was a nutcase if I sent her a picture of me and a mirror. Yeah, best not to go down that road.

"And this is your favorite?" Mac asks as he refuses to let me push him in front of the mirror.

I sigh and take in the portrait again. "Today, it is. But that can change anytime. I just always love the intimacy in the scale of her self-portraits. She's not hiding anything, you know?"

Mac studies me for a few seconds before giving time to the painting.

"And, besides, the monkey is cute." I look back at him. "And, now that I have you in the same room as Frida, I'm noticing certain similarities..." I trail off and raise my hand up to swipe my thumb over one of his eyebrows.

"Funny." He grabs my wrist and walks us unhurriedly from the gallery.

I can't help my cackle but I try smothering it with my palm.

"Okay, sorry. Now you show me your favorite."

Mac pulls out the museum map from his pocket and unfolds it. After a quick scan, he leads me by the hand down the stairs and around a few corners until we enter an exhibition gallery on the second floor.

In the middle of the room stands a sculpture. It's a simple column carved from wood, but it appears to be formed from a series of stacked and flipped pyramids in a repeating pattern. When we approach, I see it's labeled *Endless Column* by Constantin Brancusi.

It's a simple, sturdy structure, yet the repeating pattern of its construction suggests it could continue on through the ceiling and up into the sky. There's nothing particularly beautiful about it except for its simplicity and potential.

"And this is your favorite?" I throw his question back at him.

He tilts his head to the side and runs his eyes up the sculpture. "Not really."

I laugh and he turns one of his closed-lip grins on me.

"I've seen photos of another version of this in Romania. It's made from steel and it's almost a hundred feet high."

I look back at the much smaller version in front of us. "Now, *that*, I'd like to see."

Mac drops his chin in a nod.

"So, what do you like about it?" I know that's not fair.

Sometimes you just like something because you like it, but I love getting glimpses into how Mac's mind works.

"When I first learned blacksmithing, the idea was to focus on the functional. Punch holes, weld a ring, make a hinge. But I wanted to move right on past that and turn it into something new, not just a piece of iron or steel nobody would look twice at. I got a little carried away and into my own head about it, making these elaborate sculptures and then wondering why nobody wanted to buy them.

"I forgot about the basics and about how you can combine beauty and function. It wasn't until I remembered that that I was able to really discover my talent for furniture-making. I like to think I strike a good balance now."

"That's an understatement if I ever heard one. Your furniture is breathtaking."

"And it gives you a place to rest your feet." He winks like he's giving them out for free now.

"I, uh, I actually haven't been able to bring myself to sit in my chair yet."

His face freezes. "Excuse me?"

I throw my hands out. "I'm sorry, it's just so pretty and I love looking at it. I'm afraid to sit in it."

He just stares at me as people pass by us on either side. Then he shakes his head and mutters something under his breath with the words "pain in my ass," but I don't catch the whole thing because he's pulling me out of the gallery and I'm following with a shit-eating grin on my lips.

BY THE TIME Monday dawns again, I decide I'm done taking Jen Baylor's passive aggressive shit. I stop in at the coffee shop on the ground floor of the Warbey building to grab an extra big cup of coffee with enough sugar to make the spoon stand up straight. Coffee in one hand, I wave at the security guard on my way to the elevator. It's time for me to figure out a way to get Jen off my back once and for all.

When I step on the elevator, though, Naveed is waiting there. I almost trip over my own two feet at the sight of him because his hands are shoved in the front pockets of his designer suit-pants and he's looking at me like he just discovered the combination to my Hello Kitty diary and read the damn thing from cover to cover.

It's not like I can turn around and run away, so I continue walking forward until I'm standing in the back of the car and he's shifted his way through the other occupants to stand beside me.

"Well, hello there, Miss Peach."

I take a sip of my coffee and paste on a bright smile. "Hey, Naveed. How was your weekend? Sorry I couldn't do drinks Saturday." I was nailing my secret boyfriend and watching him finish a bench that would pay my rent for six months.

I can feel his eyes on me when I stare ahead at the tag sticking out from a woman's jacket in front of me.

"That's all right. What were you up to?"

My upper lip begins to sweat. Why do they allow so many people on one elevator?

"Oh, you know, just a little sightseeing." Not a lie.

"I heard as much." He raises a hand to prop a finger on

his chin and I stop breathing. "A little birdie told me you were standing on the sidewalk outside MoMA stuffing your maw with a hotdog and holding the hand of a giant brute whose description bore an uncanny resemblance to a broody blacksmith we both know."

My vision turns white and I grab the stainless-steel wall for balance, barely holding onto my coffee cup.

"Hey." Naveed wraps his hand around my arm. "Are you okay?"

I nod but the dizziness only gets worse.

Naveed gets behind me and grabs both my arms. "Move it, people. Low blood sugar emergency." The doors part on a random floor and he leads me out before grabbing the cup from my hand and tossing it into a trash can.

"Hey! That's mine," I complain in a disembodied voice.

"Coffee doesn't go well with wool." He continues steering me to a black sofa in a lobby I don't recognize and then gently pushes me into the seat.

"Here." He shoves a water bottle in my hand and I drink from it greedily until it's empty.

"Better?" he asks.

I nod and look down at my lap. I have no idea what to say to him.

"You have the worst poker face of anyone I've ever met in my entire life."

"You're not the first person to tell me that."

"I shouldn't think so." He sits next to me and shoves my knees over. "Now, are you going to tell me why you've been keeping this Angus McKinley thing a secret from me all this time?"

"Uh..." I look over at him and test the waters. "No?"

His mouth tightens and I get an angry Kardashian vibe. I try throwing one right back at him.

"Are you going to tell me who this little birdie is?"

"Tweet." He deadpans.

Well, at least that eliminates the threat of it being someone else at the magazine who knows my sweaty blacksmith secret. Someone like Jen freaking Baylor.

Naveed is still giving me the scowl and I sigh.

"I wanted to. I swear I was going to, Naveed. It's just... complicated."

He rolls his eyes. "Name something that's not."

"Mac and cheese."

"Enough with the mac and cheese, woman. Just accept the fact that New Yorkers are going to complicate the shit out of everything and move the hell on!"

"Okay, okay." I cross my arms in front of me, no longer sweating or seeing stars. "Yes, I'm seeing Mac—Angus—and I didn't want to tell anybody because you know how people talk and you know half of this Warbey crew has had it out for me from day one. I wasn't about to offer up any more fodder."

Naveed ditches his devil-may-care persona for a second and drops his voice. "But you could have told *me*."

My heart sinks and I feel like absolute shit. I reach a hand out and squeeze his arm. "I know. I'm so sorry. I guess I just got so caught up in wanting to make this new career all on my own that I pulled into myself a little too much. I didn't want anyone thinking I was behaving inappropriately. Even you."

"Pop-Tart, my middle name is Inappropriate."

I nod at him and grin a little. "I know. I'm sorry."

"And consider my lips sealed." He mimics zippering his lips and turning a key. "Now, tell me everything!"

I shove him in the shoulder. "I thought your lips were sealed!"

He just shrugs and gives me the dimple. So, of course, I share the good stuff.

Twenty minutes later, he's got stars in his eyes and I'm late for work.

"Now, if you'll excuse me, I need to go rip Jen Baylor a new one in an entirely professional manner that lets her know I mean business but won't hesitate to slash her tires if she doesn't cut this shit out."

Naveed stands and pulls me up with him. "That's a tall order, but I have faith in you."

"Thanks, Naveed."

THIRTY

"The world can be a cruel place. That's why God invented
sweet tea."
– Cookie Rutledge

AFTER I DROP Naveed off on his floor, I decide since I'm already late I may as well go back down and get another coffee. I'll need the caffeine for my planned come-to-Jesus meeting with Jen. She sent another group email yesterday and I'm done with her.

There's a long line now, though, and I'm trying to decide exactly how badly I need the caffeine when a familiar head of honey hair drifts into my peripheral vision.

I decide to abandon the coffee and flag down Elle who's just coming in the front door of the building.

"Elle, hey!" She's never visited me at work before, but it's a nice surprise.

She does a double take and I expect her face to brighten

with her usual smile, but her expression is an odd mix of determination and... exasperation. Huh?

I slow my steps as I approach. "What's the matter?"

She looks from me to the elevator and back again before sighing and signaling for me to step with her to the side where an empty shoeshine stand and a row of large potted plants line the lobby wall.

When she still doesn't say anything, I grab her arm. "You're worrying me."

She straightens to her full height in her gorgeous steel-gray and ivory dress and brushes my hand off. As soon as her eyes reach mine I know it's bad. The humor and warmth I've become accustomed to over the past few weeks since New Jersey has been replaced by a bitter cold. As has her voice.

"I suppose it's best I ran into you first."

I don't respond but just let her clipped tone hit me and try not to wince.

"The inaugural issue of *Work Home Life* magazine is running concurrent articles on Angus. The newest one is a human-interest piece on how he overcame his tumultuous background and his ties to the alleged criminal activities of one of Boston's richest families."

My mouth hangs open and, for the second time in the last hour, I grab onto something to keep myself upright—this time it's one of the giant pots to the side of us.

"No." My head shakes back and forth. "They can't do that. They *wouldn't* do that." I blink a few times, willing my brain to snap out of it. "Elle, we have to stop... *whoever* is doing this."

She sighs. "*We* don't have to stop anything." She shifts

her weight to one hip. "Look, Poppy, anything Angus told you is on the record. He signed a contract allowing you to print anything he volunteered."

She must have eaten a bad salad or something. "But he didn't. The answers he gave hardly even fill half a page and none of it is about his family," I remind her.

She smiles a sickly half-smile that has me wondering if I'm hallucinating. "Ah, but that was just in the first interview."

What is she talking about?

She unzips her purse and pulls out her phone, running her thumb over the screen.

"Not that it wasn't infuriatingly tedious waiting for you to pull the whole sordid tale out of him. I teed it up so thoroughly for you, how it took you so long, I have no idea." She shakes her head in disbelief.

"Hell, I had to resort to working the celebrity connection with that insipid starlet while you got your shit together. And that was no easy task, let me tell you. It did bring a nice uptick in sales, but I knew it wouldn't last without Mac playing ball like a good boy. I'm just happy we wrapped this up before I had to take you line dancing or something similarly gauche." Her words come out in a disdainful twist and she looks at me like I just suggested we grab lunch out back at the dumpsters. My confusion is obviously plastered all over my face.

"I admit I was annoyed when I initially received the contract to find that it was a lifestyle magazine that wanted to feature Angus. I'd heard rumors of a new design publication from Warbey and was hoping for the cover of *that*."

She swipes again with her thumb and waves a dismissing hand in the air. "But when he started panting after you and signed the contract behind my back, I eventually figured if he couldn't get a cover of a respectable industry magazine, at least we could get him attention in other ways. Imagine how the client base will be clamoring to pay whatever we ask once his story goes public." She glances up at me again. "Everybody loves a tragic hero."

Her eyes drop back down to the phone in her hand but I see nothing but red. I can't believe this is the same woman who texted me about Chinese baby fruit! "There is no way I'd *ever* do that to Mac," I hiss through clenched teeth.

She laughs but it's the furthest thing from funny. "You say that like it's your choice. You have a lot to learn about the way this town works if you think you have any control over what goes into a Warbey publication. All the juicy details have already been *conveniently* leaked to all the right people. Angus doesn't have a leg to stand on, legal or otherwise once your interview confirms it. That pesky non-disclosure agreement was threatening to be the death of me before you and your sweet little Southern accent and 'aw shucks' routine came along."

I get right in her face and have to hold myself back from decking her. "You're insane. I'll never tell a soul anything Mac told me."

She smiles and holds up her phone, assuming a fake low-toned voice. "Mr. McKinley, did you or did you not divulge the following statement to Ms. James of Warbey?"

She taps a button on her phone and I flinch when I hear my own voice. *"Why would your mama do it? Why would she push your father? I mean, what did she have against him other than him asking for money?"*

Mac's guttural voice follows, his response crystal clear. *"Because I chose him. And nobody ever puts her second."*

"I swear I thought I'd have to bug half of Manhattan before you got your act together."

I barely hear her as my mind races at a frantic pace. I need to do something. Surely Naveed would never go for this. And Kate! She can fix this. Or Athena!

"Whatever plan you're scheming, it's no use." Elle slides her phone back in her Burberry purse and flips her long fall of hair over her shoulder. "If Warbey doesn't publish the story—which they will—I've got contacts at less... reputable publishers I can work."

The dizziness threatens again but I push it down. "Why? Why would you do this to him? What did Mac ever do to you?"

She holds her purse at her waist with both hands and speaks in an entirely casual tone. "Oh, Poppy. You act like this is personal. It's not. It's just business."

Who is this woman and why would Mac have ever allowed himself or his father to be within a hundred miles of her? "What could you possibly get out of this?"

Her brows spike. "You think I took Angus on as a client because we're besties? You think I enjoy trying to make the career of a man who pushes back at every turn? Honestly, it's exhausting. He's a stepping stone, my dear. And while his pieces go for twice their current value, I'll happily take my twelve percent. Like I said, it's business."

"Not to Mac." I swallow hard. "You'll destroy him."

She shrugs like it's nothing.

"He'll quit. He'll abandon his studio and move out of the city and disappear."

And he'll leave me. I'm to blame for everything, after all.

"Not before I've made my mark. I'll be representing the next up-and-coming designer by then—one who'll be only too happy to let me work the public angle." She tilts her head and looks at me like I'm nothing but a small, dumb animal. "And, besides, you underestimate the power of money. When someone dangles a hundred-thousand-dollar check in front of Angus for a hunk of metal, it just might surprise you how quickly he could change his tune."

She doesn't know the first thing about him. He'd never take a paycheck on the back of his father's ruined reputation and his own privacy.

Elle tilts her head and looks me up and down until I feel the need for a shower. "You know, you seem to be forgetting how you'll benefit from this little scenario. Not a lot of nobodies from Georgia can show up in New York one day and have a byline on an exclusive just like that." She snaps. "And this is just the kind of springboard your magazine needs." She puts a hand to the side of her blood-red lips and pretend whispers. "I hear your little rebrand could use all the help it can get."

I hold in my gasp.

I am the human embodiment of panic. There has to be a way to protect Mac. But how? Elle is right about the dog-eat-dog world of publishing. I can think of a dozen publications that would kill for an exclusive, especially now that Mac's name is out there and all this scandal with Sterling

Pile's hotel chain is beginning to break. Mac will be fodder for the vultures and they'll pick his bones clean.

"Looks like I may be getting my cover after all. He does have the face for it, you know. And ladies love a scar." She taps her nose and slinks away like the snake she is.

My entire body is burning with fury.

I watch her get buzzed in by security and make her way to the elevators. I consider pulling the fire alarm to keep her from getting upstairs, but she already said the magazine has the story. She's probably just meeting with someone as a formality. Either that or she's here for her monthly coven meeting with the likes of Jen Baylor.

I turn to the doors of the building and start walking as I yank my phone from my purse. I need to call Mac. I need to go to him right this second. We'll talk it out and find a way to fix this.

We have to.

MAC DOESN'T PICK up so I flag down a cab like a pregnant woman who's about to crown and won't take no for an answer. I throw cash at the guy and jump out just as the car is coming to a stop outside the studio.

My fist bangs on the wood of the door till it hurts and Jonathan opens the door in exasperation.

"All right. All right." I don't even pause to say a word or decide if he's offending me today. I just rush on by until I get to the back studio. But Mac isn't there so I backtrack until I hear a loud repetitive banging.

The forge.

"Don't!" Jonathan shouts, but there's no stopping me.

I swing the heavy door open and pant from all the running around I've been doing and the adrenaline pumping through my veins. The door slams shut and I lean against it, shutting out Jonathan's voice and everything outside this room until it's just me and Mac and a room filled with noise and tools and soot. The air is thick and hot.

"Mac." My voice broadcasts my panic, but he doesn't look up from where he's focused on a steel rod with a glowing orange tip. His corded hands and arms are streaked with black and each swing of his hammer ends in a loud clang as metal strikes metal and sparks fly. He repeats the movements over and over, each bang echoing in my chest.

"Mac!" I yell and he finally lowers the rod into a basin of water with a cloud of steam and a hissing cry.

He still doesn't look up but drops the heavy items with a clash and walks over to a table against the far wall where he picks up his phone and stalks in my direction as he tears off his safety glasses. I don't know what's going on, but I have a horrible inkling that the news I came to share has already made its way here.

When we're only a few feet apart, he taps his thumb on the phone and finally meets my eyes. What I see there breaks my heart into a million tiny shards.

A disembodied voice fills the air around us. "Mr. McKinley, this is Domonique Harwood from Warbey Publishing Incorporated. We'd like to get your comments on details of an article we'll be printing, per your contract with us. It contains statements made by you regarding several incidents, including an accident involving your late father, Angus McKinley, Sr., and your mother, Margaret Tenneson-Pile. We're happy to send a copy over with interview excerpts between you and Ms. James if you'd like to read it before commenting. You can call us back or we'll try again tomorrow. If we don't hear from you, we'll just make a note that we received no additional comment."

"It's Elle." My voice isn't as loud as I want it to be, but I push it out anyway. "She—"

Mac advances a step, his damp face dirty with soot and contorted with pain—betrayal. "She what? She told me *not* to do the interview with your magazine."

"Wait. What?" It's all so overwhelming I have to remind myself that he's right. But he doesn't understand.

"When your buddy Naveed sent that contract over I was ready to give her hell for disregarding my no-interview edict. But I didn't have to. She said she was just being nice and would never agree to it." His voice is practically a snarl.

Elle's words from earlier come racing back and I put both my hands out in front of me, as if to hold Mac there so he'll listen. "That's just because she wanted an industry magazine cover. She didn't realize it was for *WHL* when she first met us. She would have manipulated you into doing an interview if it was for one of her precious design publications."

Mac shakes his head, beads of sweat from the hot room running down his temples. "That doesn't make any sense, Poppy. She was pissed when she found out I went rogue and interviewed with you on my own."

"No! She wanted you to get close to me. She wanted…" Realization crashes into me. Who am I kidding? Elle is the master of manipulation and subterfuge. She could run circles around Bunny any day. She's been two steps ahead of Mac *and* me the entire time. We both played right into her hand as she laid out all the breadcrumbs—right down to distracting me the night of the auction so she could work the JoJo angle.

Pulling in a lungful of hot air, I close the distance between us and grip his damp t-shirt. "Mac, you have to believe me! I never wanted any of this to happen. I'd never betray you like that."

He steps back and the shirt is ripped from my fingers. His jaw is stone and his eyes are turning blank.

I'm crying ugly tears by this point and I can't stop. "I love you, don't you know that?" I don't even care that I let the l-word out after keeping it so carefully tucked away in my heart all this time.

His voice is low and flat when he responds, "What I know is my life was just fine before you walked into my studio. And now it's turning to shit again. That's what I know."

He steps forward and, for only a split second, I think he's changed his mind and is coming in for a hug, but he just grips my shoulders with both hands and shifts me aside like I'm nothing but a curtain. Then he opens the door and walks out.

I turn, swiping at my tears. "Mac, no. We can fix this. We'll sue them if they try to publish any of this." Screw what Elle said! I'll find Mac an amazing lawyer and we'll figure out a loophole or something.

Right, Poppy, like you have any contacts in New York.

He pauses for a brief moment but doesn't turn back

when he says, "I used to think your naiveté was one of your strongest assets."

His words cut through me and steal my power of speech, so I stand there silently crying as the door slams behind him.

THIRTY-ONE

"Dorothy wasn't wrong, even if she was from the Midwest."
– Cookie Rutledge

JONATHAN all but shoves me out the door after that, just refraining from kicking me in the ass on my way out. I'm numb and hollow and don't know where to go, but it's only ten in the morning and I have yet to show up for work.

The last place I want to go is Warbey, but if that's the source of the imminent destruction of Mac's world, that's where I have to be. I grab a cab and am on the elevator to my office twenty minutes later when I get a text from Athena's assistant about an emergency meeting in the conference room on the twelfth floor.

I push the appropriate button and drag my ass there with no small doubt as to the meeting's purpose.

The frenetic vibe almost blows me back as I force myself to walk in the room and take a seat among the half-dozen other people present. I see Kate and Naveed and studiously avoid their eyes.

Athena struts on her four-inch heels toward the head of the table, pausing first by my chair. "Poppy, I'll need a word with you after the meeting." Her tone is stern and I want to shrink into myself. This is it.

She takes her place in the seat on the end. "Okay, people, we need to quickly redesign the inaugural issue— new cover, new featured article, new photos. You're not going to believe what we've got! This is exactly the ace in the hole we needed for our first issue. *WHL* is going to explode!"

She lays out all the facts. How our small urban artisan feature has turned into a double article with a human-interest angle and an exclusive interview. She credits me and Naveed and all I do is stare at the glass surface in front of me, ignoring the looks and comments coming my way. I don't see how Naveed reacts, but he's unusually silent, probably because he's staring at me as well.

"This one comes from the top, so no excuses—let's get this done!"

"So JoJo is getting pushed?" someone asks.

Athena straightens her stack of papers by tapping the bottom edges on the table. "Not quite. We're just giving this McKinley guy some prime real estate in the upper right."

"Did we ever get confirmation that he and JoJo are dating? What ever happened with that?" another person asks and I think it's the guy from marketing.

Naveed finally pipes up and I want to kiss him—or cry all over his expensive suit. "Dead end. No truth to it."

"Too bad. That would have been ideal."

The chatter continues but I block it all out. We're talking about layouts and page order like we're not about to rip the rug right out from under the man I love and prove to him that putting his trust in me was the biggest mistake of his life.

But it's not their fault. It's all mine. Even if I had nothing to do with this story and the details being leaked by Elle. The fact of the matter is Mac never would have signed that contract if it weren't for me. He said so himself. He signed it because he wanted to get to know me, and now I'm bringing his world down around him.

I barely make it through the next half hour of hashing out details and assigning tasks so we can hit our deadlines and ensure all our promotional and marketing campaigns reflect the adjustment in the inaugural issue's focus.

Most of it is a blur until Kate closes the door behind her and I'm the last one left in the room with Athena. She takes a new seat across the table from me and removes her glasses.

"I learned a long time ago to trust my instincts and I'm usually a good judge of character. I want to give you the benefit of the doubt because you don't strike me as a climber. But I have to ask." She pauses, maybe to give me a chance to confess something—I'm not sure. But I remain silent so she continues, "I'm curious as to why the higher ups knew about your second interview before we did." She gives her head a small shake. "I won't even begin to ask why my creative director was conducting any kind of interview in the first place, but I will tell you it took some quick talking to smooth this out."

My responding laugh holds zero humor. I wouldn't blame her if she called the state psych ward to come get me at this point.

"It wasn't an interview," I choke out.

"I don't understand."

I take a breath to steady my voice. "It was a... personal conversation."

"Oh."

I look up at her and watch her brow furrow before realization dawns. "Oooh."

I lay my hands flat on the table. "Athena, we can't print any of this. Mac never meant that story to go public. Any of it."

Her expression switches back to confusion. "Then why did you send the transcript?"

"I didn't! The wicked witch of Manhattan did."

She lifts her phone from the table and scrolls through the screen. "Your name is all over this."

I shake my head. "The bad guys always know how to cover their tracks, or so I'm discovering. But I promise you, this wasn't part of any interview, so we can't print it."

Athena returns my head shake. "I'm so sorry, but my hands are tied. The board wants a big splash and this is just the kind of thing that sells magazines. We'll all be kissing our careers goodbye if we go against corporate and sit on this."

"Even if he never agreed to it?"

She sets her phone back down and holds my eyes. "He did agree. When he signed the contract. I'm sorry, Poppy. We're running the story."

I draw my hands into my lap. "Is there anything I can do?"

"I'm afraid not." She gives me a sad smile. "Look, it can't be all that bad. He comes out of this smelling like roses. I'm sure he's just a bit surprised because he wasn't expecting it. And you're feeling protective, which makes sense. We all protect the ones we love. This will give his career just the boost every artist would kill for. You'll see."

The irony of her not caring that I forged a relationship with the subject of an interview refuses to hit its mark. All I can see is Mac's look of betrayal and devastation. He doesn't give two shits about his own image, but he'd fight to the death to preserve his dad's memory.

I muster up a fake smile. "Thanks for at least believing me. It means a lot." Especially since the man I love thinks I'm a big fat liar and a sleazy turncoat.

"Of course." She pushes her chair back. "Now, we've all got a big task ahead of us and someone has to break it to JoJo Ames that she's sharing the spotlight." Athena widens her eyes in fake horror and I force the corners of my lips back up as she gathers her things and leaves the room.

It's official. I've screwed the pooch and there's no undoing it.

I pull my phone out and text Mac.

Please talk to me. We can figure this out.

My heart lifts when three dots appear. Mac is texting me. He never texts!

MAC

It's Jonathan. Please, just leave him alone.

A tear falls on the glass surface of my phone.

Leave him alone.

Yes, I reckon it's the kindest thing to do, and it's probably the only thing he's ever asked of me. It would only be right to give him that.

"DOUBLE CHECK THE CALENDAR, ladies, 'cuz it must be my birthday!" Cookie throws her arms around me, wrapping me in a tight hug and bringing the tears right back up to the surface.

It took me twelve hours and about six gallons of water to rehydrate my body after the Big Apple Shitshow, as I now refer to it.

"Hey, y'all!" Cookie shouts, not bothering to move her head and practically making me deaf in the process. "Look who's home!"

"Poppy?" I don't have to look to know Iris just walked in the room. "Poppy!"

Then I'm in the middle of a quadruple-decker sandwich, getting crushed by Cookie, Iris, Mama, and Bunny.

"Let me look at you," Mama says, but won't stop squeezing me to allow me to step back even a half inch.

"You haven't been eating enough. You're so skinny I could snap you in two!" Bunny declares, pinching my arm.

"No, she's perfect," Cookie says back.

"I didn't say she wasn't."

"Let the girl breathe!" Iris shouts. "Mama, stop pulling my hair."

"It's caught in my watch. Hold on a darn minute."

"Grab the kitchen shears, Cookie!"

And, just like that, the tears that were threatening disappear and I'm laughing my ass off in the arms I missed so darn much.

"HEY THERE, SWEETHEART." A quiet voice sounds behind me.

I'm standing in the kitchen with my head stuck in the fridge a few hours after my arrival at the Violette. It took a good ten minutes to extract myself from my arrival hug and about two more hours for everyone to stop asking me questions. But I didn't share much. I mostly just basked in the familiarity of family and home.

I straighten and turn, a smile curving my lips.

"Hey, Bobby Lee."

My eyes scan him from top to toe and he looks good. His warm smile and perfect chin cleft make it impossible to do anything but grin back at him.

I don't even balk when he comes in for a hug and tucks my head under his chin. He smells like soap and a hint of that hair product that normally stings my nose but does nothing but soothe me at the moment.

"I take it Bunny called," I say rather than ask.

"I believe she waited a whole five minutes, though, so that's progress I reckon."

I laugh. "Yeah, I suppose so."

He pulls back and looks me over much like I just did to him.

"You look tuckered. Pretty as always, but tuckered."

I pretend to scowl. "Now, Bobby Lee, I know your mama taught you better than to utter a negative word about a woman's appearance."

He puts his hands up like he's surrendering. "You're right. I'm sorry."

I sigh. "Between you and me, I could use a three-week nap."

He smiles again and takes a step back to lean a hip against Cookie's kitchen counter. "Does that have to do with the job or the guy?" He's trying to pretend his question is casual, but he's too concerned to swing it.

I push my hair back from my face and let the refrigerator door close behind me. "Both."

His jaw ticks and it almost reminds me of Mac. "Will I be needing to book another flight to New York to break that Angus guy's nose?"

"No." I don't tell him I'll break his first if he lays a hand on Mac. I know he's trying to be sweet. "Nothing needs any more breaking than I've already done myself."

His head cocks. "What does that mean?"

And then, surprising the hell out of even myself, I tell Bobby Lee Collinsworth absolutely everything.

Including how I've been pretending to be someone I'm not; how I fell head-over-heels in love with a man who'd never for a second consider being anyone but who he is;

and how, when the game and its players showed their dirty underside and I couldn't stop the impending disaster, I threw in the towel and came back home.

THE NEXT MORNING I wake not to the sounds of horns and garbage trucks, but to the sweet song of Carolina wrens singing outside the yellow bedroom's window. A slow smile spreads its way across my lips as I stretch my arms over my head. Until I remember.

It's only Wednesday, so I know the *WHL* staff is hard at work up in Manhattan picking apart Mac's life while he either escapes back to New Jersey or spends his time hammering out his misery in his forge. I briefly wonder if he's picturing my face every time the hammer comes down.

I've been racking my brain since Monday to figure out a way to stop this story from breaking, but the truth of the matter is I have zero influence over anybody in that town. Hell, I couldn't even get the barista at the coffee shop to get my drink right half the time.

Naveed and Kate have been blowing up my phone with texts and calls. Neither one of them seems to know what happened or where I went. From their texts, it doesn't sound like Athena's told them about me handing in my resignation, but I'm sure it's just a matter of time before word gets around and Jen begins her official campaign to take over my position.

At least now that I'm gone, Mac's mother won't be knocking on my door anytime soon. Not that it's much consolation. I'd still relish the opportunity to kick that woman's ass.

My phone vibrates on the bedside table and I groan. I thought I'd shut off my notifications, but clearly I haven't. When I pick it up, there's a notification of a new text on my lockscreen.

One press of my thumb and I read a message from Bobby Lee followed by a link to an online article.

BOBBY LEE

Thought you'd want to see this.

I click through to the article and sit straight up in bed at the headline.

"CEO of Sterling Hotels Indicted on Six Counts of Money Laundering and Forgery"

My phone vibrates again and Bobby Lee has sent me another link. I quickly tap it.

"Daughter of Shipping Magnate Dan Tenneson Arrested on Manslaughter Charges"

I gasp, but in comes another link. I can't click fast enough or stop to wonder how Bobby Lee happened to find all this stuff.

The last link isn't to a newspaper article but to the celebrity section of the very familiar *WHL* website instead.

"JoJo Ames Puts a Rest to Rumors"

My hand flies to my mouth when I see the byline is none other than Naveed Shah.

"After weeks of social media tittering, JoJo Ames broke the news yesterday that she is not, in fact, dating the handsome New York blacksmith and furniture designer, Angus McKinley.

"Representatives for Ms. Ames commented that she is busy working on next summer's collection for her line of designer athleticwear and is putting romance on the back burner for now.

"When asked to comment on the infamous photo—you all know the one I mean (Hello, smolder!)—Mr. McKinley denied any relationship as well. It turns out neither had even met until that night.

"'I'm sure she's nice but I haven't so much as shaken her hand.'"

I bite my lip at that, wondering how much self-control it must have taken Mac to make the "nice" comment.

"Since Ms. Ames isn't on his radar, we asked the dashing Mr. McKinley what he looks for in a woman (You're welcome).

"'I'm partial to redheads. Southern redheads.'"

My eyes go wide and I keep reading.

"But don't get too excited, all you Dixieland gingers. When asked about his relationship status, here's what he had to say:

"'Not that it's your business but, no, I'm not single.'"

I squeal and throw the covers aside, the phone shaking in my hand when I read the last bit.

"Be sure to subscribe to WHL to read full interviews from JoJo Ames and Angus McKinley's in January's issue of the new WHL magazine."

"Omigod, omigod, omigod!" I race down the stairs in my pajama shorts and tank top as fast as my bare feet will take me.

What has that man done?!

I almost fling open the front door before I realize I need

to make a plan and can't just go rushing back to New York in little more than my drawers and a smile.

But I need to get to Mac.

"Where's the fire?"

I skid to a stop on the hardwood and look over to see Bunny sipping her coffee on Cookie's good sofa, her dyed blond hair in a genuine bouffant.

"Sorry, Bunny, I can't talk. I've gotta..." I trail off because it's too much to explain and ain't nobody got time for that.

"Come and sit over here, dear." She pats the seat next to her. "There's nothing so important it can't wait for a cup of coffee and a chat with a close friend."

I want to tell her how very wrong she is. That if I don't see Mac as soon as humanly possible, I might just die of frustration and an exploding heart.

But she doesn't look like a woman who'll take no for an answer, and all my past experience only reaffirms it.

I paste on a weak smile and go join her, sitting on my hands so I don't start biting my nails.

"Beautiful morning, isn't it?" She brings the floral-patterned cup to her lips. She's not putting out her usual hyper vibe so the caffeine must not have kicked in yet.

Come on, Bunny. Seriously? The weather? I hum my agreement while my smile struggles to stay put.

"You know, I can't tell you how lucky I am to have a boy like Bobby Lee for a son."

Here we go. "Yes, well, we're all awfully fond of him."

"So many sons fly from the nest and never come back, but not my Bobby Lee." She puts a hand to her ample bosom.

It's all I can do not to roll my eyes. Instead, I glance toward the kitchen. Where is Cookie? Can't she take over for me?

"No, he loves his mama," she continues, oblivious to my inner turmoil. "And not a secret out there he can keep from me."

I freeze in my seat. Well, shit. This is about to get messy, I can just tell.

But she surprises me by abandoning the topic and starting on a new tangent.

"You know, back in the day, I was quite the catch. I don't like to brag, but there were some summers when I had a line of suitors going out the door and down my daddy's front walk." She smooths a hand over her giant hair and my smile threatens to crack—along with my sanity.

"There was this one. A fellow by the name of Daniel. His family was from up north and used to summer down here. They were quite well-to-do and I must say my daddy was impressed with him. He had *gumption*, like my daddy used to say—aspirations in the shipping industry and, for a minute there, I admit I was charmed enough to consider him. A kind man—dashing too, with the loveliest pair of brown eyes."

My throat goes dry and, suddenly, I'm not in such a hurry to get off this sofa.

She waves her free hand. "Oh, but he wanted to take me up to Boston and I just couldn't leave Savannah. You know how firmly my roots are planted. We kept in touch over the years, though." She tilts her head down and arches her eyebrows at me for a second. "Still do, in fact."

Holy shit.

My vision narrows and my foot starts a beat on the floor while she calmly sips her coffee again.

"I eventually met Vernon and never once regretted my choice, especially once God finally saw fit to bless us with Bobby Lee. But, as you know, keeping up relationships with old friends and family is important. And I dare say, Daniel Tenneson never did quite get over me."

I know my eyes are huge by this point.

"He even told me as much when I was on the phone with him just the other night. Cheeky man."

Bunny wears a small smile until her eyes finally come to rest on my face and her expression turns soft and a bit sad. "Shame how his family has all but crumbled around him. But I reminded him it's never too late when it comes to family—or setting things right."

Holy freakin' plot twist, Batman.

"Bunny?"

She looks away again and takes a dainty sip of her coffee.

"What did you do?"

THIRTY-TWO

"So long as you can look yourself in the mirror, you're doin'
just fine."
— Cookie Rutledge

"NOT THOSE!"

"Yes, those!" I throw my red boots on top of the three other pairs I just shoved in my suitcase.

"But I've been wearing them and they're so comfy," Iris whines.

"They'll still be *so comfy* in New York when they're on *my* feet then."

"Greedy."

I hip check her on my way to grab more of my clothes.

"I can't believe you haven't burned that suitcase by now." Iris flips up the cover of the big pink case to reveal the silly phrase where the tape has all but peeled off. It looks a mess but I can't worry about that now.

"Come on, you said you'd help me!" I need to catch the first flight back to New York and go find Mac.

Bunny's story is still swirling in my head, but I believe I have her to thank for Margaret Tenneson-Pile's arrest, as crazy as that may be! I need more details and I'm not getting them here in Savannah. Then I have to find a way to get rid of Elle once and for all and hold Mac's hand while all the dust settles. Although, it sounds like his grandfather might be willing to help cushion the blow. I'll have to wait and see.

"Poppy!" Cookie's voice comes up the old staircase.

I turn to Iris who's still eyeing my red boots. "Can you tell her I'll be down in just a minute?"

Iris hops off the bed and I can hear her feet pounding down the stairs. Then they're pounding right back up again and she's standing there panting in my doorway.

"Poppy!"

I shake my head at her. "What's the matter?"

"He's here." Her eyes are about to pop out of her damn head.

When I just look at her like she's crazy, she finally exclaims, "Mac! He's downstairs sitting on Cookie's settee looking like he's about to bust the thing in two."

"What?!" I drop the stack of jeans from my hand and follow Iris as fast as my bare feet can take me. I skip the last two steps and I'm turning the corner to the parlor before I can even give the first thought as to what I'll say to Mac.

And there he is. His hair is a messy tangle like it hasn't seen a comb in a year and his dark scruff has grown into almost a full-on beard in just two days. He's stiff as a board where his fine ass is perched on Cookie's early twentieth-century embroidered settee and when his eyes find me from across the room, I see an entire world looking back at me.

I couldn't stop my feet if I tried, and I have no desire to try. I all but launch myself at him, and thank God he stands before he catches me or that settee would be history and I'd never hear the end of it.

Mac's arms come around me and he's crushing me to him, whispering words in my ear I can't even make out because I'm so consumed with relief and happiness at seeing him and feeling him against me.

I don't even realize I'm crying until he pulls back and is wiping the tears away with his thumbs while his eyes travel every millimeter of my face.

"You're here," I finally eek out through my tight throat.

"I'm here," he agrees. "And I'm so sorry."

I shake my head as I make sure nothing else on his face has altered in the last few days. "It doesn't matter. I'm so sorry too. I never meant—"

He cuts me off, his thumbs coming to rest on my cheeks while his fingers gently hold my jaw. "I know. It was Elle."

I nod and then I can't help myself. My lips are on his in a hard kiss, trying to tell him everything that needs to be said with just the press of my lips.

A throat clears and I pull back, a goofy smile forming on my face. Mac raises that eyebrow and tucks me under his arm.

"There are other people present, Poppy, if you haven't noticed," Cookie gently reprimands. "And the man just walked in the door. You can give him a moment before you attack him like a wild animal." The words are disapproving but her tone hides a smile.

Iris goes to stand beside Cookie. "Hey, Mac. Good to see you." Her grin is way too naughty.

"Iris," Mac responds with a nod, but I can still feel his eyes on me.

"All right, Iris. Let's go fix some tea and give these two a few minutes of privacy."

Cookie marches Iris out of the room with both hands on her shoulders and I turn right back into Mac's arms.

"You met Cookie." I, again, point out the obvious.

He nods and responds in his familiar gravelly timbre, "Wasn't sure if she was going to let me in at first."

I shrug and grin up at him. "She's a tad protective."

"I'm glad," he says, his tone turning serious. "I just wish you hadn't needed protecting from me. I was an asshole."

I grip his arm. "No, you weren't. You were hurt."

"Doesn't excuse it. I'm sorry for what I said and I'm sorry I didn't listen."

"Elle made it hard. She takes evil to the next level." I frown and Mac tries smoothing the lines in my forehead with a finger.

"Well, she won't be a problem anymore. In fact, I'm pretty sure her lawyer has forbidden her from talking to anyone."

"What do you mean?"

"I'm suing her for breach of contract, among other things. Well, technically, Jonathan is suing her, but it's all in my name."

"Seriously? Jonathan?"

Mac nods. "He's been onto her from the beginning,

apparently. Turns out he *doesn't* trust anybody—just like you said—luckily for me. Said he had a hell of a time holding you at bay while he tried catching her at her game."

"Oh. My. God." I drop both arms from Mac as I let that settle. Then I pull back because I can't concentrate when he's touching me. He catches my hand in his, though, and doesn't let me stray far.

"I saw your mother got arrested. And her husband."

Mac takes a deep breath and lets it out with a disbelieving shake of his head. "Yeah."

"How do you feel about that?"

"Honestly, I'm not sure it's sunk in yet."

"I'm glad your pops is finally going to get justice," I venture, telling him the truth.

"Me too. I guess I made peace a while back that it was never going to happen. I just went to live my life and keep my head down. Now that my grandfather has come forward as an eyewitness, I don't know..." He shrugs.

"Have you talked to him?" Bunny told me Dan Tenneson intended to try mending fences and get to know his grandson, but I can't see Mac just opening the door and letting him waltz right in.

Mac shakes his head. "Not yet. He called. Left a message. Let me know he wasn't going to protect my mother anymore."

I squeeze his hand, knowing there must be a lot of emotions in there and even more forgiveness to earn. But from the minute I talked to Bunny this morning I had a glimmer of hope that maybe Mac hadn't lost all his family after all.

"Are you gonna be okay with your name being in the papers?"

He looks down at our joined hands, my normal-sized one in his giant Mac-sized one.

"That depends. You gonna be with me?"

My mouth turns up and I try to give him my best "you're an idiot" look.

His lips twitch in response. "Then, yeah, I'll be okay."

"You guys are so stinkin' cute!" Iris struts in the room without making a single noise of warning first. She's got a tray of sweet tea and four glasses filled with ice.

Cookie trails in after her with a plate of shortbread, her hair freshly primped, and a coat of her signature red lipstick. She's not fooling me.

"Everybody sit," she orders and we all obey, this time Mac and I taking the sturdier sofa while Iris snatches a shortbread and drops on the settee. Cookie makes herself comfortable in a chair.

She leans forward to pour the tea and Mac whispers in my ear.

"She's gonna make me drink that awful shit, isn't she?"

I hide my smile with a hand in front of my mouth, saving my lecture about the wonders of sweet tea for another time. "Allow me to introduce you to Southern manners, Mac. Just hold your nose and think of England."

I get a good glower at that and can't help but snicker.

Cookie ignores my noises and hands a full glass over to Mac who takes it with a thank you. Once she's done passing the glasses, she settles back and focuses all her attention on Mac.

"Now, Angus, tell me, what are your feelings on gluten?"

Aaaand, we're off.

A half hour later, Mac's tea glass sits on the tray still half full and Cookie has quizzed him on everything from his preference in biscuit toppings to whether or not the Braves will have a chance at next year's World Series.

He's taken it all in stride in his quiet Mac way and I can see Cookie is a bit smitten, even if she doesn't come right out and say it.

Meanwhile, Iris has earned several annoyed looks from me and even a balled-up napkin to the forehead while Cookie went to replenish the shortbread.

But that's what she gets for not letting things go when Mac politely tells her for the third time that, no, he can't make her her own Iron Throne.

By the time we get another moment alone, it's late afternoon and we escape the inn and its oversolicitous occupants for a walk. It's so quiet compared to Manhattan, and I catch Mac turning a three-sixty more than once as he scans the nearly empty sidewalks surrounding us.

I have to grab his arm a few times to warn him to duck so his head doesn't brush the Spanish moss hanging from the oak trees. After the fourth time, I tell him he's gonna get chiggers if he doesn't watch himself, and he's careful after that.

We walk to Lafayette Square, one of the twenty-two beautiful town squares of Savannah, and stand in front of the ornate green fountain in its center.

"This fountain was given to the city by the Colonial Dames of America to celebrate Savannah's two-hundred-fiftieth anniversary," I tell him, ever the responsible home-town tour guide.

He steps around it, undoubtedly checking it out from his blacksmithing and design perspective. "Pretty."

"Mama applied to be a Dame but she got turned down when some truly scandalous behavior by my great-great-great-granddaddy was uncovered." I shake my head in feigned disgrace.

"Why doesn't that surprise me?" Mac comes back to my side.

I scrunch my nose and shrug. "We're not exactly a squeaky-clean bunch."

"You're happy here."

"I am, but I think it's because I'm finally feeling like myself again."

"But you don't in New York."

I twist my lips to the side as I think on it. "With you, I do. But I've got some serious rethinking to do as far as my professional persona."

"Ah." He leans in and mock whispers. "The shark."

I narrow my eyes at him. "Know-it-all."

His lips twitch. "If it makes you feel better, I've been doing some rethinking too."

"Oh, yeah?" I lean in, mimicking his move. "Does this have anything to do with the fact that you voluntarily gave another interview?" I tease him about his comments on the website with Naveed.

"You saw that, did you?"

"I did." I turn fully to him and put my hands on his pectorals before going on my tiptoes to drop a kiss on his cheek. My fingers flex over his shirt. God, he's firm. I'd almost forgotten how built he is under those t-shirts. It makes me want to grab his ass to remind myself exactly how perfect it is.

"Decided my pops would probably consider what I've been doing these past few years as hiding. And he was no coward."

"That's the last word I'd use to describe you, Mac. Your pops would be proud of you."

He gives me one of those half-shrugs. "Maybe, but I can do more. Gonna get the smithing apprenticeship program back up and running."

"Really?" I go back on my heels.

He nods absently and brings a thumb to my chin like he likes to do.

"And how about you? What are you gonna do?"

"Besides come back to New York with you?"

His lips turn up at that and he rubs the spot on my chin like it's his lucky charm.

"I'm not sure." I drop my eyes to the bricks at our feet. "I resigned from my job."

His thumb slides down so he can prop my chin back up and I have to look him in the face.

"I'm sorry, Poppy. I wish you hadn't done that. Not for me."

"I didn't." I shake my head. "Okay, I did, but that wasn't all. I was going about it all the wrong way."

"You lost yourself." His raspy tone caresses me.

"Didn't I already warn you about being a know-it-all?"

He grins and it's a big one. It's downright magical. I watch him as the mini parrots start chattering again, fighting over which one of them is gonna take him home. I tell them all to shut the hell up because Mac is mine, dammit, and that's all there is to it.

"Nobody ever asked me to be someone I'm not. I did that all on my own." It's time I remember I got that job in New York as a result of hard work, hours of dedication, and by trusting my gut these last ten years to put my best work forward.

I deserve that job, and I shouldn't be giving it away just like that.

"When I think about it, the only one in that damn city I've been my true self around is you. I've been pretending to be some well-bred, designer-wearing, no-nonsense boss at work; I've been lying to one of my oldest friends; and, until a couple days ago, was avoiding a new one just so I wouldn't have to lie."

"Sounds like you know what you need to do."

"Yup." I smile up at him for another second and then a thought occurs to me. "Now I just have to figure out how to explain to everyone in my department why I suddenly have a Southern accent."

A rumbling laugh sounds from Mac's chest and, after drinking in the wonderful things it does to his smile, I press myself to him in a hug so I can feel its warm, beautiful energy flow through my entire body.

THE NEXT AFTERNOON, I walk through the art department toward the center of the room. I've got on my favorite boots and a matching dress Iris shoved at me when I was on the way out the door this morning with Mac.

He slept in the green bedroom because, well, we were at Cookie's and, even though she's a smart lady who knows how the world works, it's still her inn and her rules. If I snuck in to make out with Mac after midnight, that'll be our secret to keep.

Mama, Iris, Bunny, and Cookie all hugged us goodbye at the door before we took off for the airport with my ratty suitcase in tow. But before she let Mac go, Cookie took a good long minute holding his cheeks in her hands and checking him over before she nodded her head and said, "You'll do nicely."

Mac might not know what that means, but I sure do, and it had me smiling to myself the whole way to the airport.

After an uneventful flight spent cuddling with Mac while he shifted uncomfortably in his too-small seat, we got a cab back into Manhattan where I quickly changed at my apartment and got my ass over to Warbey.

It took Athena all of two minutes to welcome me back into the fold, telling me she never even filed my letter because she knew I'd be back.

But now I've got some serious work to do. I thought on it all last night and today and decided I need to take a page out of Mac's book and be who I am with zero apologies. Mac may rub people the wrong way or get himself into uncomfortable positions, but he doesn't ever apologize for who he is. So, why should I?

I stop when I reach the middle of the room and bring my hand to my mouth where I release a loud whistle I'm sure you can hear from the executive floor. Everybody's heads whip my way.

"Attention, everybody! Attention!"

I notice Jenna exchange a glance with another designer but I block them out.

"First, I want to thank everyone for your hard work at turning things around with this last update to our premier issue. I see a lot of talent in this room, and I love the flow of ideas. Please, keep it comin'. I know from experience that it's the *ideas* that drive the product—make it a success. All the rest comes second. If you have great ideas, you'll go far in this department, no matter if you're the director or the newest design intern. I've built my career on this, and I'll stake it on it.

"Second, if you see something that could be better, by all means, I urge you to figure out a way to make it better and bring that to the next up in the chain of command. Regardless of the outcome, it's always welcome. Maybe they'll run with it or maybe it won't be quite right for reasons they know and you might not. But, take this advice seriously: complaining about something without putting your time into divising a solution is the best way to lose the respect of your colleagues. This is a universal truth. And, as a side note, where I come from, nobody ever gets far playing leapfrog and making a ruckus for no reason. Frankly, it's not only bad form but it makes you look petty."

I can see Jenna crossing her arms and looking all offended, but I don't give two good goddamns.

"Finally, I want us to be a family. No, I'm not crashing your holiday dinner, but it's my belief that people work better, are more creative and productive, when their work environment is a positive one where they can breathe easy. So, I'm instituting a sweet tea break every afternoon. We're gonna lay our work aside for twenty minutes and chat, meditate, listen to music, whatever you like to do to relax—heck, you can even dance if you want. You don't like sweet tea, that's fine. More for me. But I'll bring the lavender shortbread. I promise you're gonna love it."

I take a breath and look around. A few people look excited, probably more than a few look skeptical, and some just look plain confused.

But that's okay. I'm trying something out that feels true to me. And you can't win everybody over. That doesn't mean it's not worth giving it your best.

"Let's work as a team and kick this new *WHL* into gear!"

Two or three people start clapping, but when they realize nobody else is joining in, it fades into an awkward silence. I kind of want to laugh, but it's okay to keep some of my crazy to myself. I'll tell Mac about it later and enjoy one of his devastating laughs, because I know it'll be him laughing with me, not at me.

I stride toward my office to get down to work when I hear someone ask in a loud whisper, "What happened to her accent?"

And I smile, knowing I just added one more thing to recount that'll have Mac smiling back at me.

EPILOGUE

"All it takes is one."
– Angus McKinley, Sr.

MAC:

She's in my kitchen, her gorgeous ass swinging in a slow slide to the rhythm of her favorite song. She says it's about me and I can't say she's wrong.

"One Man Band" by Old Dominion drifts from my speakers, telling the story of a man who doesn't want to go it alone anymore. Once he finds the girl who can finish his song, that's all he needs from there on out. And that's Poppy James for me.

My girl loves to dance, and I make sure to give her every opportunity to do so. She can make any surface her dance floor and I love nothing better than to watch her body move, that fiery hair flying around her face, me knowing that later that night she'll be moving under me in just the same way.

"Kate called and said they're in for Sunday dinner, so I'm just waiting on Naveed and Jonathan," she calls over the music as she looks over her shoulder with her smile that can never hide any fucking thing she's thinking. Her face is an open book, which is how I know she's even happier today than she was two months ago when her magazine launched to impressive reviews and circulation numbers that surprised even the heads of that publishing company.

Personally, my opinion of the place ranks just above a condom factory, but I've been told I have a chip on my shoulder about these things.

Business has picked up since the articles published in the magazine. I know my girl felt awkward as shit participating in something I dreaded so much, but sometimes the chips just fall where they do and you have to roll with it. Her friend, Naveed, took a light hand, and the interest in my mother's arrest skewed the article away from anything my pops did wrong, something I'm more than grateful for.

The extra income is funding the expansion of the youth program and is getting the blacksmithing program back in line. So, even though the attention is more than a little discomfiting, I can't complain.

I'm partnering with Bastion Forge again and Paul and I are working on some new ideas to engage the kids. I'm not the best teacher, but I'm working on it. And Poppy says my face is probably enough to scare some of the kids straight.

I might be offended if she didn't follow that up with pushing her tits into my chest and letting me make her come. There's nothing better than the sight of her unravelling for me—except maybe her smile.

No, scratch that. The coming is infinitely better.

And I know she's just joking about my face. Probably.

But, yeah, my girl has been happy and I hope it has at least a little something to do with me.

She wanders over in her short sleep shorts and a sweatshirt that hangs off her shoulder. I set down my notebook and draw her onto my lap, kissing her collarbone as she settles. My dick is immediately hard like it always is when I get a taste or feel of her warm, sweet body.

"Mmm," I murmur into her skin. "Delicious."

She squirms and laughs, doing nothing to calm the situation in my pants. "You like that, just wait till you taste what I'm making for Sunday dinner."

Poppy has made it a rule that her New York family—as she likes to put it—comes for Sunday dinner at least twice a month. She goes all out, making a complete fucking disaster of my kitchen and leaving all her guests with full bellies and a new story or two to tell. There's more laughing and talking in one Sunday than I'm accustomed to in a year of Sundays, but that's okay.

It's more than okay. It's fucking perfect.

Not only has my girl brought me all the goodness of her, she's trying to make me a family like the one I lost. I wasn't lying when I told her my pops would have loved her like his own.

"Have you asked Dan yet?" Her voice is quiet and my mouth stills on her skin.

I give my head a single shake and lean it back into the cushions.

She's been gently prodding me to reunite with my grandfather. He's extended an olive branch, but there's an awful lot of water to shove under that bridge before I can invite the man into my home. He covered up the actions of my mother—the ones that resulted in my pops's death—and even though he's paid for them with a reduced sentence for cooperation, it doesn't change the fact that he knew what happened and let the bitch live free for four years.

Thank God it looks like she'll finally be paying with a good portion of the remaining years of her life spent behind bars. Her asshole husband is already sharing a similar address, a fact which makes me feel a small sense of satisfaction. Even Elle is paying for her transgressions, although hers doesn't involve any jail time.

But none of that brings my pops back, something I know Poppy is thinking about in those moments when she watches me and doesn't think I see her.

I'll probably give Dan a chance eventually, if only for her. I'd do just about anything for her. And if she wants me to have family, I'll let her bring me that however she sees fit.

But the fact of it is she's all the family I need. From the moment she ground that high heel into the cement floor of my hallway, I was done.

I watch her and she's biting her lip. Damn, that always makes me want to bite it right back. I groan and reposition her on my lap so she's straddling me and I know she feels my rock-hard cock against her.

"Next time. I promise."

She sighs and then moves her hips forward. She loves it when I start out letting her run the show. But she's told me more than once that her favorite part is when I take over and make her mine every which way I can.

"And what kind of payment do I get if you slack off and don't follow through?"

"Anything you want, honey," I tell her, even though she knows she can always have anything she wants from me.

The song switches to another Old Dominion tune. This one is "Stars in the City" and when she starts to sing along I don't tell her I know it by heart too.

"I love this one," she tells me in her soft Georgia drawl as she smiles again. She says that about every one of their songs as well as dozens of other ones by bands ranging from country to that strange zydeco shit her family made me listen to when we were in Savannah last month.

"Even more than 'Cherry Pie'?" I ask, running my hands down to her ass as she absently grinds into me a little.

"Well, that's special. It's always special when there's a memory attached."

I hate to tell her, but if that's the case then every damn song she ever dances to will be deemed special in my book.

The chorus of "Stars in the City" kicks in and she starts singing along again as I lean in to lick a path up her neck. She tastes like sweet orange and vanilla.

She doesn't know it, but she's singing about herself—about how I see her. She's my breath of fresh air, reminding me to stop and find the beauty wherever I am, whether it be in her quaint hometown or walking down the crowded city streets of Manhattan with her hand in mine.

Not that I ever have to look far.

She wraps her arms around my neck and threads her

fingers through my hair, something that lets me know we'll be moving things to the bedroom in about thirty seconds.

I bite her neck and she stops singing along only long enough to mutter, "Beast."

I feel myself smile against her soft skin.

No, I don't ever have to search far when I'm looking for beauty. Because I get it every time she's near me.

And for a man who gave up on having something good and special and right a long time ago, it's all the sweeter now that I can call it my own.

THE END

We hope you enjoyed Poppy and Mac's story!

Want a BONUS EPILOGUE with Poppy, Mac, and the whole gang? Just sign up for my newsletter bit.ly/poppynl You'll also get a FREE ebook.

Get a sneak peek of the all new *Love on Tap Series*. An excerpt from Book 1, ***Ale's Fair in Love and War***, is up next.

Want another funny, swoon-worthy read from Sylvie Stewart? Try ***The Fix*** and start the addictive *Carolina Connections Series* now!
Turn the page for an excerpt.

Check out my Poppy & the Beast inspiration board on PINTEREST to see maps, Mac's furniture, pictures that inspired both characters, and more! @sylviestewartauthor

CASH

"Blue Bigfoot Beer," I bark into the phone, tucking the receiver between my shoulder and ear. The customer across from me holds out his hand as I count his change from the drawer.

A breathy voice on the other end of the line has my hand freezing in midair.

"Is this Cash?" she purrs.

Hmm. Seems like my day might be about to turn around.

I drop the change into the customer's palm and toss him a chin lift.

"That's me. What can I do for you?" I have a few ideas if the voice matches the body.

She lets out a little giggle that has my dick twitching in my jeans. "I'm calling about your virginity."

My hearing must be going because it sounded like she just called me a virgin.

Turning away from the prying eyes of my brother a few feet down the bar, I take the receiver in hand and press it firmly to my ear this time. "Sorry, come again?"

"Your virginity," she repeats, her voice still filled with sex but carrying a tinge of amusement now. "I'm interested in relieving you of it."

I squint at my reflection in the mirror of the back bar,

wondering if I always look this tired and trying to figure out which of my three brothers is fucking with me. I settle on Denver because that asshole has been way too jolly ever since he got his girlfriend to move in with him.

"Very funny, Rosie. Tell Denny I'm gonna kick his ass next time I see him." The phone drops back in its cradle with a heavy *clang*. I don't have time for jokes today. There's a brewery to run, a taproom to serve, a newbie to train, and a pale ale release tomorrow that I'm not even close to being ready for.

I glance down the bar just in time to see my youngest brother, Miller, slosh water all over the floor mats as he drains the sink. The towel I throw at him hits him square in the face. "You *trying* to create a hazard or does it just come naturally?"

He sends a glare over his shoulder, a new eyebrow piercing glinting at me as I brush past him to serve another customer. This guy is a regular, so there's no need to ask for his order. I press a pint glass onto the cold rinse and pull back the tap on Squatch This, a smooth wheat with a sweet finish.

The phone rings again, and I'm somewhat encouraged to see Miller answer it without prompting while I finish with the customer.

"It's for you." My little brother thrusts the phone in my direction.

I gesture for him to make the rounds of the taproom as I grab the receiver. If I've got to work with him, I'm at least gonna train him right. Family can be a real pain in the ass sometimes.

"This is Cash."

"Oh, uh, hey." The masculine voice on the other end stumbles. I'd half expected it to be Denny cackling at his own stupid joke, but this voice doesn't belong to anyone I know. I wait for him to speak, but time is money.

"Who is this?" I demand, knowing I'm taking my busy day out on a stranger and hearing my mama's voice in my head urging me to be patient. It's never been my strong suit.

"Tom."

I rack my brain looking for any trace of a Tom but can't recall a soul apart from the guy who runs the smoke shop a couple spaces down. This is *not* that Tom. I know this because *that* Tom is always high as a fucking kite and only refers to me as "Cool Money."

"Do I know you?" I glance out into the taproom to see Miller parked on his ass at a four top of attractive brunettes. That little...

"Uh, no," Tom mutters.

Jesus, it's like pulling teeth with this guy. "What can I do for you, Tom?" I repeat, impatience bleeding through.

"I was, uh, hoping *I* could do something for *you*."

For the love of Larry.

My eyelids drop closed as I brace a hip against the back bar. "Oh yeah." This time it's annoyance leading the charge. "What exactly can you do for me, *Tom*?"

"Pop your cherry."

When the receiver hits the phone's base this time, the clattering echoes through the entire taproom.

Someone is definitely fucking with me.

And I'm pretty sure I know who.

Recognizing the look on my face and the mood it signifies, Miller hauls ass back behind the bar, hiking his jeans up his hips as he goes. My little brother's contempt for belts is one of life's greater mysteries.

I take my agitation out on the bar, scrubbing the polyurethane finish with my bar towel until it gleams. The ring of the phone has my molars gnashing, and I leave the receiver right where it is.

"Aren't you gonna get that?" Miller asks.

"Don't touch it!" I throw the towel onto my shoulder and stalk down the hall to the office.

If she wants to start something, I'll make damn sure she regrets it. My eyes narrow to slits as they attempt to bore a hole through the wall separating my brewery from the neighboring pet groomer.

Happy Tails Salon. The name is just as sickly sweet as her fake-ass smiles and fluttering eyelashes behind those misleadingly innocent glasses.

Miller's disembodied voice breaks through the speaker of the desk phone. "It's Mama, jackass. Line 2."

Well, shit.

"Hey, Mama." I do my best to brush off my irritation. Mama doesn't need to know about any of my troubles.

"Hello, baby. How are you?" Her concerned tone has me immediately wary. My eyes dart around the office, but I haven't one damn clue what I'm expecting to find.

"I'm great. How are you? Did you find Mango?" Mango is Mama's true baby, and everyone knows it.

She clucks her tongue. "You know, he just showed up in the kitchen a few minutes after you left. I don't know what he got himself into, but he's here now, safe and sound. *Aren't you, my little sweetheart?*" she coos at the critter, and I realize I'm just being paranoid.

"That's good to hear." I glance at my watch. "Hey, aren't you gonna be late for work?" It's already halfway through the afternoon and I haven't gotten shit done.

"I'm leaving in a few," she replies. "I just wanted to call about your... problem."

My butt drops into the desk chair, and I smile into the phone. "I wouldn't say he's *my* problem. I like to think of Miller as *all of our* problem."

"Oh hush, you. I'm not talking about your brother—although I am so glad you took my suggestion and hired him."

Took her suggestion? More like folded to her edict. Hiring Miller was not my idea at all, but the idiot crashed his bike and got fired from yet another job, so my hands were well and truly tied. Blue Bigfoot Beer is a family venture in many ways, but my oldest brother, Carter, and I are the only ones left holding the bag at the end of the day.

"Yeah, well." There wasn't much more to say than that. Mama did always teach us if you don't have something nice to say, don't say anything at all. "So, what problem are you talking about?"

"Your virginity, sweetheart."

Fuck. My. Life.

Twenty minutes later, I'm staring at a Craigslist ad on my laptop that has both my name and Blue Bigfoot's phone number on it.

"Looking for someone gentle to break my guymen. I just haven't met the right person, and it's become a burden. Please be kind because I'm hideously ugly."

"Dude, there are easier ways."

Miller's voice sends me jumping. The bastard is

leaning over my shoulder reading the screen and breathing his nicotine dragon breath in my face. I give him a good shove.

"Fuck off. I didn't post this," I grunt. "And who's manning the bar?"

Hitching his jeans up again, he snickers, enjoying this way more than I'd like. "Relax. Oscar's got it covered."

I only glare in response. There's no way I'm telling him that Mama offered the services of her buddy Regina to help me out with my so-called problem. The same Regina who runs an escort service catering to Asheville's elite and hard up.

Of which I'm neither, thank you very much.

"Any idea who did it?" Miller flicks his tongue ring against his teeth, sending my already raw nerve endings buzzing.

There's only one person on this earth who can get under my skin and make me take my eye off the ball like this.

I grit my teeth around my growl of an answer. *"Hollis."*

Find out what happens next in ***Ale's Fair in Love and War: An Enemies-to-Lovers Romance***
www.sylviestewartauthor.com

LANEY

I ran my tongue around the shell of his ear and sucked his earlobe. Apparently that was the last straw. Nate physically picked me up and headed to my bedroom with his hands on my ass, and I had no choice but to hang on for dear life. This was shocking and a bit embarrassing on many levels, the least of which being the chronically untidy state of my bedroom.

Let me explain.

In all these romance novels, the buff guys are constantly picking the girls up and throwing them on the bed or having vertical make-out sessions—all while not straining a single muscle. I am not that girl. I have tits and I have ass, and I'm not saying that in some cute little "oh, look at her perky booty" kind of way. I have triple Ds and a very proportionate ass to match. That very often puts me into the plus-size department and then on to a tailor to fit the smaller parts of me. Everyone loves to talk about boobs and booty like they are thrilled the old bombshell figure is back in style, but I can tell you two things: (1) a rack like this wreaks havoc on your back, and (2) tailors are not inexpensive.

So Nate carrying me to my bedroom, an event which should have been a romantic milestone complete with "Up Where We Belong" playing in the background, was instead an episode that filled me with self-doubt and imagined trips to the emergency room. A hernia, at the very least, was a distinct possibility in this little scenario—how romantic can you get?

Amazingly, though, we made it without injury and he deposited me gently on the bed. He honestly didn't look any worse for wear, and his lustful look implied I'd better kick my insecurities to the curb. Shit was about to get real. *Yowza!*

Grab your copy of **The Fix** and start the award-winning
Carolina Connections series today!
Also available in audiobook
www.sylviestewartauthor.com

Then Again

Happy New You

About That

Full-On Clinger

Nuts About You

Booby Trapped

Love on Tap Series

POPPY & THE BEAST PLAYLIST

As I'm sure you can tell, a lot of this book was inspired by music (as usual). If you haven't listened to Old Dominion, you must go do so right this minute—I'll hold your beer. At the very least, give "One Man Band" a listen. It will always be Mac's song to me. Enjoy!

Listen to the *Poppy & the Beast* playlist on Spotify: https://spoti.fi/2XIkhzY or just search for Sylvie Stewart

- One Man Band - Old Dominion
- The Feels - Maren Morris
- All on Me - Devin Dawson
- Beautiful - Akon, Colby O'Donis, Cardinal Offishall
- Shut Me Up - Old Dominion
- Something Beautiful - The Noms
- Dance with Me Tonight - Olly Murs
- Hotel Key - Old Dominion
- Southern Girl - Tim McGraw
- Seeing Blind - Niall Horan

- Bad Liar - Imagine Dragons
- Cherry Pie - Warrant
- Better When I'm Dancing' - Meghan Trainor
- Southern Nights - Glen Campbell
- Georgia on My Mind - Ray Charles, Willie Nelson
- Hammer to Fall - Queen
- Written in the Sand - Old Dominion
- Trust Me - The Fray
- This Road - The Noms
- Stars in the City - Old Dominion
- Company You Keep - Maren Morris

Thank you so much for reading *Poppy & the Beast*. I hope you enjoyed all the Poppy and Mac hotness.

Want to hang out with me and my other readers? Join my **Reader Group** on Facebook: www.facebook.com/groups/SylviesSpot

Subscribe to my newsletter and you'll get a BONUS EPILOGUE from *Poppy & the Beast*! You'll also get a FREE ebook.

Stay up to date and keep in touch!

- www.sylviestewartauthor.com
- sylvie@sylviestewartauthor.com
- Facebook: SylvieStewartAuthor
- Twitter: @sylvie_stewart_
- Instagram: sylvie.stewart.romance
- BookBub: sylvie-stewart

- Goodreads: bit.ly/ss_gr
- Pinterest: @sylviestewartauthor
- TikTok: @authorsylviestewart

XOXO,
Sylvie

ABOUT THE AUTHOR

USA Today bestselling author Sylvie Stewart loves bad jokes, hot HEAs, country music, and baby skunks—preferably all at the same time. Most of her steamy romantic comedies take place in North Carolina, a.k.a. the best state ever, and she's a sucker for hugs from her kids and a good laugh with her hubby. She also cusses like a sailor and can't seem to bring herself to feel bad about it. If you love smart Southern gals, hot blue-collar guys, and snort-laughing with characters who feel like your best friends, Sylvie's your gal.

Stay up to date on all things Sylvie!
www.sylviestewartauthor.com

facebook.com/SylvieStewartAuthor

twitter.com/sylvie_stewart_

instagram.com/sylvie.stewart.romance

bookbub.com/authors/sylvie-stewart

tiktok.com/@authorsylviestewart

pinterest.com/sylviestewartauthor

ACKNOWLEDGMENTS

I'm mixing it up a little bit this time. My first and biggest thank you is going to all the musicians out there. Whenever I talk to my fellow authors, we all agree that music is such an inspiration to our stories. When I get writers block, I turn to music; when I need to spark a specific vibe for a scene, I turn to music; and when I want to get to the heart of a character, it's music that helps me dig deep.

For *Poppy & the Beast*, I found myself going directly to my favorite band in the land, Old Dominion, and they didn't let me down. In fact, if you noticed, I dedicated this book to them and their beautiful talent. So, thanks to them and to all you amazing musicians out there inspiring us all!

I also can't go without sending my thanks to Heather (my wonderful editor and friend), all my author buds (you know who you are, you crazy hobags), and my family (you wonderful, delicious bunch).

More thanks go out to my Facebook reader group (Sylvie's Spot)!

Lastly, thank you, my readers, for spending a few hours with my book babies and the characters I love so much. None of this would be possible without you!

XO,

Sylvie